DOMUS NIGER

Family and History

John Hunter

ISBN 13: 978-0-578-53843-3

Library of Congress Cataloging-in-Publication Data

Printed in the United States of America

For my parents, Louise and John, Jr.,

and

The Hunter, Owens, Robinson, Sykes, Taylor, Kooden and Weissberg Families iv

CONTENTS

BOOK ONE

PORTAL
OF
NO RETURN

SWEE SELLABIE

My family is one of the oldest black families in Pachacuti, Georgia; older, some say, than most of the white families in town. I, Swee Sellabie, am the self-appointed historian of my family, and with the intent of recording its history, I have gathered as much information as I could about its genealogy as well as stories of individual lives. However, what I record here is not simply, or even essentially, only my family's history. While this is a story about folks with whom I am related by blood, it is also a record of people who married or sometime just had intimate relations with me and my family members. "Family" here is used broadly because all kinds of folks have willingly or unwittingly bound themselves up with my people. Some of these folks I never knew personally but many of them I did know and a few of them I still know. There are lots of names recorded here and many individual stories. Some are more important than others because of their greater interest to me. Most of the folks in this story are black but a good number of them are white. In all honesty, some are both. In my family it is not possible to record a true history without crossing racial lines because the folks—black and white—crossed those lines again and again.

I am recording this history in 1970 after having lived a long life—59 years—but I am only one of the many characters in it. I know my own story as well as anyone can know herself and I've tried to be mostly honest about myself. I've also tried to be as honest as possible about everyone else. There is a lot here that I've gotten from other people and I trust that what they've told me is true. However, I know that truth is not always the best, or even the most prudent story to record for posterity. I've talked with many folks over many years; some have also given me personal letters and documents so that I could tell this story as completely and authentically as I feel necessary. I have faith that they have not lied through their teeth (but I suspect some did) and, although some facts may be missing or incorrect, I think that there is more truth here than not. I can only hope that my own memory is trustworthy as well. Memory is a slippery thing and, even when being honest, folks—including me—sometimes get things wrong by accident or by design. C'est la vie.

C'est la vie is, in fact, my family name or, in the pronunciation and spelling by the uneducated black folks of south Georgia—Sellabie. It is, of course, French for "That's life." My grandfather,

Fairfax, would always say: C'est la vie, and folks began referring to him as Sellabie. He chose that name for himself and my family in the hope, perhaps ironically, that our people would understand life as it was. That's not the same, of course, as accepting it; but understanding was essential to our survival. Our life was hard even after Emancipation and we didn't see how it could be any better although we certainly wanted a better life. We went along to get along. It was fatalistic for sure. But it was also as rational a way to survive as any in a hostile, often violent environment. You can't fight forces that are so much stronger than you and your people. You cannot change what other folks (I'm talking about white people) don't want changed. And when everything that you know is contained within a radius of a few miles of a little town in the rural Deep South, you have a fairly well-defined world view and that world has you fixed at the bottom of the pile with no easy way to rise up or get out. *C'est la vie.*

Sometimes, though, what we assume will be is not what happens. This history begins with "C'est la vie" as a way to describe a world I and my family had no other way to describe. We were fish in water unaware that the water might be different elsewhere or that we might become different fish in another pond. Our pond was called Pachacuti. It was home to many of the folks in this history, including me. As far as most of us were concerned, it would always be our home, generation after generation. Never assume.

5

I

OUTWARD PASSAGE

PACHACUTI I

Mosey DeBobo was, and still is, a handsome man. Tall and thin as a stalk of celery and tough as a boiled owl, he was a heart-breaker who turned his back on nearly everyone who wanted him. He has only one arm; the other was lost in an accident. His missing arm always made him feel different and stand out from others. But it wasn't just his arm that made him the way he was. No. There were other reasons, lots of other reasons, and they begin with his family.

Every family has a history—some long, some short—but each of us is a product of their ancestors whether we know about them or not. In Mosey's case, we know a lot about Mosey's people and they have a pretty long history. The DeBobo, lived in Georgia—that's red clay, hot, southern Georgia. However, the earliest family member, at least the one that most of us knew anything about lived in Louisiana. This was Midah who was enslaved on a plantation and died in 1865. His wife, Jubelie, was sold to a distant plantation before Emancipation and was never heard from again. One of Midah's children, Nattea, who grew up in Louisiana, created the family name of DeBobo. She came to Georgia after Emancipation although nobody knows for sure why or when. The name was originally something like Des Beaux which black rural folks in Georgia, because they were unfamiliar with French or Cajun, turned into DeBobo—"The most beautiful of the beautiful." Nattea settled in Pachacuti—the name of the town taken from an Inca ruler. She didn't have a husband but black folks suspected that, by a white man, she had at least two children—Deerie and Bear. Nattea's son, Bear, was Mosey's grandfather. He was also tall and lean like Mosey; so, his name—really a nickname which he was always called—marked his character not his appearance. He was like a bear, strong and fearsome, a man not to be messed with. He kept the DeBobo as a family apart from others. Town folk, including whites, didn't cross Bear DeBobo or his kin. Bear and his wife, Ardeah, had four children, the oldest of whom was Adelpho, Mosey's father. Adelpho married Loissey Sellabie who was Swee's older half-sister and that marriage is how two families became intwined. The Adelpho Debobo were a typical black family in Pachacuti—farm workers—field hands really. They worked hard and got by. They had five living children to feed. So, when Mosey came along, he being the first boy after four girls (two had died young), people were doubly circumspect about his shyness, about his distance from everyone.

There were maybe two thousand people in town back in 1929 when Mosey was born, both black and white, about equal in number. The whites had their side of town and so did the blacks. The blacks lived mainly south of the main east-west street that passed through the center of town. The whites lived north of the street. A few whites, about a couple dozen, who had money from big farms or businesses, built large homes on a bluff to the west and above the railroad tracks that ran parallel to the main north-south street. At the center of town where the main streets crossed was the place where black and white Pachacuti came together. The center of town was not much. Some stores, shops, and a little movie theater clustered east of the main intersection. Further east of the center was a dense woods cut through by a stream flowing south. Surrounding the town were extensive farms owned by wealthy white Pachacuti landowners and small plots owned by Pachacuti blacks. Most of Pachacuti's black residents were farmers. Pachacuti was a place you might want to leave if you had any other place to go. Mosey didn't want or have any other place to go until the time came that he had to find someplace else. Pachacuti was his home.

When he was young, he already seemed different from other members of his large family. He was quiet, shy, and distant. But in such a large family as his, there were too many kids and too many everyday tasks for anyone to pay attention to Mosey. His parents worked their own small fields outside of town as farmers. Loissey, his mother, like so many women, also did laundry and sometimes worked as a domestic in the homes of the wealthier white townsfolk. Loissey's entire extended family, the Sellabie—Swee's people—thought that she was odd; they stopped short of saying "crazy" of course. Swee just accepted Loissey, her older half-sister, as strange. Loissey's mother, Soonie Fleet, had always been a whispered secret in Swee's family and around Pachacuti. Her short life had a far-reaching and lasting impact on nearly everyone in this history.

The history of the Sellabie began with Sesto, Swee's great-grandfather who died enslaved. One of his sons, Fairfax, although born enslaved, when emancipated, moved from Louisiana to Georgia and established a branch of the family with the name Sellabie in Pachacuti. His older brother, Ajax, also moved to Georgia—possibly with his brother—and also adopted the name Sellabie. However, he settled in an all-black hamlet of Sokodé near Pachacuti. Fairfax married a local woman named Clara and they had three sons, the two youngest died early. His eldest son, Hanton, married twice. His first wife, Weela Bay, gave him two children, Maena and Littell, before she died, and his second wife, Darissa McKree, produced three more offspring, Prellis, Daphet, and Swee. But, in between his two wives, there was his mistress, Soonie, whose child by Hanton was Loissey, Mosey's mother and Swee's half-sister.

Soonie was a Fleet, one of the middling white families in Pachacuti. Her parents, Murray Fleet and Sutreen Moore Fleet, had three daughters and a son; Soonie was the eldest. When Soonie became a teenager, she learned that her father liked black women and had fathered children by several of them. She had heard arguments between her parents about his women, and kids at the all-white school she attended had also talked, without any specific detail, about whose parents were doing what with whom around town. Maybe, the stories about her father piqued her interest in black people who, after all, were everywhere in town despite the color line (the official but superficially observed segregation of the races). She had noticed an older man of color who behaved more like a white man than the subservient and deferential blacks she usually encountered. Hanton Sellabie was smart, clever, and self-assured, and Soonie found him attractive. He was handyman and deliveryman for the town's biggest grocery store. When he accompanied her home one day with a box of her purchases, she let him know that she wanted to see him discreetly in the woods. And, so, as they say, one thing led to another, and Hanton impregnated Soonie. If either of them had intended this consequence, no one really knew, maybe, not even Soonie. Surely, if they had thought about what might happen, they would have been more careful. Soonie told her father about Hanton and the pregnancy. Since Murray Fleet knew quite a bit about secret sex with black folks, he helped his pregnant daughter to leave Pachacuti temporarily and took her to the nearby, small, all-black community of Sokodé where the other branch of the Sellabie—Hanton's distant kin—lived and farmed. There, she gave birth but, sadly, died soon thereafter; she was only sixteen. The Sokodé Sellabie buried her in an unmarked grave in their own family plot. They returned the child, named Loissey by her mother, to the baby's father in Pachacuti to be raised by Hanton after he married his second wife, Darissa, Swee's mother. The Sellabie treated the child well enough but something was wrong with her, something that made her distant and unloving, something that made her own children, especially, Mosey, like her but also wary of her. Maybe, it was because of his mother that Mosey was different, always shy, always apart from the others. He was such a good-looking kid who everyone wanted to like; but no one could get close to him, not his parents, family, or friends.

When Mosey was about to turn ten—this was in 1939—his family had planned a little birthday party and invited relatives. However, Mosey's father, Adelpho, died suddenly that year (Loissey had died in 1934), and Mosey's eldest sister, Serriah, took charge of her parent's household. With a funeral to plan, there was no money for, or interest in, a birthday party. Knowing of the financial straits of her kin, Mosey's aunt, Xantha, invited him to her house as a birthday treat. Xantha DeBobo Pendle was Adelpho's eldest sister. She had married Murty Pendle, and they had, to everyone's amazement, only one child, Trique, who everyone called Trick except Xantha who, somewhat pretentiously, always called him "Tree-kay" as if his name were Spanish. Trique Pendle was the same age as Mosey. But, unlike Mosey, Trique was a fireball—a charming, mischievous, and bright boy. He was the kid to whom all the other kids gravitated. Not quite as tall as Mosey but almost as good-looking, Trique was seductive and keenly aware of his charms to win over other children as well as adults. Trique had known Mosey most of his life but he had not spent any time with him until his mother's invitation to Mosey to celebrate Mosey's birthday with them. Xantha made a cake with candles. She also made Trique buy a twenty-five cent present at the dry goods store for Mosey which she wrapped in fancy paper with a ribbon. As usual, Murty was not home because he worked long hours as a janitor in Pachacuti's single factory on the edge of town, so only Xantha, Trique, and Mosey were at the party. They sat at the dinner table, and Mosey blew out the candles of his cake. Trique watched him, completely fascinated. He noticed Mosey's long neck, fair complexion, short curly brown hair, and widely spaced gray eyes. He was smitten. Mosey, however, was in agony. He had never spent any time previously with his aunt and he was unsure why his cousin, Trique, was watching him so intently. He only knew that he wanted to go home as soon as possible. When the meal was done and Mosey had had two big slices of cake, Trique asked permission to take Mosey to his room. And that's where they went. Trique showed Mosey some of his treasured things: a couple of old books that he found discarded in a bin outside of a store in town; a dried-up toad that died behind his house; and a magazine picture of a young white man in a tight-fitting bathing suit that he secreted in one of his old books. At first, Mosey couldn't understand why this was such a special and hidden treasure until Trique pointed out the bulge in the man's crotch and told Mosey that when they both grew up, they were going to be like that man. Trique went on to say what men did with the bulges in their pants. Mosey, of course, had heard all of this kind of talk before. Kids and adults were always joking about sex; it wasn't anything special or unusual at his house. And Mosey knew that men and women had sex because they liked it, and it was how people made babies. But Trique's interest was different from everything that Mosey knew. Mosey couldn't figure out what that was exactly but he felt himself becoming intrigued and frightened. It didn't take long for Trique to terrify Mosey; he said that sometimes men had sex with other men. Mosey couldn't imagine how Trique knew such a thing as this or how, in fact, one man could have sex with another man. He knew that men and women were different—he had sisters; he could see the difference. Then Trique stood, turned his back to Mosey, and pulled down his pants and underwear, grabbing and spreading his butt cheeks while turning his head to see Mosey's reaction. They were too young—ten years old—to actually succeed in doing what Trique vividly described that evening. But as they grew up over the next few years, they tried it and found that they both enjoyed the act a lot. Mosey and Trique not only became friends after that birthday party but later, as teenagers, they also became lovers.

After the party and after Mosey returned home, his life soon changed, partly because he now had a friend, his first, and he and his friend shared an intimacy; but mainly because his sister, Serriah, told him that he would have to go live with relatives; she and the next oldest girl, Habboey, couldn't, on their own, take care of him and also the two youngest boys. To Mosey's surprise, he wasn't sent to live with a DeBobo, like his Aunt Xantha, where he could be with Trique; instead, he was to live with his aunt, Swee Sellabie, his mother's half-sister.

Sweet Tea was Swee's given name. Sweetie or Swee was a nickname. She never liked the name Sweet Tea because, when she was young, other kids made fun of it. So, in the town's only black school, she began referring to herself as Sweetie. It was Amity Lowe who first called her Swee. Swee and Amity met when both worked as domestics in Pachacuti. When they decided to live together, Amity moved into a little house belonging to Swee that was adjacent to the property of James Morton, a prosperous black man who owned the only black funeral parlor in town. His property, on the periphery of the black section of town, had a big house and two smaller houses that had been used by members of his family. A house, adjacent to his property, became Swee's and Amity's home.

Swee, who was born in 1911, was a stout woman with full breasts and buttocks. She was quite a contrast to the woman who lived with her. Amity was skinny, practically no breasts or butt and narrow, bony hips. She was also ten years younger (born in 1921) and pale with long straight brown hair while Swee's hair was short, black, and curly, and Swee's skin was very dark. Amity was tall and Swee was short and rotund—a diet of fried chicken and black-eyed peas cooked with ham hocks will do that to you. However, Swee was the dominant of the two. She had a confidence and determination that allowed the two women living on their own to survive. Their work as domestics in town provided them a little extra cash that they saved in the town's only white-owned bank. Swee was enthusiastic about Mosey coming to live with them, Amity less so. She wasn't happy about a male in the house, even if he was only 10 years old. She also didn't like someone else competing with her for Swee's attention and affection. So, it was a surprise for everyone that Mosey stayed with the two of them for so many years, six in fact. Trique may have been the reason why everyone settled into a harmonious routine. The women noticed how often Trique and Mosey were together, like boys, of course. But they sensed something more, something like Amity and Swee had between them. Trique began to spend the night, with his parents' consent, at Swee's house in Mosey's room and bed—there was nothing unusual, at that time, about cousins sleeping together. And the women could hear them talking in a low voice, then giggling, then silent. As the boys got older, entered puberty, there was the rhythmic squeaking of the bed, and, of course, the stained sheets. One day, when Mosey and Swee were home alone, she decided to talk to Mosey about Trique. She wanted to know if, and how, they planned to stay together now that they were getting older and they would have to leave Swee's house. She also knew that Trique's parents expected him to find a job, get married, and raise a family. What would happen to Mosey? Mosey didn't have answers to any of this. He knew that he wanted to be with Trique, the only person besides Swee, who made him feel alive and excited about life.

Mosey turned sixteen in 1945. Some black people were leaving Pachacuti for the North. There was talk of jobs, lots of jobs in factories that paid good money, even for black people. Mosey and Trique talked about possibly going north together. Mosey's elder sister, Habboey, who had met Critton Gant—a reject from the military—had already moved north to Detroit with him in 1944. They got married, found work, and much later bought a house. Critton had a good-paying job at the Ford Motor Company's River Rouge factory complex. Habboey worked downtown at the main post office as a cleaner. Just knowing a family member in the North gave Mosey some hope of a little help to find his way. Trique wanted to go too but he had his parents in Pachacuti even though he spent less and less time at their house since he met Mosey and since Mosey began living with Swee. He began to feel that Mosey would leave without him because Trique didn't know how he could part from his family, how they would let him, a sixteen year old, leave. Trique was thinking about all of these things when, one day, he stopped at the town's general store where he encountered Martalee Boston; she was seventeen and white. She had often seen Trique on the main street. She thought that he was cute even if he was black. She also knew that to talk to him would bring trouble. But she decided to take the risk. Trique was a little surprised that a white girl said hello to him, and he said hello back and left the store. Martalee followed at a distance when she felt no one was watching. Trique headed out of town into the woods; although Martalee was some distance behind him, she caught up with him when she thought they were both out of sight. She asked him his name, and he told her. She made him promise to meet her the next afternoon at a place she knew in the woods where they would be alone. Trique and Martalee kept their date and many after that. At some point, in their youthful sexual enthusiasm and disregarding all of the realities of the time and place where they lived, they decided to stay together. And that's why Trique decided to leave Pachacuti.

It is funny how, in a small town like Pachacuti, people can know so much and so little at the same time. Black folks knew Billy Holliday's song, *Strange Fruit* (first recorded in 1939) because it speaks of "Southern poplar trees with black fruit, burnt and hanging from branches with bloody leaves." But even they didn't know that that could come true. The Sellabie witnessed such a tree, as did much of the rest of Pachacuti. Prellis, Swee's brother, the younger son, was lynched in 1945. He was accused of violating the first commandment of the racial code for blacks: Don't even look at a white woman. It wasn't clear what Prellis did or did not do. Supposedly, he accosted the teenaged Myra Charles who even outdid Martalee Boston in bold recklessness. Some white people said that they saw him do it although black people could not and would not believe that a black man—especially a middle-aged man—could be so stupid as to accost a young white woman in town, in daylight, with white people as witnesses. But that was the accusation, and Prellis' main mistake was not to escape town as fast as he could. He lingered at the scene of the alleged accosting, then started for home. He never made it. A posse of white men quickly formed, overtook him in a car, attacked, beat him, and dragged him, still alive, into the woods where they strung him to a branch of a tree and set him on fire. He died there and his body remained until his family cut it down and buried it in the family plot. The murder took place while Trique and Martalee were taking leave of their senses in the same woods.

Swee was making dinner in the kitchen at the rear of her house. The entire house was raised above the ground and open underneath because the nearby stream in the woods sometimes flooded. That same space under the house, unfortunately, was often a refuge from the heat for snakes and other creatures that came from the woods. A front porch, the width of the house, was the main entrance. All of the rooms were on one floor flanking a central hallway from the front door to the back door. To the right of the hallway was a sitting room and to the left two bedrooms each separately entered from the hallway. The back porch was also the width of the house with a small walled enclosure for a toilet—actually just a wooden bench with a hole and bucket underneath. Bathing was done in a metal tub on the back porch. There was no running water; it came from a well in the side yard. The kitchen was separate from the house proper but was connected to it by the back porch. A stair between the kitchen and the rest of the house descended to the side yard. Amity was in the rear yard collecting eggs from the chicken coop. Mosey was in the rear bedroom. Amity was the first to hear the sound of someone coming through the woods behind Swee's house. Then she saw Trique running towards the house. Then she saw that Trique was pulling a white girl by the arm behind him. As they headed toward the house, to the rear stair, so did Amity. All three arrived at the kitchen causing Swee to stop cooking. A quick explanation by Trique established Martalee's identity, Trique's and Martalee's relationship, and the fact that Martalee's brothers, who had just become aware of that relationship and of their most recent tryst in the woods, were in pursuit. Mosey came into the kitchen, after hearing the commotion and learned, somewhat abruptly, of Trique's other love. Swee knew immediately what everyone had to do to avoid a disaster. Trique would have to leave town, immediately, running as fast as he could through the woods heading north. The recent lynching of her brother, Prellis, made it clear to her that Trique should not dally but, to evade pursuit, catch a freight train in the switching yard north of town. Martalee would have to turn around, intercept her brothers, and try to give Trique some time to escape. Trique bolted the house for the woods. Mosey, without thought, took off after him. It was a long time before they knew what subsequently happened at Swee's house after they left just as it was some time before Swee and Amity knew what had happened to Mosey and Trique.

This is, in fact, what happened: Martalee, spotted her brothers coming out of the woods and, afraid to confront them, ran into the sitting room. Swee and Amity followed. Simultaneously, the brothers—Hamilton, Oliver, and Finn, Jr.—stomped up the front stairs of Swee's house. Martalee peeked through the front window. Swee came onto the front porch and said: What do you boys want?

Oliver, the talkative one, shouted: We're looking for that nigger boy who was with our sister.

At that, Martalee, suddenly feeling confident, came out of the house and pointed out the obvious: He ain't here. He's gone for good, and you can't find him.

We're coming in, Oliver replied, and the boys started through the front door.

Swee said: All right boys have a look around. And they entered the house, surprised to see how nice it was with lots of furniture, even some rugs on the floor.

This stuff is too good for you niggers. What did you do, steal it?, said Finn, Jr.

Y'all go home now, said Martalee. That boy ain't here. I told you.

Come on; you're going with us, insisted Oliver.

No, I ain't. I ain't never going back to that house. So leave now.

Martalee, you don't wanna be with these niggers, said Oliver. You've gotta be with your own people. So come on.

Martalee, go with your brothers. It's the best thing for everybody, Swee said.

You better go before there's trouble, Amity added.

There's already trouble, said Hamilton. Come on, Martalee.

Can't I stay?, Martalee pleaded with Swee.

You really better go.

So Martalee reluctantly left with her brothers. As he was descending the front steps, Finn, Jr. picked up a rock and hurled it through a window.

We ain't finished with you two, Finn, Jr. added. That nigger is going to hang from a tree like the other one.

As the Boston boys literally dragged their sister home, Mosey and Trique raced through the woods heading north. Both were petrified that they might be followed but their potential pursuers were busy with their sister while plotting revenge on Swee and Amity. Despite his anxiety in flight, Trique remembered what Swee had said: Head to the rail-yard north of town and catch a freight. Running as fast as they could through the woods they came upon the open fields surrounding Pachacuti. They sprinted across the fields to the north-south road, crossed it, and continued their flight until they reached the north-south rail line. Trique felt that the rail line was a safer path to follow than the road in case someone in a car should pursue them. After a few miles at nearly breakneck speed, they reached the rail-yard and promptly climbed inside of the first open boxcar. They checked to see if anyone was around who might have noticed them. There was no one. Both were startled when the train they were on started up with a jerk. They were now moving slowly away from Pachacuti, which was a good thing, but they had no idea where the train was heading, which could be a bad thing. But, at least, they had escaped the present danger. What was ahead, they couldn't begin to contemplate since neither of them had ever been far from Pachacuti.

They sat quietly in the empty boxcar watching the passing fields. Both were trying to catch their breath after their breakneck run and the overwhelming fear for their lives. As minutes passed, they began to relax.

Where do you think we're headed?, Mosey asked.

I think north because the sun is in the west. Yeah. North. That's good.

Do you think we're okay? Do you think they followed us?

If we got this far without seeing anybody, I don't think they can find us.

You sure?

Yeah. We're okay. I think we're okay. How are you feeling?

Tired.

Yeah, me too.

Trique . . . Who was that girl?

Some girl.

She's white. What were you doing with a white girl?

You know how white girls are with us. They've heard about black dick and want to try it.

No white girl ever talked to me.

That's because you scare people.

What do you mean? How do I scare people? How could I scare a white person?

You're a DeBobo. People know to stay away from you.

Why?

Because that's what folks say. Don't fool with DeBobo.

I never heard that.

That's what they say.

Do you think that?

With me, you're not that way. But with everybody else, I don't know.

Trique, I didn't scare you. We've been together for a long time since we were kids. We've had fun together. We've had a good time. We've done stuff together in bed. You liked it. I liked it. Why did you go with that white girl?

Mosey, that was nothing. I told you, she wanted some black dick. I just thought I would see what it as like. You know. White pussy is the forbidden fruit. She wanted me. I didn't think it was anything like we do. It wasn't as much fun. I just did it because she wanted it and I couldn't stop myself.

But what about me? What about us?

We're here together. We'll be together.

We're only here together because I followed you. You were going to leave me. I bet that if that girl's brothers hadn't found you out, you would have been with her.

No. No. Mosey, you're my boy. You're what I want.

But you were going to leave me.

You know I had to run. Swee told me to leave right away. I didn't have time to think about everything. I had to run. We would have gotten together later after I found a safe place.

Would we? Or would you have waited for that white girl? Would she have followed you?

No, she wouldn't follow me. She doesn't mean anything to me. I told you that. I like you. I want to be with you. We're here now together. We'll stay together wherever we are. You know that.

No. I don't know that. I don't know what you will do or who you want to be with. Maybe, I shouldn't have followed you.

Oh, Mosey. You know I want you. I want you right now. Can I show you?

With that, Trique had sex with Mosey and their conversation, for the time being ended.

That night the Boston boys returned and set fire to Swee's house. Amity and Swee, who were anticipating trouble, got out safely but there was nothing to be saved from their house in Pachacuti. Amity and Swee stood in the yard and stared at the smoking ruins of what was their wood frame home. All of their possessions were gone—their clothes, their dog and cat, and for that Swee wanted to kill the Boston boys. But that was not going to happen. The Boston boys had even opened the chicken coop and slaughtered all of the birds. Smoke rose from the ruin and wafted through the neighborhood. A few neighbors ventured out of their houses in the dark and stood at a distance from Amity and Swee. When it was certain that there was nothing left to salvage, Amity and Swee headed toward the center section of town where most black folks lived, including the Sellabie. The Sellabie family home was no bigger than Swee's house that was just burned to the ground but, at one time, it housed Swee's large family—her father, his two wives (not at the same time, of course), and six children. Of her parents and many brothers and sisters, only her sister, Daphet, and brother, Littell, were still living and they occupied the family home alone. Neither had ever married. They were standing on the porch when Swee and Amity arrived because, like every other black person in Pachacuti, they already knew what had happened. The three women passed into the house and went into the small sitting room. Littell remained on the porch with his shotgun to keep watch for any white vigilantes.

What are you going to do now?, was Daphet's first question.

We lost everything, Sister, except our money in the bank. Amity wants to go to New York City and live in Harlem. She's heard that colored people live well there, that there are opportunities for colored people, and that there are other women like us. I don't want to go that far from Pachacuti. I thought we could go to Atlanta or Birmingham. But Amity thinks that those places wouldn't offer us as many opportunities, and two women living together would always be in danger. It's only because Pachacuti is such a small place that we've been able to live in relative peace, that is until Trique and that Boston girl ruined everything. I wasn't convinced about New York until Amity said that she would go there without me. We've already decided to use our money in the bank to leave Pachacuti and get ourselves set up in New York City. There's nothing for us here. We can start over in New York because Amity has family there. Maybe, they can help us to figure out where we can live until we can afford to get something of our own.

Daphet asked: Who are your people, Amity?

This was a funny question because Swee realized that she had never told her sister much about Amity. It was doubly funny because Swee suddenly was aware that she, herself, had never asked Amity about her family.

Amity began: My family lived in Tallahassee, Florida. My daddy, Nisan, was a Jewish man but he was born in New York City where his brother still lives in Harlem. There is also an aunt in New York who was married to another brother who is now deceased. My momma was part colored and part Seminole Indian. Her name was Edouit Long-Green. She and my daddy lived together but never married. They couldn't. They had two children who have survived—me, the elder, and my little brother, Richard, who still lives in Tallahassee. After both of my parents died, I left Florida and ended up here in Pachacuti because, well, I met a colored man in Florida who took a fancy to me and he brought me here where he could work in the fields. We broke up after a while because he fell for another women. I got a job cleaning a white family's house and that is where I met Swee. She told me that she had her own house and I could come live with her, and I did. That was in 1938. We've been together for almost seven years.

You know that colored folks in town talk about the two of you.

We know that, Sister, but what folks say don't mean nothing to us. We work hard. We've saved a little money. We keep to ourselves and don't bother no one.

What about that boy, Mosey, and what about Trique? What did you do to them?

We didn't do anything to them. I gave Mosey a home when his own family couldn't raise him, and Trique is Mosey's cousin and his only friend. Mosey and Trique wanted to be together and we had nothing to do with that. We tried to do our best for those boys and let them be.

Yeah, and now they had to leave town before the white folks could hang them from trees like they did our brother, Prellis.

Yes. But that was Trique's fault for getting involved with that white girl. Trique, not Mosey, caused this mess. Now, they're both gone and I hope that they are safe. We've got to leave now too and all we ask from you is to let us stay here a couple of nights until we can get our cash out of the bank. We'll be out of here as soon as we can get ourselves together. I hope that we aren't bringing any trouble to you here.

Swee, we know how to handle white folks. If they mess with us, they'll end up with some bullets in their ugly fat butts. Those crackers that killed our brother know that we're ready for them. Sister, you and Littell are my only living relatives now. Everyone else in this Sellabie family is dead. You're not the sister that I wanted but you're the only sister that I've got. Stay here. You'll be safe enough for now and you can get your money tomorrow and go to New York. I want you safe out of this town, even if it is in New York City.

Daphet, I know I'll be safe with you and Littell here until we can leave but I'm more concerned now about Mosey and Trique. I hope that they took my advice and headed north to the rail-yard. If those Boston boys followed them or if they got you-know-who to help them hunt Mosey and Trique, they will be in big trouble.

That mother-fucker should be dead.

His time will come someday. Meanwhile, find out what colored folks know and tell me after we get to New York.

Maybe someday I can come and visit you. I think I would like that.

Daphet, you would always be welcome wherever my home is.

With that, Daphet showed Amity and Swee to a bedroom, gave them some bed clothes, and said good night.

When Martalee and her brothers reached home, her brothers explained to their father, Finn, Sr., and mother, Olive, what had happened. Finn, Sr. told the brothers to leave the living room and close the door. He told Martalee to sit on the couch while he and Olive remained standing. He began to interrogate his daughter while Olive remained silent.

So, what exactly did you do with that boy?

I had sex with him.

Tell me the whole story. Everything.

I saw him at the general store and said hello. He said hello back then he left headed towards the woods. I followed and when I caught up with him where no one could see us, I told him to meet me the next day at the old oak. He did and we had sex. And we had sex again a couple of times for the next few weeks at the same place. My stupid brothers must have been following me and when we saw them coming, we ran to this house where Trique was staying. My brothers came and made me leave with them. They brought me home. That's it.

His name is Trique?

Yes, sir.

Is that Xantha's boy?

Who is Xantha?

Xantha DeBobo Pendle.

I don't know. Maybe.

I hope not. We don't want to make trouble with the DeBobo. What I don't understand, Martalee, is that there are lots of white boys in this town. Why a colored boy?

I think he's cute.

Well, what you think and what you did are going to bring you and this family a lot of trouble. It was stupid, Martalee. That boy could be killed by folks in this town. You're in danger too.

Daddy, he's gone. He ran away and left town with another boy. They ain't coming back.

I've told you not to use "ain't". You're not some poor, uneducated cracker. You've had schooling and should know better.

Yes, sir.

Finn, Sr. sat down in a chair.

You're going to have to leave town too. That's clear. It's now too dangerous for you to stay here. You're in big trouble. I want you to go to your room. Your mother and I will have to talk this over and decide what is the best thing to do. You can go now.

After Martalee left the living room, Olive sat down in a chair near her husband.

Olive, what do you think?I agree that she is in great danger especially if her brothers start talking to folks, especially my brother. You'll have to warn them to keep quiet. I doubt that they will so Martalee has to leave town as soon as possible. But I don't know where to.

I don't either. We don't have any close family that she could stay with who would be far enough away from Pachacuti so that she could be safe. Olive, this never would have happened if you had been more strict with her.

More strict? Do you mean that she should be like her brothers who have been encouraged by you to disrespect the coloreds? You, of all people, should have explained to your children where they come from.

Olive. You know what this town is like.

Yes, I know what this town is like. Martalee is the only one of your children who hasn't been poisoned by the hate in your family and in mine and I'm glad of that. I'll find a safe place for her to go. I have to talk to some folks I can trust tomorrow. Good night, Finn.

The next day, Martalee left the house saying to her parents that she was on the way to school but never returned home. She hitchhiked a ride out of town heading north, reached the next town, and hitched another ride with a woman who was driving up North to get a job in a factory. Martalee could go with her all the way with her and, maybe, get a job too.

The next morning, Swee and Amity got their savings from the bank, bought train tickets to New York, a few clothes and other necessities, and a day later they were on their way. They reached New York City via Atlanta and Cincinnati in three days and rode a subway for the first time in their lives to Harlem.

In 1945, five people left Pachacuti precipitously. Mosey DeBobo and Trique Pendle fled north by freight train fearing that a posse would form to revenge Trique's transgression of Southern mores. Their house burned to the ground, Swee Sellabie and Amity Lowe took a train for New York City. And, Martalee Boston, losing her boyfriend and cutting ties to her family, hitched a ride heading north but only as far as Atlanta where she decided to stay a while.

ATLANTA I CINCINNATI CLEVELAND

Fortunately for Mosey and Trique, the freight train that they hopped at the rail-yard north of Pachacuti headed north to Atlanta although Mosey and Trique did not know this at the time. When it reached the central rail-yard just outside of the city, Mosey and Trique got off figuring that they were now far enough away from Pachacuti to rest and take stock of the situation. They discovered that they were in Atlanta, after talking with a black yardman and, at his suggestion, headed to the eastern part of town near Auburn Avenue where he told them they could find their own kind. Hungry, they hung around outside the back of a small restaurant. The cook, a middle-aged black woman, came outside to empty some garbage. Trique, turning on his charm, asked if they could get something to eat. Kind woman that she was, Vereatha Osgood gave them both a plate of food and asked where they were from. She decided, after some hesitation, that they could help out in the restaurant. With the end of war in 1945, soldiers were returning home, business was picking up, and more help was needed. With the promise of jobs and some advice from the woman, Mosey and Trique got a room together in a house of Vereatha's neighbor nearby and resumed being lovers. Although Trique had explained his sleeping with Martalee as her seduction of him which was true, in part, he failed to divulge to Mosey his own desire and enthusiasm for her sex. And his adventure with Martalee led Trique during the next months to find other women to sleep with while he was having sex and living with Mosey. Mosey soon realized that Trique was running around with women as well as, he soon discovered, with other young men and, although he wanted to stay with Trique—he loved him—he was profoundly hurt and dissatisfied with their life together. He then also sought sex with other young men, one of whom was Waite Carvey, another black fellow a few years older who was visiting Atlanta. After several casual encounters, they became lovers. Waite fell in love with Mosey but he had a dilemma: He had to return to his job in Cincinnati and he wanted Mosey to come with him. Mosey told Waite that he still wanted to be with Trique. He wanted Trique exclusively as they had been, he thought, in Pachacuti. Hearing this, Waite reluctantly returned to Cincinnati alone but told Mosey, that if he changed his mind, he should come to Cincinnati and live with him. Without Waite, Mosey tried again to gain Trique's exclusive love by giving up his own affairs. He told Trique what he wanted from him and for the first time in his life revealed his true feelings for and to another person. Trique, however, could not give up his pursuit of other men—and women—despite his love for Mosey. He made promises which he knew he wouldn't keep and he tried to conceal his affairs. Mosey was willing to deny the obvious deceptions but, when he finally realized that Trique could not or would not change, he broke up with him. He told Trique that he was leaving and, in 1948, after living for three years in Atlanta, he contacted Waite and moved to Cincinnati to rejoin him.

Waite had been born in Cincinnati to a good working-class family. His father, Horton Carvey, was a mechanic and his mother, May Easter Carvey, was a domestic. He was the second oldest of four children and much beloved by his mother. His father, however, suspected that Waite was not going to carry forward the family name and devoted his attention to the younger son, Cassius. Although Waite's parents had modest incomes, they did send their children to school, and all four —Arleeta, Waite, Cassius, and Willa—graduated from high school. It was two years after high school, in 1947, when he was twenty, that Waite met Mosey.

Waite's family had sent him to Atlanta to stay with his aunt, Ornella, his mother's older, widowed sister. She had no children and often kept Waite, when he was a child, during summers when he was out of school. He had come this time, however, to stay with her while she mended from a broken hip. His was a temporary stay. He had temporarily left his job, as a dishwasher, and his flat in Cincinnati for a few months until his aunt could manage on her own. Some evenings, he would go downtown to a movie and bought a ticket to the colored section in the balcony of a movie theater. He had seen Mosey downtown at one of the movie theaters. Mosey was with Trique and, although Waite could see that Mosey only paid attention to Trique, he did acknowledge Waite. Then, one day, he saw Mosey without Trique and went over to him to introduce himself. Waite was more muscular in build than Mosey, but not as tall. Waite was also darker than Mosey and wore his wavy hair heavily pomaded so that it looked very shiny. It took a long time and many casual meetings before Mosey began to hint at his relationship with Trique. But Waite already suspected the truth and helped ease Mosey's disclosure. By the time Mosey decided to leave Trique, he was already frequenting the few places where black men met for companionship and sex, and he was having liaisons before meeting Waite. When they started seeing each other and talking, and Mosey felt that Waite might like men too, he took Waite to a small joint for black men and introduced him to the homosexual world. When Waite learned of Mosey's unhappiness with Trique, he asked Mosey to come live with him in Cincinnati.

Waite's second floor flat on the west side of Cincinnati had two small rooms—a living room and bedroom—with a tiny kitchen and bath. They shared a narrow bed. Other than a few chairs and one table, there was little else in the flat. Waite had lived there since finishing high school. He was encouraged to move by his father who preferred that Waite's younger brother, Cassius, occupy the center of the family's attention. Mosey was more sexually adept than Waite because

Waite had hesitated to act on his impulses. He didn't know other men who liked men and he didn't know how to meet them. But he allowed Mosey to show him what men could do sexually, and Waite followed his own urges as well. Waite discovered that he liked anal sex, encouraging Mosey to penetrate him. With Trique, Mosey had submitted to being penetrated as well as penetrating Trique; he found that changing positions made him realize how much he liked this different role.

Waite worked at a black restaurant where he got Mosey a job as dishwasher. This had been Waite's job until he was promoted to busboy and janitor. Now the two of them settled into a life together; they both got what they wanted—an exclusive lover. Waite and Mosey spent most of their days at the restaurant, Waite bussing tables and Mosey in the kitchen as dishwasher. They went to work together and came home together. Since they ate most meals at the restaurant, they kept very little food at home and did hardly any cooking. Waite introduced Mosey to his family, but not, of course, as his lover. Waite's older sister, Arleeta, liked Mosey and tried to encourage him to come around and see her. But Mosey excused himself because of his work. Waite's father recognized Mosey's disinterest for what it was and during one of Waite's and Mosey's visits to the family home, told Waite that he didn't want them around the house. Waite's mother protested and told Waite that he was her son too; he was always welcome home, and he could bring Mosey or any other friend regardless of what his father said.

Mosey had some experience as a cook from his years in Atlanta and, soon, he was also assisting the cook, a man called Slide but whose real name was Otis Black. Slide was a very talented and fast cook. He made dozens of breakfast dishes in the morning and then prepared several different meals for the lunch and dinner crowd. Mosey learned a lot about cooking by watching Slide, and then began to help him. When a new dishwasher was hired, Mosey became the cook's assistant. He and Waite came to work together and left together each day. Mosey got along with Slide except toward the end of the breakfast rush when Slide would become irritable. Mosey noticed that Slide left the kitchen every day just after the morning rush and before the lunch crowd. He figured out that Slide went behind the restaurant to drink because when he returned, Mosey occasionally smelled the booze, and Slide always seemed more relaxed after a couple of drinks. Around dinner time, however, Slide became irritable again and, sometimes, mean until he took another break behind the restaurant and returned to his duties calmer and more relaxed.

Slide was finishing the lunch orders when the owner, who ran the dining room and cash register, stepped into the kitchen. Slide was in an irritable mood and told the owner: Get out of my fucking kitchen. The owner, Bates Green, told Slide he needed to cut out the drinking. He had been messing up lunch orders all day. If things didn't improve, he would replace Slide with Mosey who didn't drink and who was becoming a good cook.

That fucking punk?, Slide sneered. They fuck each other, him and Waite. You're gonna let a fucking punk run my kitchen?

Slide grabbed a huge meat cleaver and swung it at Bates who jumped back. Mosey rushed forward to block Slide but Slide was already swinging the cleaver again and struck Mosey's left arm between the shoulder and elbow slicing through the muscle to the bone which cracked. Slide dropped the cleaver and ran which, under the circumstances, was his best move and his last contribution to the restaurant.

Waite rushed Mosey to Charity Hospital in a car driven by the owner, and the doctor told Mosey that they would have to remove most of his arm below the break. After the surgery and a week of recuperation in the hospital, Waite took Mosey home to his small upstairs flat. Mosey couldn't return to work in the restaurant so he stayed home while Waite resumed his job. Waite made very little money, only enough to cover his needs and pay the rent. Without Mosey's income, he could barely provide for both of them. Mosey decided that this arrangement was unfair to Waite and wanted to move out but his options were limited. He didn't want to return to Pachacuti to stay with one of his siblings now that he had lived in Atlanta and Cincinnati. He couldn't go to New York to stay with Swee; she was making a new life for herself. Returning to Atlanta to partner with Trique, as much as he might have wanted that, was out of the question. Trique, he felt, would never give up chasing other men, or women, for that matter. Mosey wanted one lover, like Waite. But he couldn't ask Waite to take care of both of them when Waite had so little himself. So he told Waite that he had decided to leave for Detroit where he might live with his sister, Habboey, and her husband, Critten Gant. Waite was dumbfounded and pleaded with Mosey to stay but Mosey was determined. Mosey wrote his sister, Habboey, in Detroit. He asked her if he could come and stay until he could find work and get his own place. She wrote back and said he could stay as long as necessary. Since she and her husband were making good money and had their own home, Habboey told Mosey he could come and stay until he could work out a new life for himself. Mosey packed his one travel bag, caught a train with money Habboey sent him, and said goodbye to Waite. Mosey took a train to Detroit; Habboey met him at the station. They took a streetcar and bus to the Gant home. Now twenty years old, Mosey was ready for whatever his new life offered.

Waite understood why Mosey left but he wasn't happy about it. He didn't want Mosey to go but he could do nothing to stop his leaving. Waite also had few options. Needing to share his distress, he told his mother about his relationship with Mosey. She had already surmised her son's love interest and understood how hurt he was by not being able to support Mosey to keep him in Cincinnati at their flat. But she also saw an opportunity that she had long nurtured like a fragile plant; she wanted Waite to go to college. He would be the first in the family to do so. Arleeta wasn't smart enough nor was she interested. Waite was smart but his mother thought that he wasn't motivated. She revealed her plan:

Waite, this would be good for you. You could be something. Working in a restaurant is a decent job; your father and I have decent jobs but you could be something and make a good living. I always thought that you could be a teacher. Teaching school, that would be good for you and your people. You could help raise up the race. You're smart, good looking like your momma, and I know that you won't get married to a woman. I know that. So, make something more of your life and go to college. Become a teacher and live well however you want to live. If it's with another man, that's okay. You know I don't believe all that church talk about sinning. If you can be a good person, and I know you are, you deserve a good life. Your daddy is wrong for saying you can't come to your own home with whoever you want and he knows that I would rather leave him than shut out any of my children, including you. If he wants Cassius to be his favorite, that's okay with me. But he can't run you out of this family. Never. But if he won't accept you, that's your ticket to make your own life as you want it. And, Waite, your momma wants things for you that you don't even know yet that you want. I want you to go to college. I can see in the white families that I work for, that their kids go to college, and they can make something of their lives. They can do things even their parents can't do. So, if it works for white folks, it can work for colored people too. I know it. I heard that Oberlin College takes colored with white people. No difference. You could go there. Mr. Adelman, my boss, says that colored can get scholarships; that's free money for school. You could do it and get a job to support yourself there too.

Waite was moved by his mother's words but he couldn't see college for himself. He liked his job. He liked having his own place even if Mosey wasn't there. And, he liked Cincinnati. All he knew about Oberlin was that it was in a small Ohio town and probably didn't have many men who liked men. He would stay in Cincinnati.

Waite's father died in 1949 a few months after Mosey left for Detroit. Waite told his mother that he would move back to the family house to help with expenses and with his younger siblings. She agreed, and Waite moved into May Easter Carvey's house. But his mother's willingness was her opportunity to continue to preach her vision of his future. She figured out that her son didn't want to be without a boyfriend and she argued that, once he finished college, he could live wherever he wanted and meet whoever might fill his life. He had to see the bigger prize than someone in his life now. He had to have a larger life, wider horizons, and many more possibilities. She was unrelenting until he made an application, was accepted, and began college the next year, 1950.

Waite's four years in Oberlin were exciting and transformational. He met people from all over the country and from all backgrounds. There were some Negro students and lots of whites. There were also a few Asian and African students. Waite had some difficulty adjusting at first but many of the other students and his professors seemed to accept him and encourage him. He was always reminded that he was a Negro. However, he seldom felt that that was something that held him back. In fact, some white students wanted to know him because he was a Negro. Before he graduated with his teaching degree, the Cleveland public schools offered him a job. His assignment was in a Negro neighborhood on the east side of the city. He found an upper flat in a house in the same area and settled down to a comfortable but unexciting life.

Waite's sister, Arleeta, had tried marriage and found it not to her liking. Cooking, taking care of someone, cleaning house, letting a man have her body when he wanted, not when she wanted, these were not things she could appreciate. She asked Waite if she could move to Cleveland and live with him. Their brother, Cassius, would look after their mother in Cincinnati. Waite didn't hesitate; he told her to come as soon as she could. Waite's mother wasn't so happy about the plan, not because she minded having two of her children living some distance from her, but because she thought Arleeta was a useless human being and would spoil Waite's life. She would suck him dry with her needs and contribute nothing. Waite wasn't worried. He knew what Arleeta was like and even if she was at her worst, he wouldn't mind having some family nearby.

Arleeta arrived at Waite's flat with her clothes, some possessions, and her cat, Miss Lena. She took Waite's second bedroom. She also decided, after a few weeks, that she wanted to redecorate his flat. Waite didn't mind since he hadn't spent much effort or money on the place. With Waite's money, she bought new furniture and drapes and rugs. Waite finally had to caution his sister to hold off any further purchases because his salary couldn't cover what she already ordered. Arleeta's feelings were hurt because she thought that she was doing her brother a favor. But, by intent or not, Arleeta and Miss Lena gradually took over Waite's flat, making Waite feel like a tenant in his own home.

Waite's intermediate school was orderly and subdued. The principal ruled with commanding and unchallenged authority. Teachers, like Waite, wore suits or sport coats; the women wore dresses or suits. All of the students were black. Waite's social studies classes were filled with mostly attentive, if not overly bright, students. Waite felt that they weren't really stupid but so lacking of any knowledge of the world beyond their humble neighborhood. Of course, Waite had not known much of the world before college so he knew that the students' limitations were not their fault. He worked hard to help them overcome their deficiencies but, with thirty-five students per class and six classes a day, there wasn't a lot he could do.

Waite was attracted to another male teacher who was a few years older. Woodward F. Templeton was short, stocky, and balding. He also wore rimless glasses that accentuated his large, seductive eyes. Woodward wore expensive suits, sport jackets, and ties that made him look prosperous and important. He probably was impressed by his own image more than anyone else. Woodward was friends with some of the other teachers. In addition to everything else, he was witty and outspoken. He was a natural leader and became a faculty spokesman to the principal. Many of the teachers were black, but about a third were white, as was the principal. Woodward was forceful in speaking for himself and his colleagues. It was this that attracted Waite. He saw Woodward as an articulate, sharp, and fearless man who demanded respect. Waite was also impressed by the fleeting glimpses he got of a significant bulge in the crotch of Woodward's carefully pressed and pleated slacks.

Waite asked Woodward out for dinner on a Friday night after he had discreetly determined that Woodward was not married or dating women. Gaining this information had taken patience and time. Woodward refused, however, without any explanation.

While Arleeta had taken over Waite's flat and, essentially, made it into her own, she had not contributed anything to its outfitting or upkeep. She expected Waite to pay for everything including all of her personal needs and wants. Her mother came for a visit, and May Easter was outraged. She told her daughter that she had way overstepped the bounds of family. She had to get a job immediately and contribute her share to her new home. Arleeta whined that there weren't any good jobs and, besides, Waite didn't mind their arrangement because he had a good job and paid all of the bills. May Easter had a talk with Waite and explained that giving his sister a free ride was not in his sister's best interests because she would always be lazy and expect others to take care of her. And it was not in Waite's best interest because he couldn't live his life freely with his sister and her cat filling his home. She was adamant. Arleeta knew that she wouldn't win an argument with her mother so she thought she would find a way to humor her until she returned to Cincinnati. Arleeta, with minimal effort, got a part-time job in a beauty parlor, Jonetta's Beauty Palace. She knew how to straighten and style hair although she didn't have a license. The shop's owner, Jonetta Blount, felt that, if an inspector came by, she would say that Arleeta was just a temporary assistant. Besides, with a little work and study, Arleeta could get a license. May Easter was anxious to set Waite's home back in order. With her shiftless daughter now working, she insisted that Arleeta also find her own place to live; May Easter wanted Waite to have his place to himself, without Arleeta or May Easter. When she felt that everything was in order again, May Easter announced her plans to return home.

Waite, I was wondering if you've met anyone.

Well, there's a very interesting teacher with a very snobby name: Woodward F. Templeton II— the F. stands for Franklin. He's kind of the leader of the teachers, black and white. I've talked to him, and he seems interested. But when I asked him out to dinner, he refused.

Are you sure he's not married or something?

I'm sure.

Where does he live?

What are you going to do? Pay him a visit too?

No, I was just wondering. Something might be going on that he doesn't want you or anyone else to know.

I can't imagine.

Well, you see, that's the problem. You can't imagine. Find out where he lives. Pay him a visit.

I can't do that. If he doesn't want to go out, that's his business. We can be friends at work.

May Easter was not satisfied. Before she returned home to Cincinnati, she wanted to know all there was to know about Mr. Templeton. She made up her mind to a direct approach. She convinced Waite to take her to his school for a visit. When she was introduced to Woodward, she asked him if she could talk to him privately before school ended for the day. So, after Woodward's last class, he met May Easter in his office, a tiny but tidy space with a few books, two chairs, and a desk.

What can I do for you, Mrs. Carvey?

Mr. Templeton, I don't believe in wasting folks' time. Waite asked you out to dinner, and you refused without explanation.

I would have been happy to go to dinner with your son but my Fridays and Saturdays are always booked.

Is that because of someone else?

Mrs. Carvey, you may not be aware that public school teachers are under very close scrutiny by their fellow teachers, the principal, and parents. If any one of us was involved in something, however harmless and legal but not approved of by most people, their job and career would be in grave jeopardy.

Does that mean that you are doing something harmless and legal but questionable?

Do you think, Mrs. Carvey, that, if I were, I would admit it to you, a complete stranger?

But I already know what you are doing. You work at a little nightclub weekends, the Blue Jewel. You see, all of the old ladies, like me, like to go there, and those ladies talk to each other at the beauty shop where Waite's sister now works. Those old ladies like to see the shows and they love the amazing men dressed as women. One of those old ladies showed me some pictures she took. She was very proud of them. I was very impressed with one well-turned lady, Delores DeVore, who reminds me a lot of you.

I would like to deny your assertion but it would probably be pointless. You're quite a detective. Congratulations. Thank you, by the way, for the compliment. Yes, that is my secret, and I hope that it will be our secret but I suspect at a price.

Yes, of course, it will be our secret, Mr. Templeton. But the price is this: Go out to dinner with Waite. He likes you, and he will keep your secret too if you tell him. He's a lovely man, and so are you. Make a boy's mother happy.

And, so, Templeton went to dinner with Waite; May Easter returned to Cincinnati a happy woman; and Arleeta Carvey become a useful person.

NEW YORK

After Swee and Amity arrived in New York City from Pachacuti, Amity telephoned her father's bachelor brother, Aaron Lowe, who lived in Harlem, and he invited her to his apartment. When they arrived, he could hardly suppress his surprise to see his niece with a black woman. Nevertheless, he asked them to be seated in his living room and offered them tea and cookies. They explained their situation and asked if he could help them. Although he was not a devoutly religious man, he was uneasy with the idea of two women—one black—staying in his apartment. Nevertheless, he was sympathetic to their plight and offered his living room to them for a few days until they could find someplace else to live. And, so, for their first days in New York, Amity and Swee had a safe haven and the possibility of re-starting their lives.

Amity suggested that they go to a church and ask some of the ladies about a room, and that's how they found their first place. It was a lot less space than the house in Pachacuti but it was big enough for the few things they brought with them. Now they had to find jobs. The ladies at the church told Swee that they knew a white family that needed a domestic. Amity, on her own, got a job as a waitress in a Harlem restaurant. Swee called the family, made an appointment, and went to the family's apartment, a big spacious place overlooking Riverside Park and the Hudson River. The family had three children, two of whom were too young to go to school. So, the couple wanted a live-in nanny for the children and a housekeeper to clean and cook. Swee would have her own room and one day a week off. She took the job.

After Amity and Swee arrived in New York City, they began moving in different directions. Swee wanted her life to be as much like it was in Pachacuti while Amity saw that there were new opportunities for her. It wasn't that she and Swee didn't care about each other; it was that, for Amity, New York was not Pachacuti. She discovered ambition that she didn't know she had and she wanted to take a chance to find out what she could do.

Amity and Swee, therefore, only saw each other on Saturday, when Swee's employers went to worship with their children. Amity liked her work, and her customers liked her. One of them, Hiram Brown, told Amity that she was as pretty as a pitcher of cream. He said he knew a white guy with a nightclub in Harlem who was looking for light-skinned colored dancers. Amity said that she didn't know how to dance. Hiram said that she could learn. And she did. But that meant that she couldn't be with Swee on her day off. So Swee stopped going to their room in the apartment building and stayed, instead, with her employers all week.

Amity became a good dancer. She had a natural grace and the dancing, as such, wasn't demanding. She could kick, twirl, and move her arms in a coordinated way that looked as professional as some of the other women who had been dancing longer. In fact, Amity began to improvise new dance movements that the dance captain adopted into their routine. Hiram Brown stopped by the nightclub periodically and saw that Amity was a natural. She also seemed to become more attractive—her body filled out—and she clearly was one of the favorites with the audience probably because of her fair complexion and long straight hair. He began to ask her out on dates but she always refused with a polite excuse. Mostly, she said, she was too tired working two jobs, as dancer and waitress. Hiram persisted and, eventually, she agreed to go to an after-hours place for a drink one night. From then on, Amity and Hiram became lovers; she gave up the room and moved into his apartment.

Hiram Brown made good money as a salesman in a Harlem furniture store. Although his real interest was show business, the opportunities were too limited for blacks, even in New York City. So, he hung around clubs like the one where Amity worked as a dancer. She took over the job of dance captain. Hiram seemed to recognize Amity's potential before she did. He worked his contacts in Harlem to see if he could get her a break downtown. Black dancers were not unknown in downtown clubs, but they were rare and usually not integrated into the choruses. Hiram kept working his contacts. He also suggested that Amity adopt a stage name. Amity Lowe had no marquee potential.

Amity, what about something sophisticated like Alexis Lowe?

You ever heard of a colored woman called Alexis? Don't be silly. That's a white name. Who do you think we would be fooling?

Well, Ella, Pearl, and Mahalia are already taken.

You know what? I've always liked the name Claire.

Claire? Well, that's neither black nor white.

But Claire Lowe doesn't sound good. How about something French-sounding like Claire Lamere?

Hey! Claire Latour.

That's not bad. Claire Latour. I like it.

When Amity discussed it with Swee, she didn't like it.

Claire Latour sounds a little phony. It's too, I don't know, sham.

Well, it's just a stage name, just so that I can get a foot in downtown, Swee. It won't hurt anything.

But people back home in Pachacuti won't know who you are?

My brother in Tallahassee will always know who I am.

Amity, you don't need a new name. With your talent, someone, sometime, is going to discover you and give you a chance. And I am going to come and see you.

Hiram convinced his friend, a Harlem club owner named Darius Dommel, to bring a downtown club owner named Mark Wise to see Amity. The show that night was crisp and electric. The moves and steps were quite original, and Wise recognized immediately the potential of the choreography. When, after the performance, he was introduced to Amity, he asked if she were Jewish with a name like Lowe. You could be, he said. Keep it. It will work for you. Claire Latour was immediately retired although Amity sometimes thought that her mother's last name, Long-Green, could be tried on for size. She never did though.

After Amity moved in with Hiram, Swee began to meet other women, mostly doing the kind of work she was doing. She talked with them when she took the youngest children to Riverside Park. One woman in particular, Gulley Atkinson, was friendlier than most. Gulley was also from the South. Swee explained how she came to New York and how she was now unable to see her woman friend. Gulley suggested that, since she also had Saturday off, they could get together. Gulley was from the Delta and, like Swee, was attracted to women. But, unlike Swee, she had been married to a man in the Delta and had three children, two of whom were with their father. The youngest lived with Gulley. She left, but did not divorce, her husband. He expected that she would return some day but Gulley knew that she wouldn't and probably would never see her other two children again. Gulley and Swee became lovers.

Swee found another person very much like herself. They were happy with their lives and decided how they could live together with Gulley's youngest child, a girl named Meer. Swee would inform her employers that she would no longer live in their apartment; they agreed. With luck and a good tip, Swee and Gulley found an inexpensive apartment in Harlem with a living room, two bedrooms, a kitchen and bath. There, they established a life together until Gulley found out from relatives in the Delta that her husband had died, and her two children were living temporarily with his folks. Gulley asked her employer for a leave to go get her other children. Her employer agreed because Swee stepped in to take care of the family in Gulley's absence. After a week, Gulley returned with her other two boys, Bone and Donald. Gulley's husband had named Bone as a joke that Gulley never appreciated. Neither did Bone who fought kids about his name and had, himself, become quite a tough, thuggish kid. His younger brother, Donald, feared and admired him. When Gulley arrived back in New York with the two boys, the Swee/Gulley household was turned upside down. Three rooms for five people was too little space so both women had to take drastic measures to integrate the boys into their lives. Swee had some experience with this since Mosey and Trique had lived with her and Amity in Pachacuti. But Bone was difficult and belligerent; Donald generally did what his brother did to stay on his good side and only added to the turmoil.

Bone was intelligent but not interested in school. Donald was not as intelligent but a better student when he was not around his brother. Bone quickly found a group of boys his age to roam the neighborhood. Soon, he was in trouble for vandalism, petty thievery, and bullying other kids. Gulley and Swee tried to help Bone but he was unreachable. When he was fifteen, he was sent to juvenile detention for assault. After six months, he was released. Gulley and Swee didn't know what to do with him. They didn't want him back in their apartment but he had no other place to go.

Swee went with the flow. Her life with Gulley Atkinson and Gulley's three children, especially the troubled and troubling oldest boy, Bone, was exhausting. In fact, life was hard as well as raucous but Swee went with the flow. Gulley was sweet and loving when she had a moment away from work and child-rearing. But such moments were, well, few. Swee was philosophical. She had a decent job as housekeeper and nanny to a nice, considerate middle-class white family, and she had her own home life with Gulley. So, she couldn't complain. Life in New York was at least as good as it had been with Amity Lowe in Pachacuti. It was not quite as peaceful but black folks weren't hanging from trees in Riverside Park like burned fruit. She and Gulley agreed that Bone was a serious disruptive factor in their lives and home. Constantly in petty trouble, belligerent to his mother and Swee, abusive to the two younger children, Bone was the ticking time-bomb threatening to blow up everything. His mother tried reasoning with him. She tried rewards. She tried threats and punishments. She could not banish him, however, because her maternal instincts couldn't conceive of that. Swee had become so attached to Gulley that she didn't consider leaving their home for a more tranquil place, like returning to her employer's apartment. She went with the flow.

Bone ran with a tough crowd of boys his age. But they were not the toughest in Harlem. Bone's smart talk and violence brought him and his gang face to face with the 127s, a gang of boys a little older, a little more violent, and a lot more street-wise than Bone's crew. They jumped Bone and his boys one evening and left Bone on the sidewalk bleeding from a stab wound in his side. Police were called. An ambulance came and the broken Bone was carted away to a hospital. When his mother was eventually notified late the same night, she and Swee went to see him. He was close to death having bled so profusely on the sidewalk. But, after a few days, he rallied, and within two weeks returned home.

Swee tried to cover her job and care for Gulley's other children while Gulley stayed with Bone in the hospital. But her excuses for being late or leaving early began to irritate her employers, Sarah and Benjamin Weiss. They were annoyed that their household routine and the care of their children were disrupted by Swee's increasingly erratic schedule and distractedness. Sarah and Ben finally had a late night talk and decided to give Swee a week's termination notice. They would look for a more reliable housekeeper. Ben was tasked with the pruning.

Swee, my wife and I have noticed that you are not performing to our expectations. Although you've been a good housekeeper and taken excellent care of the children, lately you've been unreliable and not focused on your duties. We've decided that we have to let you go and find a new girl. You have another week with two additional weeks pay, and then we'll bring in someone new.

Mr. Weiss, I know I haven't been all here lately but you and Mrs. Weiss have never complained about my work in the past. I know that this is a temporary situation because of some problems at home and I'll be back on track in a day or so.

May I ask: What are the problems at home?

The woman I live with—we share an apartment in Harlem—has a teenage son who is a hellion. He was stabbed a few nights ago by some neighborhood hoodlums, and he nearly died in the hospital. His mother has been staying with him while I have been looking after her other two children. That's why my schedule has been so messed up and I've been pre-occupied with my friend and her family. Everything will be back to normal in a day or so.

Are you sure?

Yes, I think so.

Well, my wife and I have been happy with you up until now but we can't risk the well-being of our family because our employee can't do her job properly.

I'm telling you that this is a temporary thing. As soon as my friend's son is better and can go to school, and my friend can return to work, everything will smooth out.

But when will that be?

I can't say for sure but within a week or so.

But that means you'll continue to be distracted with your work here, your schedule will be uncertain, and we will be in a situation where we won't know if you will be here or not to take care of our children and our home.

Surely, Mr. Weiss, you and your wife could find a way to let things slide just a little for a short period of time until I can get back to my regular routine?

Swee, that's not our job but yours. You're asking a lot. We're both busy; that's why we have you. The children cannot take care of themselves, at least, not at this time. So, if you can't be here, then we will have to have someone more responsible and dependable.

I'm telling you that this is temporary; it's an emergency. Surely, you can understand that and appreciate that I have given you one hundred percent up until now.

But, "now" is a problem with no resolution in sight.

A week or two more! Is that too much to ask?

I'm afraid so.

Well, you know what Mr. Weiss? I've been practically begging you. But I'm not begging anymore. You can keep this fucking job. You've never had a problem with me before. I admit I've fallen down these past few days but you've not asked me why I can't do my work as before. You're just ready to toss me out because I'm just another nigger to you, a lazy, unreliable, shiftless nigger. Well, get yourself another nigger. Sweet Tea Sellabie has survived worse than you.

Really, Swee, that's awfully strong and unnecessarily vulgar talk from a woman. I can't have that kind of language in my home. I can't imagine why you would suddenly start talking to me like that. I've never used derogatory language with you. I've never even thought of the things that you are turning into accusations of me. I'm really hurt that you even believe that I would think that way. What have I ever said or done to make you talk like that to me?

I lost it Mr. Weiss. I'm desperate. I'm trying to do right by you and Mrs. Weiss and the kids and I'm trying to do right by my girlfriend and her children. You just don't know what we are going through. You live so far away from our kinds of problems. You don't seem to understand what we colored folks have to deal with every day. We are just your servants, your help. We have lives too, you know. And, often, they are very difficult not because we choose to live that way but because we don't have a lot of choices. I was taught to stand up for myself and be an honorable person. I've been honorable with you and your family but now I'm having difficulties and I need some understanding and some flexibility. I will more than make up for my irregularities as soon as I can. That's all that I, Sweet Tea Sellabie, asks.

Sweet Tea? Excuse me, that's your name?

Yes, that's my real name. My people now call me Swee but to some folks I'm still Sweet Tea, and a Sellabie. My people in Pachacuti have lived through more shit than you can imagine. White folks burned down my house, killed my cat and dog, and drove me out of my home. I need your job; there may be other jobs somewhere but I'm happy here with you. I just need a break.

Swee, I'm sure that if you had explained things to Mrs. Weiss and myself prior to all this, we could have understood and made other arrangements until all of this tragedy was past you. But you simply put us in a difficult situation. We aren't trying to be unreasonable but we need a solution too. By the way, how is your girlfriend's son?

Bone? His name is Bone, and my girlfriend's name is Gulley Atkinson. He's home now and she is nursing him. I'm looking after the other two, Donald and Meer.

I think that Mrs. Weiss—Sarah—will understand when I explain things to her. We wouldn't want to cause you further distress on top of what has already happened. In fact, what can I do to help you?

That would be enough. Just let me work through this difficult time.

Okay. A deal. By the way, why were you named Sweet Tea?

It was my momma, Darissa McKree's, idea. My daddy, Hanton Sellabie, loved my momma's sweet tea and, so, when I was born, she thought that he would love me like he loved his sweet tea. And he did.

Swee settled back into her work routine once Gulley could leave Bone on his own again. But Gulley had to find a new job because her employer, who was not as understanding as Swee's employer, had let her go when she began to miss work. The Weiss family started taking an interest in Swee, seeing her as more than just a hard worker. Sarah Weiss had wondered what exactly Swee had said to her husband that had resulted in such a quick reversal of their plans to fire her. When she asked Swee, Swee said that she warned Ben that she would kick his white ass into next week if he tried to separate her from the Weiss children. Sarah immediately understood that this nondescript colored woman that they had hired was replaced by someone far more sharp, colorful and profane.

Swee turned forty-nine in 1960. She voted for John F. Kennedy and felt, like many, that a new age had begun when he became president. The Weiss had also voted for Kennedy and they, too, were hopeful. With the Weiss children in school, however, Swee was not needed six days a week. Swee thought about something she had long put out of her mind. She wanted to return to school. In Pachacuti, she had only completed high school. The crash of 1929 didn't greatly affect folks in Pachacuti but opportunities diminished. She was happy to make a life with Amity and then came Mosey whom she treated like an adopted brother. But now at forty-nine, she wanted to try for more. She asked Ben and Sarah about school. They volunteered that they had friends at several schools and found a program that would take Swee.

Swee was interested in social work. She wanted to help women—black women especially—like herself with limited education and means. She wanted them to overcome their gender, race, and social status so that they, too, could live like the Weiss family.

School was a shock to Swee. She was unprepared in so many ways except for her determination and intellect. But her academic preparation was so weak and it had been so distant in the past that her determination faltered. Her English teacher, Natalie Benson, a decade younger than Swee, and a somewhat prim and sarcastic professor, saw Swee struggling, unsuccessfully. She called Swee to her office for a conference.

Miss Sellabie, you're not doing well in my class. You don't seem to understand the material that you are reading; your papers are confused, rambling, and completely ungrammatical.

I know Professor Benson. I can't seem to figure this out. I never wrote before, just letters to my family.

What do you write about in your letters?

I write about what I'm doing here in New York. That's all.

Well, I want you to write more, and I think that writing will help you with the books you are reading.

How so?

When you write, you organize your thoughts and find the best way you have to express your thoughts. Then, when you read, you begin to see how someone else has done the same thing. How big is your family?

Oh, there were lots of us but only a few alive now.

Well, I'll tell you what I want you to do. Write the story of your family, a kind of history. Go back to your earliest ancestors. Do you know anything about them?

Some. There are lots of family stories.

Well, write about them all. Start at the beginning and bring the story up to the present.

But I don't have all of the facts and dates.

That's not a problem for now. Write what you know. Make it clear what you don't know and why. That's all part of the storytelling. Can you have it for me next week?

With my other school work too?

Yes.

Maybe, I think so.

Swee was surprised how quickly she completed her family history. She let Sarah Weiss read it first and this is how it began: My family is one of the oldest Negro families in Pachacuti, Georgia; older, some say, than most of the white families in town. Sesto was the first person in our family whose name we know. He was an enslaved man who died in 1853 before Emancipation. He had a son, Fairfax, who was born into slavery in 1849 but died a free man in 1902. I never knew him because I wasn't born until 1911 but my father, Hanton Sellabie, told me about him. My father also let me know why our family was called Sellabie; Grandfather Fairfax always had this to say about difficulties—*C'est la vie*. I don't know how he learned any French but *C'est la vie* became Sellabie, our family name, and our motto.

After she finished reading Swee's paper, Sarah Weiss made some suggestions and corrections.

Swee, I think that telling your family's story worked very well for you. But, I have another suggestion that I want you to think about. Your storytelling is good, but you could have a better grasp of the structure of language, and I have an idea that might help.

What's that, Mrs. Weiss?

I think that you should take Latin because knowing Latin will help you understand the fundamental structure of English. Besides, knowing another language, even one that isn't used anymore, except in literature, will also help you understand the meaning and richness of words and their relationship to one another.

I don't know, Mrs. Weiss. Latin, that's sounds awfully hard.

Well, it will be hard at first but you're a smart woman. Nothing can stand in the way of your learning except you. Give it a try. I bet your professor knows a really good teacher who can coach you. Anyway, give it some thought.

Alright, I'll think about it.

Swee left the Weiss apartment and headed home. She couldn't wait to show Gulley her story. Gulley read it after dinner and liked it. Swee also wanted Amity to read it so she called her.

Amity had been hired as a dance captain and assistant choreographer for an Off-Off-Broadway show. She was busy with rehearsals but had Swee meet her at the theater in Greenwich Village. Swee had never been in a theater other than those showing movies. She entered the small auditorium and sat in the back. Amity was onstage coaching the dancers. When they took a break, Swee walked to the stage and called Amity.

Hey, girl. You look good. Can you teach me to dance like that?

Are you kidding? You taught me how to dance. You danced with me all those nights in Pachacuti. I didn't know it then but that was what I was born to do.

Amity, you could have done anything you decided to do. You just needed a chance. Here you are.

And, what about you, Sweet Tea Sellabie?

Read my paper for my English professor. I'll leave it for you. Can you get it back to me by Monday?

Sugar, that's gonna be hard. We're working all the time, late at night, too. But, for you, I'll stay up late. Hiram can sleep without me one night.

How is Hiram?

Sweetie, Hiram Brown is a good man but he's not much in bed. In fact, he doesn't seem much interested in sex.

So, how about you?

I'm okay. Work keeps me busy and focused. I can live without sex. For now.

Don't let the well go dry.

Girl, you make me laugh. How is Gulley?

She's my rock. But those kids of hers are wearying, especially Bone. He's been beat up, cut, arrested, jailed, and he hasn't slowed down yet.

I'm really sorry to hear that but listen, Swee, I've got to get back to these dancers. I'll read this tonight and give it to you tomorrow. Give me a kiss goodbye, Girl. Ummm. No wonder they call you Sweet Tea.

Swee's paper was not only a big success with her professor but the things that Natalie Benson also had said about writing and reading started to click. More importantly, Swee saw herself overcoming her fears, fears about the larger world; she hadn't consciously realized that she had those fears. Literature for her had always been for white people. She didn't know history or religion or art or anything beyond the very narrow worlds of her youth and now middle age. She still didn't know much but she wasn't as fearful of discovery. And she could repress the instinct to reject white culture. And through her study of white culture, she stumbled on the hidden treasure of black culture. She went with the flow.

The day that Swee decided to stop straightening her hair and leave it naturally curly was a sign to everyone that she was becoming a new person. Gulley wasn't sure that she liked the change. Gulley's kids, Donald and Meer, were at first surprised and then enthusiastic. Meer coerced Gulley to allow her own hair remain natural. Donald, who had always had his hair cut right down to the scalp leaving only a faint shadow, let his hair grow out into a tightly curled mass. His and his sister's Afros were becoming popular among their classmates at school. Swee approved. Gulley eventually let her own short, cropped, and straightened hair go natural.

Swee continued writing, encouraged by Natalie Benson and other professors whose intermediary and advanced writing classes she took. Although still intending to complete her studies in social work, she knew that writing touched something in her unlike anything else she had experienced. She tried to think how she could write more. But social work was the practical thing to do. She was good at her social work studies and she could see that she would finish them, get a job, and write on the side. Maybe, some day, she would get a break like Amity. In the meanwhile, she made up her mind to follow Sarah Weiss's suggestion and study Latin. The flow would take her; she only needed to be ready.

The downtown theater scene was exactly what Amity needed. But, it was almost completely white, and that bothered her. Nevertheless, the opportunities were greater downtown than they were uptown. Amity suspected that her acceptance into the downtown scene was due to her appearance. She didn't look like a Negro by white people's standards. Most whites thought that she was, perhaps, Latin or Middle Eastern. Amity realized that it was to her advantage not to correct anyone's perceptions. If she could pass, she would. Within herself, she knew who she was and she would never let go of that. Her home life with Hiram in Harlem immediately reminded her, if she somehow would forget, where she came from and where she belonged.

Amity made friends easily because she was vibrant as well as attractive. Although she rebuffed male advances with the fact that she had a live-in boyfriend, she was drawn to certain male dancers who didn't seem romantically interested in women. She struck up a conversation with one of these men during a break in rehearsals for a new musical.

Hi. I've seen you dance and you're really good. My name is Amity, what's your name?

People call me Zipper. Zipper Schiele.

Zipper? That's an odd name.

Odd maybe but accurate.

What do you mean?

Oh, I have a fondness for zippers or, shall we say, unzipping zippers. I like to see what's inside of those zippers.

You're not talking about women's zippers, are you?

No. Ma'am. Strictly male. I'm a cock-sucker. Does that surprise you?

Not really. I know something about men, and men liking sex with other men. I've had similar experience with women.

You bite the clit?

Guilty. A pussy-eater. Although my main squeeze now is a man, if given the opportunity, I could bite another clit?

My, my. A sister, indeed.

And a brother. Welcome to the family. Where are you from? You have a strange accent.

Mississippi.

Oh, lord.

I know. I couldn't wait to get out of there. Where are you from because you have a little accent too?

Georgia.

Oh, lord. Two country bumpkins.

In the big city.

Zipper and Amity became good friends and remained so even after their gig in the new, but terrible, musical ended after only a few performances. During the following months of looking for new work, both were hired for a downtown musical review that quickly gained an admiring audience. One night after a show, Zipper asked Amity if she would like to accompany him to a party in a downtown artist's studio. A large crowd was expected of artists, writers, and performers. She would have a chance to meet a lot of people who were beginning to make names for themselves in their fields. Amity accepted the invitation. When they arrived in the cigarette smoke-filled studio, the place was already crowded with whites and a few blacks and Asians. Most folks were standing and talking while smoking, drinking, and eating the abundant cold-cuts and cheese. Amity noticed a strange odor, one that she had experienced previously. Before she could sort things out, someone passed her a joint. She looked at Zipper and he smiled.

Never tried it?

No. I don't smoke.

Go ahead. It will give you a buzz. Just inhale. Hold it in for a minute and exhale. You may like it.

Amity did as suggested. Coughed. Teared up. Coughed again. Then, bravely took another drag on the joint.

See, that wasn't so bad, was it?

As Amity and Zipper moved through the crowd, they came to a group of people sitting in a corner of the studio on the floor. Amity had never been anywhere socially where people sat on the floor. Negroes did not sit on anybody's floor unless forced. Somehow, it seemed funny to her and she started to laugh.

What's funny?

People are sitting on the floor.

So?

I've never seen that before.

Come on. Let's join them.

Okay.

Amity and Zipper sat down. Amity was already feeling the effects of the joint and felt very relaxed.

Zipper, can I tell you something?

Sure.

I've never been to a party with white people before?

What do you mean? You've never been to any party before?

No. I've never been to a party with white people. I'm not white.

What are you? You look white.

I'm mixed race—black, Indian, and Jewish.

Wow.

What do you think about that?

I'd say that you're a triple winner. I thought that I was an outsider. You are outside of the outsiders. I'm a homo and that makes me not only an outsider but also mentally ill and possibly a criminal.

I say, good for you.

Sister.

Brother.

Amity and Zipper went to many more parties and Amity met more people in various art fields in New York. She became popular among the crowd and that, in turn, opened doors for her for more work. She came to know the downtown theater scene better and began attending avant-garde dance and theater performances. She also began taking workshops with individual dancers to improve her technique and develop her choreographic ideas. Zipper persuaded her to bleach her hair blonde. Amity became part of the scene

ATLANTA II

By hitchhiking from Pachacuti, Martalee made it as far north as Atlanta which wasn't very far north. But that is where the car she hitchhiked in broke down a few miles from downtown. Martalee considered what she would do next; she didn't have many options. She had no money. She didn't know anyone, and she didn't know where to go. So she walked for a while towards downtown. She passed a corner grocery store that had a sign in the window for Help Wanted. She went inside and asked the clerk at the cash register about a job. He asked her if she could lift boxes and restock the shelves. She said she could but soon proved that most of the boxes were too heavy for her. But she quickly learned the produce and was very good with the customers who asked for help. Eventually, she got stronger and could even move most of the boxes. She was referred by the storekeeper to a room in a lady's house nearby, a woman who was one of the store's customers, in fact. She settled in and, after a few months, realized that she was pregnant. As her pregnancy became more apparent, her landlady convinced the owner of the grocery to let Martalee operate the cash register until after her baby was born. Meanwhile, Martalee suspected that she was pregnant with twins, a fact that she kept secret from everyone. Thinking ahead, she had decided to have the twins delivered by a black midwife in case their color revealed their paternity—a dangerous and unforgivable transgression in the white South. The twins were born in 1946. When she returned to her rooming house, she brought only one child with her and named him Dunn; she never mentioned to her landlady that the other twin, whom she named Alfred, was left with a wet-nurse. Martalee was eighteen.

Her landlady, Arista Crimm, became a kind of surrogate mother to Martalee and a grandmother to Dunn. She had learned the story of Martalee's hasty flight from Pachacuti but, significantly, not the precise details, and wondered if Martalee's family should know the whereabouts of their daughter. Arista knew the danger of such contact, however. She was impressed with the violence visited upon Swee's house by Martalee's brothers. What she didn't know, because Martalee deliberately didn't tell her, was that Trique and Swee were black, and had Arista known, she wouldn't have been so motherly to Martalee and Dunn. Baby Dunn didn't give away his mother's secret because he looked white. When Dunn was four months old, Martalee returned to the grocery store. But she began to develop plans for herself and her son. She wanted to finish high school, go to secretarial school, and get an office job. With Arista babysitting Dunn, she started night courses and completed high school in one year. Then she enrolled in secretarial school, also at night. By 1950, she was ready to find an office job. Several companies were hiring; Martalee made a list from the newspaper want ads. She took off a couple of days from the store and went to interview. Everyone was impressed with her typing and shorthand but they also liked her personality. She was easygoing, confident, very quick and attractive. She took a job with the third company she interviewed and started work immediately. She stayed with Arista for a while longer then found her own flat nearby on the south side of town. She continued to let Arista babysit Dunn while she worked.

Trique was heartbroken when Mosey left him. He knew that Mosey had taken up with Waite Garvey. Yet, he hoped, somewhat unreasonably, that he and Mosey could remain together. Trique moved around from job to job, usually at small restaurants. But then he got a dishwashing job at a big restaurant downtown. There, he met some other fellows his age, a few of whom were recently discharged from the Army and Navy following the end of the war. Trique sensed that none of these guys slept with other men but he liked them anyway. And since he was dating women, while still secretly sleeping with men too, he seemed one of the guys. The men who had returned from the war and who had been overseas, talked a lot about how they were treated there as opposed to here. One of them, Waltus Moore, spoke angrily about how he was no longer treated like a man as he had been in the service and overseas. Trique listened carefully and asked questions. He thought about having to leave Pachacuti not just because he had slept with some guys' sister but because he had crossed the racial divide to do it. Then he felt remorse that he had left Martalee behind, and he felt anguish that Mosey had left him. He began to experience the full conflict of loving men and women and transgressing so many prohibitions to find love and sex.

Like Martalee, Trique also had ambitions; his mother, Xantha, had coached him from childhood to achieve success. From his co-workers, he learned about evening classes. He, too, wanted to finish high school. So he enrolled in a school for blacks. His teachers recognized that he was exceptionally quick to learn and urged him to take college courses. One of his teachers who had attended a black college nearby put him in contact with a black professor of English, Dalton McIntyre. When Trique first met Professor McIntyre, he knew that there was something different about him. Elegant and sophisticated, he was also a northerner. He helped Trique enroll, saw that he was eligible for some financial support, and also began sleeping with him. Trique was able to leave his dishwashing job. He moved into a house for students on the campus. And he finished college in exactly four years, 1950.

Trique had majored, not in English, but Economics. He wanted a job with a bank, and there was a small black bank, Citizens Trust Bank, where he was hired as a teller. With his degree and job, he felt more his own man, and his relationship to Dalton McIntyre began to change. Both men were seen in public with women but now Trique began to arrange dates with Dalton. He pursued Dalton who, by now, was more interested in his younger students than with Trique. Trique, pursued by women, charmed them really, but returned their interest with callous, indifferent seduction that they didn't seem to mind.

Trique's supervisor at the bank sent him on an errand to deliver a bank document to a downtown office in a department store. As he approached the reception desk, he noticed a familiar woman. He said to her: Do you know where Mr. Wright is located? The woman stopped to listen and looked directly at him. Martalee Boston recognized Trique Pendle immediately. She glanced about her and mouthed the words: Meet me at six o'clock tonight outside. He was prompt, as was she, but where could a black man go with a white woman in Atlanta? Not a segregated movie house, restaurant, or hotel, and certainly not her neighborhood. The color line was so much more rigid in Atlanta than in Pachacuti. There was no place they could be together so Martalee quickly passed Trique a piece of paper with a telephone number, a day and time, and she departed for home.

Trique called; Martalee answered. It was the phone at a friend's house, and she had given a story to her friend so that she could take the call at the appointed time. She started the conversation with news of her son, Dunn; Trique was the father. He was stunned and wanted to see the boy, now four years old. That was difficult for now, Martalee cautioned. She filled in the rest and then Trique told his story, omitting Mosey, Dalton, and all of the other men in his life. Martalee wanted to see Trique but she didn't see how. Trique suggested that she come to his neighborhood. No one would know her or bother her. They agreed to meet at a bar late at night. Martalee was nearly unnerved being in a strange black neighborhood, something she had only done once before in Pachacuti, to tragic consequences. But no one said anything to her. And Trique was waiting. They held hands. They talked more. He leaned over to her and kissed her cheek. She turned her head so that their lips met. They continued to meet in the bar for some time and, in doing so, fell in love. Trique wanted to see his son. They decided that they would meet downtown. Martalee would bring Dunn. On the appointed day, they were there, and from a short distance, Trique saw his son. Martalee handed Dunn a piece of paper and told him to walk over to a man that she pointed to, hand him the paper, and then come back. He did as he was told and, when he reached Trique, he said that his mommy told him to give him this piece of paper. Trique said: What is your name? The child replied: Dunn.

It was Trique's good fortune that there was a man at the bank who could pass for white but considered himself black. Trique made friends and, when he felt confident, explained his situation. Alton Sturdivant was amused by the deception he was asked to play. Trique drove Alton's car as if he were a chauffeur. His passengers were Martalee, Dunn, and Alton, all pretending to be a family. That way, they could go to the park and be together and talk. And

Dunn got to know his father. It was a temporary and unsatisfying solution so Trique dared another plan.

When Trique found Martalee in Atlanta and met his son, Dunn, he decided that he would become a family man if he could find a way that he could live with a white woman and a white child. He knew he couldn't stay in Atlanta because of the color line so he made plans for all of them to move west to Los Angeles where, he heard, black and white people could legally marry and were not as restricted as they were in Atlanta. He was still attracted to men, as well as other women, but he tried to restrain his impulses. Trique contacted his former professor, Dalton McIntyre, and made arrangements to meet him. He wanted to discuss his plans with someone who could fully grasp the complexity of his problem and plan. Dalton was gracious and sympathetic. But he warned Trique that trying to live in so many worlds, black, white, heterosexual and homosexual, was bound to come crashing down on him. Trique thought that he understood the difficulties and he wanted to try but was seeking the older man's knowledge and experience. Dalton said that it might be easier to live with a white woman than to be a homosexual. Trique thought that he could manage both. Dalton hesitated, then said good luck.

For a long time, Arista Crimm, Martalee's former landlady and occasional babysitter, resisted contacting Martalee's parents to tell them about their daughter and grandson because of her knowledge of the violence of the Boston boys. But she gradually began to convince herself that, if she could speak to the parents, they would be more reasonable than the boys. A long distance phone call was expensive; she decided, instead, to write a letter. She knew the parents' names, Finn Boston, Sr. and Olive Boston. So she wrote them with no more address than Pachacuti thinking that, in a small town, the post office would know where they lived. Olive saw the letter first, when it was delivered, opened and read it, and immediately decided to keep the information to herself. She would go to Atlanta some day with a false excuse to Finn, Sr. and to the boys. She would wait and plan.

When she felt the time was right, Olive took a train to Atlanta and went to Arista's address. Arista was pleased to meet her. She was, at that time, babysitting with Dunn. Olive spoke to him and explained that she was his grandmother, something that didn't mean anything to him since he was so young. Arista told Olive that Martalee would arrive soon to retrieve Dunn. And she did. She was startled to see her mother after so many years and became very angry when she realized what Arista had done. But her mother assured her that it was alright. She had come to Atlanta alone and had told her husband a lie about why she was there. He and the boys had no idea of the real purpose of her visit. Besides, she was not upset with why Martalee abandoned her family, and she certainly wasn't upset with Dunn whom she thought was adorable.

So, Martalee took Dunn and her mother home to her flat. Martalee made dinner and put Dunn to bed. Martalee wanted her mother to know that she was surprised by her favorable reaction. Olive said it was time that she knew something more about her own family.

She began:

I'm sorry that you didn't know any of your own family history, Martalee, because I think it might have made a difference about the way you left Pachacuti. Your brothers behaved badly, and I'm sorry that at the time I couldn't step in right away to assure you that I would protect you. Your father is a good man but he is afraid of his own world and so I was silent when I learned of your situation with that boy, but I shouldn't have been. You needed to know what I'm about to tell you because you're not the first person in our family to have a colored lover.

You know my brother, your Uncle Griffin, and you know I had two sisters—one is deceased; that's your Aunt Soonie, and the other is your Aunt Calla, who still lives in Pachacuti with your Uncle Griffin. Well, we—my sisters and I—were the three Fleet girls. Soonie was the oldest, then me, then Calla. Our daddy—your grandfather—was Murray Fleet. He was married to your grandmother, Sutreen Moore. But he also had, as a mistress, a colored woman named Estah Pendle and they had a child called Murty. Now this is the really important part: Murty was Trique's father.

What? Doesn't that make Trique's father your half-brother? Did I get that right?

That's right.

Then, Trique is really my cousin. We're related?

Well, yes, some kind of cousin, I guess.

And that means that we are related to colored people?

In a way, that's right.

So, that's why you're not upset about Trique?

Well, Honey, there is a lot more to this story than that about our family history but that is reason enough for now.

Does Daddy know this?

Sure. It's one of the reasons he wasn't too upset about what you did. But we'll talk about that another time.

After all of these revelations, Martalee felt sure enough to tell her mother about Trique and their plan to move to Los Angeles to be a family; but she was not sure that she was ready to tell her mother about the black twin, Alfred. Olive was surprised and disappointed by Martalee's plans;

now that she found her only daughter, she didn't want her so far away. Martalee explained that it was the only way they could be a family. Olive didn't want her daughter to go. Martalee said that they didn't have a choice. Olive suddenly said that she wanted to meet Trique; she had a right to meet the man who had fathered her grandchild whom he was going to take away to California with her only daughter. Martalee explained why that was difficult. Trique would not want to play the chauffeur. The only possibility was for them to go to the colored section of town and meet Trique at a restaurant. Olive was reluctant and decided, instead, to return to Pachacuti. She would keep their meeting a secret from her husband and sons but she thought that Trique could return to Pachacuti to see his family and they could, perhaps, meet at Trique's family home where such a visit wouldn't cause as much comment. Martalee wondered if it wouldn't be dangerous for Trique to return to Pachacuti. She worried that her brothers might find out. Olive was confident that no one would know except his family and they certainly wouldn't say anything.

Something about her mother's understanding and acceptance of her plans encouraged Martalee to tell the rest of her story. Hesitantly, at first, she explained that she had had twins—two boys but one was black. Olive did not react with surprise; she listened quietly. Martalee continued and broke down in tears as she revealed how distraught she was that she felt she couldn't keep the other twin because of his color. Olive was suddenly distressed: What had Martalee done with the other baby? Martalee then divulged her arrangement with a black wet-nurse who promised to keep and raise her child. Olive relaxed and asked many questions about the wet-nurse. Who was she; where did she live? She assured her daughter that she had done the best she could do and told her not to worry; somehow, all would be made better some day. And, that's how matters stood when Olive Fleet Boston said goodbye to Martalee and Dunn, and returned home.

Trique had long been in contact with his mother, Xantha Debobo Pendle. His father, Murty, had died suddenly in 1945 after Trique left Pachacuti, so Xantha lived in their family home alone. She frequently saw her brother, Teatus, and sister, Zennana, both of whom lived nearby. Since her older brother, Adelpho, Mosey's father, had died in 1939, these three were the surviving siblings. She was delighted and fretful when she learned about Trique's impending return to Pachacuti, lest the Boston boys hear of it and cause more trouble. Therefore, she didn't even tell her siblings of her son's visit. When Trique arrived by train, she forgot her worries and welcomed him home. Xantha had kept his room intact. She had made him a huge dinner of his favorite dishes. He told her about Martalee and Dunn and their plans for Los Angeles. Xantha was as saddened as Olive. But she also knew that moving west would be a good, safer way for them to be a family than to live in the South. However, she was not thrilled to learn that Olive would be paying a visit the next night. When Olive arrived at dusk, to avoid the curious, she entered the house and noticed how tidy and attractive it was. It surprised her because she had never been inside a Negro home. She talked at length with Trique until she was satisfied that he had good prospects and would care for her daughter and grandson. After an hour, she said goodbye. She would later report to her husband that the sick friend she had visited was doing better. Finn, Sr. was unconcerned as were the Boston boys. None of them paid much attention to Olive.

After Olive left, Xantha asked Trique more questions about his plans for Martalee and Dunn. When she was satisfied that he had thoroughly considered all of the possibilities, she diverted the conversation in an unexpected direction; she inquired about her nephew, Mosey. Why did Mosey leave Atlanta for Cincinnati?, she asked. Trique said he didn't know why. He said that he thought that Mosey had met a guy named Waite Carvey and was living with him. Mosey had not written so he didn't know anything more. Xantha then told Trique that she knew more than that. Mosey had contacted Swee's sister, Daphet, to find out about Swee. Then he wrote her. He had also written other members of the DeBobo family, including   Zennana and Teatus. But Swee, a Sellabie, knew the most about Mosey's life, and she told what she knew to her sister, Daphet.

Daphet said that, after Mosey arrived in Cincinnati and moved in with Waite, he found work in a restaurant where Waite was already employed. There was some kind of crazy cook there, a drunk, who got all fired up one day and took a meat cleaver to the owner. But Mosey got in the way and lost an arm. The doctors couldn't save it. You know those white doctors didn't even try. After that, Mosey left for Detroit without Waite.

Trique was shocked and anguished.

He lost his arm? He is living in Detroit?

Yes and yes. One arm and living in Detroit. He went to live with his sister, Habboey, and her husband.

What's he doing there?

He found work as a janitor in an apartment building.

A janitor?

Yes, he didn't have a chance or the wherewithal to go to school, like you did. Mosey was kind of a lost child in the DeBobo family. Thank god, Swee took good care of him. But he didn't have the advantages you had. I was always pleased that you and Mosey were such good friends. That's why I let you stay at Swee's house. I thought both of you needed a good friend. So, when all of that happened with Martalee and the Boston boys, and you left Pachacuti so hastily—but you probably saved your life—I was glad that Mosey went with you. In Atlanta, from what you wrote me, the two of you remained good friends. So, why did Mosey leave you and move to Cincinnati with another boy?

I don't know.

I think you do know, Trique. It's time for you to be honest with your mother because she has always been honest with you and has always loved you, maybe too much. Why did Mosey leave you?

He was upset about something.

About what?

Something.

Trique, tell me, honestly. Tell me what upset him.

He was jealous because I was dating.

Why would he be jealous?

Momma, I don't know why he was jealous. We were good friends. We worked together. We got along. We've been friends a long time and I was happy that he left Pachacuti with me. I don't know why my dating made him jealous.

Well, I think you do, Trique, and I'm disappointed that you can't tell a mother who loves you and who would love you no matter what. Here's what I think: You and Mosey have been like Swee and Amity ever since you were kids. Do you think that I didn't know that? Why do you think I let you stay with Mosey at Swee's house? Because I knew how you were, Trique. You've always been a very seductive boy. You didn't care if it was another boy or a girl. Mosey loved you just like Martalee. That's why he went with you when you ran away from the Boston boys and left Pachacuti and your parents and your pregnant white girlfriend. Trique, what are you up to now? You had a boyfriend and girlfriend. Are you now ready to be a father and a husband—to a white girl—in this country and leave your boyfriend behind you?

Momma, I think so. I can. I want to. That stuff with Mosey was just kid stuff. I can be a good husband to Martalee and a good father to Dunn. That stuff with Mosey is over. That's all.

I don't think so, Trique, and I think you really need to look at all of this before you get into a big mess in California. I hope that you're making the right decision and don't ruin your life or Martalee's or Dunn's. You may think that Mosey was just something in your childhood but don't fool yourself. If you ever want to talk further about this, I'm here. I'm your mother and I will always be your mother. And, with that, Trique said goodbye and returned to Atlanta.

LOS ANGELES

Trique's plan to move to Los Angeles was simple. He would buy a used car and drive it out of the deep South, like a chauffeur, with Martalee and Dunn in the backseat. They would head to the Watts section of Los Angeles and stay in a motel until they found a place to live permanently. Maybe two days at the most. That plus about four or five days to drive west would mean that in a week they could be settled and start looking for jobs. It wouldn't be easy but it wouldn't be that hard. And they could get married now that inter-racial marriage was legal in California. Martalee was skeptical that the plan would work but she was willing to try. They would follow two and four lane highways across the southern tier of states with the exception of the first leg. For that, they made a big detour by driving north from Atlanta to Tennessee and then west to avoid Alabama and the dreaded Mississippi.

By the time they crossed northern Texas into New Mexico, they felt a loosening of the color line for the first time in either of their lives. The first word out of white folks mouths wasn't "nigger." White people were almost polite and everyone accepted Trique's role as chauffeur. After all, he wore a taxi driver's hat for his disguise. Martalee could hope that Trique's plan might work. She still didn't dare to ride beside him but she let Dunn sit in the front seat so that he could see the countryside and be nearer his father. Crossing into California after five days of driving, they saw a new world opening for them in Los Angeles.

Finding a motel in Watts was easy. After a few days, they also chose a garden apartment in the Crenshaw neighborhood and signed a lease for three months as Mr. and Mrs. Pendle. Next they both found jobs, Trique in a branch bank in Crenshaw and Martalee in an office downtown, a long commute but worth it. They found a Mexican woman who would babysit Dunn. So, with all the pieces in place, they got married at city hall.

Trique made a good father but a terrible husband. He loved his son but could not feel genuine romantic emotion for his wife. He liked her and enjoyed the sex but his infatuation with Martalee was not love, not, at least, as he could now understand how he once felt about Mosey. Mosey, he loved. He missed that feeling and, although, he didn't dwell on it, he knew that he would at some point start searching for real love.

Martalee was nobody's fool. She could see what was happening. What she didn't understand was why. Maybe Trique was experiencing a kind of freedom he never knew in the South. Maybe he was preoccupied with work. She could sense that he would be a success. He was smart, attractive and ambitious. Plus, he had the imagination to bring them to Los Angeles to a new life. She, too, was ambitious and she, too, was experiencing a freedom she never knew, not just living openly with a Negro but living free of the conventions and restrictions of life in the South. Wasn't that what attracted her to Trique in Pachacuti, the sense of transgression against all those stupid things that dumb white people believed? People in the West were smarter because they didn't give as much support to restrictions and conventions. In her office, women were freer to be themselves, wear what they wanted within limits, date whom they liked. It wasn't total freedom, whatever that was. But it was more than in Atlanta or Pachacuti.

Martalee decided to put freedom on like a new dress. She started calling herself Lee dropping the Marta. It sounded more modern and not so country, small town and old-fashioned. Lee also, and more importantly, decided to go back to school. She didn't want to be a secretary forever, and she figured that she might have to raise her son by herself someday, maybe sooner than later. She also wanted him to enjoy all of the freedom of their new life. She told Trique that she would begin night classes at a small local college. She wanted to study law eventually. So, she would take coursework with the idea of applying to law school. Trique wondered who would take care of Dunn. Lee replied that Dunn was his responsibility as well as hers. He could babysit or find a babysitter if he had to go out at night. Trique could not miss the implications of Lee's last remark: If he had to go out at night. He said nothing.

Dunn had reached the age where he could go to pre-school. There was a decent school in the neighborhood and either Lee or Trique would drop him off in the morning. Xiochimara Tiextera, their babysitter, picked him up in the afternoon and took him to her house in the neighborhood. Sometimes, it was very late before one or the other parent picked him up and took him home. His parents had told Dunn that Disneyland would open soon, and they would take him to see it. Dunn had watched the television all afternoon with Xiochimara's three children and saw the Disney program that promoted the new amusement park. He was excited. When the day came and they drove to Anaheim, the crowds were overwhelming. Trique eventually found a place to park and, after paying admission, they entered the gates. Dunn knew that he wanted to go to Sleeping Beauty's Castle to ride with Peter Pan through London and Never Never Land. Then, he wanted to take the water ride through Adventureland. By the time they had walked, waited in lines, tried the rides, ate hotdogs, gone to the toilet, everyone, especially Dunn, was exhausted. They exited the park and began to search for the car.

Lee was an outstanding student; her professors encouraged her to attend school full time on scholarship. So, she left her secretarial job, finished her pre-law studies and was admitted to law school. Trique also advanced rapidly at his bank. He was transferred from the branch to the main office downtown. His easy grasp of banking, his tasteful, professional appearance, and his quick wit helped him overcome some of the objections to blacks in the lower ranks of the bank hierarchy. He would not rise to the top; he knew that. But he was rising higher and making more money than he ever could in Atlanta.

Lee spent many nights studying. She was good at it and worked hard to master tort law. Although she and Trique continued to have sex and seemingly a relatively congenial conjugal life together, they were intimate but not close. Lee thought that it was the difference in their races but she knew that they came from very similar backgrounds despite their races. She also thought, as she had even considered from their days in Atlanta, that Trique was interested in other women, probably Negro women. She mused that, maybe, her own ambition had taken too much of her time from Trique and Dunn. But what was she willing to do about it?

Lee noticed a used pack of matches in the trash of the wastepaper basket in the living room. The name Keyhole was on the cover; it was some kind of bar or club in Hollywood for men. It would prove to be a portent of her future but she wouldn't know its implications for some time.

Dunn graduated high school in 1964. He was a smart kid like his parents. To most people, he seemed white, of medium height, with sandy colored hair and blue eyes like his mother. He could easily mix with other white kids at school but didn't. He was not on good terms with black kids who suspected that he wasn't quite white but not black either. He dated both white and black girls but could not really feel comfortable with groups of either blacks or whites. His best friend —and that really doesn't describe their relationship because Dunn was a loner—was Charles Silk, another loner. They occasionally palled around together especially since Dunn had a car that his parents gave him when he turned sixteen. Before Dunn began high school, the Pendle family moved from Crenshaw to Baldwin Hills, a middle class black enclave in Los Angeles. Dunn's mother, Lee, had lived for a while in the new house but, after she began practicing law and began making a good income, she separated from Trique and found her own apartment in Hollywood. Dunn had never understood what caused the breakup of his parent's marriage but he knew that his father was withdrawn and remote. Dunn shuttled between his parents' homes on weekends and considered that his own life needed to be more independent of his family.

Dunn's high school friend, Charles Silk, decided to attend college and started classes at UCLA. Dunn wasn't ready for college. He didn't know what he wanted to do. He had jobs as waiter and store clerk; he was making some money; he was dating girls occasionally; and he lived with father. While sitting in front of the television one night waiting for his father to come home, the telephone rang.

Hello.

Are you next of kin to Mr. Trique Pendle?

Yes. I'm his son.

Your father is in the emergency room of Wilson Memorial Hospital. He was attacked and battered but is now bandaged up. You should come and get him.

When Dunn reached the emergency room, his father was in the recovery area. Bandages covered his face and right arm. He had been slashed with a knife. Dunn took Trique to the car and drove him home in silence. Trique's car was impounded and could be reclaimed the next day.

At home, Trique went to bed. Dunn called his mother to tell her the story.

Dunn, she said, I guess you need to know that your father has sex with other men and he probably was beaten up by one of them. I always thought that he slept with other women, which he did. But he also likes men, maybe, more than women.

Is that why you two broke up?

Partly. Your father just isn't honest about himself and that keeps him closed-up and distant from you and from me. But even if he could change, I couldn't live with him anymore.

So, daddy's a faggot?

Yeah, I guess so. But that is not all that he is so don't judge him just on that account. I couldn't live with him; maybe you can.

Does his being a fairy make me a fairy too?

I don't know, Dunn. You'll have to find out for yourself.

The next morning, a Saturday, when his father got up, Dunn asked him about his injuries.

What happened to you last night?

Some guy jumped me.

Where did it happen?

At a park. I stopped on the way home to use the public toilet, and a guy pulled a knife on me and tried to rob me.

So, you weren't having sex?

What do you mean?

Mom told me when I called her last night that you have sex with men and that you're a faggot; that's why she left you.

Trique started to cry.

Dunn, this is hard to explain and I can't say I understand it myself. You see, when I was young in Pachacuti, I started fooling around, like kids do, with my cousin, Mosey DeBobo. We had sex together. And I spent a lot of time with him. But, then, your mother came along. She was sexy and wanted to sleep with me. In Pachacuti during segregation, sex with a white girl was a big deal, not to mention dangerous. Anyway, her brothers found out and came after me. Me and Mosey left Pachacuti and went to Atlanta. I left your mother behind but she later came to Atlanta, too, but I didn't know it. By the way, your mother's brothers burned down the house where Mosey was living with his Aunt Swee and her girlfriend, Amity. I stayed there a lot, too, and that's where I went when your mother's brothers were after me. Me and Mosey got jobs in Atlanta and started living together. I got a scholarship and started school. Meanwhile, I was seeing other women; Mosey got mad and left me. I graduated and got a bank job. I found your mother in Atlanta and she told me that she had had you. I made up my mind that we would be a family and we all moved to Los Angeles. I was good to your mother, and she was good to me. We both loved you and didn't want to do anything to hurt you. But, I needed other people, Dunn. At first, it was women but I couldn't stop feeling that I wanted a man. It was different. I felt satisfied. I felt like it was what I was supposed to do but I know that men are supposed to want women and I did. But a woman couldn't give me what a man could. You probably don't understand. I don't understand. But I know what I need. So, last night, I stopped at the park and I picked up the wrong guy. He seemed like he wanted sex but he really just wanted to beat up a faggot. That's happened before and that is what made your mother decide to leave me. I'm sorry.

Maybe, you can get help. See a doctor, you know, a psychiatrist.

I've tried it, Dunn. I don't want to change. If I did, I would still be with your mother.

But you can't go on like this. I don't want a faggot for a father.

What can I say, Dunn? I am a faggot. I've met a lot of faggots, and they like who they are. They like sex with men. Sure, some of them don't like themselves or what they do, and a lot of them I don't like. But being a faggot is what we are.

But you had sex with women too. You had a kid. What was wrong with that?

There was nothing wrong with it. I liked being with your mother and other women but I can't seem to really want that or just that. I need a man, a man's body, a man's sex.

Does that mean that you have faggot feelings for me?

Dunn, you're my son. I'm not interested in incest. I've never had those feelings for you. I love you as my son not as a sexual partner. They are different things, and I could never mix them up.

But you mixed up your feelings for women and men.

I know. I've tried to explain that. But you're different, Dunn. There is nothing about me that would ever feel the wrong way about you.

I can't live with a faggot. I've gotta leave here.

Dunn, you're my son. I moved from Atlanta with your mother to raise you where you could have a better life and a family.

This is some family. I'll get some things and go to my mom's place.

Please, Dunn. Don't go like this.

Goodbye.

Dunn moved into his mother's apartment temporarily. Since he often stayed with her, it wasn't much of a move. But he removed all of his things from his father's house. The more he brooded on his father and his parents' relationship, the more he felt that he wanted to get away from them and Los Angeles. His only friend was in college and studying all the time. None of the girls he dated really interested him, and he wasn't finding anyone new whom he liked. He really didn't consider his options because he didn't feel that he had any. He didn't feel like he had a family. His only relatives, on both sides, were in some backwater town in Georgia. He didn't know them and he wasn't interested in getting to know them. Going to college somewhere still wasn't for him. He didn't want to study like Charles Silk did. He didn't have any idea of what he would study. He didn't want to stay in some dead-end job like waiting tables or clerking in a store. Making it in the movies—the big obsession in Los Angeles—was a joke. He wanted to go far away for a long time. See things. Have some interesting experiences. Maybe meet someone he would like. He enlisted in the Army and left for basic training in August, 1965.

Trique and Lee were stunned. They were unprepared for Dunn's decision and distraught that their only child was in the Army and possibly headed to war. Lee blamed Trique for not being a better father and husband. Trique blamed himself. He pleaded with Dunn not to sign up. Both parents had a foreboding. Lee decided to divorce Trique. Trique tried to stay away from men, unsuccessfully. After the divorce, he found a younger man, William Bass, who moved into his house. Trique, Lee, and Dunn Pendle had fractured into three parts, each headed in a different direction. There was also a fourth part that only Lee knew and she continued to keep that a secret.

PACHACUTI II

When Mosey left Pachacuti with Trique in 1945, he also left his father's branch of the DeBobo family behind. Both his father, Adelpho, and his mother, Loissey Sellabie DeBobo, were deceased. His oldest sister, Serriah, was now head of the family. She had been married to Norwood Fox but her husband had died soon after they were wed from a congenital heart condition; she never remarried. The next sister, Habboey, had married Critton Gant and moved to Detroit. Mosey was the next youngest then there were two other boys, Cullios and Phessin, who were fourteen and twelve in 1945. Two other children, Micutia and Amelia, died young. After the death of her father, Serriah sent Mosey to live with Swee so that Serriah could raise the two youngest boys. Both went to school, and Cullios graduated high school in 1949. He was drafted into the army during the Korean War and trained in the infantry. He shipped out to Korea and came home in a coffin. He was buried in the colored cemetery of Pachacuti near earlier generations of DeBobo. One of these was the founder of the DeBobo clan, Mosey's great-great-grandfather, Midah. He was an enslaved man who died in 1865. His wife, Jubelie, was sold during slavery to a white family somewhere and was never heard from again. All that the family knew about Midah's and Jubelie's daughter, Nattea, Mosey's great-grandmother, was that the father of her two children was a white man. One of those children was a son called Bear. He and his wife, Ardeah Person DeBobo, were Mosey's grandparents. They had four children: Adelpho was Mosey's father; Xantha and Zennana were his aunts; and Toetus was his uncle. Of the surviving children of Mosey's parents, Adelpho and Loissey, only Serriah and Phessin remained in Pachacuti; Mosey and Habboey lived in Detroit.

Adelpho's three siblings all lived in Pachacuti. Xantha DeBobo Pendle had a home built by her late husband, Murty Pendle; her only child, Trique, moved to Los Angeles with his wife, Martalee, and son, Dunn. Zennana, who never married, lived in the DeBobo's ancestral home. The youngest sibling, Toetus, who married Iolithe Watson, had his own home and a large family —five children of his own and one adopted child.

These offspring of Bear DeBobo were the main branch of the family. There was another branch that was seldom acknowledged because it was on the other side of the color line. Bear had a sister named Dearie; she lived in the house of a white man, Roy Boston, and gave birth to his four children. One of Roy Boston's granddaughters was Martalee Boston Pendle. Although she was related by blood to the DeBobo through both of her parents, she didn't know this when she met Trique. Her mother, Olive Fleet Boston, did know this history, however, but hadn't informed Lee when she told her about Olive's own family ancestry. Roy Boston had ignored southern rules about bloodlines that decreed that Dearie was black. Since she looked white, her children, fathered by Roy Boston, also looked white and permanently crossed the color line. Consequently, neither the DeBobo nor the Boston ever publicly claimed kinship to one another but they did transmit this history along to some family members of the next generation.

All of Roy Boston's children easily identified as white. When Finn, Sr., Roy's youngest child, married Olive, he told her about Dearie but demanded that she not disclose this to her own children. Finn, Sr.'s admission and prohibition didn't trouble Olive because, of course, she had a similar ancestry. Her own father, Murray Fleet, had as his mistress a black woman, Estah Pendle, and Olive's eldest sister, Soonie, had a child, Loissey, by a black man, Hanton Sellabie. Thus, the bloodlines of five families—DeBobo, Sellabie, Pendle, Fleet and Boston were intertwined. That was life in segregated Pachacuti. All of this and more Serriah knew. She instructed her youngest brother, Phessin, in this family history because, she felt, one day all of these families would sit down together for a nice family reunion.

Now that is your true family history, Serriah DeBobo Fox told her youngest brother, Phessin.

Crackers in our family! Phessin could hardly believe what he was hearing. They've been part of our family for generations and know it, and those Boston boys would rather die than admit they have colored blood and colored kin?

That may be but I hope to live long enough to see their ugly cracker faces when they hear the good news. Meanwhile, you've got to finish school. I want you to go to college when you're older. There's a school in Little Rock. You'll go there. There's a man in town who will pay for your schooling because he knows that you are the only male of our family who can carry on your father's line of the DeBobo name.

What about Mosey?

I don't think that Mosey is up to the job.

Why do you say that?

Your brother, Mosey, left town with his cousin, Trique. That's who he loves.

What? He loves Trique? He won't take a woman? What's wrong with him?

Nothing. He's just that way. That's how he is. Maybe our mamma, Loissey, had something to do with it. I don't know but I love him anyway. He's your brother. Your only brother now and you may have to take care of him someday.

Phessin, like the other DeBobo, was handsome. Tall, like his brother, Mosey, with hazel eyes and silky straight hair, he was olive complexioned and could be mistaken for a Cuban or an Egyptian. Unlike Mosey, Phessin was aggressive and short-tempered. He often tipped toward anger and expressed his feelings in sarcasm. His eldest sister, Serriah, cautioned him repeatedly to never let his mouth get him into trouble especially with white people because he could get himself and others killed. So, Phessin learned to suppress his anger and control his tongue except around his sister and closest friends who grew accustomed to his biting remarks and flashes of temper. Born in 1933, Phessin was almost twenty when his brother, Cullios, was killed in Korea. The next year, he went to Little Rock to college and studied mortuary science. He would become an undertaker and return to Pachacuti to work in the town's only Negro funeral parlor and eventually take over the business. That was his plan.

As he was finishing his studies and prepared to return to Pachacuti, he heard about the US Supreme Court decision that ruled public school segregation unconstitutional. So, even Little Rock's schools would be integrated. That meant that Pachacuti's schools would also be integrated which was something he wanted to see.

Phessin's return to Pachacuti as an undertaker went as he planned. James Morton welcomed him to the town's only Negro funeral parlor. With an exclusive lock on business, Morton's House of Funerals was prosperous and in need of a younger associate. Morton had no children who could follow him in the business so Phessin's long-planned entry into the company was timely. Phessin quickly learned the routines and he was especially adept with grieving families. He could lead them through the choices of casket selection, body preparation and burial services. While he was adept at embalming and applying the cosmetics to make the dead flesh resemble a living person, he relished the office work of consoling and cajoling the bereaved. He was also an excellent money man.

Phessin reconnected with his childhood friends, most of whom had not left Pachacuti. In particular, Patton Creedy and Jaydell Waxton were his constant companions after work; their revelries often went on well into the night. Phessin had moved back to the family house where his sister, Serriah, lived, but he thought about a place of his own now that he was earning good money. This was a constant source of discussion with Patton and Jaydell.

This town is gonna change, I tell you, said Phessin. Negroes already outnumber white folks. Integration is coming. The schools will change. More Negroes will get a better education and start more businesses. One day we could take over this town.

Negro, what have you been drinking?, said Jaydell. White folks ain't gonna let Negroes take over nothing except burying Negroes. So, you're in the right business.

You're a dumbass motherfucker. You don't know shit. You ain't never been out of this town. You don't know as much as Patton's dog, and that dog is dumb as a turd.

Listen, I know, Negro, that white folks is white folks. Integration may come but white folks ain't gonna change. Your black ass won't mean as much to them as Patton's dumb dog.

Jaydell is right, Phessin. You may be a college man with a good job and good prospects but you're always gonna be just another nigger to white folks just like Jaydell says. And if you ever let that mouth of yours go off on some cracker, you're gonna be a dead nigger in one of those caskets at Morton's House of Funerals. And no amount of fixing will put you back together so that your sister will recognize you.

Listen, dumb Negroes, you're right. Crackers ain't gonna change. We're always niggers to them but I ain't no fucking nigger to me. Change is gonna come and when it does, I'll be ready. I'm gonna grab that change like I grab my dick and I'm not gonna let go until I come all over Pachacuti.

You're a crazy nigger. Just make sure that the white man doesn't stick his dick up your ass until it comes out of your mouth because around here whitey always has the biggest dick.

Phessin, Patton, and Jaydell liked to visit the neighboring town of Oglethorpe in Phessin's new used car. There was a joint where young Negroes met, drank, and danced to records. Luma Arden, who lived in Oglethorpe, was there one night with her girlfriends. She was pretty, dark skinned, and thin. She noticed Phessin, not for the first time, and came over to where he was seated with Patton and Jaydell. She asked him to dance and he did. They started dating after that, and Phessin drove to her house a couple of times a week to take her out and had Sunday dinner with her family at her house. They were engaged by the end of the year and married in 1958. By the time John F. Kennedy became president, they had had two children, Diedre and André. A third baby was stillborn and, after that experience, Luma decided not to have any more children. Phessin took over Morton's House of Funerals in 1962. He built his family a new house on the outskirts of Pachacuti in an area that had been farmland and owned by Negroes. Other Negro families followed his example as Phessin became the wealthiest Negro in town. He also built a dry cleaners, a grocery store, and a nightclub, all for Negroes in the still segregated Pachacuti. Phessin learned that the only movie theater in town was for sale because the owner, Haley Reese, had died, and his heirs didn't want to continue the business. With a bank loan from Citizens Trust Bank in Atlanta, the bank where Trique had worked before leaving before California, he purchased the theater. One of the reasons Reese's family didn't want to keep the theater was that they didn't want to integrate it. Black and white people had always sat in separate sections—

whites on the main floor and blacks in the balcony, with separate entrances. Phessin knew that change was coming and he was ready.

Pachacuti's largest business was the farm implements warehouse in town. It was owned by the richest man in town, T. Reardon Post. Phessin had his mind set on owning that business and becoming not just the wealthiest Negro in Pachacuti but also the richest man in town. He started making plans and waited for the opportunity. The U.S. Civil Rights Act of 1964 nudged aside strict segregation. Phessin's theater became integrated but whites abandoned it, refusing to sit side by side with Negroes. But black patronage was sufficient to keep the place going. Phessin, though, could see that, with change, some things didn't change. He talked again to the bankers in Atlanta. They needed to open a branch in Pachacuti. All of the town's Negroes had their savings in the town's only bank which was owned by whites. Phessin laid out the economics of blacks from Pachacuti and surrounding towns that might transfer their accounts to a Negro-owned bank. After the Voting Right Act of 1965, the bankers could see that Negroes in rural Georgia could become more prosperous and powerful. That was a strong incentive to establish a presence in Pachacuti. As the town's wealthiest Negro, Phessin also convinced the bank to set up a loan to finance Phessin's purchase of the Post Farm Implements Company through D.B.B. Enterprises. At the conclusion of the deal, Phessin DeBobo realized his dream. And then he had another. He wanted to be mayor of Pachacuti. In the election of 1968, that dream also came true.

DETROIT I

After Mosey arrived in Detroit, he slept in the basement of the house of his sister, Habboey DeBobo Gant. He had a cot, some crates, a chair and little table. With one arm, he found that he couldn't get a factory job although they were plentiful. Most tasks were too difficult for a one-armed man, even if he could do many things with that one arm. So, it seemed that Mosey's stay at the Gant's home would last somewhat longer than anyone could have guessed.

Mosey was sitting on his cot when Critton came into the basement to retrieve a pair of pliers. Critton was dressed in slacks and an undershirt.

Hey, Mosey.

Where's Habboey?

She's out with her girlfriends. How's it going?

Okay, I guess. How about with you?

Hey, I'm good. Real good. I gotta fix a lamp upstairs so I'm looking for my pliers. They must be in cabinet with the other tools. How do you like it here? Are you making yourself comfortable?

You and Habboey are being real nice to me. I appreciate it.

You're family. Our home is your home. You won't be going back to Pachacuti, will you?

Not likely.

Hey, I hear that you had a real close friend down in Pachacuti. What was his name?

Trique. Trique Pendle. He's a cousin, my Aunt Xantha's son. She's a DeBobo.

Yeah, I heard that from Habboey. What happened? He got into that white girl's pants, and her brothers burned down your Aunt Swee's house. Right?

That's what I heard. I left Pachacuti before I knew what happened.

Swee was one of those man-women, living with another woman. Right?

I don't know about man-woman but she did live with another woman. Her name was Amity. Amity Lowe. She was nice to me, and so was Aunt Swee.

So, what did you and Trique do together all the time?

What do you mean: Do together?

I mean he used to stay with you, right, and you two lived together in Atlanta? So how did you live together, like Swee and Amity?

We did live together in Atlanta until I moved to Cincinnati.

You know what I mean. Habboey says that Swee and Amity ate each other's pussy. Did you do something like that with Trique?

Like what?

You know. Go down on him and stick it in him.

Why do you think that?

Hey, man, don't get upset; it don't bother me. I'm just curious. You're living in my house and I just want to know the deal. You understand? You know, maybe you want to bring some punk stuff here and do him. It's okay with me. I just want to know what's going down in my own house. You know? You know, you could do me. I ain't never done nothing like that with a guy but I could try it. I ain't scared. It don't mean nothing to me. You want to do me?

Critton moved closer to Mosey's cot and undid his trousers. Mosey did the rest. And that started a regular routine whenever Habboey was away. Critton was a good lover but not serious, and Mosey knew it. Having sex regularly with his sister's husband made him feel bad for her but, then, she seemed to have her own life with her girlfriends while leaving Critton on his own most of the time. Mosey went out of the house during the day. He met a few guys his age in the neighborhood. One of them, Parker Patterson, liked Mosey and felt sorry for him because of his arm. He told Mosey that his uncle was a custodian for an apartment building, and he knew that the neighboring building was looking for a full-time custodian. Mosey talked to Parker's uncle and met the landlord, Shelton Wise, who was skeptical of hiring a one-armed man but, given Mosey's youth, good looks, and earnestness, decided to give him a chance. The building had four floors and a basement with laundry room, storeroom, and boiler room. There was also a tiny live-in room, more like a cell, with a toilet and sink for the custodian next to the boiler room. In addition to his other duties for the nine apartments, he would be the boiler's human controls. Mosey told Habboey and Critton that he was leaving and moving his things, in a car that his

friend, Parker, borrowed, to his basement room in the apartment building. And there he worked
for the next twenty years.

Mosey had few friends after he settled in Detroit but Parker Patterson initially remained his best
companion. Although Parker never seemed to have a girlfriend, he was not sexually interested in
men. Mosey had sensed this in their conversations and kept his own interests to himself. Mostly,
on Mosey's day off, when he could leave the apartment building, he and Parker would frequent a
local bar. Men and women, single, in couples, and in groups filled the place with loud talk and an
occasional fight. There was always the danger of someone pulling a knife and cutting someone
but usually the constant noise was the only thing that cut through everything. When Parker
wasn't with him, Mosey sat by himself at the bar. The bartenders, Coral and Vivian, would chat
with Mosey. Everyone knew how he lost his arm, where he came from, and where he worked.
But no one knew about his romantic life, his love of men, or the places he frequented far from
the neighborhood of the bar and apartment building. One of these was called The Plantation, an
ironic name of a tiny club for black men that was patronized by a few white men who wanted sex
with Negroes. All of the racial stereotypes and status roles were often inverted in this club. Black
men could and did dominate white men but only within the confines of the club because black
and white would not be seen together outside of the club. The Plantation had two rooms—the
front room with tables and chairs, a bar, and a minuscule area for dancing; and a back room
completely darkened for casual, often anonymous sex. Mosey spent time in both rooms and often
went to the back when a particular white man came in and sought him out. Mosey didn't know
his name—nor did the man know Mosey's name—but Mosey thought of him as Red because of
his hair which was naturally reddish-blond. Mosey and Red met off and on for months, never
talking about much, just having a couple of drinks and then heading for the back room. After sex,
they went their separate ways. Besides Red, Mosey often coupled with Lucille. That was what
Lucius Collins called himself. Lucille was quite attractive and a very effeminate black man. It
was an act for the crowd at the bar but Lucille was not afraid to carry the act outside of this small
safe world. Lucille told Mosey that Negroes had to be bold and stand up for themselves. And
fairy Negroes had to be fierce because everyone, not just white folks, wanted to crush them.
Lucille wore bright colors—purple, orange, yellow—and tight pants. And he loved to take
Mosey into the back room and shed those clothes for Mosey's pleasure.

At the apartment building, Mosey was virtually unseen. He stayed in his room in the basement
after he completed the morning cleaning of the hallways and stairs, removed the trash, and
checked the boiler room. One of the children in the building, Donny Bryant, would come to
Mosey's room with a note from his mother—there was no heat; there was no hot water; there
were mice or roaches in the kitchen; there was a leak in the bathroom—and so on. Donny was
always frightened to go to the basement which was dark, and the rumbling, hissing boiler room
gave him particular pause because he thought that the Frankenstein Monster hid in there. He

would knock cautiously on Mosey's door which was steps away from the boiler boom and quietly call Mosey's name. Sometimes, he would peek through the keyhole to see if Mosey was inside. He was relieved when Mosey opened his door and light filled the corridor that was, otherwise, darkened. Mosey's room was a wonder. Big enough only to hold a metal cot, a wooden cabinet with drawers and a hot plate on top, a sink, and metal pole suspended horizontally from the ceiling on which hung hangers with a few shirts, pants, a jacket, and overcoat. There was a makeshift wooden enclosure in the corner of the room with a toilet that Donny could see through the open door. A single light bulb hung from the ceiling in the middle of the room. Donny stood while Mosey read the latest note.

So, no hot water, huh?

Yes, we don't have hot water.

Okay. I'll look into it. Tell your momma.

Donny turned and raced out of the room and down the corridor and up the stairs. Mosey checked the hot water heater and discovered a leak that he fixed, went back to his room, and closed the door. He sat down on his cot and pulled out a notebook that he kept under his pillow; he had been keeping notebooks, a journal actually, since he lost his arm. He opened it and read: What is Trique doing? He won't stay with Martalee. Not in California or anyplace else. I want to see him again. Aunt Swee is happy with Gulley but not with those children. She says that Amity is doing well, not big time, yet. But she might be someday. I miss Waite. He's still attending school in Oberlin. Then, Mosey wrote in his book: I'm meeting Lucille tonight. I hope that Red shows up. He likes the three of us together.

On his next night off, Mosey knocked on the door at The Plantation which had no sign or any indication of what it was. A peephole in the door allowed the door attendant to observe who was outside and whether or not to open the door. Mosey, a regular, was let in. Just inside there was a small vestibule and then another door to the front room. Several men were already there, drinking and talking in the dim light. Lucille sat at the bar dressed as usual. Mosey joined him.

Hey, baby, is your one hand ready for business tonight?

I'm ready as ever.

Do you think that Red will come?

He might. It's hard to say but I think he will.

I love that red hair. I've never seen what color it is down below. Have you?

What can you see in the back room? Besides, it's not the seeing that I like.

Oh, Mosey, baby, you and your one hand. You're better than a man with three hands.

Well, don't they say that most men have three arms?

Get outta here, bitch. You're just awful. So, I guess that means that you still have two arms.

Two strong arms.

Oh, talk to me; I like that. Do you think that we could adjourn to the recreation room in back or are you waiting for Mr. Red?

I'd like to sit here a while longer, if you don't mind. I would like to see him and, if he comes in, we can all go to the back room.

Well, your prayers have been answered. Look who just came in. Mr. Red.

Hi, Red. Sit next to me.

I'll sit here next to our friend.

How are you doing?, said Mosey.

Just fine. You?

I can't complain. I need a drink though.

Otis, a beer, please.

Oooh. See what a gentleman he is, Mosey? You could learn something from Mr. Red here.

Red got his beer. Mosey and Lucille also got drinks, and all three sat for a while until a table became free and, then, they sat there. Lucille chattered. Red was nearly silent but he watched Mosey as he responded to Lucille's running commentary on everyone and everything. Red reached over and put his hand on Mosey's leg. This was usually a sign to go in the back room. Mosey turned slightly to Red and with a slight tilt of his head signaled if he wanted Lucille to join them. Red shook his head slightly to indicate no. Mosey and Red then stood, turned and started towards the door to the back room. Lucille crossed his legs and said, Well, leave a girl all alone. It's a good thing I brought my knitting because . . .

He never finished the thought. There was a loud crashing of the front door that made everyone freeze. This was followed by the commotion of several people rushing through the vestibule into the front room.

Oh, shit. Police, said Lucille.

The police moved swiftly through the room.

Niggers, line up against the wall!

Everyone complied. The police continued into the backroom and encountering total darkness, turned on their flashlights. Several of the men inside, in varying states of undress, panicked and tried to push past the police to the exit. The melee spooked Mosey and Red and they tried to run as well. The police began randomly clubbing men and yelling at everyone to stand against the wall. Red was hit on the head and fell to the floor. Mosey tried to help him, Lucille came to his aid as well. When the situation began to settle down, the police checked identification and escorted out the men who were still partially dressed, leaving the rest, including Mosey, Lucille, and Red behind with a warning to stay away from The Plantation.

Red was bleeding from his head and was dazed.

We can't leave him here, Lucille.

What are we going to do with him?

Red! Red! Listen, can we take you somewhere? You're bleeding.

Red was too confused to reply.

Check his wallet, Mosey.

Red had a driver's license.

Red, do you have a car? We'll drive you home.

Come on, let's get outta here, Girl, before there's more shit.

The police were gone as were all of the other customers. Only the bartender and bouncer stayed behind. Once Mosey and Lucille got Red on his feet, he seemed to be able to orient himself.

Red, do you have a car?

Yes, it's that black Chevrolet, there.

Where are your keys?

Red pulled them out of his pocket.

Lucille, can you drive?

Of course, Miss Lucille can drive. She's a modern girl.

Do you know this address?

Honey, I've been all over this city; I can find it.

Red lived in a mostly white area of four story apartment buildings in the posh Boston-Edison neighborhood on the city's westside. The streets were wide and lined with trees. The area was quiet. It was quite late. Mosey and Lucille took Red up the elevator to his apartment on the third floor. Lucille left when they got Red washed, bandaged and in bed.

Red, will you be all right if I go too?

I think so but could you stay awhile?

I can't. I have to be at my job.

Where's that?

A building about three miles from here and I don't even know if there is a streetcar or bus to get there.

If we can't go back to The Plantation, how will I see you?

I don't know.

Would you come back here?

Sure, why not?

Call me when you want to come by. I'll pick you up in my car.

Okay. Good night, Red.

You can continue to call me Red but my name is Steven. Steven Schiff.

I'm Mosey DeBobo.

Goodnight, Mosey.

And, Mosey left for home but, first, encountered the stares of a white couple who were entering Red's apartment building. The woman said to the man: What's he's doing here? And they hurried to the elevator.

Mosey looked at the telephone number Red had given him. It was his only way of contacting him now that another raid had closed The Plantation permanently. It seemed that the municipal authorities were not so much intent on putting out of business a bar for black queers as it was their determination to prevent contact between blacks and the white men who desired them. A few other clubs for queer black men survived but they did not encourage white patronage. If Mosey wanted to see Red again, he would have to call him. Mosey went about his work. Little Donny Bryant brought complaints from his mother about roaches, mice, and no heat. Mosey noticed that Donny, who was ten years old, was always a little nervous when he came to his room but he was, apparently, also attracted to something that caused him to linger longer than to deliver his message. Mosey was always careful not to say or do anything that Donny might misunderstand. And, after a few moments of polite conversation, he would suggest that Donny return to his apartment.

Mosey met Lucille at another black fairy club on Hastings Street. They didn't like the neighborhood, which was notoriously dangerous, or the club but the choices were limited. This club had only one room with a bar, tables, and a dance floor. But since it was a fairly dark place, men did engage, discreetly, in sex on the periphery of the room and in the toilet.

Mosey, Baby, what are we going to do with all of these sisters? They are out of control! Look at that bitch over there. Does she think that she's a python trying to swallow that man whole? Really. You shouldn't bring me to places like this. I'm a lady.

You're a lady all right once you pull your dress up over your head.

Oh, you're so rude. You shouldn't discuss in public things that you've seen in private. I'm completely offended. But, listen, my dear. What about Red? That little fire engine can run his hose up me anytime he likes. That is, when he's not putting out your fire.

I haven't seen him since we left him at his apartment. I have his telephone number but I didn't call him. He said that he could pick me up if I wanted to meet him at his place.

So?

Lucille, it's one thing to fall together in a back room; it's something else to go to his place. In the back room, we're all the same, just dicks and butts.

Honey, please don't forget the oral cavity. Just look at Miss Python over there.

Come on, you know what I mean. Anyway, at his place—you saw it—I'm in his world, the white man's world. I'm black and he's white.

But, Sweetie, it's still dicks and butts, and I know he likes your dick and you like his butt.

Lucille, none of that matters if all he can see is black and white.

Miss Mosey, of course, he sees the world in black and white. That's how it is. You have to put that aside, Baby.

Lucille, ain't no way me, him, or anybody else, can put that aside. It's what we live in; it's who we are, and I ain't saying that can't change. I'm saying that, in his world, in his white world, I'm just another nigger. Oh, he likes my dick. But in his world, he's in charge of my dick, me, and everything else. In the back room, none of that matters.

Baby, you're full of shit. If the man gave you his telephone number and invited you to his home, yes, his white home, then he wants to see your black dick and your black one-armed self because, surprise, he likes you! This isn't complicated. Listen to Mother Lucille. Call that white boy. Get him naked and pound his ass until he yells: Thank you, Jesus!

Don't think that you've changed my mind.

Honey, buy Miss Lucille a drink and shut the fuck up. Pardon my language; you've got me all upset now with this nonsense about black and white.

Mosey's second visit to Red's apartment was also at night. Steven opened the door, turned on the light, and escorted Mosey inside. After Mosey called him, Steven drove by the building where Mosey worked and lived and picked him up. Mosey was waiting on the sidewalk in front. Mosey now noticed Steven's apartment, something he hadn't done during the first visit when he and Lucille brought the bashed man home. The apartment was large. An entryway opened onto a living room directly ahead. A dining room was off the entryway on the left. Mosey knew that at least one bedroom was on the left from the living room because that is where he and Lucille took Steven the night of his injury. There was a lot of furniture, rugs, paintings, and beautiful art objects. Steven led Mosey to the living room couch and offered to prepare him a drink that he then went to the kitchen to pour and retrieve. Steven turned on the stereo and played a Johnny Mathis album. Mosey was surprised that Steven had music by a Negro singer but then he noticed that most of Steven's music was by Negro musicians.

I guess you like Negroes, huh?

I think they make great music. I like other music too but I thought that you would like to hear this.

Why?

Because he's a good singer, and the music is romantic, and it gets me in the mood for something sexy.

I see that you have a Tony Bennett record too. Why didn't you play him?

Would you rather hear Tony Bennett?

No, not really.

Mosey, I'm just trying to seduce you. I don't care what music we listen to. You seem a little on edge tonight, not relaxed like you were at The Plantation.

The Plantation was a club; this is your home. I've never been here before as your guest. I've never been in a white person's home before. I didn't know white people had Negro records. This is all new to me. Do you bring other Negro men to your home?

No, I don't usually have anyone else here. If I want to be with someone, I go out to clubs.

Do you go out with white and Negro men?

Sometimes I do. I've been out with both. Why?

I thought you just like Negroes, you know, black dick.

Well, I like your dick but not just because it's black. I like you, Mosey. I thought that you knew that was why I came back to The Plantation. There were nights when I was there and you weren't. Most of the time, I left the club if you didn't show up.

So, you didn't go into the back room with the other guys?

Well, sometimes. But I was looking and waiting for you.

Why?

I like you; I've always liked you. You're very different.

I'm different for a Negro?

Maybe, I don't know for sure. But you're different to me. You're very self-contained, very sexy and, I think, but I don't know, very perceptive.

What do you mean by that?

I think that you can see things other people can't.

I don't think that's true.

Well, maybe not but I would like to find out by getting to know you better.

Don't you just want to fuck?

Sure I do but that's not all.

Well, why don't we get the fucking out of the way? Your bedroom is this way, right?

That's right.

Let's go.

Mosey's work routine never varied. He worked all day; often there were emergencies at night and on the weekends. When he could, he got away from the apartment building. Most often, he met Lucille for drinks at a club. Sometimes he saw Steven whom he continued to call Red. They only met at Steven's apartment now, and Mosey went there on a streetcar and bus. He refused to let Steven pick him up again or take him home in his car. Mosey also saw other men whom he met in the clubs, including The Plantation which re-opened. There was a change in city government to a more tolerant administration that restrained the police from raiding clubs if there were no signs of criminal activity. The re-opened Plantation eliminated the back room and expanded the seating and dance floor. Mosey and Lucille frequented The Plantation but Red never showed up there.

Darling, how's Mr. Red?

He's good.

Well, give a girl some details!

I see him a couple times a month at his place.

And?

He's good in bed, creative, a little freaky.

Now, you know I want to hear all of your business. So, tell Miss Lucille about Mr. Freaky Red.

He wants to sit on the stump of my arm.

Get the fuck outta here! Lord, I'm having hot flashes. I need a fan. What did you say? Sit on your stump? That red-headed motherfucker isn't just freaky. He's a fucking circus act. Wait. Did you do it?

No. Not yet. I'm saving that one.

Saving it for what, television?

I'm saving it for our goodbye session.

Wait a minute, Miss Stump-of-the-Month. You've got this circus freak and you're planning your goodbyes?

There's nothing but the sex.

Nothing but the sex! Honey, why do you think all of these Negroes are in this club? They want what you've got.

Well, I guess I want something more.

More like what?

Like my Aunt Swee. She lived with her girlfriend in my hometown. They went to New York and stayed together for a while. Now, Aunt Swee lives with her lover and they have her three kids. They are a family. That's what I want. I want a family. Trique and me were like a family until he started fooling around with everything that walked or waddled. Waite and me were a family until that crazy nigger cut off my arm.

Honey, Miss Lucille is your family now, and Miss Henry, and Miss Anthony and Miss Thomas. No, Miss Thomas is out; that ugly, mean bitch can't be in our family! Excuse me. I got a little carried away.

You're right. In a way, you and the rest of the guys are my family. But we live separate lives, like me and Red. I want a life with someone.

With Red?

That's not gonna happen. Do you think that Red would have me move into his nice apartment in a white building in a white neighborhood? They hung niggers from trees in Pachacuti for less than that.

Baby, this ain't Pachacuti. I grew up in the South too. People are different here.

Lucille, that is the dumbest of the dumbass things you've ever said. White people are white people. They'll fuck you but don't expect to be invited to dinner.

Wait just a damn minute. Didn't your friend, Trique, marry a white woman?

That's different.

What's different about it?

She wanted him. They had a baby.

And they moved to California, got married and live together. See, you don't know what you're talking about. White and black folks can make families if they want. How did you get all of that white blood in you, Honey? You told me your grandmother, Soonie, on your mother's side was white. Didn't she live with your grandfather?

No. My Aunt Swee told me that my grandfather, Hanton, and Soonie had my mother, Loissey, but they didn't live together; Soonie left town before she had my mother. Then Soonie died. The baby was brought back to Pachacuti and raised in Swee's family.

And your great-grandmother on your father's side had a white man. Didn't you tell me that?

Yes, that is what my sister, Serriah, said. Great-Grandmother Nattea had two children by a white man, my grandfather, Bear DeBobo, and my grandmother, Dearie DeBobo.

So, Baby, you got white folks everywhere in your family. You're carrying on the traditions. It's the American way! Praise the lord!

That still doesn't mean that Red could be my family. And that's what I want or else.

A few nights later, Mosey and Steven lay in bed. Mosey looked at Steven then got up and took a shower. Then he dressed. Steven woke up and asked him why he was leaving. Mosey reminded him, again, that he had a job and had to return to the building to check on the boiler. Steven knew all of this.

Mosey?

Yeah.

Could you leave that job?

Yeah, but what work can I do with no education and one arm? I'm thirty-eight years old. You're what, thirty-five, educated, white. I can't even work in a factory. And I haven't seen any one-armed garbage men.

What if we lived together, here? I make enough money at my accounting firm to support two people. It wouldn't be hard.

Are you crazy? What about me living here? Your neighbors already give me dirty looks when they see me, like I'm here to rob them or something. What if I was here all the time? What would they do? And what would we do? We don't do nothing now but fuck. We've never done anything but fuck. We've never been outside of this apartment together, never to a movie or a restaurant or a ball game.

But, Mosey, you never have the time. You're always working. I've never sensed that you wanted to do anything else or had the time.

You never asked me.

You're right. I'm sorry for that but you've also never mentioned wanting to do anything. I didn't have any idea that you were interested or, really, what interests you.

What about you? Did you ever mention doing anything except having sex?

You're right again. I've thought about restaurants and movies but I was afraid to say anything.

You were afraid? What did you have to be afraid of?

Mosey, I don't know much about Negroes. I don't know what they do, what interests them.

Whose fault is that?

It's my fault. I'll admit that. I'll also admit that I wanted you. As long as we could get together for sex, yes, I wanted the sex and I really wanted to be with you. If you want to do other things, too, we can do them. Whatever you want, we can do. I want to spend as much time as I can with you.

Listen, Red. I think that we've gone as far as we can go. I'm not leaving my job. I'm not going to depend on you for nothing. I don't want nothing from you. You got your stump tonight. Move on to something else. I've got work to do. Goodnight. Goodbye.

Mosey? Are you walking out on me? Are you saying that you don't want to get together anymore, even for sex?

Yeah.

Why is that?   What happened? Couldn't we talk about this a little longer at least? I don't understand how you can say that I got what I wanted and now everything is over. I thought that we could get to know each other better by having sex, all kinds of sex. But, I really didn't feel that you wanted anything more than sex. Maybe, it's my fault for not suggesting dinner or a movie or anything else but I thought that you knew that I liked you, and I thought that you liked me. We had a good time together. Did I misunderstand something?

You didn't misunderstand me, Red. You don't understand me or any Negro. You can only see this situation from your point of view. You're a white man who likes sex with Negro men. You go to bars where Negro men are, and you fuck them. That's what you want and that's what you get. You don't look for Negro men to go out with to dinner or to a movie or to be with your friends. There's only one thing on your mind when it comes to Negro men, and I've done what you want. You say you like me. You've been polite to me; you've driven me here to your place and back to my home; you've had me in your apartment. But you haven't had me in your life. What does liking someone mean if they are not in your life or a part of your life? And, do you want to be in my life? Do you want to be with niggers, in our homes, at our places, doing things that we like to do? Do you?

Mosey, I don't think that I've really thought about all that but I could. What I have thought about is that you are the one person that I like and want to be with. I'm offering to share my home with you and support you. Doesn't that show my feelings? Isn't that a place to start? We can find out about other things that we could do now that we are talking about them. I think that everything that you've mentioned, we could do. Why not, unless you don't really like me?

Everything that you've said, Red, ignores one important fact: you're white and I'm black. We live in two different worlds, and those worlds don't come together in a way that I want. Yes, we can have sex; blacks and whites have been having sex ever since the slavers dumped us in this country. But can blacks and whites live together? It doesn't happen. It's not going to happen, and I'm not wasting my time pretending that it could happen. I don't have much but what I have is mine. I won't give that up to be your houseboy. Maybe, you can pay for some other Negro but not this Negro. Good night, Steven.

Mosey, you're breaking my heart. I want you more than anything.

I'll see you, Red.

Despite his decision, Mosey thought about calling Steven again but didn't. They saw each other occasionally at The Plantation but didn't speak. Steven always came with another young white guy, and they would often leave with a black man.

You know, Lucille, maybe some Negroes could make a family with white people. I just haven't figured out how.

Miss Mosey, let this queen tell you something: You still have Trique and Waite on your mind. You can't go back to them. Move on, Baby. If Red is not the man for you, look around and find another one, someone you can be with and who can be with you. Look at me. Miss Lucille is available and I'm a beautiful black queen. So, there, nigger!

Lucille, if I could go back to Trique or Waite, I would. Meanwhile, you're here and I'm here. Tonight, you look real good to me. Let's go and see what you've got.

Oooh! I get the stump! Thank you, Jesus!

II

MIDDLE PASSAGE

DUNN'S CHRONICLE

Dunn knew about the South from his parents but he never thought that he would ever be in the South, particularly in South Carolina. That was where he began his basic training at Fort Jackson. He quickly adapted to the routine after the initial shock of having his head shaved down to his scalp and outfitted with ill-fitting fatigues and too-big boots. The barracks was a two story wooden building with rows of single metal beds on both floors. At one end of the building on the ground floor was a latrine with a long line of sinks on one side and another line of toilets on the other without partitions between them. There was a separate gang shower room in the latrine with several nozzles. The place was old and decrepit, a relic of the Second World War. There were broken windows, malfunctioning lights, and cranky plumbing. And the new soldiers were all young, scared kids from all over the country. Dunn kept to himself. He excelled at the physical conditioning—the calisthenics and running with full gear—and he quickly learned to shoot his rifle, master hand-to-hand combat, and understand the rudimentary techniques of infantry warfare. He did not like the complete lack of privacy in the sleeping area and especially in the latrine where grunting soldiers took a crap side by side and showered in groups. The horseplay, snapping towels at someone's butt or joking about their cocks, really bothered him and he remained distant from everyone.

It was several weeks before he and the other new soldiers received their first pass to go on a day's leave into Columbia, the city nearest Fort Jackson. Dunn went by himself, ate in a restaurant, and went to a movie before returning at curfew. Since only Dunn knew that he was mixed race, everyone else assumed that he was white. Because he stayed aloof, neither blacks nor whites befriended him. When he went into Columbia on leave, some white girls would flirt with him. He occasionally would go to a movie with one and kiss and finger her, if she would let him. One girl took him to wooded area of a park and let him fuck her standing up. Unlike the other soldiers, he never talked or bragged about his real or imaginary sexual exploits. Some of the other soldiers began to suggest that he was a faggot but not to his face.

Basic training passed quickly and Dunn was sent for advanced infantry training to Fort Benning, Georgia. As far as he was concerned, it was more of the same only the pace was more lax and less strenuous. He couldn't imagine how combat soldiers could be prepared for battle with such lackadaisical preparation. He received letters from his mother letting him know that both of his grandmothers, Xantha DeBobo Pendle and Olive Fleet Boston, wanted him to visit them in Pachacuti. So, he made arrangements during his first weekend leave to see them at Grandmother Pendle's house. He rented a car, drove from Fort Benning to Pachacuti, and arrived in the town in the early afternoon. The drive through southern Georgia was uneventful but when he reached Pachacuti, he wasn't sure which way to proceed. His grandmother's directions had been clear enough but the streets didn't all have signs. He pulled over when he saw a couple of Negro boys walking on the sidewalk.

Hey, fellas. I'm looking for the Pendle house. Do you guys know where it is?

Sure. Turn right at the next corner then left. Do you know Mrs. Pendle?

Yes, I'm her grandson.

Then Martalee Boston must be your momma.

That's right.

Welcome to Pachacuti, soldier. Hey, Trique Pendle is your daddy, right?

Yeah. That's right.

Where is he?

He lives in Los Angeles. So does my momma. But they are divorced now. I'm here to see my grandmothers.

Well, I'll bet they'll be glad to see you.

I hope so. Thanks, guys.

Dunn found the house. It was larger than he imagined—two stories and lots of lawn surrounding it. The other houses on the street were spaced at a good distance so that each one was set in its own landscaped park. The Pendle house was all white with a broad one story porch. People were sitting on the porch and, when Dunn pulled up in front and stepped out of the car, everyone got up and started down the stairs to greet him. A woman called into the house: Xantha, your boy is here! Several people, black and white, came out of the house.

Dunn. Dunn, baby. Come kiss your grandmother.

Dunn was swarmed with folks hugging and kissing him but they gave way to Xantha.

Honey, I'm glad to see you. Did you have any trouble finding us?

No, Grandma. I did ask a couple of guys where your house was, and they knew all about me.

Of course, they did, child. This is a little town. Most folks know almost everything about everybody. Now, I want you to meet your family. Come on in the house.

When nearly everyone was inside, the introductions began.

First, this is your Grandma Boston, your momma's mother. Give her a hug and a kiss. Don't shake hands. She's your family too.

Olive said to Dunn: These are my sons—Hamilton, Oliver, and Finn, Jr. They are your uncles and your mother's brothers.

So, you're the guys who burned down Aunt Swee's house.

Dunn, that was a long time ago. They were young and, well, times have changed. We're trying to let all that go. We're here because we're all families together. Olive continued: This is Hamilton's wife, Deanna, and their daughters, Alice and Mindy. And this is Oliver's wife, Matricia, and their son, Winston; and Finn, Jr's wife, Kimmie Beth.

Dunn shook hands with all.

Dunn, we Boston are happy that you're here and want you to enjoy yourself and get to know us all.

Zantha interjected: Now, Dunn. It's our turn. These are the DeBobo. This is my sister, your Great Aunt Zennana. And this is my brother, your Great Uncle Teatus; his wife, Iolithe, and their children, Ottice, Melivia, DeLanna, Ornton, and Wentell. Their youngest, Alfred, isn't here; he's your age and also in the Army. This is Ottice's husband, Benny Robinson, and their children, Iris and Camden. This is Melivia's husband, Johnson Baylis and DeLanna's husband, Hudson Brandt. Here is Ornton's wife, Wilma, with their children, Payton, Setteria, and Dylmar; and finally, Wentell's wife, Dorena. And if you think that this is a lot of family, there are other kinfolk of yours that couldn't come. But let's go outside in the backyard. We have tables set up and lots of food to eat. Everybody brought something; so there's fried chicken, meatballs and spaghetti, ham, and chitlins, collard greens, green beans, potato salad, sweet potatoes, corn on the cob, steamed cabbage, rolls, cornbread, pies and cakes, and lemonade. We're gonna fill you up so you can't move. I'll bet that you've never eaten chitlins before.

You're right, Grandma. I don't even know what they are.

Pig intestines.

You're kidding.

No. Try them. You might like them.

We'll see.

The entire crowd of family went to the backyard and sat at tables. Teatus and Iolithe accompanied Dunn and sat on either side of him. The Boston sat together at their own table. Zennana remained in the house with her sister, Xantha.

I didn't realize that he would be so white, Xantha. Did you know he looked white like his momma?

I knew that he had to look white; otherwise, Martalee couldn't have kept him when he was born. He is white like his momma, not black like Trique. If he had been black, well, you know what would have happened. That's what decided everything. It was a hard decision for Martalee but she did what she had to do. When she and Trique got together again in Atlanta, what was done was done. There was no going back. Anyway, as white as he is, I can tell that he's not a Boston.

Well, he looks like a Boston, not like a Pendle.

That's true, Sister.

Isn't it too bad that Alfred isn't here?; it would have been good for them to meet.

I'm not so sure that a meeting now would be a good idea. Dunn has got enough here to think about. He's meeting all of his relatives for the first time; he's got a lot of family history to learn. The rest of that can come later.

If there is a later . . .

What are saying?

Well, they are both in the Army now. Something could happen.

Sister, let's pray that both of them come out of this safely. I want Dunn to learn everything about the Pendle side of his family.

Including Murty?

Including Murty. He should know about his grandfather.

Xantha, I hate to keep on saying it, because you've certainly heard all of this before, but I was glad when Murty died. He was a mean son of a bitch. He was mean to you, to Trique, to all of us. I hated him. To this day, I don't know why you ever married such a man.

You know I wanted to get away from Papa just like you; only you didn't. Our daddy, Bear DeBobo, was something else. He protected us from everyone; he kept us safe but I felt like I was his prisoner. When Murty came along, he was a lot like Papa, strong and determined. But when I married Murty, I left one jail for another. Murty was a mean man but he did take good care of me and Trique. When he died, I felt that I was finally free, and I wanted that freedom for the rest of my family. That's what I've worked for and will work for until my last day, Sister.

Amen to that. Should I call those useless wives in here to take this food outside?

Go ahead.

In the garden, Teatus and Iolithe chatted with Dunn.

Dunn, you're in the infantry?

Yes sir, Uncle Teatus.

I missed the Second World War because I was too old and had a family. Besides, my heart is bad and always has been, and they wouldn't take me because of it. Looks like you might see this war.

Yeah. I guess that's possible. We'll see after I have my first assignment.

Where's that?

San Francisco, at the Presidio. I'm getting a desk job though.

What will you do?

Oh, paperwork. The Army has lots of paperwork. That's what I'll do.

Not bad. Say, how's your daddy and momma?

My mom is fine; she's working hard at her law office. She's dating a nice guy, she says. I think she's happy. I haven't talked with my dad but my mom says that he's doing well at a bank.

You know your daddy left town because of Martalee and her crazy brothers.

Yeah, I know they burned down Swee's house.

Well, like Mrs. Boston says, they were young and times were different then.

Were they?

Oh, yeah. You wouldn't see black and white folks having dinner together then like now. And no white folks back then would admit they had black kin although down here nearly everybody does. But I give it to Mrs. Boston. She never ran away from or hid the truth. She and Xantha have been friends since about the time you were born. Anyway, your daddy ran away so that the Boston boys wouldn't lynch his black ass.

Teatus, don't talk like that; it isn't proper. Dunn doesn't want his family trash-talking. This is the first time he's meeting all of us so make a good impression and, maybe, he'll come back to visit us again. Won't you, Dunn?

Yes, Aunt Iolithe.

I'm sorry, Honey. Excuse me, Dunn. Anyway, your daddy ran away to Atlanta with our nephew, Mosey. Then Mosey went on to Cincinnati and Detroit. That's where he is now. Your daddy got schooling and a good job and hooked up with your momma again after she had you. Then all of you moved to Los Angeles. You know how folks talk. I hear your momma and daddy split because he was a punk. He and Mosey were punks. Mosey lived with Swee; she and that woman who lived with her were that way too. They were all funny. My sister, Xantha, accepted that shit.

Teatus! You are out of place talking like that. What will Dunn think of you talking about his folks like that?

Xantha did accept that stuff! She still does. But I don't. It ain't right. It ain't how God intended. Man and woman are supposed to be together, like us. That's what's right. Not two men or two women. That ain't right. You didn't turn out that way did you, Dunn?

No, sir.

That's good. Now I know that your daddy is your daddy but he ain't right. So, it's good that you don't have anything to do with him. He's my nephew, too, but he ain't part of my family. You're welcome here and your momma. But Trique knows to stay away from here. I don't care what my sister, Xantha, says.

Okay, everybody. The food is on the table. Let's eat, Xantha announced.

Olive intercepted Dunn after he filled up his plate and invited him to her table. She pulled him aside for a private conversation.

Dunn, come sit with me so that we can talk. Your Grandmother Xantha's family really loves you. They've gone to a lot of trouble to plan this party.

Yes, I know. I appreciate everything and I like them a lot, too.

Well, Dunn, I want to make sure that you understand that we Boston are your family, too, and we love you.

I know that you do, Grandma, but I'm not so sure about my uncles.

Dunn, the men in my family have had a hard time seeing around everything they've been taught about black people and white people. They have changed from when your mother left town. But some things just stick with folks, and they do the best they can in new circumstances. We are living in new circumstances but the old teachings are there, inside them. Quiet for now and, maybe, forever. But give your uncles a chance to try being different even if they don't think different. But I can tell you when they look at you, they see a white man, one of them. They know Trique is your father but they don't see him in you; they only see someone like themselves, someone like your mother. They'll accept you like they will never accept someone who looks black. I'm not saying that this is right or the way it should be or the way it has to be but it is what's true. Right now, it's true. Can you give them a chance? It would mean a lot to me. And I hope someday your mother can come here and be a part of her family again. You're here and you can start it, please.

Okay, Grandma.

Now, let's sit down. Boys, Dunn is going to join us.

So, what's it like in California?, asked Hamilton.

Not like here, at least in Los Angeles. The city is big with freeways everywhere. There's mountains and the ocean and palm trees. And Hollywood and movie studios. Where I lived is just miles of houses and apartments. Nothing really special. But there are all kinds of people. Black, white, Mexican, Japanese, Chinese. All mixed together.

You like that?

Well, you know, Uncle Hamilton, that's how I grew up. Not like you down here in segregation.

Hey, Pachacuti ain't segregated no more.

Really? Don't white people live on one side of town and black people on the other?

Well, that's because people on both sides prefer it that way.

I thought it was because that is how white people want it.

Maybe, that's the way we wanted it at one time but we even got us a Negro mayor now. I tell you that's something. White folks around here know times have changed. And we're here with the DeBobo. The mayor is their relative. I understand that he's coming by here to pay you a call. He's your Grandma Xantha's nephew. That makes the mayor some kind of cousin of yours.

Say, Dunn, you know that you look like a white man?

Yes, Uncle Oliver. I know it. But why do you say I look like a white man instead of I am a white man?

Well, your daddy's a Negro. That means you're half Negro.

But I look white?

Yeah.

So, what does that mean to you?

It means you ain't white like we are but you look white.

And, so, what does that mean to you? Am I different than you?

I don't know how to say it. You could be just another white man but I know you ain't because I know your Negro daddy.

Oliver, stop right there! Excuse me, Dunn, but I have to explain something again to your uncle. Oliver, your grandmother, Dearie DeBobo, was part black just like her brother, Bear DeBobo. So, you know that the DeBobo are your ancestors too. Now, what does that make you? Are you a white man or do you just look like a white man? You've been white only because your granddaddy, Roy Boston, told your father and you that you were white. Folks around here didn't contradict them because all of Roy Boston's children passed for white. They also say that things are changing but some things, like white men making babies with black women and, yes, black men making babies with white women, remain the same. What do you think, Dunn?

Well, Uncle Oliver says he's white but I only look white. He's right. I'm really black because inside that's what I feel. If that changes things for us, so be it. I guess I'll excuse myself for now, Grandma.

Dunn left the table and walked through the yard past his relatives. He took a cigarette out of a pack in his pocket of his dress uniform, lit it, and took a deep breath. A car pulled up in front of the house, a recent model Chrysler. A man and woman exited. Dunn's grandmother, Xantha, came over to him.

That's your cousins, Phessin DeBobo and Serriah DeBobo Fox.

Phessin is the mayor? He's so young. He must be thirty-something.

Well, yes, he's a firecracker, that one.

Afternoon, Aunt Xantha. Thanks for inviting us. This must be our cousin, Dunn. You look mighty good in that uniform.

Dunn, give your cousin, Serriah, a kiss. I told you, you don't need to be shaking hands.

My. My. You are a handsome fellow, Cousin Dunn. You don't favor your daddy at all, as I remember him.

Well, you're right, Serriah. I look more like my mother.

I should say you do. Well, come on with us and sit down. Aunt Xantha, can we get some of that food; it looks awfully good?

Of course, Phessin. We are honored by the presence of Pachacuti's leading citizen. You and Serriah sit here with Dunn. Phessin, where's your wife?

Luma and the kids went to visit her folks in Oglethorpe. Her mother is ill. She sends her regrets. So, Dunn, how long are you gonna be in Georgia?

Not much longer. A few weeks and then I go to San Francisco, to the Presidio.

Any chance you might be shipped out overseas?

Sure. There's always that chance later on.

Oh, Dunn, I hope not. Well, not someplace where they're shooting, like Viet Nam.

Well, Serriah, that's what can happen in the Army. If I have to go, I have to go. Can't say that I want to go but I'll take my chances. I'll have a desk job in any case so there's really no chance I'll see any fighting.

Honey, how are your folks?

They are okay. Thanks for asking. My mother is dating and my father is, well, living his life.

What are you saying, Dunn? You say "living his life" in a funny way.

Serriah, you know that your brother, Mosey, and my father stayed together when they were young and went together to Atlanta. Well, my father is living with another man now.

Is that why he and your momma parted ways?

Probably.

Not because they were black and white?

No, I don't think that black and white had anything much to do with it. It was my daddy's fooling around that my mother didn't like, especially fooling around with men.

So, Dunn, what do you think?

I don't know, Mayor DeBobo.

Just call me Phessin.

Okay. Phessin, it seems like it's not right, a man wanting a man.

Well, Dunn, let me be frank with you. I agree; it's not right. Our brother, Mosey, was that way with your father, and our aunt, Swee, was that way with that woman, Amity. Seems as though that's the way it is with some folks. That's the way they are or the way they want to be. Now, I don't think it's right. I mean I don't approve because the Bible is against that sort of thing but your father, Mosey and Swee seem to be that way.

I don't see that. I think that they can choose. My father married my mother; that was a choice. He could have stayed with that choice. He didn't need to be with a man.

Your daddy is kind of a special case because he, well, got your mother pregnant and had you but that happened even while he was with Mosey. He must have loved your mother because all of you moved to Los Angeles and he married her. And you know, Dunn, it ain't easy for a black man to live with a white woman in this country and especially in this part of the country. Damn, our uncle, Prellis, was lynched in this town because he was accused of molesting a white woman. Believe me, this family hasn't forgotten that, and you white folks better understand that those days are over.

Excuse me, Phessin, but what do you mean by "You white folks?" Why are you including me?

Dunn, all I have to do is look at you and listen to you. You're as white as the rest of those cracker Boston, and you don't even respect your black daddy who made you.

Phessin, my father being black is not something that I'm ashamed of; it's the fact that he is a faggot that I can't accept. Now, my uncles don't even think that I'm white because of my black daddy. Even I don't think that I'm white.

But you look white, not black.

Yes, I look white but I don't feel that I'm one of the Boston.

So, you're a DeBobo?

I'm a Pendle—part DeBobo and part Boston. So, I'm not black or white.

Phessin, you can't make Dunn choose sides.

Serriah, the side has been chosen for him; he looks like a white man and he can't be anything but a white man.

But, he feels something different. Your brother, Mosey, looks like any other black man but he only likes other men, not women. So, how a person looks doesn't say how that person feels inside. You're being worse than the worst white folks when you can't let a person be what they want to be.

Listen, Dunn, I don't mean to make you feel like you don't belong. You're a part of this family but you look like a Boston. Somewhere back in time, I guess, we were all part of the same family. If, as Serriah says, you have to be who you are, you be that. Your Cousin Phessin, the mayor of Pachacuti, welcomes you, even if you are a cracker.

Oh, Phessin, stop messing with him. Let's eat.

The family said their goodbye's by evening. Dunn stayed and helped Xantha and Zennana clean up. When all was put away, Zennana said good night to her sister and to her great-nephew, Dunn. Xantha and Dunn went out to the front porch and had a seat in two white wicker chairs.

Grandma?

Yes, Baby.

What do you know about the Pendle?

Oh, Dunn, I knew that we would come to this. It's a long story and I hate to put so much on you on top of everything else today. The DeBobo and Boston were having a time this afternoon trying to figure out where you belong. Do you really want more complications right now on top of that?

Yes, I want to know. Until today, the only family I had were my mother and father. Now, I know the DeBobo, Boston, and Sellabie but I don't know the Pendle.

Well, Dunn, you're a grown man. You've got a black daddy who loves men and a white momma who loved a black man. And here you are, one of Uncle Sam's soldiers about to get himself into who knows what. Let me think for a minute about the Pendle to get my story straight because this is important history for you. Let's see. Okay, let's start with my husband, Murty Pendle, your grandfather. He died in 1945, the year before you were born. Lord, 1945 was some year around here. As I said, Murty died, Prellis Sellabie was lynched, and your daddy, Trique, left Pachacuti with Mosey. Murty and I only had the one child, Trique, because I got an infection after Trique was born and couldn't have any more children. But Trique was special, real smart. That's why he's a banker. And he had a way about him that the girls and, I guess, the boys liked. Your grandfather, Murty, was completely different from your father. He was kind of quiet and closed up; he had a terrible temper and could be very mean. He was mostly good to me and to Trique; he built us this house because he worked hard and started his own little restaurant that served black folks. He did a good business and I took it over after he died. I still run it but I've got folks now to do all of the work. I cook sometimes when people ask for special things or have parties. White folks now come to the restaurant because they like good food too. A lot of the food today came from the restaurant; those Boston nearly ate everything in sight today.

Anyway, Murty was a decent man but, like you, he had a world of hurt to live with and that, I think, made him mean. His momma was Estah Pendle; she kept her family name because she never married. The Pendle were not a big family. Estah had two brothers; one they called Cutt and another was Wheeler. Their momma was Medan Smith, a mixed-race woman. I never saw her because she died before my time but I have a picture of her from Murty. I'll show you. I don't know anything about Cutt and Wheeler because they left Pachacuti as youngsters. You see Murty's mother, Estah, was really a beautiful woman with long wavy black hair like her momma. And she had a nice brown color like coffee with a little cream in it. So, there was this white man named Murray Fleet. He was married to Sutreen Moore at the time and had four children with her, including your grandma, Olive. He took up with Estah on the side. Murty was born when Estah was twenty-four. She also had five other children before Murty by various men. Now, I won't say that she was an easy woman but she wasn't hard to get either. She liked her men, and they liked her; they kept her clothed and fed, and the kids too. The other children all died eventually from one thing or another.

Now, when Murty was born, something strange happened. As I said, Murty's father had four children by Sutreen Moore—three girls and one boy. The oldest girl, Soonie, found out about this baby, and talked Estah into letting her take care of it. Soonie couldn't have been more than fourteen but she took care of Murty like he was hers. Somehow, while she was tending to him at Estah's house, she met Hanton Sellabie. You know the Sellabie because that's Swee's family; Swee was his last child by his second wife. It was in between his first and second marriages that Hanton took up with Soonie and got her pregnant. Their daughter, Loissey, was born the year after Murty, and when that happened, Soonie left Pachacuti with Murty to have her own baby and lived with some Sellabie in Sokodé, not far from Pachacuti. She probably intended to raise Murty and Loissey as siblings. But when she died after Loissey's birth, the Sellabie took the baby away to live with her father, Hanton, his new wife and his other children. Murty was left behind in Sokodé with Hanton's kinfolks. Now, I don't know for sure what happened to Murty all those years that he was growing up an orphan in someone else's family but he became tough and hard. He came back to Pachacuti; we met, and he wanted to marry me. I saw that he was strong like my father so I went with him. Then we had your father, Trique.

Dunn, when we're young, we don't know a lot of things. The things we do know often cause us to make bad decisions, decisions that we might later regret. I wanted to get away from my father and my home so I married a man who could get me out of that home. We had a good life but was it the life that I wanted to have? I can't say that it was. However, that's the past and the past can't be undone. We only have now. I have my family, my own child and his children. That's what concerns me today.

Grandma. Wait a minute!. You said "children." You said "his children!"

Dunn, I must be tired. I meant his child. Trique's child. You. Let me finish this story before my mind goes completely tonight.

Folks say that the reason white folks came down so hard on Prellis Sellabie and lynched him was to take revenge for Soonie going over to black folks. Anyway, Murty and Loissey were raised with the Sellabie, and when Loissey married my brother, Adelpho, and I married Murty, the DeBobo, Sellabie and Pendle became one big family. But what all this means to you is that you didn't become white and black just through your momma and daddy. That happened generations ago. I'm just so sorry that you don't have any other Pendle in your life. But you've got a mess of DeBobo and Sellabie.

And Boston. Grandma Olive told me today about Dearie DeBobo. So, I'm not the first in this family to have one foot on each side of the color line.

No, Sir. Not by any means.

Grandma, I'm happy that I have you, the DeBobo, and grandma Boston too. It's like I have people with me out in the world. Other than my mother and father, I haven't really had a lot of people in my life. It's kind of hard when people think that you are one thing and you, yourself, don't know who you are.

But, Dunn, everybody has to figure out who they are. We don't just know that because we look black or white. Sure, having people around us who accept or reject us helps us to find ourselves. But we all have to work at it. You have to work harder than some others. But you can do it. You will do it and you will be a glory in this world. Now, let's get some sleep. Get your things from the car and I'll show you your room. You'll need a good rest to drive back to your base in the morning after I fix you a big breakfast. Come on now. I'm tired. It's been a long day.

Dunn left the next morning after breakfast and returned to Fort Benning. He completed the remaining weeks of his Advanced Infantry Training and flew to San Francisco to report to the Presidio in the shadow of a pylon of the Golden Gate Bridge. He was assigned an office job for a year that passed quickly. Before the year was completed, he received a new assignment with the Fourth Infantry Division in Viet Nam. He was to report to an airbase in Oakland for a flight to Saigon.

The Braniff Airlines chartered aircraft was like any other commercial flight except that there was only one class. There were male and female cabin attendants in Braniff uniforms. But all of the passengers were military in dress uniform. A meal was served on the first leg of the flight to Honolulu. Then, another meal on the next leg to Guam. Finally, breakfast was served on the last leg to Ton Son Nhut airport in Saigon. Upon disembarkation, the heat and humidity penetrated every part of Dunn's body. It was much hotter than his stay in the South. He began sweating profusely. Overhead, huge columns of clouds sailed across the intensely blue sky. The sun was brighter than anything Dunn had ever experienced. He tried to find shade but there was none on the tarmac until he reached the terminal. Buses were waiting for him and the others to take them to the processing center for new arrivals in-country at the American military compound at Ton Son Nhut. The Braniff crew was bussed separately, presumably to a hotel. Dunn spent three days at Ton Son Nhut. His only diversions were the post-exchange (PX), where he did some shopping for gifts for his mother that he mailed to her, and the bar and mess hall where the other enlisted men congregated. Like so much of Army life, the waiting was tedious, interminable and there was never any information. On the other hand, he was apprehensive about his next assignment. It was a combat unit and, although he would have a desk job, he didn't know what dangers were ahead. So far, though, everything was quiet, orderly in that strange military way—so unlike life outside. But it was also so restricted and regimented by rules that were explicit and yet often absurd—and tense because of the uncertainty and the sense of imprisonment in this world. It took three days before an aircraft was available to transport a dozen newly arrived soldiers to a base camp of the Fourth Infantry Division. The flight took an hour in a two-engine propeller craft. As the plane rose into the sky, the land below appeared flat, covered sporadically with vegetation. Clusters of buildings and roads were clearly visible. Rising in the distance was a curious conical mountain on the plain that rose above it like a female giant's well-endowed breast. The plane's engines changed pitch in preparation for a landing, and the craft skimmed the short runway. To either side of the landing strip was what seemed like a small city of wooden buildings, all uniform in layout as if some very unimaginative child had decided to create the most boring community possible. This was a typical military base camp; it did not house the entire Fourth Infantry Division, as Dunn thought, but only one detached brigade. Nevertheless, there were several thousand men billeted there; however, only a portion of them were combat troops. The rest were support staff—mechanics, clerks, artillery gunners, pilots, and cooks. The camp was built next to and partly incorporated the town of Dau Tieng; so, everyone called the camp by the town's name. Flanking the camp and the reason for the town's existence was the giant Michelin Rubber plantation. It was a holdover from the French colonial era and consisted of mile after mile of uniform rows of equally spaced rubber trees, a kind of maniacal forest identical in every spot and a perfect complement to the rigid geometry of the military camp. All of this Dunn saw while descending in the plane but it would be a while before he understood what he saw and what, now, would be his home.

His assignment was Company B of the Second Battalion, Third Brigade, Fourth Infantry Division. He became the newest company clerk replacing a man who had just completed his one-year tour of duty and had returned stateside. His immediate supervisor was First Sergeant Donald Smith, a black man from Alabama with fifteen years of active service. Sergeant Smith did not like Dunn and he made this clear immediately. His last clerk had been white too and white boys didn't seem to understand that they had to answer to black bosses just like black men had to obey white bosses. This is the Army, soldier. So, no shit from you. Dunn wanted to say that he was black but, once again, it didn't seem to matter what he said or did. Other people already made up their minds about him.

Sergeant Smith directed Dunn to his barracks which housed thirty-two men on double-decker metal bunks beds, eight double bunk beds to each side of a central aisle. Each bed had two footlockers on the aisle, one for each man's personal belongings. There was no running water or electricity. The latrine, a four seater was a wooden outhouse some distance from the barracks and serving several buildings. A gang shower, enclosed in corrugated metal and supplied by plastic water tanks overhead, stood off by itself away from the barracks and latrines. All barracks were sandbagged up to the height of the horizontal, screened opening that ran completely around the exterior of the barracks. There were entrances at both ends of the longitudinal buildings. Corrugated gabled roofs capped the building. This design was the template for nearly every barracks in the camp except for a cluster of two story concrete mansions built by the French to house managers of the Michelin plantation, when it was still in operation, before the Americans joined the war. Military officers now occupied these stately buildings.

Dunn stowed his belongings in his footlocker, went to the battalion quartermaster to receive his jungle fatigues, boots, and M-16 rifle. After storing those items and changing into his fatigues, he reported to Sergeant Smith to learn his duties. The Sergeant explained the reports the company clerk prepared and he outlined the daily, weekly, and monthly routines. He warned Dunn to treat all of the soldiers politely because it was not uncommon for an abused soldier to toss a grenade at a rude clerk or officer. So, that white skin of yours is no protection here, soldier. Do you hear me? Yes, Sergeant.

Despite Sergeant Smith's hostility, Dunn liked this new assignment. The commanding officer, Captain Edwin Matthews, who was white like most of the officers, was said to be smart and friendly. Dunn hadn't met him because the captain and all of the company's foot soldiers, except for two men who were sick, were in the field on some kind of operation. Dunn's area of the base camp was virtually deserted. The mess hall, another wooden, corrugated roof building just like all of the others, fed only a dozen or so personnel. Dunn sat at a table with First Sergeant Smith and four other non-commissioned soldiers, one of them, Justin Torrebella, seemed the friendliest. Justin was white; the others were black.

So, you came in today?

Yeah, I arrived three or four days ago in Saigon and flew out here today on transport. The sergeant, here, has got me settled in.

So, what do you think? Is this a shit-hole or what?

I don't know. It doesn't seem so bad so far. Actually, it's a lot better than I thought it would be.

But, it's a shit-hole, man. The food is crap. They treat you like a turd, and the fucking gooks look like they want to kill you all the time.

Gooks?

Yeah, the Vietnamese civilians who burn the shit pots and haul the garbage.

Burn the shit pots? What's that?

Oh, man, wait till you have to take a crap. The latrines here are on a high water table so they can't dig pits for the shit in the outhouses. Instead, the turds and piss fall into big metal cans under the seats and the gooks take the cans out and burn the crap with gasoline. Uncle Sam's ingenuity. Sometimes, I think, though, that they empty those cans into the kitchen and serve it to us for dinner. This stuff looks, tastes, and smells like crap. Hey, where are you from?

Los Angeles.

Oh, yeah. I'm from Brooklyn, best place in the world. Can't wait to get out of this shit-hole and get back home. I'm a short-timer here, seventy-two days to go and then I only have six months duty stateside after that. How about you?

I enlisted for four years. I've got a year here, three hundred and sixty-one days, I guess, and then another year and half stateside.

You enlisted? Are you crazy?

I wasn't going anywhere, not doing anything. I didn't think that this would be so bad.

Well, you've stepped into it now, man. Sam is gonna show you what a fucked up world is really like. I mean the Army is bad enough, all these fucking rules and shit and assholes in charge of everything—not you, of course, Sergeant—but Nam is the shit-hole of the world. This place ain't got nothing but gooks, mosquitoes, and ants that can snap off your dick and make you wish you were dead which you probably will be before they haul your sorry enlisted ass out of here in a box. Man, you are in it deep. Don't cross the sergeant here because he can send your ass out in the field with the grunts and you and Mr. Viet Cong Gook Supreme can fuck each other over. Maybe, Charlie will only blow off your fucking head because that's the stupidest shit-for-brains part of you for enlisting in this fucked up fucking shit-hole fucked-over turd graveyard.

So, what do you like about his place?

Good pussy ain't bad but watch out for razor blades in their cunts.

What?

Yeah, they say that some of those fucking whores are Cong and they put razor blades in their pussies so that you, Specialist Fourth Class Pendle, puts his dick in there and it comes out sliced in two. Real insidious. Hey, they say it happens. So, give the cunt a finger first just in case. That's what I do. Hey, you wanna go to the canteen for beers?

Sure, let's go.

It's a walk but, hey, we got time.

B Company returned from the field after a two-week operation patrolling the supply road between Dau Tieng and Tay Ninh City. All of the renewed activity of hundreds of men transformed the company compound. Dunn met the company commander, Captain Matthews, who welcomed him and told him to do a good job for the first sergeant and for the men because they needed a good clerk to handle their paperwork and requests and orders from headquarters. Dunn promised to do his best to help the first sergeant.

Dunn's daily routine was easy. He was good at the paperwork and could be very helpful to the grunts who never spent more than a week at a time in the base camp. Usually they were in the field on road operations or security for the bridge over the Saigon River, or guarding some other operation like the mining at the laterite pit where army trucks went to get road building material. After the workday, Dunn stopped by the canteen to watch television, drink beers with Justin or talk with clerks from other units. This was the routine for months. Justin's time finally ran out and he shipped back to the States. A guy named Jimmy Clegg became Dunn's closest friend. Jimmy was also a clerk but with Headquarters Company of the Second Battalion. He was from Chicago and black. Jimmy had been to college but dropped out after two years and was drafted. He thought that Dunn wasn't like other white guys—didn't put up the same kind of barriers, didn't seem so smart-assed and condescending. Dunn was okay.

You ever been to Chicago, Dunn?

Naw, Never been north but I've got family in New York and Detroit. I might see them someday after I ship back.

How many days you got left now?

Two hundred and seventy. How about you?

One hundred and fifty-three and counting. Everyday I cross off one more on my short-timer's calendar. It seems like the days pass so slowly. Back home a week could go by like, it seems, in a flash. Here, every day is like a week.

What's the scuttlebutt in headquarters, Jimmy?

They're talking about something big, some kind of big operation during the dry season, maybe the whole battalion. The major has been going to a lot of meetings at brigade headquarters and he's been meeting with the company commanders. Something's up. We're also getting a lot of new guys, fresh off the boat. Most companies are up to full strength. That means a big operation. Charlie's in for it.

Any idea when?

Not sure but soon, probably. You want another beer?

Sure.

On me.

Okay, then it's my turn.

So, Dunn, you got a girlfriend back home?

No, I dated in Los Angeles and went out some after joining the Army but nobody steady. How about you?

No, didn't date much. You know black women want to get married and I'm not ready.

So, have you tried the Vietnamese women?

No. Have you?

No, I don't trust them. I mean some of them are pretty enough but they all could be Viet Cong. How can you trust them? This is their country and we're blowing it up, killing their people because we don't like Charlie. It's crazy man, a crazy place and a crazy situation. When I first came here, I thought that we were supposed to be doing good things. But no good is coming from this. We treat the Vietnamese like they were dogs.

You mean like white people treat black people back home?

Yeah, like that. You mean that you, a white dude, understand that?

I do because I'm not really a white dude, Jimmy. My mother is white but my father is black. They're both from some little town in Georgia and had me and moved to Los Angeles. So, I'm either black and white or not black or white.

Man, your father is black? He must be a pretty white-looking black man.

No, he's a pretty black-looking black man.

Man, I need another beer now.

Sergeant Smith passed a stack of papers to Dunn. They had not been on friendly terms but the sergeant had ceased being outright hostile when he saw that Dunn did everything as he was told and never challenged, contradicted or questioned him. Dunn was perfectly docile and deferential. So, the sergeant left him alone. Most of the men in the company also left Dunn to himself. They treated him politely but indifferently. Dunn did his daily office work, ate dinner in the mess hall and then headed to the canteen where Jimmy Clegg usually showed up for beers and television.

Hey, Jimmy. What that on the news?

I don't know. Looks like some kind of riot or something. Hey, private, did you catch what's on the news?

Yeah, it's a riot in Detroit. The whole place is burning. People got killed. Lot's of houses burned. It's crazy. Just like Nam.

Oh, shit, Jimmy. I have a distant relative who lives in Detroit. He's a janitor in an apartment building in the black ghetto. Jesus, I hope they're not burning his neighborhood. Hey, private, did you catch any mention of where in Detroit this is taking place?

No. They didn't say.

Dunn, don't worry, man. You can write your folks and find out. There's nothing you can do from here.

But isn't it strange, Jimmy, to be here in this war and another war is going on at home?

Well, you know, Dunn, somebody is always fucking over someone else. There, white folks beat down black folks. Here white and black folks are beating down yellow folks. It's all the same world. The only difference is we're doing the beating, not being beaten.

Listen, I gotta go, Jimmy, and try to call home. I'll see you.

The big field operation began in November. The whole Second Battalion was airlifted by helicopters to the field for a ground sweep of the jungle terrain between Dau Tieng and the Cambodian border. Only the support staff remained in camp.

Jimmy, who is that guy over there? I've seen him here a lot lately. He must be new.

Which one?

The blond guy.

Oh, him. He's a new company clerk. Another Jimmy. James Westley. They say, he's that way.

What way?

You know, a homo.

A homo?

Yeah. They say he sucks cock and doesn't care who knows. They also say he takes it up the ass.

How can he get away with that in the Army?

Are you kidding? Look around, man. It's nothing but dudes here. The only pussy is Vietnamese and a lot of guys would rather get sucked off or fuck a homo before messing with Miss Victor Charlie.

Would you?

If I can be honest here, yes. I've thought about it. But I'm holding out and beating off. My hand is my best piece of ass right now. Why do you ask? Does he interest you?

No! No! Shit no. My old man is a homo and he's one big reason why I left Los Angeles and joined the Army.

A homo? How did he have you?

Well, he was going both ways when he got my mother pregnant but the older he got, the more he only swung one way.

So, you've never thought about guys here in the all-guy Army?

I can't say I haven't thought about it but, like you, I'd rather beat off than fuck a guy.

So, why do you ask about Westley?

He just looks interesting. I wouldn't mind having a beer with him.

Listen, Dunn, you have a beer with Westley and the next thing you know, you're ramming it up his ass and every guy on this base is going to know it. But, Man, you do what you want to do. One thing about this place is that we don't know if we have another day. Charlie could drop a mortar on our heads tonight and that would be that. So, introduce yourself and let it go where it goes.

Naw. You're right, Jimmy. There's no real curiosity on my part. I'll just have another beer with you and fuck you tonight.

Get outta my face, nigger.

Reports of casualties flowed into company headquarters—a soldier in the first platoon had his foot blown off when he accidentally dropped a live grenade on it. Another soldier's back was lacerated by shrapnel from the same grenade. A soldier in the fourth platoon was killed by a sniper who was never caught. And another soldier in that platoon received a deep gash in his leg when he tripped over some bungi sticks set as booby traps by the Viet Cong. Dunn saw the reports on all of these men as he processed the paperwork for hospital stays, transfers out of country, or next of kin notifications. All of this paperwork was forwarded up the chain of command to the battalion and brigade headquarters.

Considering the scale of the operation, casualties were light. So, the buzz among the office staff was not about the operation but about a rumor that the Third Brigade would rejoin the rest of the division at the division base camp in distant Pleiku.

How the hell are they going to do that? March the brigade north to Pleiku?

Seems crazy but you know the Army. If it's crazy, that's the Army's way to do it.

Dunn, I don't think even the Army is that nuts.

Well, what do you think they will do?

I don't know.

Hey, I heard you guys talking. I think I know the answer.

And what is that, Specialist Atamara?

Call me Jim.

Okay, Jim. I'm Jimmy. This is Dunn. What are you, Atamara? Chinese?

No, Japanese. Japanese-American.

Hmmm. Okay. We beat them last time.

Yeah, whatever. So I was saying the brass are going to rename our brigade.

What?

Okay, it's like this. We're Third Brigade, Fourth Infantry Division, right? Well, we'll become Third Brigade, Twenty-Fifth Infantry Division since the Twenty-Fifth Division Headquarters is just down the road in Cu Chi and the current Third Brigade of the Twenty-Fifth will become the Third Brigade of the Fourth. Got that?

Jesus fucking amazing. I hope you're right, man.

Oh, I'm right. I'm a clerk with brigade headquarters and I've heard the brass talking. It's a done deal.

Great. Have a beer on me.

So, Jim, Where are you from?

Nebraska. Lincoln. I got drafted. How about you guys?

I'm from Chicago.

My home is Los Angeles.

Two big city guys. Well, I'm just a farm hick. By the way, Jim—actually James—is not my real name. My first name is Henry, Henry James, some fucking joke of my mother who named all us kids after authors.

Who the fuck was Henry James?

Dunn, man, you need some education. He was a famous writer. You know, Henry James?

Sorry. I never got into that stuff.

Well, try it, you ignorant asshole so we can talk about intelligent stuff instead of Army crap and pussy.

So, Henry James Atamara, a toast to the Third of the Twenty-Fifth! Hey, did you hear something?

In all of this noise?

Yes, there was a thump-thump. Oh, shit, incoming!

You sure?

Get down!

Three mortar rounds crashed into buildings surrounding the canteen. Everyone hit the floor and tried to get under a table. More rounds crashed in the distance. And then silence, except for the television that was still on.

I think that's it. Charlie hit us and now is on the run before the helicopters scramble and sweep the area. That was close. But the thing about mortars is that if you hear them launched—and that means that Charlie was not more than a kilometer or so away—you got a few seconds to take cover. And did you hear the whistle as they came in?

Barely.

Well, this is something new. Welcome to Nam, Baby. Welcome to Nam.

Dunn sat on his bed. He had the lower bunk. He had taken his short-timer's calendar out of his footlocker. Already he had crossed off two-hundred and fourteen days. He still had one hundred and fifty-one days to go. But now he would spend a week of that on R and R—rest and relaxation—in Bangkok. R and R was about the only perk that came with Viet Nam. Now, he and Jimmy Clegg were headed on an adventure to a place where there wasn't a war. Bangkok was one of the most popular destinations for enlisted men. He wasn't much interested in Tokyo or Singapore. He had heard that Bangkok was fun; fun and change from the Army and Viet Nam were what he needed. On the flight to Bangkok from Ton Son Nhut, Saigon, Dunn saw that James Westley was among the military passengers. They were all staying in the same Patpong area hotel in Bangkok.

Hi, fellas. I've seen you guys in Dau Tieng at the canteen. James Westley. I'm with D Company, Fourth Battalion. How about you guys?

Dunn Pendle, B Company, Second Battalion.

Jimmy Clegg, Headquarters Company, Second Battalion.

You sound like northern fellas.

Yeah, Chicago.

Los Angeles.

Well, I'm from Savannah.

I have folks in Georgia.

Really? Where?

Well, my mother and father are from Pachacuti.

Pachacuti? Ain't nothing there but boll weevils and rednecks.

I've been there and it's not so bad.

Well, how about you, soldier? What's Chicago like? You have fun there?

Chicago's great. Black people have it pretty good. My family lives on the south side. Nothing but black folks but we do all right.

You seem like a college boy.

I went a couple of years. Oh, I did well. Learned a lot but I couldn't afford to continue. There are six kids in my family and the money ran out. Then, I was drafted.

Well, me too.

Dunn, here, enlisted. He's a fucking jerk.

Listen, guys. I know a place where we can get a good meal; some of my friends have been there and they recommend the place. We can eat and have some drinks.

Sorry. Dunn and I already have plans.

Okay. Well, another time because I would like to know you guys better. See you later.

I think he has an eye on you, Jimmy.

Yeah, dark meat. That homo can find a Thai boy. I'm not on his menu. There's plenty of pussy in Bangkok and I'm getting some. You game?

Sure. Let's go fuck our brains out.

Some of the guys say that this is a good place. You buy the girls some drinks, talk with them. Feel them up. Then they take you to a room and you bang her till you can't walk anymore.

Yeah. That sounds good.

What's up, Dunn? You don't sound exactly enthusiastic.

I'm not real happy about whores.

Man, it's just getting your rocks off. Give your hand a rest. You might catch a dose but they got penicillin for that.

Okay. Let's do it. It's no big deal.

Hallo, G.I. You want to meet nice girl? Marie there is nice girl. You, what's your name?

Jimmy.

Jimmy, you go to Marie. And you?

Dunn.

Done? What you mean, you done? You no start, yet. That joke.

Yeah, okay. Done.

You go with Alice over there. You treat her nice and she treat you nice, make you forget Viet Nam.

We go in this room. You take off clothes and put there on chair. You want another drink?

No, thanks.

You like me?

You're pretty.

I make you very happy. Come lie down on bed. I put you in my mouth. You like that?

Yeah, that's nice. Go easy. It's been a long time since I've done this. Wait! Wait! I feel like I have to come. Let's go slow. Okay?

Okay. I rub you with hand. Slow. Like this.

Yeah, okay. Wait Hold on. That's making me come too fast. Can we just lie here for a while?

Yeah, but just a little. I got other customers tonight.

Oh, okay. Can I fuck you?

Yeah, but not in front. I got something. An infection. You can fuck me in back. Is that okay with you?

I don't know. I never did that.

You never fuck your friend? You G.I.s sleep together in Viet Nam. No women. You fuck each other?

I never did.

You try sometime. You might like. You try me. You see.

Alice took some lubricant from the nightstand beside the bed and rubbed it on Dunn's penis. Then she guided him into her anus. Dunn had barely started to thrust when he came.

Boy, you come fast. You come back tomorrow and we do this again. Slow next time. Okay?

Dunn waited for Jimmy Clegg in the lounge. When he finally emerged from his room with Marie, he had a big smile on his face. Well, my friend, shall we go to dinner?

Dunn and Jimmy did return to the girls' club the next night and the night after that. Each time Dunn took longer and he tried different girls.

Hey, Dunn, for our last night here, let's try something new.

What's that?

Let's get two girls together in the same room.

Why?

I think it would be a kick to switch off. You know, more variety.

You mean just the girls, right? You're not going weird on me and thinking you and me might do something together?

Hey, let's just go crazy and do whatever moves us. Dunn, we could go back to Nam and be blown away before the end of the week. If something happens, it will happen because we are friends and friend can do shit.

Wait a minute. You've said that you wouldn't do a guy. What are you saying now?

I'm just saying that I don't know if I have a week, a year or what. If you and me got it on, it would just be between friends. Not homo. Just friends and fun but if it scares you, it's cool. We'll just do the women. Okay?

Okay.

Lisa and Carmen were assigned to Dunn and Jimmy. They had explained to the girls what they wanted to do, and the girls were hardly surprised since lots of G.I.'s did the same thing. After everyone undressed and got in bed, the women took charge and the men were compliant. Both came and lay back on the bed side by side while the women dressed. Jimmy leaned over and kissed Dunn on the mouth. Dunn didn't resist. They dressed and left.

I'm sorry you fellas never had the time to get together but I hope that you had a good time.

I did. Did you, Dunn?

Yeah, me too. How about you, Specialist Westley?

Why so formal? Well, I'm glad that you asked. I went to a club where there were only rent boys.

Rent boys?

Yes, you know. Boys that you can hire for sexual pleasure.

Boys?

Yes, young men. Beautiful brown men like you, Jimmy. So, I hired myself some boys and had a great time.

Tell me, James, how can you talk like a homo in this man's Army and get away with it?

What are they going to do? Send me home?

They could put you in the brig.

And if they did? The brig is run by men, and men like sex. Sometimes, they take what they can get and don't worry too much if it comes with a cock and balls instead of a cunt and tits. Tell me, Mr. Jimmy Clegg, specialist fourth class: You ever considered a little man-on-man sex? I'll accept your lack of a response as an affirmative. And what's the harm? It's only sex. A man and a woman, two women, two men, three men, if you guys are ever game and can get over your tight ass hang-ups. Listen, one day faggots will do what they do and nobody will think anything about it. They already do it that way in Bangkok. It's no big deal. Get over it. And come to me when you're ready.

On their return to Dau Tieng, Dunn and Jimmy Clegg took up their routines. One night, Dunn had one beer too many at the canteen and, as he headed for his bunk in the barracks, he had to steady himself. Then he realized that he had to pee and backtracked out of the barracks to the latrine. There was a foul shit odor because the barrels that collected refuse needed to be burned by the Vietnamese attendants the next morning. Dunn lifted a toilet seat lid, steadied himself and pissed. After giving himself a good shake, he headed back to the barracks. He came up to one of the above-ground sand-bagged bunkers and thought he saw some kind of small dark creature run out of the entryway. Maybe, it was a lizard or something. He stopped again and noticed that there was no moonlight. All of the shadowy barracks lined up in neat rows looks like some kind of housing development for the poor. There were no clouds but lots of stars, so many and so bright. No one else was moving about because the company was out in the field. The office staff and a few sick call grunts were in the barracks. There were no lights on. It was 9 pm and still hot and completely silent when he reached his bunk and undressed to his Army boxers and T-shirt. He pulled back the blanket and top sheet and sat on the bed. His head was spinning. Finally, he laid down resting his head on the pillow. He moved his hand somewhat absentmindedly to his crotch and he scratched. Touching himself, he felt slightly aroused. He began to imagine that club in Bangkok and the girls. One of them was fondling his cock. He was getting hard. She then put him in her mouth. He tensed and grabbed her head. Now, another girl was kissing him. But he didn't remember a girl kissing him. No, Jimmy Clegg was kissing him. He pulled away and turned his head. When he looked back, he saw that he was holding Jimmy's head in his hands. Jimmy was sucking his cock. He could feel himself losing his hard-on. As he looked past Jimmy's head, still buried in his crotch, he saw James Westley behind Clegg, naked with his hands on Clegg's upraised hips. Westley was fucking Clegg. Dunn suddenly got hard again and realized that he was coming. He squeezed his eyes shut as his body shook. A few seconds later, with his heart pounding, he opened his eyes and stared at the bottom of the top bunk overhead. None of that happened, he thought. But, maybe I wanted it to happen. Okay, I wanted it but it didn't happen. Clegg did kiss me, and I let him but that didn't mean anything. We're good friends. Close. We were in a whorehouse. We talked about sex. Westley came on to us. We were excited, with strange women, not women we really liked or could trust. We were . . .

His thought was interrupted because he heard a weird whistling sound. It was unlike anything he had heard but he knew what it was. He rolled out of bed onto the floor and then crawled under his bunk just as two rockets hit the barracks next door. The concussion of the blast peeled away the corrugated metal from the roof overhead. The sandbags outside of Dunn's barracks split and popped as shrapnel tore into them. The blast hurled something that thudded to the floor of Dunn's barracks. He curled into a ball and covered his head. More explosions crackled in the distance. Then a final barrage of four distinct blasts fell closer to Dunn's barracks and vibrated the building. Silence followed. Dunn waited a few minutes. He decided to make a run for the nearest bunker. He crawled from under the bunk. The wooden plank floor was littered with debris. He couldn't worry about cutting his feet. As he headed to the door, he felt something soft and wet under his foot. He kept going in low crouch. Already the metallic smell of blood from the corpse on the floor was strong. He dashed out of the barracks to the bunker. Two other soldiers were already there in the dark. No one spoke. After ten minutes, someone said, Who's in here? Pendle. Wisnewsky. Frankel. They answered in turn.

What the fuck was that?

That's the war, man. It's come home. Rockets. Viet Cong rockets.

But I thought they only had mortars!

Well, not anymore. We're in deep shit now. Deep.

You think Charlie got in the base?

Man, I hope not. We really are fucked if he does. Hell, that fence and guard posts around the camp don't seem so reassuring right now. No. If Charlie wants to get in, he will, man. We're fucking fucked. Let's get out of here and get our weapons at least.

Okay. Let's go.

They ran to different barracks.

When Dunn got back to his bunk, he got his boots, fatigues, ammo belt, helmet and weapon, dressed and went to the company headquarters. Sergeant Smith was there and on the radio.

Dunn, they're attacking bases all over the country. It's a coordinated attack. Probably North Vietnamese and Viet Cong. Division headquarters is under attack at Cu Chi. There's no ground attack here. Just the rockets. We've got casualties.

There's a body in my barracks, Sergeant. Blown over from the third platoon barracks.

Maybe, it's that guy on sick call. Roberts. Could you do anything for him?

No. He was a bloody pile.

Well, soldier, you can expect that you and every other grunt with two legs will be headed to the field. They need replacements out there more than they need company clerks. Your vacation days are over. I hope that you remember how to use that weapon of yours. You didn't expect that this was going to be a great big pussy party did you?

No, Sergeant. But this is a bad time to jump in.

Tough shit, Soldier. Be ready to move out tomorrow.

Orders to move out didn't come the next day. The remaining soldiers in B Company began to clear away the destruction. The third platoon barracks with its bunk beds, footlockers and assorted equipment was wrecked. Private Roberts dismembered body was removed from Dunn's barracks as was the corrugated metal roof that was peeled back and exposed the ceiling beams, some of which were splintered. Tarpaulins were spread over the gaping hole in the roof. Damage throughout the base was significant but limited to the areas directly impacted by the fourteen or so rockets. Sergeant Smith reported that the rockets had been fired from a distance of about three or four kilometers which meant that the North Vietnamese or Viet Cong could easily escape into the countryside without detection. The accuracy of the rockets was a surprise since they were fired from such a distance. Obviously, the war had changed. A ground assault on Cu Chi breached the perimeter but Twenty-Fifth Division forces drove back the invaders and reinforced the perimeter. Helicopters were ferrying the Third Brigade, already in the field, to reinforce Cu Chi. All available infantry personnel in Dau Tieng were joining the brigade soon in Cu Chi.

Dunn stood on the helipad at Dau Tieng. Troops were gathering in full battle gear. Some, like Dunn, had never worn it except for periodic barracks inspections by the unit commander. It was hot and the gear was heavy. Dunn surveyed the landscape. He had a panoramic view from the helipad which was on the highest ground of the camp. To the east were the green tops of the rubber trees of the plantation. To the north spread the camp proper, like some shanty town, nearly identical buildings, all one story high. Beyond the camp, which was demarcated by fences and watchtowers, was a random array of trees in clumps with patches of open land. In a northwesterly direction beyond the camp were a series of hills, all in a line and one slightly larger and higher than the next. They looked like the spine of some subterranean creature slithering under the plain. To the west, towards distant Cambodia were more rubber plantations, and thrusting above the tree-line some twenty kilometers distant, the green-gray tit, Nui Ba Din, the sacred mountain that dominated the landscape. The southern view was obscured by the broad rising plane of the helipad. But the red clay tile rooftops of the village of Dau Tieng poked above the distant margins of the asphalt surface. About two hundred soldiers, like Dunn, massed on the western edge of the helipad standing carefully behind a yellow strip that marked off the waiting area. As they waited, clouds swiftly swept in from the west, scudding over Nui Ba Din and speeding towards Dau Tieng. Then, rain in gentle but steady waves drizzled over the helipad. The sky darkened. In the distance, what first seemed like thunder, morphed into the rapid staccato of helicopter rotor blades. To the southeast, the swarm of Huey helicopters advanced under the clouds, their rotors becoming ever louder. At first they looked like insects but as they came closer, their brown metallic carapaces suggested something more deadly than mosquitoes. The choppers arrived at the helipad quickly hovering in place above the tarmac without their skids touching the asphalt. Dunn stepped onto a skid of his assigned chopper and pulled himself into the cabin with six other soldiers. He was soaked from the rain and had to wipe his face to see. The chopper rose and headed forward then banked right to the east rising higher as it passed over the camp and the bordering rubber plantation on the east, higher still beyond the range of gunfire until the landscape resembled a kid's model train layout. But there were no trains. Only a few roads cutting through patches of forest, fallow fields, and scattered rooftops of villages. The chopper lurched from side to side as it was buffeted by warm and warmer air currents. Dunn held onto the handhold beside the open side of the chopper. A machine gunner, with his gun pointed out and down, kept a keen eye on the landscape. As the chopper began to descend, Dunn tensed. They were approaching Cu Chi. He knew that Cu Chi was a massive base camp with three infantry brigades and support units, four times as big as Dau Tieng. It was a veritable city of tens of thousands of soldiers. And it was under attack. The buffeting of the chopper became more pronounced. Dunn looked out and down and couldn't make sense of what he saw. The landscape was aflame. Plumes of smoke and fire billowed up from the ground. Tracer rounds, like streaks of lightning, criss-crossed the landscape. If he had known the paintings, he might have been reminded of Hieronymus Bosch's scenes of Hell. Several tracer rounds zipped past the choppers. As the gunner prepared to return fire, he got a Negative, Negative. Friendlies down there. The chopper moved on, crossing over the perimeter of Cu Chi and hundreds of wooden, metal-roofed buildings to the helipad. As it hovered, Dunn and the other soldiers stepped onto the skid and jumped to the ground, moving rapidly away from the chopper as the rotors sprayed him in the downdraft with rain.

The disembarking soldiers were directed to troop-carrying trucks that, when full, lumbered away some distance to a compound within the base camp. This was a processing center composed of several barracks-type buildings. Dunn got his assignment, found an empty bunk, piled his gear beside it, and waited. At lunch, he went to the mess hall, got a metal tray, and filled the several depressions with roast beef, mashed potatoes and carrots. He picked up a can of cola from a drum filled with ice and other cans of soda and beer. As he scanned the hall for an open place at one of the long tables, he saw the three Jimmys.

Well, Pendle, we were wondering when you would get here.

Dunn took a seat next to Jimmy Clegg. Westley and Atamura sat across from Dunn and Clegg.

What do you guys know?

Charlie is kicking the shit out of Sam. Heavy casualties. Heavy. The worst yet. Charlie doesn't seem to care how many gooks go down. Sorry, Atamura. Anyway, Charlie is sticking it to Cu Chi. They can't take the base, of course, but they are showing that Sam can't sit on his fat white ass and piss all over these people. Charlie is pissing back and when he's made his point and killed lots of GIs, he'll fade away like always. Then, later, he'll do it again until Sam gets tired and walks away, of course, after shitting big time on everyone and everything.

I heard that us company clerks and all of those sick-call fuckwits are going to take the place of the recently blown away until Mr. Army gets more grunts in here from stateside. I'm telling you boys, our days are numbered. None of us will be sitting around telling stories about this twenty years from now.

They may get your ass, Atamura, or yours, Clegg, or yours, Pendle, but they won't get me. I'm gonna blow the executive officer and keep him happy here.

Good luck with that, faggot.

Did you see that shit when we came in on the choppers?

No, I missed it, asshole. Are you fucking kidding? Of course, I saw it. How could I miss it? I thought that the whole fucking world was blowing up. You know when their rockets hit Dau Tieng, some grunt got blown up and his body landed right in my barracks. He was a piece of raw meat.

If you have to go, at least that's a quick way.

Who gives a fuck about quick? I just don't want to go out in that hellhole.

Do you think we have a choice?

Man, we're already here. Westley thinks he has a way out but nobody's getting out of this shit. This is it, man. Charlie's got us by the balls and he's not letting go till we are dead or every gook is dead. So, a lot of us won't be around next Tet.

The quartet left the mess hall and headed to their barracks. Word quickly spread that the new replacements were shipping out immediately to join units in the field. Dunn grabbed his gear and went outside to see a convoy of trucks lined up with soldiers climbing into the rear of the transports. He took his place on a bench the length of the truck cargo area and facing directly across to another bench that was rapidly filling up with soldiers in full battle gear. Everyone was quiet. Someone slammed the rear flap shut, and the truck started up with a lurch. Soon, the buildings of Cu Chi camp passed slowly by, as seen from the rear opening of the camouflaged canvas-sided truck. Dunn could see another truck directly behind. The driver and armed shotgun riding next to him were visible through the windshield of the truck's cab. Since the ground was wet from the recent rain, there was no dust but the rear wheels of Dunn's truck splattered mud on the windshield of the truck following so that truck's windshield wipers were swinging back and forth to keep half moons of glass clear. The trucks suddenly stopped. Dunn could hear the rumbling strain and metallic clacking of tanks and armored personnel carriers. He assumed that that armor was joining the convoy to provide escort and firepower. The truck lurched forward again and Dunn could see that the convoy was passing through one of Cu Chi's gates and around several barbed-wire barricades. They were now on a road passing through flat farmland that looked as if every tree and bush had been leveled to create an un-obscured fire zone around Cu Chi. After some distance from Cu Chi, clumps of trees and bushes re-appeared. We're fucking sitting ducks, Dunn heard the guy next to him mutter. Indeed, they were.

It took about an hour for the convoy to reach the forward base camp of the Second Battalion of the Third Brigade. Dunn was surprised that there had been no weapons fire during the convoy. And now as the soldiers scrambled down from the trucks, all seemed calm. He and the rest, however, were quickly hustled to their units. Dunn joined B Company again and was assigned as rifleman to the third platoon headed by Lieutenant Daniel Graff. He welcomed Dunn and introduced him to first squad leader, Private Otis Manning. Manning told Dunn first of all to dig a foxhole trench. That would be his defensive position in a firefight. It was then that Dunn noticed that there were a series of one man trenches creating a line that defined the circular perimeter of the base. On one side, in other words his side of that line within the circle, was the company and the rest of the Second Battalion. On the other side, in other words outside of perimeter, was the rest of the world, namely the VC, Victor Charlie—the Viet Cong. It struck Dunn that he and the rest of the battalion were cavalry on the Great Plains huddled in a defensive circle and out there were the Indians, hidden until the first arrow took down some dope taking a crap while squatting near a bush. He made a note to himself to hold his bowel until dark.

All remained quiet although artillery could be heard in the distance. Dunn and the rest broke out their C-rations for dinner. It was dark now, and he was assigned to the first watch in his foxhole along with other members of his shift. Since the water table was high, Dunn actually was squatting in water up to his chest. He held his M-16 rifle in front of him scanning his section of the perimeter for any movement. In the moonlight, he could see for quite a distance but, then, he realized that he could also be seen from a distance. About two-thirds of the men had spread their plastic ponchos on the ground and tried to sleep until it was their turn for guard duty. After four hours, squad leader, Manning, came over to Dunn to tell him his shift was over and he could go to sleep. Dunn crawled out of the muddy water of his foxhole, spread his poncho on the ground, took off his wet boots, socks and helmet and clutching his rifle laid down and fell asleep. Manning awoke him at dawn, told him to get ready to move out. B Company was assigned a forward sweep through the countryside. The company was moving out in an hour. Dunn took a quick piss and shit behind a bush, ate some C-rations, and brushed his teeth with water from his canteen. At 0700 hours, the company assembled in formation—two long, parallel files of men— about thirty feet between the two files—with the third platoon in the lead. Four men from each platoon formed two pairs, one pair to the left and another to the right of the main files. These two pairs—one man at point and the other behind him as his cover—were about thirty feet to either side of the main files. In this way, the outlying pairs could serve as an early warning as the massed formation moved forward. The other three platoons followed the third in a similar formation. B Company commander radioed to move out and the formation, in two files with the two pairs of point men, started forward through the defensive perimeter of the battalion base camp. Dunn was assigned to the left-flanking pair as cover for the point man. It was as if he was walking all by himself through Charlie's front yard. The point man was twenty feet in front of him. The left file was thirty feet to his right. They were walking slowly and silently. He was instructed to watch for signals from Lieutenant Graff who followed his radio operator and two riflemen and was followed by a machine gunner, ammo man, and more riflemen. There were twenty men from the platoon in all in both files, eighty men in the company. This was the first time Dunn had been on an operation in battle since arriving in country nine months before. He was a short-timer, only three more months to go. What the fuck was he doing in the field? He should be arranging stacks of forms in the office. He had never even fired his rifle and wasn't sure, in fact, if it worked. This was so crazy; it didn't seem real. Was he really walking through fields and woods in Viet Nam? Whatever happened to Los Angeles? To Pachacuti? Where is Jimmy Clegg? Where's Charlie? He must be out there somewhere. The company continued its sweep for some hours traveling several kilometers until they came upon a village. The Lieutenant signaled the outlying men to rejoin the main files as the company approached a cluster of houses. Each platoon was assigned a sector of the village to search. The third platoon searched several houses and found them empty. The families' belongings were still in place, however, chairs, beds, framed pictures on tables, dishes in the kitchen. As Dunn and his squad moved through houses, he was surprised at how well the local people lived and suppressed an urge to snatch a souvenir of someone else's belongings. When the village was searched, only a few old women, several children, and various animals were identified. All of the adult women had their identification cards and were allowed to remain in their houses. Word was passed that the company would spend the night in the village as the Vietnamese civilians would provide cover from the Viet Cong. Third platoon was assigned a large two story house whose front and most of the roof were destroyed in an earlier bombardment. Aside from looking like a cracked-open egg, the house had most of its furnishings intact, including sofas, chairs, and a grand piano in what must have been the living room. Two women in the household went about their chores as if the soldiers, who were camping out on their upholstered furniture and teak wood floors, weren't there. Dunn and two riflemen claimed the top of the piano as their bunk. After the commander posted guards around the village, the company settled in for a quiet night's sleep.

Dunn was aching in the morning. The piano had been a bad idea because he was aware all night long of trying to avoid rolling off the top onto the floor. However, he had lain on his back most of the night and watched the stars. There were so many, he realized, because of the absence of ground light. How could the world be so beautiful and fucked up at the same time? One of the women in the household, perhaps a servant, carried a pot which she emptied in the path outside of the house. Dunn wondered if it was a chamber pot although he had never seen one. He realized that he had to attend to that business too and stepped outside the house, dug a hole in the garden and took a shit. Word passed that the company was re-forming to move out. He was assigned again to the left flank but the second platoon would lead the formation. Third platoon was now last. The spacing was tighter between men as they left the village and headed to the lightly wooded area beyond. As they reached the woods, the lieutenant signaled for the formation to spread out. Dunn and the point man in front of him moved to the left of the left file and the point man increased his distance from Dunn. He momentarily entered a thicket of brush. Dunn's attention was distracted by a Vietnamese man on a bicycle off to his left who pedaled nonchalantly towards him. There was the crackle of gunfire. Everyone dropped to the ground. The man on the bicycle dropped his bike and rolled on the ground too. The gunfire had come from the thicket in front of Dunn into which the point man had entered. The lieutenant signaled Dunn to go forward to the thicket. He crawled forward with his rifle pointed ahead of him until he reached the thicket. There, just inside in a little clearing was the point man on is back. Blood puddled in his mouth which was wide open. Blood also soaked his chest. He didn't move. Suddenly, three more riflemen entered the clearing with the lieutenant and radioman. The lieutenant was calling the company commander to report the casualty. The platoon was to stay behind while the remainder of the company moved forward. The lieutenant radioed for a medevac helicopter. He instructed the men of Dunn's platoon to move to the nearest clearing and throw a smoke grenade to identify their position when the helicopter approached. Two men lifted the body and the lieutenant reorganized the platoon to move to the clearing. Dunn became the point man on the left flank with a new man assigned as his cover. Something flashed out of the woods and there was an explosion and another. Parts of bodies landed near Dunn; they were bloody and burning. Then there was screaming, and more explosions. Dunn hugged the ground. He tried to spot the lieutenant. Everyone was on the ground in the undergrowth. Still, there were cries and screams. A jet roared over the treetops. Someone popped some smoke grenades to signal their position. Dunn felt an earth-shaking explosion. Something was whistling through the air tearing leaves and ripping bark from trees. Shrapnel. The jet had fired a rocket too close. A piercing scream. Then silence. Minutes passed. The lieutenant called for everyone to check in. Six men didn't respond. The lieutenant called in the flank men. When Dunn reached the rest of the platoon, he saw one man propped against a tree. A large jagged piece of metal was imbedded in his face. The man had no nose or upper jaw. There was just a bloody, gapping cavity. The man was still breathing and his eyes were open but unfocused. He was alive though grievously, probably fatally, wounded. Dunn could hear movement in the undergrowth. The rest of the company had come back. Third platoon rejoined the formation which moved to the nearest clearing. A medevac chopper's rotors could be heard. Smoke grenades were released. The dead and injured were loaded, and the chopper swiftly moved away. The company commander told the remaining men to dig in for the night. The rest of the battalion would arrive tomorrow as reinforcements and a sweep of the area would continue.

Dunn dug his foxhole in the perimeter that was partly in a wooded area and partly in a clearing. He was on the clearing side. He ate his C-rations and started his guard watch from his foxhole. He wondered how Jimmy Clegg was doing. He doubted that he would ever see him again. He wouldn't see his mother or father again. Not his grandmothers. None of his family. He wanted to cry but that seemed pointless. This was the way it was. He was a soldier. He chose this. Why? Because he wanted to be away from his father? Because it was hard being black and white? Because he never found anyone or anything else in his life? So, how would it be different if he survived this hell? He would tell Jimmy Clegg that he was the best friend he ever had. He would tell his father that being a faggot wasn't such a big deal. Hell, he had let Jimmy kiss him and that was okay. If they had had a chance to go farther, he might have. It was okay. Everything is okay if you're not hung up about it. We can all decide for ourselves. If his daddy liked men, so what? The fact is that his father, liked someone, like Dunn liked Jimmy. He remembered that he was attracted to another soldier his age at the Presidio; he wanted to talk with him but didn't have the opportunity. He knew that he really liked women just like his father sometimes did. He could get married and have children. That would be nice. He could go back to school. Start a business. Buy a house. Travel. Maybe, someday he could even come back to Viet Nam after the war was over because, someday it would be a nice place. He could be happy.

Dunn, his squad leader said, you can sleep now. The next shift is taking over. Okay. Dunn pulled out his notebook from his pack and wrote about all that had happened that day and what he was thinking. When he finished writing and returned his notebook to his pack, he realized he had to take a piss. Dunn found a bush and peed. He heard the single rifle shot and felt the slug hit him in the chest. He slumped to the ground. On his back looking up at the sky at the stars. It could have happened, he thought. He could have done those things. But not this time. He was done for now. Last of the Pendle. Twenty-three years old. Done, just like the girl in Bangkok said. I'll be one of the stars now

CONNECTIONS

May Easter Carvey sat in her tidy living room. She looked quickly around at the modest furnishings, particularly the upholstered faded purple sofa on which she sat, and asked herself once again what she was thinking when she agreed to take it from her sister who had purchased a new sofa. Ornella Easter Crimson, May's older, widowed sister, had redecorated her house in Atlanta and offered to ship her old sofa to Cincinnati for May, and May had agreed to take it because her sofa was even older and rattier than Ornella's cast-off. May resolved to have that gift re-upholstered as soon as she could afford it. Meanwhile, as her attention refocused on why she had come into the living room to sit down, she picked up the telephone from the end table and dialed her son, Waite's, number in Cleveland. It rang three times before it was answered.

Hello!

Hello, Woodward, this is May Easter.

Well, hello, Mother May. How are you?

I'm fine, Baby. And you?

Just dandy. I had a birthday yesterday, and Waite took me out to dinner downtown. We had quite a good time. That boy of yours is a sweetheart, like his momma.

Oh, you sure know how to make an old lady feel good. By the way, is he there?

Sure, let me get him.

May Easter could hear Woodward Franklin Templeton II, Waite's boyfriend and roommate, put down the phone, walk a short distance, then call Waite.

Pick up the phone. It's your mother.

Hello, Momma?

Hey, Baby. How's my boy?

Fine. And you? What's up?

I'm okay. I'm thinking about this couch that your Aunt Ornella gave me. I want it re-upholstered. What do you think?

What color is it?

Purple.

Oh, definitely. How about a nice dark blue? That would look nice in the living room.

Oh, maybe. Anyway, that's not why I called. You'll never guess who called me yesterday.

You're right. Who?

Mosey. Mosey DeBobo. You still there, Waite?

Yeah, Momma. I don't think that I've heard Mosey's name in nearly twenty years. Where is he? Why did he call?

Well, he's in Detroit.

Still? That's just hours away from Cleveland.

But Waite, he had some bad news.

About what?

Some distant cousin of his was killed in Viet Nam.

That's a shame.

I know. This distant cousin was Trique Pendle's son.

Trique? Mosey's old boyfriend, the one he had when I met him?

Seems so. The boy . . . I'm saying boy but he was twenty-three years old . . . he got killed during that mess we've been watching on television.

Do you know any more details?

No, Mosey didn't know much himself.

How did Mosey find out?

Well, Trique called him from California. Trique lives in Los Angeles now. He was married but now he's divorced. Mosey said he was feeling really down and was crying.

Funny he would call Mosey after all this time.

Well, not so funny after all. He had wanted to call Mosey but something kept him from doing it. Who knows? Well, the important thing is that Mosey wants to talk to you.

But why?

I guess, like Trique, he wants to hook up again. You know, a lot of time has passed. Everyone is older, more settled. It's time to look around and look back. People you thought were part of your past life are somewhere still in you and you want to accept that. I'll bet you might want to see Mosey again.

You know what, Momma? I'm not sure.

Well, he asked me to give you his telephone number, and said that you should call him.

Okay. I'll see. I need to discuss this with Woody. I'm not sure I want to bring an old boyfriend back into my life.

Well, you decide. By the way, how is your sister?

Arleeta is actually doing quite well. She and her husband and kids seem to be fine. They're having me and Woody over for Sunday supper tomorrow.

Good for her. And you too. Listen, Baby, I've got things to do so I'll say goodbye. Give Woodward my love.

Bye, Momma.

Woodward was shoveling snow from the driveway of their suburban acre lot when Waite searched the house for him. Waite opened the screen door from the rear entry to the house and called Woodward inside to tell him about the conversation with May Easter. Woodward wasn't interested in Waite's old boyfriends and told him to do what he wanted. Waite was intrigued to re-establish contact with Mosey but after all of this time, surely, they were both different from when last they saw one another nearly twenty years ago. What would they have to talk about? Not the past; they were just kids. The present? Why would it even matter now?

Well, I guess he wants to talk about his distant cousin's death. But, why with me?

Waite waited. The following day, before he and Woodward headed out to dinner at his sister's house, he sat down at the phone in the little study off the living room and closed the door. An oak desk against the wall served as his work place at home where he graded papers and exams for school. There was a stack of them now although it was early in the semester. Waite believed in demanding work of his students, short papers, surprise exams. Keep them working and on their toes, couldn't hurt, might even help. He dialed Mosey's number. It was answered on the first ring.

DeBobo here.

Mosey? This is Waite. Waite Carvey. You called my mother, and she gave me your number. How are you?

Waite? Oh, Waite, you called. Waite. Waite.

And Mosey started crying.

Mosey, my mother told me your cousin died in Viet Nam. I'm sorry. Is there anything I can do?

Waite. Excuse me. I'm so happy that you called. I wanted to talk to you. You mean so much to me.

Mosey, thank you. But all that was a long time ago. I'm surprised you even thought to call me. What happened to your cousin?

Oh, Waite. You called. I feel so bad about how things ended between us. You were so kind to me, as kind as anyone in my family has been. I didn't thank you.

Mosey, what happened, happened. It was a long time ago. I did the best I could. But I think I let you down. I couldn't help you when you needed it the most.

No. No. Waite. You saved my life. You took me to the hospital when I lost my arm. You took care of me afterwards too. You couldn't afford to keep both of us forever. I had to move on. Take care of myself. And I'm doing that.

Mosey, I'm happy for you. What are you doing now?

Well, I was a janitor for an apartment building but the fools here had a riot and set the city on fire. My building burned but nobody died. Thank god. But folks had to find new places to stay. I'm with a friend temporarily until I can get new work. That's the number you called. His name is Lucius Collins in case you call here again. He likes to be called Lucille though. He's a silly old queen but he's my best friend. What about you?

Well, my mother convinced me to go to college so I went to Oberlin here in Ohio and then I got a teaching job in Cleveland. I met my boyfriend, Woodward—I call him Woody—Templeton. We live together in a house we bought in a new suburb that's mostly black. It's very nice and we're happy together.

So, you've done well. That's good. You're a good person, Waite.

Mosey, you didn't tell me about your cousin.

All I know is he was killed somewhere in Viet Nam. Trique called me after he talked to his mother, my Aunt Xantha, in Georgia. I had called her after the riot to let her know I survived and to give her Lucius's number. She gave it to Trique and he called. He's really low. He wants me to come to Los Angeles for the memorial service.

Do you need money?

Yes. But no. My brother, Phessin, who is pretty rich, will pay my way.

So, you're going?

Yes, we all are. The whole family. The DeBobo and Sellabie are all that Trique has. His ex-wife will be there and her folks, the Boston, too. So, it will be a reunion on a sad occasion.

What about you, Mosey, are you with someone?

I've had boyfriends but no one serious except for this one white guy I call Red.

Does everyone have a nickname in Detroit?

Maybe, I don't know.

When is the memorial service?

Next Saturday. I'm going out there with my sister, Habboey, and her husband, Critton.

Well, as I said, Mosey, I'm sorry about your cousin's death in that stupid war but it sounds like you'll be seeing your family again, and Trique. Is that what you called to tell me?

Yes. But, Waite, I wanted to say that I wished we could have had a life together.

That's a nice thing to say, Mosey, but that isn't what happened. So, now, we have our different lives.

Do you think that you and Woody might come to Detroit sometime? I would like to see you.

I don't know. Maybe. We can talk about it later, after you come back from California.

Okay, Waite. I would really like to see you again. I really would. Okay? Well, goodbye for now.

Waite continued sitting at his desk. He glanced at the framed photograph of him and Woodward taken on vacation in New York with the Empire State Building in the background. That was three years ago. He wondered what Mosey looked like now. Mosey. How strange that he should have called his mother. Well, Mosey. They had some good times before the accident. Maybe, he would talk to Woody about a little trip to Detroit. He got up, opened the door.

Woody?

Yeah.

Are you ready for dinner?

When the phone rang in Swee's office, she was tempted not to answer. It had been a crazy week with too many clients, and too many problems. Her caseload had exploded. There were pregnant teens, homeless women, hopeless drunks, and junkies. It seemed like the whole fabric of the city was coming apart. She shared an office with a co-worker in an old fourteen story office building on West 37th Street. City social services had its midtown branch there. Old metal desks, wooden filing cabinets, and florescent ceiling fixtures with burnt out bulbs defined the crowded space. Snow and ice streaked the grimy windows. And it was much too hot in the office with no way to turn down the heat. So, Swee had propped open a window for a little relief of cool air. On the fourth ring she picked up the phone.

Sellabie, here.

Swee, I got a call from Mosey.

Mosey? What did he want, Gulley?

Bad news. Trique's son, Dunn, was killed in Viet Nam.

Oh, poor Dunn. He was a beautiful boy. Trique must be crushed. He loved that boy more than anything.

I think he did. Mosey says that Trique wants you to call him.

I will when I come home. I can't use this phone for personal long distance. I'll be home after six and call then.

Well, you'll have to wait until about ten because of the time difference.

Oh, That's right. Okay.

I gotta go now. I'm swamped with work.

Bye.

Gulley was fixing dinner for Donald and Meer when Swee walked in the door.

Hey, Sweetie.

Hey, Gulley. Hey, kids. How ya'll doing?

I'm finishing my homework.

Me too.

Swee took off her coat, scarf, hat, and boots and went into the kitchen and gave Gulley a kiss on the cheek.

Hey, Honey, smells like chili.

It is. Hot, like you like it. With red beans and ground beef. You want some cornbread with that?

Sure do and a salad. That's good too.

So, set the table. Tell the kids to get ready. We'll eat in a half hour.

After washing the dishes and going over some paperwork she brought home, Swee sat down at the dining room table. Gulley sat next to her. Gulley had put on weight and was fairly thick around the waist and butt. Her breasts rested on her belly. Swee, on the other hand, had lost weight. She was still matronly but held her weight well. Gulley tried feeding her but Swee only nibbled at meals. So, Gulley ate more than she wanted so that the food wouldn't go to waste.

What are you going to say to Trique when you call him?

I'll try to console him. What else can I do? I wonder if he and Martalee are talking? It's strange that he would call Mosey. From what I know, he and Mosey haven't spoken since they broke up in Atlanta over twenty years ago. Maybe, I should talk to Mosey first and see what's up.

Hello?

Hi, this is Swee Sellabie, Mosey's aunt. Is this Lucius?

Yes, my dear.

I've heard so much about you.

Pleased to make your acquaintance at last. You can call me Lucille.

Lucille, may I speak with Mosey? I hear that you've taken him in temporarily.

Yes. The niggers have burned down Detroit. Mr. Mosey's building was burned out but you know that. Lucille will take good care of him until he gets it back together again.

Well, bless you, Miss Lucille.

Here he is.

Mosey?

Hey, Aunt Swee.

How are you doing, Mosey?

Lucille is taking good care of me.

Are you going to get another job and a place to live?

I hope so, Aunt Swee. I hope so. Things have to settle down here first. Everything's in turmoil. Homes and businesses are gone. People are in shock. There's no plan. No help. No nothing.

Well, I can understand that. Our government is wasting all that money in Viet Nam blowing up things and killing people. We should be taking care of our own.

How do you mean?

I mean that this government and the people who have the wealth and power are more interested in destroying another country because they don't like their politics than they are in making life better here for poor black and white folks.

But, Aunt Swee, if we didn't fight against their politics, they would spread that stuff all over the world and then where would we be?

Mosey, that's the lie they want you and people like you to believe. Politics is politics. What's important is how people live. They need jobs to feed their families and have a decent place to live. Do you think that you lost your job and home because of niggers, as Lucille puts it? You lost everything because the people in power don't give a shit about you. You're just another nigger. I'm just another nigger. But I know the game. And poor Dunn was caught in that game and died. For what? Politics? You think that Dunn is dead because the USA wanted to stop communism in Asia? Communism isn't the problem.

Maybe, you're right, Aunt Swee. But I don't know.

Mosey, you've got to get yourself some education. You've got to wise up and rise up. Get control of your life or you'll be another casualty of the war, the war on dumb niggers. Now, tell me, what did Trique say to you when he called?

He just said that Dunn was killed. He didn't know where or how except that it was in Viet Nam. He and Martalee are having a memorial service a week from Saturday in Los Angeles. Phessin is paying for me to go. Can you go too?

Oh, Mosey, we don't have much money with the kids and all. I don't think so.

Well, please call Trique and talk to him. He cried on the phone. That really scared me.

Okay, Mosey. Take care. We'll talk again soon.

William Bass, the man who lived with Trique was taking dishes from the dishwasher and tidying up the kitchen after preparing dinner. A pot of beef stew simmered on the stove. The kitchen was large and sunlit. There was a neatness about the room that reflected William's sense of order. When he met and moved in with Trique, the kitchen and house were chaotic, at least in William's opinion. He had gradually asserted himself over the Pendle household and brought the kind of order that he wanted and to which Trique was frankly indifferent. Trique focused only on two things. Well, three. He was obsessed with his work at the bank and had become a low-level executive. He worried constantly about his son, Dunn, and now that Dunn was dead, he seemed to lose himself in frenetic and rough sex, mostly with William but occasionally with someone he brought home for threesomes.

William was ten years younger than Trique and raised in California. At twenty-nine, he had had his share of sexual adventures and he didn't mind Trique's threesomes. In fact, he thought that life with Trique was satisfying and secure. He didn't mind being kept by Trique while he attended college to complete his long-delayed degree. He kept Trique's house and warmed Trique's bed and entertained Trique's tricks. But Dunn's death had changed the household dynamic. Trique was no longer emotionally present. He went through the same routines but he wasn't connecting with William. William glanced at the kitchen clock on the counter next to the toaster and Mexican clay pot full of wooden spoons and spatulas. Trique should be home soon. William got out plates and silverware and cloth napkins and set the table in the dining room. He heard Trique's car pull into the driveway. The motor was turned off, and Trique came into the house through the laundry room off the kitchen. William waited for Trique to speak. He didn't. He went directly to the hallway that connected the kitchen to the front door, left his briefcase on the hall table, and hung his trench coat and suit jacket in the hall closet.

Trique?

Yeah?

Mosey's Aunt Swee called from New York. She wants you to call her back.

Swee?

Yes.

Did she say when?

She just called a little while ago. It's about eleven pm. in New York. She said she would stay up until midnight because she has work to finish.

Trique sat down in the hallway chair and dialed Swee's number.

Hello? Aunt Swee?

Trique? Hey, Darling. I just heard the news today from Mosey about Dunn. How are you doing?

I can't . . . I can't . . .

Take your time, Honey. Cry if you have to. Swee is here for you.

Trique let out a wail that caused William to come into the hallway. Trique was holding the phone in his hand with his head thrown back against the wall. William took the phone from Trique.

Hello, Swee. This is William.

Hi. He's taking it hard, isn't he?

I'm afraid so. Wait. He wants the phone back.

Swee. Dunn is dead. They killed him. Why didn't I stop him from going into the Army? I knew this would happen. Lee knew this would happen. I didn't stop him. He's dead. My beautiful boy is dead. Why? Why did they kill him? Why did I let him go? He's dead, Swee. Dead.

Go ahead and cry, Trique. That's all you or anyone can do now. You gotta cry until you can't cry no more.

But they killed him.

Trique, it's a war, a senseless war. People get killed. Dunn was one of them. How could you have stopped him from going into the Army if that's what he wanted to do?

Swee, he went because he hated me for being a faggot. That's what he said, Swee. I never wanted to be queer. I like women. I got one pregnant, Dunn's momma. I've been with women but I keep . . .

He looked at William who was leaving the hallway.

But, I don't know. I keep finding men. I keep wanting them. What's wrong with me?

Look, Trique, what is it? Is it about Dunn or is it about you?

It's about Dunn, Swee; we are devastated about Dunn.

But it sounds to me, Trique, like you're not living in yourself. You like men; you like women. There's nothing wrong with that. I like women. Mosey likes men. You like both. You're not settled with that, and you couldn't get Dunn to understand that who you sleep with is not as important as who you love. And, I think, you loved Dunn as your flesh and blood. He might have understood that if he had had more love in his life. But did he know you and Martalee? I don't know how much love there was there. And, maybe, Dunn never fully felt the love you had for him, and he may have never found another love in his life. But, Trique, all that is past. It's done. You can't change any of it. You can feel sorry about it but it's over. Grieve for your child. But don't grieve for your life or for who you are. Do you hear what I'm saying, Trique?

None of this makes sense, Swee. I can't seem to see it straight. I don't think I can keep this up. I don't want to keep this up.

What are you saying, Trique?

I want out of everything. I've lost my son, my wife.

But you've got your career, a house, a boyfriend.

It's not that important anymore. Dunn should still be alive. I should have been a better father. I don't know, Swee. I can't go on like this.

Trique, are you saying suicide?

No. I don't think so. I'm just saying I want out. I don't know.

Okay, Trique. Mosey told me the memorial service is a week from Saturday. I'm coming out to it. We'll talk.

Okay.

Swee will talk with you. Okay? Mosey will be there too. We'll all talk. Let me speak with William, Trique.

Trique went into the kitchen.

Swee wants to talk with you.

Hello, Swee.

Listen, William. Trique's on the edge. He could go over at any moment. But my guess is that he is good until the memorial service. At least I hope so. Keep an eye on him. Watch for any change in his routine. Talk to him. Let him cry. Comfort him. If you know a therapist, talk to him about seeing one. He's on the brink. And if we don't hold on to him, we'll lose him. He needs professional help and the support of his family. I'm coming for the memorial service. I'll have to ask my nephew, Phessin, to help me financially. But, I'll be there. Take care of him and love him. Goodbye.

I understand and will do my best. Goodbye, Swee.

Luma Arden DeBobo was not a good mother. Her two children, Diedre and André, were spoiled. It was her husband, Phessin, who gave the children everything they wanted and then more. But it was the DeBobo, particularly Phessin's aunts, Xantha and Zennana, who blamed Luma for not exercising more control over her husband and children. Luma, frankly, didn't give a fuck. She had married well; Phessin was not only rich but he was also still mayor of Pachacuti and likely to remain so for a long time. Black folks were beginning to prosper in town, building new houses to replace the shacks that generations going back to Emancipation had occupied. Life was good, and Luma enjoyed it. Her two story mansion was as nice as any of the homes the old white families had. In fact better because everything was new and modern. They even had a housekeeper, a black woman, of course, who kept the place spotless and cooked the meals. Phessin was home. He had decided to forego working another Saturday and relax because he was to be at a community event on Sunday at the main black Baptist church. That would be an all-day affair with everyone bending his ear about every problem that he, as mayor, couldn't do anything about. But he would listen sympathetically, shake hands, give hugs and kisses, and be the mayor everyone expected him to be.

The mayor's large family room, as big as the living room that they only used for guests, was comfortable with windows overlooking an expansive lawn at the rear of the house. A dense forest of trees screened the house from the not-so-near neighbors. There were two couches in the family room. The brown leather one belonged to Phessin. The other, a beige upholstered model, was Luma's and the children's realm. Luma was reading the newspaper. Phessin was taking a post-breakfast nap. The children could be seen outside on the lawn tossing a ball back and forth.

Luma answered the phone.

Mayor DeBobo's residence.

Hello, this is Swee Sellabie. I'm calling from New York and I would like to speak to my nephew, Phessin, the mayor.

Oh, hello, Swee. This is Luma, Phessin's wife. What a surprise to hear from you. I guess you've heard about poor Dunn.

Yes, that's why I'm calling. I need to ask your husband a big favor.

Well, Swee, he's taking a nap now. How have you been, Girl?

It's been rough lately. I don't know if you know but I'm a social worker now with the city and we've got a lot of hard cases. There's so much misery in this city that it weighs me down. It seems like there is so little that I, or anyone, can do. This damn war in Viet Nam is part of the reason. It makes me so mad I could kill someone. All of that money wasted on killing people when our own people are dying of poverty and neglect. It gets me down but, Honey, I somehow keep going. How are you and the kids?

We're too comfortable if you ask me. Phessin makes good money and he's a big nigger around here so everybody is always kissing his fat ass. Hold on, fat ass just woke up. He wants to talk; he's going to pick up the extension. Let's talk another time.

Hello, hello, Aunt Swee.

Hello, Phessin. Listen, I don't want to take up much of your time. I know that you're busy being mayor and all but I would like to go to Dunn's memorial service next Saturday in Los Angeles. But I just don't have the money now to fly out there and stay. And I talked with Trique yesterday and I'm very concerned about him. Dunn's death has pushed him to the breaking point and I want to be with him to see if all of us can help to heal him. I'm only asking for a loan. I know that you are helping your brother, Mosey, to go out there and you probably have the expenses of going there yourself with your family so I know I'm adding to the financial burden. But, I've got to go out there for Trique and help him through this.

Well, Aunt Swee, the money is not a problem, especially if it's just a loan. You tell me how much and I'll get you the money. But I have to say that, although my family is going and all the DeBobo and Sellabie—hell, I think, Olive Fleet Boston and some of her clan are going too—I'm not doing this for Trique. When Dunn visited us in Pachacuti, I told him that he should honor and respect his father. I believed that then. Now, I think that there is nothing honorable about Trique and I don't respect him. I don't approve of him and his life and just between us, although I'm not holding this against you, I believe you and Amity contributed to the mess Trique and even Mosey are in. You encouraged them. You set an example living with another woman. You let Mosey and Trique live together in your house. That's where all this shit began. It was a good thing those Boston boys burned you out of there but I'm glad they didn't hurt you. But you lead a sinful life, Swee, and you helped those men to sin. That's what killed Dunn, a sinning father. Dunn was a beautiful young man. Now he's dead, and it was sin that killed him. That's what I believe. Now, how do you want me to send you some money?

So, that's how you feel? When did you get all of this self-righteous religion, Phessin? Do you know what? I've changed my mind. It was a mistake to call you. You've got your life, your family, and your view of things. I can't argue with you about something that I see completely differently. There is no sin in two people loving each other, man and woman, woman and woman or man and man. What I am, what Mosey and Trique are, is how we are. It can't be changed any more than you can be changed. I'm not a sinner; neither is Trique or Mosey. Trique may not have been the best father or husband but he's no sinner because he can love men and women.

Now, Swee, you know in your heart that just isn't right.

Phessin, as I said, I can't argue with you. I won't argue with you. I'm sorry to have interrupted your day. Say goodbye to your wife and stay well.

What was that about?

Swee wanted a loan to go to Los Angeles for the memorial service. But, damn it, she let the devil in this family with her dyke girlfriend. She let Mosey sin with Trique and now the devil has both of them. Mosey with one arm and Trique divorced with a dead child. You know, I realize now that the kids aren't going with us to Los Angeles. We'll get a sitter. I'm not exposing them to all that sinfulness. They can stay here.

Phessin, sure the kids can stay here but you can't go out there with that attitude. You're only going to cause trouble and this is not the time or place for it. Leave it be, Honey. We'll go and give our support with the rest of the family. But, I'm warning you, Phessin: Don't make trouble because you are the one who will pay the price. You will be evil yourself if you let your feelings show to your family, and evil has a way of coming back on itself. Let it go. Do you hear me?

I'm cool, Baby. I'm cool.

Amity Lowe sat in a booth of the midtown diner. A black turtleneck sweater acted like a pedestal to her fair head with her now blonde hair pulled tightly into a bun. Swee, her round face topped by her graying Afro that looked now more like a mane, clutched at her plaid cardigan and leaned forward. The waitress arrived and they ordered coffee and sandwiches. The waitress immediately brought the two cups of coffee.

So, why did you want to see me, Swee?

I wanted to see you in person instead of telling you what's on my mind over the phone. Dunn, Trique's son, was killed in Viet Nam. We don't know how yet but his body is on the way back to the states, and Trique and his ex-wife, Martalee—she calls herself Lee, now—are having a memorial service on Saturday. I need to be out there not just for Dunn's memory and the family but because I'm also worried about Trique. I talked with him, and he could be suicidal. I want to help him.

Suicidal because Dunn was killed?

Partly. He feels that he wasn't a good father and, maybe, he wasn't. But he feels that way because he never has accepted his own sexuality. He has a live-in boyfriend and, knowing Trique, he's probably still fucking around, maybe with other men and women.

So, you're saying he's suicidal because he bisexual? Hell, I'm bisexual and loving it.

No, that's not it. He can't accept whatever he is—homosexual, bisexual or heterosexual. He's not at peace with himself and, I think, because of that he couldn't be a completely loving father. Trique was a pre-teen when he started hanging around our house so that he could be with Mosey. Maybe, we shouldn't have let them do that, Amity.

Dear, you know those boys would have done what they wanted to do regardless of being at our place. I thought, and you agreed, that since they were loving each other, our home would show them that it was okay.

Still, I don't think that it worked for Trique.

Right.

And that's the problem—Mosey never had doubts about being a homo; neither did I. You are harvesting both sides of the garden. Trique, on the other hand, never settled into his own skin. Maybe, it was because his own daddy was such a hard man and, you know, his mother was too loving. I mean that in a negative way. She didn't establish good bounds for Trique. She let him go his own way.

But, Swee, all of us have kind of gone our own ways. I don't understand why you think things were so different for Trique?

Okay. Trique is one of those people who can't find satisfaction. He'll try men or women or both. No one satisfies him. He's always on to the next one and the next one.

Well, that's a theory. So, you're going out there to work your miracle?

Yes, I'm going out there but it won't be a miracle. Trique needs support and some straight talk.

Straight?

You know what I mean. But, here's something. Oh. Here are our sandwiches.

Let's see, tuna for you, ma'am and a BLT for you. Anything else I can get for you ladies?

No, that's all.

Then, I'll leave the check for you; you can pay at the register.

Thank you. Now, Amity, I'm going out there but Gulley and I don't have the money. I asked my rich nephew in Pachacuti, and he was willing to give me a loan. But, then, he starts in about faggots being sinners and all that shit, and I told him to go fuck himself.

In those words?

Of course not but now I'm stuck so I'm asking you for a loan.

How much?

Six hundred.

Whoa! That would be tough. I've got a couple thou in the bank, and I can give you what you need but I will really need it back. It's all the cash I've got to keep me going until my next dancing gig.

Oh, Amity, thanks. Can I pay you back about a hundred a month? I'll take some of that writing work I've been putting off and pay you back early if I can.

I know you will, Babe. You go do your thing. Save Trique. Make the world right and who knows, maybe, you'll write about all this and become famous.

Sure. Let's eat. I have to get back to work.

FOUR DAYS
Thursday

Lee Pendle, born Martalee Alice Boston, lived in an apartment in Hollywood on Franklin Avenue. The four story building, set in luxuriant landscaping of palms, succulent shrubs and deciduous trees, had two wings embracing an entry courtyard. Her apartment was a two bedroom with a large living room. All of the windows were on one side of the apartment so that from each of the rooms, Lee looked out into the courtyard of the building. The apartment was not air-conditioned. But it had plenty of louvered windows to catch whatever breezes wafted in. Since her apartment faced west, she was spared direct sunlight most of the day and her rooms stayed relatively cool. In the late afternoon when the sun shone on her windows, the venetian blinds managed to block direct sunshine while allowing light to enter the sparsely furnished apartment. The living room had a beige upholstered couch, a blond Scandinavian coffee table, a floor lamp, and two blond wooden chairs with green cushions. There weren't pictures on the walls or rugs on the oak floors. The place looked like the occupant either hadn't finished decorating or didn't plan to stay put very long. Lee thought of herself as too busy to bother with furniture shopping, and she didn't spend much time in the apartment except to sleep. Otherwise, she was at work or with her best friend, a woman and another lawyer, with whom she worked named Brenda Lessinger. She spent a lot of non-work time at Brenda's apartment in the Silver Lake section of Los Angeles. Hers was an upper of a two family house approached through a side yard and exterior stair at the rear of the building. The entrance was through the kitchen and then into a dining room off of which were two bedrooms and a bath. Through the dining room was a living room. All of the living spaces were small and crammed with an odd assortment of second-hand furniture, ceramics, wood carvings, paintings, prints, and exotic textiles. The place looked like a very untidy but welcoming thrift store.

Brenda was taller than Lee and thinner. Her hair was dark while Lee's was naturally blonde. It was also short while Lee's was long. Both women dressed fashionably for work at the law office but wore slacks and blouses at home. Brenda cooked; Lee had stopped cooking when she separated from Trique. Both liked red or white wine with dinner. Lee sat on Brenda's sofa, a somewhat tattered cushioned relic with a brilliant South American textile draped over the faded, stained and frayed floral upholstery. A bottle of red wine and two glasses stood on the wobbly nondescript wooden table in front of the sofa. Lee had just replaced her glass on the table after having taken a long drink. She rubbed her eyes which were still damp and red from an earlier bout of tears. From the kitchen, Brenda announced dinner would be ready in five minutes.

The chops and rice are done. I'm finishing the string beans. Shall I serve your plate?

Thanks, Brenda. Not too much, please.

Okay.

Lee stood for a moment, stretched her arms to the side. Rolled her head and then sat again on the sofa. Brenda entered the living room with a tray of two plates of food, silverware and napkins.

Here, take this one. I served you less than mine.

Thanks.

Brenda sat at the opposite end of the sofa.

So, fill me in on the plans, Lee.

Lee tried balancing the plate on her lap while cutting her chop into bite-sized pieces.

My mother arrives tomorrow. She'll stay with me and sleep in my bedroom; I'll sleep on the couch. My brothers, Hamilton, Oliver and Finn, Jr., are also coming, at my mother's insistence, but they have hotel rooms downtown.

Just them, not the wives or kids?

The wives are coming too but not the kids. It was too expensive for all of them. So, it's my mother, the Boston boys, and the Boston wives.

That should be fun. How old is your mother now?

She just turned sixty-five. My brothers are forty-seven, forty-three, and forty-two. I haven't seen my brothers since I left Pachacuti. The last time I saw my mother was when she came to Atlanta to talk to me and that was in 1946, twenty-two years ago. Dunn had just been born. My mother was so understanding. I think that if I had known how she felt, I might have told her I was leaving Pachacuti. My brothers were awful, hateful and, of course, they were young and just acting out what they learned growing up in the South. Our daddy encouraged them as did my uncle, Griffin, and that was another reason I left. Even if I had known how my mother felt, I don't think she could have stood up to my daddy and my brothers. She had to lie to them about why she went to Atlanta. Well, that was then. Daddy is dead; he died in 1955. The Boston boys are grown and my mother says that they have an understanding of a new reality in Pachacuti and the South. She doesn't say that they like it but they know now there are consequences where twenty-two years ago there weren't any.

Have you talked to your brothers?

No, Hamilton called a couple of times but I hung up. I'm afraid I can't forgive them for what they did to me and Trique, and Swee and Amity.

You know, Lee, it's hard to believe that that kind of thing even went on in this country.

Brenda, what are you saying? Do you think that things have changed that much? I don't think so. Los Angeles may be a lot more progressive than the South but I hear racist remarks all the time at work and not just about blacks. I'm sure you do too.

Well, yes, sometimes. But I think that is just the occasional bigot speaking.

Brenda, bigots are not occasional. Racism is America.

But threatening people's lives, burning down their houses, that's a thing of the past.

I don't think so. You may not see much of it now but it happens.

All right, I see your point and since you married a black man, you probably are more sensitive to it than me. What has your mother said about Dunn?

Lee began speaking, wiping her eyes again: She could hardly say anything except that she would be here and stay with me as long as I wanted. You know, I'm glad that she is coming. I appreciate your love and friendship and you have helped me through this. But my mother knows what this is doing to me in a way that I don't think that even you or I can understand. An important part of our family—the Boston—was destroyed with Dunn. Trique's mother, Xantha, and her family, the DeBobo, have suffered a great loss too. The Pendle, however, were annihilated when Dunn died. I doubt that Trique will have another child since, as a far as I know, he's only fucking other men and they sure aren't going to give him another child. Of course, Trique is only forty-four and could give it another try for the family name.

Come on, really?

It's something that Trique could do. Not likely. But he could. Anyway, his mother arrives tomorrow, too, and the whole DeBobo clan. They are also staying in a hotel downtown.

Is Trique bringing his boyfriend to the memorial service?

You know, I hope so. That would at least say that he has decided what he wants to be.

Lee, I've always been curious about your lack of anger towards him. He cheated on you and he's homosexual. How can you be so understanding? I would have fucking killed him.

Don't think that I couldn't have killed him too. But Trique did something not too many men in his situation might have done. He made a family with me and Dunn when he didn't have to. He left a good job in Atlanta and moved us to California where he could marry me. He made a home for us. That's where I really became a mother and a wife. He loved Dunn even though it was hard for him to show it; that's something I never understood until I realized he was a homo. He didn't want to affect Dunn's life and his growing up. But Trique's caution and distance still had a negative effect on Dunn. I don't think that Dunn was like his father—he had his own problems because he couldn't decide what race he was—but I do know that his sex life wasn't settled. He dated girls—as did his daddy—and liked them, I think. But he was troubled about his father's sex life and probably believed he was susceptible to it too. I told him before he went into the Army that he would have to work out his feelings for himself.

Is that why he went into the Army, to be with other men?

You know, that's funny. That never occurred to me. I only thought that he wanted to get away from us—his father for being homosexual and a cheat, his mother for being complicit in his father's dual life.

But you didn't know, did you, Lee?

Sometimes, I wonder. You see, I was confused because Trique was black; his behavior and attitudes seemed explainable by his race. I didn't see it any other way until I realized that his race had little to do with how he was sexually.

Really? I always heard that black men were, in fact, more sexual than white men.

Maybe, some are, like Trique. But his working both sides of the street is not a black or white thing. It's a bisexual thing and I didn't get that until it literally hit me that he was queer.

So, you simply accepted that about him? Didn't you want him to change? You know, just be with you and heterosexual?

That's the thing, Brenda. I don't think it's a choice he could, or can, make. That's just the way he is and, for all I know, that is how all of those bisexuals are. Why would they risk the scorn, arrests, beatings, discrimination to be queer?

Maybe they like the risk and thrills.

Well, Maybe. But in my heart, I know Trique is, by his nature, homosexual or bisexual. He could, and did, have sex with women. But that's not what drives him.

So, he gave you a child and now that child is dead.

My beautiful Dunn. My Dunn is dead, killed in that stupid war. One of the boys who knew Dunn wrote me a letter. His name is Jimmy Clegg, and he was in Dunn's unit but he wasn't with Dunn when he was killed. He found out about it later and got my address somehow and told me what he knew.

What was that, Lee, if you don't mind telling me?

It happened during this Tet thing—the Tea Offensive—a few weeks ago. Before Tet, Dunn had an office job. This Jimmy did too, and that's how they got to know each other. But when this Tet happened, most of the soldiers in the offices were sent out to fight. Dunn went to one unit and Jimmy to another. Dunn's unit got into a lot of fights with the Viet Cong or whoever but he got through that okay. But one evening when nothing was going on—there wasn't fighting—Dunn was shot in the chest. He died on the spot. There was nothing that anyone could do to save him.

Excuse me? Shot in the chest? When there was no fighting?

I know it sounds like something else was going on but Jimmy says that everyone thought that an enemy sniper shot Dunn.

A sniper, eh? Do you buy that?

Why not? What else could have happened?

I don't know. The circumstances seem strange.

Brenda, it's a strange war. It is war. Stuff happens. I can't begin to think anything except what I was told. Dunn is dead. What else matters? Do you think that someone other than a sniper shot him? Why?

Lee, I don't think anything except that this is a tragedy, and your only son is dead. We'll honor and celebrate his memory on Saturday. I have to say, Lee, that you're doing well with this news. I know it's hard for you but you're still putting one foot in front of the other. I'm proud of you.

Thank you, Brenda, but we've talked so much about me. What about you?

Me? Nothing, really. I'm dating this guy who's kind of nice but it's not serious or long term. We go out. Have fun. Fuck. That's about it. By the way, do you want me to come to your place tomorrow after your mother arrives?

Can I give you a call? I don't know how things will work out. I'm picking her up at the airport. My brothers and their wives will arrive on the same flight but they are renting cars to drive to their hotel downtown. We may all have dinner together somewhere near the hotel before I bring my mother to my place.

I get it. So, I'll be here. Call me if you can. But keep me up to date about the plans for Saturday.

Don't worry. I want you there by my side with my mother. It's going to be tough. We'll get through it.

Are you finished eating?

Yes, I guess I didn't eat much.

No, but you did eat something. I'll take your plate to the kitchen. Pour yourself another glass of wine. Relax. I'll do the dishes and rejoin you.

Thanks, Brenda, but I think I'll leave now. I've got a lot on my mind and I should try and get some sleep, if I can.

Both women stood and embraced. Brenda kissed Lee on the cheek. Lee took her jacket and walked with Brenda to the kitchen. They held hands briefly then Lee opened the door, descended the wooden stairs to the backyard, walked alongside the house to the front, to the street and unlocked her car, a 1964 Ford, started the ignition and pulled into the empty lane between parked cars along both curbs. The night was cool. Streetlights illuminated the street intermittently. Driving beneath them was like passing in and out of spotlights. Lee navigated instinctively towards home.

FOUR DAYS
Friday

Lee had difficulty deciding what to wear to meet her family. Standing in the terminal concourse, she pulled at her suit jacket and smoothed her skirt. She wore navy blue with a white blouse and black high-heeled pumps. Her outfit suddenly seemed too formal, too businesslike, too conventional, but she felt this was a solemn occasion and she wanted her family, her brothers, in particular, to see her as an adult and a serious, grieving person. The last time her brothers saw her she was a teenager, a horny, devil-may-care rebellious hick. Now, she was a professional woman, a mourning mother, and estranged ex-wife. Yes, a serious suit was the best choice. The concourse was crowded with people like her, waiting for passengers from the arriving Delta flight from Atlanta. There were also lots of people with luggage waiting to board the same flight which continued on to San Francisco. There were many men, young men, in military uniforms. She recognized some of them as being Army enlisted men from photos that Dunn had sent her of himself and with some of his buddies. She suddenly wondered if that Jimmy Clegg, who had written her, had been in any of the photos. She couldn't remember seeing any black men in the pictures but, then, she had no reason to make note of it. Why hadn't she paid attention? She had always noticed before if Dunn's friends were black or white. It was such an issue for him and for her. She had encouraged him to have black friends. It made her feel better about her own choices. Her mother was the first family member she recognized coming off the gangway and through the double doors into the waiting area of the concourse. She waved as her mother scanned the crowd. Her mother spotted her and, with her radar on, homed in on her daughter. They embraced and kissed. Her mother then turned back towards the gate and waved to a group of men and women emerging through the double doors. Lee realized that these were her brothers—the Boston boys —Hamilton, Oliver, and Finn, Jr. She was surprised at how handsome they were, all in business suits, carrying trench coats across their arms. Their wives accompanied them, each brother paired, advancing through the crowd towards Lee. Lee quickly glanced back to her mother and noticed that she was wearing a dark gray suit with a black blouse. As she turned her attention back to her brothers, they were already upon her. Finn, Jr. spoke first.

Martalee, my baby sister.

And he started to cry as he hugged her. Hamilton and Oliver also teared up and took their turns hugging her. Hamilton spoke.

Martalee, it's been so long. Too long. We missed you. We're sorry about everything. We were crazy kids. We loved you. We didn't know what we were doing.

Oliver added: We thought we were protecting you. We are honestly sorry. To this day, Momma won't let us forget what we did until you forgive us. Please, Martalee, let's put this past us. Let's be a family again. Especially, now. We are so sorry for your loss. We met Dunn when he came to visit Pachacuti. He was a good-looking, smart man. We're sorry we didn't get to know him better and now he's gone. He was our nephew. We came here to be with our sister and stand with you, as your family.

Lee had started to cry as well, provoked more by the shock of reunion than by what her brothers were saying. She took a hanky from her clutch purse and wiped her eyes. Each of her brothers retrieved handkerchiefs from their pockets, blew their noses and dried their tears. After this pent-up display of emotion, the brothers thought to introduce their wives who had stood unmoving. Hamilton started.

Martalee, this is my wife, Deanna.

Pleased to meet you.

Likewise.

This is Oliver's wife, Matricia.

Thank you for coming.

Honey, it's my pleasure. I just feel so sad for you.

And this is Finn's wife, Kimmie Beth.

Pleased.

Thank you.

Where are the children?

Oh, they are all staying at our house. The oldest, Hamilton, Jr., is in charge. They're having a great time.

Well, thank you all for being here. I wasn't expecting this.

Martalee, it's a new world and I'm making sure these boys are a part of it. They mean what they say. You'll have time to think it over and discover if you can forgive them. You've got a lot on your mind right now so let's get our bags, get these boys and their wives to their hotel, and get me to your place.

Well, I was wondering if we all wanted to go to dinner together tonight. We could eat in the hotel's dining room and then you and I, Mother, could drive to my apartment which is a long way from downtown.

That's fine, Sis. Oliver assured her nodding to his brothers.

Yes, let's do that, Hamilton added.

Okay, let's go to baggage claim, get the bags and find our rental cars.

The group, with Lee and Olive in the lead, made their way through the concourse to the escalator down a level to baggage claim. Hamilton spun off from the group and approached the rental car desks, completed the paperwork, and rejoined his family that had collected all seven suitcases. The brothers and wives headed to the rental car lot; Lee and Olive, with Lee carrying her mother's bag, walked to the parking garage to find her 64' Ford.

The dining room of the Biltmore Hotel was large and elegant. Tables were set with white linen, heavy dinnerware, and sparkling glasses filled with ice water. Lee sat between her mother, on her right, and Hamilton, on her left. Finn, Jr. and Oliver faced her with the wives beside each of their husbands. Most of the dinner conversation was catch up with each brother discussing his family, job, and life in Pachacuti since Lee left home. Hamilton acknowledged that he had been the ringleader who convinced his brothers that they had to find their sister at Swee's house and, yes, they intended bodily harm to Trique. It was as much a matter of family honor as race although all of them were angry that their sister was seeing a black boy. It was part of the times, Hamilton concluded.

I'm not saying that as an excuse but it is an explanation. Burning down Swee's house was inexcusable. We don't know what we intended but when we got there, we just wanted to do something bad to punish them. Thank god nobody was hurt. That's the truth and I'm ashamed to say it. But it's the truth. We were ignorant crackers, as black people say. All that's changed, at least for us. Besides, all of us, especially you, have been through a lot. Let's be a family again.

Lee turned to Hamilton but she was speaking to them all.

Our mother has been one of the most loving people I know. She came to Atlanta when I had Dunn. She encouraged me and showed me that I wasn't the first in the family to cross the color line. Fleet and Boston seem to have a thing for black people. Having my mother come to me like that and telling me I was okay, that things would be all right, made me determined to do whatever I needed to do and not feel bad about anything that I had done.

Lee suddenly turned to Olive.

Isn't that right, Mother?

Olive nodded affirmatively and held her daughter's gaze for what seemed like a very long time. Lee slowly turned back to Hamilton.

So, since our mother has helped me come to terms with my life, I can appreciate that she's done the same for you boys. What's done can't be undone. It's all the past now. Swee's house, Trique and Dunn. I will have a new life, childless, divorced but with my mother and brothers. I'm glad to have you back.

During the drive to Lee's apartment, Olive chuckled.

I wasn't sure how you were going to handle your brothers. It seemed a little touch and go there for a while. Do you really forgive them?

No, Mother, I don't. Some things can't be forgiven.

Then, I guess our task is to get you to forgive yourself and me.

Mother, we haven't talked about that in over twenty years.

But, after we get settled in your place, we have to.

When does Dunn's body arrive?

Sometime next week. It takes a long time for the Army to process everything and ship the body from Viet Nam to here. Trique and I have made burial arrangements and we'll be the only ones present beside my friend, Brenda, and Trique's boyfriend, William.

I wish I could be there too.

So do I . . . but as his parents, we'll have to close this chapter by ourselves.

They remained silent until Lee reached the street outside of her apartment building. She carried her mother's bag up the courtyard through the lush gardens to the entrance of her building. Using her key, she opened the outer and inner doors, walked the short corridor to the elevator, pushed the fourth floor button, and listened to the nearly silent swoosh of the closing doors. Then the ding-ding as the floor indicator signaled four. She turned right on the wall to wall carpeting until she reached 4D. Turning the key in the lock, she opened the door and switched on the vestibule light giving a glimpse of her under-furnished apartment. She showed her mother to her room and helped her unpack. Later, they settled on the couch with a bottle of white wine and two glasses.

Honey, you know I don't drink much wine. I never got used to it. Church folk kind of frowned on it.

Mother, you're in Los Angeles, not Pachacuti. This isn't the church social hall, and I don't remember you being much of a church lady.

After you left, and that mess with your brothers, and your father dying in 1955, I guess I got religion. You know your father was only fifty-three years old. Cancer. It came on so sudden. He went down fast. The boys rallied around but I missed you.

I missed you, too, Mother, but it has taken me all this time to figure out my life, what with Trique, Dunn and all.

What's the "all," Martalee?

The baby, Alfred, the other baby.

That's what I wanted to discuss with you.

I thought so from that remark you made in the car and the look you gave me in the restaurant.

Martalee, you have to forgive yourself, especially now. Especially since Dunn was killed. You did the best thing you could do at the time. You were single, pregnant by a black boy, no prospects, and living in a segregated society. All of this came about because white and black folks, but mostly white folks, couldn't get along. There was so much hatred. Look at your brothers. Think about the lynching in Pachacuti. It was much worse then. Maybe times have changed for the better but not you, I, or anybody else could have seen that it might be better. You did what you had to do for that baby. How could you keep it? It looked like a black child. You were a white mother. Dunn you could keep. He looked like a white baby. If you had kept the other one, you would have had to leave the white community—the only people you knew— behind, like my sister, Soonie, did. I once told you how my father, Murray Fleet, got a black woman pregnant. That was Estah Pendle, Trique's grandmother. What I didn't tell you was that my sister, Soonie, fell in love with a black man, Hanton Sellabie, Swee's father, and got pregnant. She left Pachacuti to live with Sellabie in another town and died after giving birth. She felt that she didn't want to stay among her own people with a black man's baby. It just wasn't possible then. You were lucky to have a white baby. You couldn't keep the black twin. At least, you gave it away and didn't kill it.

Mother, how could I have killed my own child?

Folks can do such bad things; you didn't. You gave that baby a chance by leaving it with that black wet-nurse.

It's funny; a black woman named Delores cleaned the rooming house where I lived. When I was due, I asked her if she knew a midwife because I couldn't afford to go to a hospital. I thought that I was carrying twins and the birth might be difficult. After talking with her, I thought that I could trust her; you know how black women are—they treat us so kindly. I told her that my baby's daddy was a black boy, and that seemed to convince her. So, she found a midwife named Ethel. I went to that midwife, to her house, and she delivered the babies. Both of us were surprised that one was white and the other black. I cried not because I didn't want both but because I knew I couldn't keep both. That midwife, Ethel, knew a black wet-nurse named Callista Collins. She was young, had two children of her own—one of them still nursing—but no husband, like me. She took to my baby and he sucked her like she was his real mother. Callista kept Alfred and said that she would raise him. Mother, I hope she did because that means I still have a child in this world.

Martalee, have you ever tried to find out what happened to that child?

Mother, as long as I had Dunn, I was afraid to inquire. I didn't know how to go back and enter that family's life or know if they would let me. I didn't know if that child was still alive. If it had died, I didn't want to know. Now, with Dunn's death, I feel paralyzed. Mother, Trique doesn't even know I had twins. What would happen to him if he found out?

Well, my dear, we are going to find out tomorrow.

Lee looked at her mother as if she had just said that a man landed on the moon.

What are you saying?

At dinner, I told you that you would have to forgive yourself. And me. I didn't say anymore, at the time, for fear of giving away news of your black child before I could tell you.

Tell me what?

What I did. When I came to see you that time in Atlanta and saw you and Dunn—and came, by the way, because your landlady wrote us, and I read her letter without telling your father or brothers and, especially, your uncle, Griffin—you told me about the twins and the wet-nurse. After I left Atlanta and returned home to Pachacuti, I made up my mind to bring that black baby back with me to be with his people, the DeBobo. When Trique came to visit his mother, Xantha, I stopped by her house to become acquainted with her and Trique. I learned that he loved you and would take care of you and Dunn. I was confident that he could handle himself with a white wife and child in California. I also saw that Xantha was a strong upright woman, that her people were hard-working and going places. They impressed me.

You met them?

All of them. I had a plan to bring that black baby to Pachacuti. I went back to Atlanta with Xantha and her brother, Teatus, to see Callista Collins. She let us in to her house, and we saw the child. As much as Callista loved the child, she knew that she couldn't raise him properly with her own children because she was sick and poor, and was relieved that the child would be with his own people. So, after a couple of days, we brought him back to Pachacuti, and he became part of Teatus's family. Now Teatus and his wife, Iolithe, already had five children but they felt that another child wouldn't be a problem. And Xantha, the child's grandmother, would help out. So, she actually kept the child a lot at her house.

Mother, Dunn was at her house when he visited that time and never mentioned a thing.

Well, that's because the child you named Alfred was also in the Army and away somewhere when Dunn was in Pachacuti. He never met his twin and no one among the DeBobo said anything to him.

Does Alfred know I'm his mother?

Well, my Dear, he knows now. He knew that he was not born a DeBobo and that Teatus and Iolithe were not his birth parents. He was told that his mother couldn't keep him and so the DeBobo raised him. And, frankly, because of all the love he's gotten, he's never shown any interest in knowing his birth parents. The other DeBobo children were only told that he was an orphan and that they should treat Alfred as their little brother. And that's how it went.

Mother, you said something about me finding out what would happen to Trique if he knew about the twin.

I did, Martalee, because Alfred will be here, in Los Angeles. He is supposed to arrive today with the DeBobo. All of them will be at the memorial service. All of them! You'll see your other son, Alfred. Teatus, Iolithe and Xantha expect you to tell him you are his mother and Trique is his father. He knows now that he is a Pendle and Dunn was his brother.

Oh, shit, Mother. I can't believe this! One son that I raised is dead and gone from my life; another I've never known, not even if he was alive, will come into my life! Tomorrow! Mother!

And Lee started to cry. Olive put her arms around her.

Martalee, the DeBobo and I have agreed that we should wait until Sunday to tell Trique so that the memorial service won't be spoiled.

But, Mother, how can I even look at him without wanting to tell him everything?

Simple. Tomorrow is for Dunn. Not you. Not Alfred. Not Trique. No one else. Sunday is soon enough.

Mother, I can't be as, what, calm about this as you are! You've had twenty years to think about this and you never said anything to me! Why did you keep this from me? What were you thinking? This is, I don't know, so unbelievable.

Calm down, Honey. Martalee, do you think that you could have had the life you've had, having made the decisions you made—dropping your drawers for a black boy in the segregated South; running away from home without even telling me where you were going; having twins and giving the black one away to a stranger like breaking up a litter of puppies; moving to California with a black man you came to suspect was sleeping with other men—you say I should have told you that your mother and your mother-in-law rescued your child from a sick, poor woman and raised him among his own people? My dear, Martalee, you are, pardon the expression, full of shit. But I don't blame you. I was too much under your father's thumb and fearful of my own sons and their uncle. But I've only tried to put things right. Now times have changed. I've changed. If I made a mistake here, I apologize but we can only start now and that's why I said earlier you will have to forgive me. Anyway, let's sleep on it. We'll talk, the two of us, if you want, on the way to the service. I'm going to bed now. Goodnight, Dear.

Lee sat stunned. She cried and laughed and then got sick.

FOUR DAYS
Saturday

St. Paul's Episcopal Church stood close to the curb on Wilshire Boulevard at Alvarado Street. A surface parking lot for the congregants filled the space to the right of the church and behind it on the otherwise commercial strip with one story stores selling hardware, groceries, vacuum cleaners, sandwiches, and mattresses filling block after block. The mission-style bulk of St. Paul's dominated its block as if it were trying to assert that it was, indeed, the center of some colonial town. But instead of a quiet pedestrian-filled plaza in front and stone buildings all around, there was the street with its endless traffic of cars, trucks and motorbikes. And parking lots. The morning was warm and sunny. The still rising sun streamed through the stained glass windows on the apse at the eastern side of the church warming the interior and casting stains of multi-colored light on the interior. Lee Boston Pendle sat midway back from the altar and on the right hand side of the aisle. Beside her sat Brenda Lessinger. Both wore black—Lee in a suit with skirt, Brenda in a long dress with sleeves. Each had a black hat, Lee's had a veil which was now pushed up. Their black gloves rested on their handbags which nestled between them on the cushion of the pew. Lee had been crying and still dabbed at her face to dry her tears. Brenda stared ahead at the altar where Olive Fleet Boston was arranging bouquets of flowers.

Brenda leaned towards Lee and, in a lowered voice that one uses in church, asked if she could get Lee a coffee. Lee shook her head no.

Is there anything that you would like before everyone starts arriving?

No. If I have anything else to drink, I'll have to pee. I'll wait until the reception after the ceremony. I'm really doing fine, all things considered. I'm on edge about meeting Alfred. I can't imagine what it will be like to see him; after all, the last time I saw him he was no more than a few weeks old. After he was born and I decided I couldn't keep him and that lovely wet-nurse, Callista Collins, offered to raise him, I thought that I would never see him again. But I went back several times to see how he was and, when I saw how much Callista loved him and took such good care of him, I made up my mind to put him out of my thoughts and focus on Dunn. Now, he's back thanks to my mother and my mother-in-law. He'll be here on this day when I should be thinking only about Dunn. He'll be here, and his father will be here; Trique doesn't even know he has another son.

And you're going to introduce yourself to Alfred as his mother and introduce Trique as his father? This will be worth the price of admission, Lee. Maybe, I should go get you a bottle of something or should we go to my car and smoke a joint? Seriously, you need something to help you through this.

Brenda, my mother, up there, made me realize last night that I've made some pretty bad decisions. I guess I'll have to face, at last, the results of those decisions—Trique, Dunn, and Alfred. Shit! Oh, god! Can I say that in church?

Uh oh. Get ready. People are arriving. Thank god, it's only friends from work.

Several women and men, all in dark clothing, advanced down the aisle to where Lee and Brenda were seated and whispered greetings and condolences and took their seats. Her mother, having finished the flower arrangements, took a seat beside her.

Martalee, I've changed my mind, Olive whispered.

About what, Mother?

I'm going to mention Alfred when I speak.

Why now?

Dunn's and Alfred's lives go together; rejoining them must start now with all of these people here.

Mother, it's too much.

Martalee, you're tough. Be tough now.

I may be sick.

Bullshit.

More guests arrived and came to the front to greet Lee and then seated themselves. Lee's brothers with their wives arrived and sat in the pew behind their sister. A large group came through the front door with Xantha Debobo Pendle in the lead. The group followed Xantha to the front of the church. Xantha touched Lee on the shoulder, and Lee stood to be introduced. In a low voice, intended only for Lee to hear, Xantha called forth each member of the group in turn.

Lee, this is my sister, Zennana.

Pleased to meet you.

And this is my brother, Teatus, and his wife, Iolithe.

Thank you for coming.

Their children—Ottice, Melivia, DeLanna, Ornton and Wentell.

Pleased to meet you all.

And, this is my niece, Habboey; she's my late brother, Adelpho's, child, and this is her husband, Critton Gant. They've come from Detroit. And this is Habboey's brother, Mosey. Maybe you remember him from Pachacuti.

Nice to meet all of you. It's been a long time, Mosey.

Mosey is also from Detroit. And this is Phessin, another of Habboey's and Mosey's siblings. He's the mayor of Pachacuti. You can tell by his big fat head.

Thank you, Aunt Xantha. It is with sadness that we are here today but me and my wife here, Luma . . .

Pleased to meet you both.

We wanted to stand with you and our family on this sad occasion.

Thank you, Mr. Mayor . . . Mrs. DeBobo.

And this is Sweet Tea Sellabie and her friend, Amity Lowe. They came all the way from New York City but you may remember them from Pachacuti. Your brothers burned down their house, didn't you, boys? But that's over and done now.

Swee, Amity, thank you for coming. We'll talk afterwards?

All took seats across the aisle. Lee leaned towards her mother.

Mother, did I somehow miss Alfred's name?

No. He wasn't in the group.

What do you suppose happened?

I don't know.

Several more guests arrived, among them was Trique and trailing behind him William Bass, Trique's lover and housemate. William took a seat at the rear of the church. Trique walked to the front, leaned down and gave Lee a light kiss on the cheek. He shook Olive's hand and glanced at the Boston boys without acknowledging them. Then, he took a seat in the front pew by himself across the aisle.

At 11 am., the Reverend Morris John Cunningham stepped to the lectern and announced that the family and friends of the late Army Specialist Fourth Class, Dunn Murton Pendle, had gathered to honor his life and memory and to show, during this time of grief and sorrow, their solidarity with Dunn's parents, Mr. Trique Pendle and Mrs. Lee Pendle. After the reverend's opening remarks, there followed an organ arrangement of the title song from *Lost in the Stars*. Reverend Cunningham invited Xantha to the podium. When she arrived there, Lee noticed how tall and elegant she seemed. Her graying hair was pulled back into a chignon. Her large black hat with a very wide brim was pushed back to show the angular features of her dark brown face. Her black dress was tubular and only showed her bosom over which the dress flowed.

The woman has no hips. Just like her son. Lee was struck, in fact, by the resemblance of mother and child. Trique could be the male version of his mother. Xantha talked about Dunn's visit to Pachacuti before he went to Viet Nam. She mentioned his charm, manners, and intelligence and returned to her seat. Reverend Cunningham then called Olive Fleet Boston to the lectern. Olive, like Xantha, was elegant, also in black, a dress fitted at the waist with a shawl over her shoulders. She wore a black pillbox hat. Lee had never noticed how long her mother's fingers were, and they seemed so white against her black dress. Olive talked about her love for Dunn. How she had visited her daughter surreptitiously after Dunn had been born in Atlanta, so that her husband and sons wouldn't know. She thought Dunn was a beautiful child and a handsome man, like his father. . . She paused to wipe her eyes with a handkerchief and then continued: And like his brother. She left the lectern and returned to her seat amid a low murmur of voices. Lee looked at her mother in alarm. Trique started up and headed across the aisle towards Lee.

What did she say? Did she say "like his brother"? What brother? What is she talking about?

Trique, sit down. I'll tell you and everyone else.

Lee pushed past Trique to the lectern. Trique took his seat.

Dear family and friends. We are all here today for my son, Dunn, and I'm grateful to see all of you, especially, those of you who have traveled so far and at great expense to be here. Dunn was a beautiful child. My heart is broken that his life ended so abruptly and tragically before he had a chance to make a place for himself in this world and to have his own family. He had so much to give, and he gave so much to me. I can't face that I will never see him again. Never hear his voice. Never hold or kiss him. Never be able to show my love for him or accept his love for me. None of that for Dunn changes but my mother brings news that changes a lot of other things for me and everyone here, especially you, Trique. As my mother said, Dunn has a brother who, to tell the truth, I'm not sure that I would recognize because I haven't seen him or known his whereabouts since he was a baby. The truth, Trique, is that I had twins; Dunn had a brother. But one baby was white—that was Dunn—and the other was black and his name is Alfred. At the time, in 1946, in the South, as a single mother who had run away from her family because she slept with and got pregnant by a black boy, I didn't know how I could raise a black child without jeopardizing the future of the white child and, frankly, my future. I was stupid, selfish, and a lot of other things that I'm sure the rest of you already know. Whatever you think of me I deserve. But I gave up my black child to a black wet-nurse to raise as her own. Unbeknownst to me, my mother went to the wet-nurse, a lady named Callista Collins, and convinced her to give the baby to the baby's family in Pachacuti—the DeBobo. My mother-in-law, Xantha DeBobo Pendle, found a home for my child with her brother, Teatus, his wife, Iolithe, and their children. My son was raised as their son where he was loved and cared for as I could not do. That child is your child, Trique. You are the last to know this story. I will have to ask you and everyone else here to wait to discuss the child that lives until we finish remembering the child that died.

Lee took her seat.

The St. Paul's choir's soprano, accompanied by piano, sang a hymn. Following the song, Reverend Cunningham called Trique to the lectern. Trique wore a black suit, white shirt with gray and black stripped tie. He looked at Lee, then at Xantha.

Lee says that her heart is breaking. Mine has exploded. I came here to grieve my son only to learn that I have another son. Alive. Teatus! Is he here?

Teatus shook his head, no.

I have to apologize to all of you. I just can't quite get my head clear. Dunn was, as his mother says, beautiful and wonderful. He was becoming his own man. We didn't have as good a relationship as he had with his mother. There were things about me that he couldn't accept and I don't blame him. I was not a good father although I tried as best I could. But I know that wasn't enough. I blame myself for his death because I feel he went into the Army, in part, to get away from me. I tried to change his mind, to step back from his life, but he made up his mind. And, now, that smart, wonderful man is gone, another casualty of this hateful war. I don't know what else to say except I'm sorry, Lee. I haven't been a good husband either.

And Trique returned to his seat.

The program continued with more musical selections. Family members were invited to the lectern to make brief remarks. Finally, Reverend Cunningham delivered his homily about loss and healing and invited, on behalf of the family, all present to adjourn to a reception in the basement social hall.

Ten round tables, five to each side of the hall, were encircled, each with eight chairs. Several long tables at the end of the hall formed the serving area. A ladies group of the church had covered all of the tables with white linen and flower centerpieces. They had also prepared the meal of baked chicken, mashed potatoes, green beans, salad, and assorted desserts.

Nearly all of the guests stayed for the reception. Some of Lee's co-workers excused themselves claiming other obligations. Trique's friends from the bank mostly stayed and claimed a table for their group. The guests tended to gather in clusters based on familiarity. The DeBobo took two adjacent tables. The Boston sat together with Lee and Brenda. Trique took a table with William Bass and his friends from the bank. When the serving pans were uncovered, the guests spontaneously formed a line to take plates and sample the food. Unobserved, a young man descended the stairs to the social hall and scanned the room. He spotted Teatus, Iolithe, and their adult children and walked over to them as they stood in the serving line.

Hey, Daddy. Hi, Momma.

Alfred, Teatus turned and responded. You made it.

Yeah, it was close. My flight from Atlanta to Denver was on time but the flight from Denver to Los Angeles was delayed. I got in about two hours ago and I knew I wouldn't get here in time for the ceremony and then it seemed to take forever for the taxi to get here. The traffic in LA is crazy. I've never seen so many cars. Hey, Sis. Hey, Sis. Hey, brothers.

You look so nice, Alfred, Iolithe joined in.

I bought this suit to come out here.

Honey, let me fix your tie. It's not straight.

Okay, Momma. Anything else?

Yes, let me pat down your hair; it's sticking out on top.

Is that it?

That's it.

Big crowd here.

Well, some folks had to leave after the ceremony.

How was it?

Nice. Simple. Your Aunt Xantha spoke and Olive Boston. Also, Martalee and Trique. And, of course, the Reverend.

Where's Trique and Lee?

Trique's at that table over there with those men. He has the black and gray tie. Martalee, I think, you can guess, is with the Boston clan. You know Olive and the boys. They do stand out here.

Yes, but they are here. Olive made sure of that. She's made sure of a lot of things. Alfred, here, take a plate. Fill it up, Baby. You look too skinny.

Sure, Momma.

Everyone returned to their tables to eat. As they were finishing, Lee began to make the rounds to thank everyone. When she arrived at the table with Teatus and Iolithe, she thanked each person in turn but stopped when she encountered a face she had not previously seen. She stared a moment too long and then started to cry. Loudly and convulsively. The room went silent.

Trique!, she screamed.

Trique, who had already been looking in the direction of the crying, stood and walked with a hesitant pace towards Lee. Although his eyes were fixed on her, he glanced in the direction she was staring and saw the young man in a dark blue pinstripe suit. He was dark complexioned, handsome with broad forehead, prominent nose and black curly hair. The young man stood and extended his hand.

I believe that you're my father. And you're my mother. It's been a long time. Pleased to meet you at last.

Lee launched herself at him, gripping him in her arms, bawling. Trique stumbled a few steps backward, sank to the floor and started to cry. William Bass ran over to him and with a handkerchief, tried to wipe his face.

Swee, who was sitting with Mosey and Amity at the adjacent table, leaned over to Mosey and said, Well, that's that. Now the fun begins.

Trique, with William Bass's assistance, had prepared his house for a family gathering after the church reception. The DeBobo and Boston were invited along with Swee, Amity, and Brenda Lessinger. As Phessin DeBobo, the mayor of Pachacuti, walked up the front steps of Trique's house with his wife, Luma, he remarked: I've never been in a faggot's house before.

Phessin, if you say one thing that you shouldn't say in front of Trique or anyone else here, I'll take a knife and cut your fat tongue right out of that ugly mouth of yours.

Be cool, Luma. I'll be dignified, as befits my place in the family.

Negro, don't even think about saying anything. Just grin and nod, something I know you do very well. Otherwise, shut up. Do you hear me?

Yes, dear.

Oh, hi, we haven't met you. You're William Bass, Trique's roommate. I'm Luma DeBobo and this is my husband, Phessin.

Come on in folks.

Oh, what a nice place this is.

Thank you. Have a seat and I'll get you a drink. Beer, wine or liquor?

Oh, I'll have a double bourbon on the rocks.

Luma, how about you?

Just a soda, if you have one.

A soda?

You know, a cola or something like that. We folks in the South call soft drinks sodas. No alcohol for me, please. I'll have to drive us back to the hotel.

Oh, okay.

There's Habboey over there. Habby, come on over here.

Nobody calls me Habby anymore, Phessin. You sure are getting fat. All that money and power are going right to your big stomach. Hi, Luma.

Hello, Habboey. Hello, Critton. Isn't this a nice house?

Yes, very nice. Trique must make a lot of money at the bank.

Well, I guess there are two incomes here.

Easy, Phessin. Don't go there. Habboey, we'll move over so you two can sit next to us. There. This is a nice leather couch. Very nice. Critton, what do you do for a living?

I work at the Ford Motor Company. I've been there twenty-one years.

Luma, we're also a two income family. I work for the post office.

Do you, Habboey? I wish I had a job but the mayor, here, wants me at home with the children and available for official duties. I do sometimes help out with his businesses though. You know, helping with the paperwork.

What's it like in the South these days since desegregation?

Oh, a lot has changed but some things are still the same. Black folks have more opportunities, like Phessin, here, but I feel, at least, that white folks will always be white folks, you know. They always have a way of letting you know that they think they are better.

Yeah, I know, they think that they're smarter and cleverer. But look at those Boston. Excuse me for saying so but that Martalee is trash and, as far as I'm concerned, the whole bunch is lowlife.

Girl, I know what you mean. Imagine, giving away her baby like that, just because he was black and an inconvenience to her. She should have thought about that when she had Trique's black dick inside of her.

Habboey, that's a bit crude.

Critton, you don't know these white women. Remember, I grew up in the South before I met you. I know what they're like. Sneaking around, chasing black boys. Those white boys did the same thing with black girls. Those same Boston boys were after me but I told them to go fuck a pig.

Habboey, watch your language. People will hear you.

Do you think I give a shit? I'm just telling it like it is, Critton. Nobody in this family can get high and mighty. What do you think this house is, full of saints? Look around, Critton. There's a lot of shit going on here.

Habboey, we know all that family history. Everybody in this room is related to each other by blood or marriage, sometimes both.

And there's also this queer stuff.

Habboey, not now.

Why not now? Our brother, Mosey, is queer. Trique is queer. Swee and that girlfriend of hers over there are queer. That's a lot of queer people in one house, if you ask me.

Habboey, I told Phessin not to start that kind of talk and I'll tell you too. Cut it out. It's none of your business; it's not any of our business. People have a right to be who they are. And there's a lot of sadness in this house right now.

What kind of bullshit is that? Be who they are? Do you think they should disgrace this family with their behavior? Well, I say no.

Habboey, you're talking a little too loud. People can hear you.

Do I give a fuck?

Habboey, please.

Swee stepped over to the group.

It's okay, Critton. I've heard all of that before.

Hello, everyone. Let me tell you something, Habby.

It's Habboey. My name is Habboey.

To me, you're still the same old Habby with the same ugly mouth. Listen, my sister, Loissey, was your mother, Phessin's mother, and Mosey's mother. I know she loved all of you. She treated you the same, raised you the same and, yet, Mosey was different. You could say he chose to be different or that I chose to be different but that wouldn't be the truth. Neither Mosey nor I could be any way other than how we are. Habby, you didn't choose to be how you are; we are all what we are supposed to be.

The lord didn't make queers, Swee. You made yourselves.

The lord did make me, Habby, as surely as he made you. I am a child of god as much as you are. And what may I ask is wrong with being queer?

The Bible says it's wrong.

The Bible says a lot of things. If we believe everything in the Bible, you would still be a slave because your people were slaves.

Don't change the subject. The Bible says that a man should not lie with another man as he would a woman. That's what it says.

Listen, Habby, I know my Bible as well as you do. I grew up in the South too, you know. As I said, the Bible says a lot of things that folks believed were right a long time ago but now they see things differently. I don't expect to convince you. I don't even care about convincing you. But I think that you need to keep your comments to yourself while you are in Trique's home, or if you can't, then leave.

Who are you to tell me what to do, Bitch? Get your pussy-eating mouth away from me. You're the one who should leave. You and that skinny-assed woman are a disgrace.

Habboey, please, that's enough. This is not the time or place for this.

Critton, go get me another drink. I've had enough of this crap.

And Habboey left the living room.

Swee, I'm sorry that my wife made such a scene.

Listen, Swee, not everyone agrees with her. I don't and I've told her so.

Thanks, Luma.

Excuse me. I'll get my wife that drink.

I'll talk with you later, Luma, Phessin. And Swee rejoined Amity and Mosey.

Thank you, Phessin, for not saying anything.

You know, coming from my sister, that stuff about queers sounds pretty crazy. Is that how I sound?

I'm afraid so.

So, I can keep my fat tongue?

Just for now. Sometimes it's useful.

Luma, you're something else talking like that. Maybe later, you'll let me use my tongue. It's been a while.

Well, we'll see how that tongue behaves here today.

Out behind Trique's house on the patio, the tables were set with drinks and snacks—bowls of chips, peanuts, and pretzels. Lee and Trique were seated at a table with Xantha, Olive, Teatus, Iolithe and Alfred. Alfred spoke:

So, my grandmothers decided when Dunn was killed that it was time for me to know about my parents. I had always been told that Teatus and Iolithe were not my real parents but they have been as good to me as they have been to their own children. I was never really curious about my true parents so when I was told a few weeks ago, I wasn't that excited. I had a family; the two of you were complete strangers. My grandmothers told me the whole story of how I was born and then returned to my family. I did try to find that wet-nurse, Callista Collins, but I couldn't trace her. But, in all honesty, Trique and Lee, I wasn't dying to meet you. I am so sorry I didn't meet Dunn or know that he was my brother when he came to visit Pachacuti. I was stationed at the Presidio in San Francisco at the time. But I guess that I'm glad to see you both at last. Lee, you're a beautiful woman. I see where I get my good looks from. And you, Trique, well, I'm darker than you. No wonder I was a hot potato. But, listen, my being here is a surprise to you both. I've had some time to think over all of this. You're still dealing with the death of one son and the sudden discovery of another one. I'll be around a while so that we can get to know each other better. Who knows, maybe, I'll come to Los Angeles to stay a while after I'm out of the Army. It's pretty nice out here. Perhaps, you can help me find a job. I want to go to school, make money, and have a family. I could learn to like this place.

Trique said: Alfred, you're a very confident and well-spoken young man. Teatus and Iolithe have done a fantastic job of parenting, much better, I think, than I did with Dunn.

Trique, you're not being fair to yourself or anyone else. You and Lee did the best you could. There were some bad decisions, true. But I don't think that, given the circumstances, anything could have done differently. I think that things turned out pretty well for me.

Xantha said: By the grace of Teatus and Iolithe, Alfred has a generous heart, a forgiving heart. We, I think, can forgive ourselves as well.

Habboey lurched into the gathering.

What's all this forgiving crap? Martalee, you'll never live down the shame of abandoning your own black child, and now the white one you kept is dead, dead because his black daddy is a faggot. He ran away from this cesspool of sin and got himself killed. Well, that's what happens when you don't stay with our own kind, and you sin against the lord with perversions. He strikes you down and crushes you. You're two sinful people; god hates you and everyone like you.

That's enough, Habboey, said Xantha. I won't stand for you or anyone else in this family talking like that. You don't speak for god. You certainly don't speak for anyone in this family; you are speaking only for yourself, and you are the one who should be ashamed. On this day of mourning and rejoicing, you're bringing nothing but hatred into this home. There is no solace, no good tidings, just evil and wickedness. Now get your things and leave this house and this family.

You can't tell me what to do!

I am telling you what to do. I'm the head of this family and I'm telling you to leave now or else I'll have the police escort you out. Do you understand? I won't tolerate your evil tongue in this house, in this family. This family has survived a lot. All of the hatred and violence in Pachacuti didn't bring this family down and, now, it won't be brought down by someone who can't see what's right and what's wrong. I'm telling you, you are wrong, Habboey, wrong about Trique, Lee, Mosey and Swee. They are good people. Some of them have made mistakes, like all of us. But, they are good. Now, show how good you can be and leave. Take all of that hatred with you. Goodbye.

When were you appointed god? Who put you in charge of this family? How do you get to decide who is right and who is wrong? You're nothing, Xantha. You're just another old lady who thinks that because she's old, she's knows everything. Well, you don't know shit. You've been bossing everybody around, oh, all ladylike for sure, all genteel and well-mannered. But, you're just a bossy bitch who wasn't much of a wife or a mother. Murty never loved you; he had his piece of ass at his restaurant—that silly, ugly bitch, Dolly Taylor, while you were at home with your precious Trique. You did nothing while your own son was fucking his cousin at Swee's nest of corruption. Oh, you were being the good woman, the upright pillar of the family and the community while everyone around you was sinking into the slime and muck of degradation. You brought all of this about, Xantha, you, who claims to be so righteous and good. You are the devil's handmaiden, the one who has brought all of this misery on this family. You did it all by yourself with your stupid, above-it-all superiority. If you know so much about so many things, how did you allow all of this to happen?

Xantha remained silent.

Well, now you're suddenly quiet. All of you are quiet because you know I'm telling the truth here. I know that you want to say that the liquor is talking. The liquor is talking but that doesn't change the truth! This family has been mixed up for generations with these no-good crackers and it is fucked up. It's degenerate. And death is god's punishment. But each and every one of you is to blame for bringing down god's wrath on Dunn.

Alfred stepped forward.

Sister Habboey, I can't speak for anyone in this family but myself but I have to say something here. A long time ago, I found myself in a family that was not my own. For as long as I can remember I was told that I was an orphan, that my own parents couldn't keep me so I lived with Teatus, Iolithe, and their children. I got whatever their children got. If they got new clothes, I got new clothes. If they got a treat, I got a treat. If any of us misbehaved, we were all punished in the same way. If we needed help or comfort, we got it. When we visited Grandma Xantha or Grandma Zennana, I was treated just like the other grandchildren. I was praised when I did good work in school; I was scolded when I disobeyed. I've always felt like I belonged to this family; it is my family. These people have helped me become who I am and I wouldn't even be here without them. When I learned that Dunn was my brother and that Lee and Trique were my parents, I didn't feel that my life had changed because I still had my family. Instead, Lee and Trique became another part of my life; I'm sorry, of course, that I've lost my brother, Dunn. The reason I'm telling you and everyone else here all of this is because I don't care if my family is black, white, green or yellow. It is my family and I love every one of them whatever their faults. If my father loves another man or my cousin loves another woman, all that means to me is that they love somebody. Love is what has kept me in this world, and love, Sister Habboey, is what we all need now. You're entitled to your feelings but you can't deny the love that is here today. A loving god doesn't punish love or loving people. Dunn's death was a consequence of war, not god's wrath. That's all. Love is what heals us from the sorrow of death.

Well, Alfred. You're certainly a DeBobo. They've filled you up with the same crap that is bringing down this family. But, I'm done here. I'm leaving because I don't want to be around any of you anymore. Critton, let's go. Now!

When she was gone, Alfred went to Trique.

Trique, I meant everything that I said. I can see that you and William have a nice home here. I hope that you'll let me stay and visit sometime.

Trique grabbed Alfred in a bear hug.

Can you come for breakfast tomorrow so that we can talk?

Sure. I also want to visit with Lee here today before I leave.

Can you come tomorrow at ten for breakfast?

I'll be here. Thank you.

Trique broke off his embrace. Alfred turned to Lee; she was talking with her mother. As Alfred approached, Olive excused herself: Lee, there's someone I need to talk to, and left.

Alfred turned to Lee and suggested that they sit by themselves in the garden. They walked to a corner away from everyone else. Iolithe called to Alfred as he and Lee were walking. When she had his attention, she gave him some kind of look, like a warning, and he shook his head as if to reply: No!

I wanted to talk to you, Lee, alone right now even though this might not be the best time with everything else going on here today.

I understand, Alfred. This has been a tough day but I want to hear whatever you have to say. You're so handsome, like Trique.

Thank you. I said a little while ago that I understood why you did what you did when you gave me to that wet-nurse, when you left me, well, actually abandoned me, because I was black. You're my mother and you gave me up like I was nothing to you. Nothing. Just because I was black. Why did you do that?

Alfred. And she started to cry. Alfred. There's no answer that I can give you that will ever make sense to you or me. You don't know the world I grew up in. You don't really know my family. You don't know what the South was like back then. You don't really know any of these things.

What are you talking about? I'm black. I know all of those things. I live in the South. I grew up with black people, my people. I've seen how white people treat black people. I've heard the stories. I read about it. I've seen it with my own eyes. I've lived it too. So, don't say I don't know what it was like. The Reverend King and all the protests didn't change that much in white America. White people are still white people despite laws.

You don't know what it was like for me back then. I was a young white girl who got pregnant by a black boy because I wanted him; I wanted sex with him and I wanted his child. But I was too stupid to know what having a black baby would be like.

Well, you never even found out because you got rid of me as soon as you could.

Alfred, I didn't get rid of you; I didn't have an abortion. I didn't abandon you; I left you with someone who I thought would love you and protect you like I didn't know how to.

You, a white woman couldn't protect me? What are you saying? White women are the top of the pyramid in the South. You're goddesses.

Not when we cross white men. When we cross white men, we are nothing. A white woman with a black man, with a black baby is less than any black person. She shouldn't exist and she might not exist. She is cut out of white life. She has no place to go.

You had black people who would have cared for you just like they did with Soonie. You just didn't want to give up your privileged white life! You were safe in Atlanta. Your family wasn't there.

What black people could I have gone to? There were no Pendle or Sellabie or DeBobo in Atlanta. I would have had to go back to Pachacuti and that wouldn't have helped me or my children, not with my father, his sons, and his family there.

These are all excuses. Your children come first. A mother takes care of her children.

But how does she take care of her children if she can't take care of herself? I was a single mother living in white Atlanta. I had to survive somehow to take care of my children.

Child. One child. The white one.

Yes, the white one because the black one would have killed all of us.

A baby can't kill. It can't do anything. It must be cared for. If you couldn't care for me, then maybe you and Dunn should have died. But, no, you had to save your and Dunn's whiteness.

Alfred! You, like Dunn, would rather be dead now instead of alive and having a loving family? You've had a loving mother, Iolithe. I wasn't that loving mother. I left you to have the only life I could imagine then. It may have been a bad decision but it was the only one I knew. I'm sorry that I could not have been your mother, like Iolithe, but I'm happy that you are alive today. You may never understand or accept what happened to me, what I did to myself, but you have a life, a good life. If I could undo what I did, I would. If my dying now could somehow make your life better now, I would, Alfred. I would give my life for you if I had to but I hope that I can just be in your life and that we can make what we have ahead of us better for both of us.

I'll never forgive you.

Then, I've lost both of my sons?

You lost me a long time ago.

Excuse me. Iolithe joined Alfred and Lee. Alfred, if you are talking about what I think you're talking about, I have something to say.

Lee, did he ask you why you gave him up?

Yes.

And did he tell you that he can't forgive you for that?

Yes.

I want you to know I told him not to say those things to you, especially not today. I told him but he's like his birth mother and father; he does what he wants to do and doesn't consider the consequences. No, Alfred, with you, nobody else gets consideration. It's only you, only your feelings. Not mine, not Teatus, not Lee.

I put on that show for you today, Momma, just like you told me. I did everything you told me to do.

Except for the most important thing: Lee, here, has enough guilt and sorrow. She doesn't need more from you. I didn't give birth to you but I loved you like no other mother could. A child is lucky to get the love of a mother. Lee decided that she could not be your mother; she cannot change what we all know happened. You, Alfred, are black. A black family raised you. We loved you. We still love you. This white mother of yours raised the white child she could. That was it, plain and simple. That's the world she lived in, that we all lived in. That was how she faced the world, and survived; that's how you survived. If that isn't clear to you, if that doesn't put your mind to rest, if that doesn't tell you that life comes on life's terms, then we haven't been as good as mothers as I thought.

Momma, it hurts to know that my birth mother threw me away.

Alfred, we've talked about this for days. All of us have talked to you—me, your daddy, and your brothers and sisters. You're going to have to get over this or you'll be crippled for life. That's all there is to it. Do you understand?

Maybe, I just had to say what I felt. Maybe, that's all. Maybe. Lee, my mother is usually right. There's no answer to this.

Alfred, listen. Whatever I can do from now on, I will do. I'm not asking you to love me or even accept me, only let me be part of your life. Please.

We'll see.

Alfred left Lee sitting in a chair and went with Iolithe back to the table with Teatus. Meanwhile, Olive had entered the house and walked over to Swee who was sitting with Mosey and Amity.

Swee, may I talk with you for a little bit? Privately?

I'm good to go. Where to?

How about outside, in the front? We can go for a little walk down the street.

The two women were both about the same stature, matronly, one dark, the other pale. Swee was fifty-seven and Olive was sixty-five. Swee was grayer. Olive took Swee's arm and guided her down the sidewalk of the quiet residential street. Olive began:

Swee, I have a lot to be grateful for. I have my children and grandchildren. Although my husband, Finn, Sr., died thirteen years ago, I've been comfortable and reasonably content. Life in Pachacuti is fairly simple for white folks of a certain class especially, and predictable. All of my boys are married now and have their own homes and families. Lee is settled and now has recovered the child she so regretfully gave away. I've tried to do my part to repair that damage. With Xantha's help and Teatus and Iolithe's love and generosity, Alfred was raised to be a lovely young man who, I think, will make his families proud. Prouder, I should say, because they're already proud of him. But, there's one big thing that still troubles me, Swee, and that is the terrible and inexcusable tragedy that my boys inflicted upon you and Amity in 1945. That was a horrible day twenty-three years ago. When I found out what they did and how so many innocent lives were so profoundly affected, like you, Amity and Mosey, Martalee and Trique, I was beside myself with shame and grief. I vowed that day to do what I could no matter how long it took. That's why I did what I did for Alfred and now I want to do for you.

You don't need to do anything for me, Olive. What happened in Pachacuti freed me. I would never have gotten my education, met my current girlfriend, or do the work I'm doing for poor folks, like me, in New York. In a weird way, I'm grateful to your boys; they made me get up and do something with my life. Amity, too. She would never have gotten into show business if she had stayed in Pachacuti. Mosey is the only one who really suffered and I plan to talk to him tomorrow about that. He lost Trique; he lost his arm. He's lost his way. He's the real victim of your sons and we need to help him find a good place in this world.

I know some of that, Swee, and that weighs on my heart too. But it's you that I must remove from my conscience. I told my sons today what I intend to do and they are very angry. Finn, Jr., in fact, has left with his wife. But, I'm not concerned about their anger. They've acted out of anger before. If they still feel they need to act out of anger again, then I have really failed with them. I can't and won't do anything more for, or with, them. They have their father's sense of self-importance   and entitlement and I'm sure that they'll make their children just like them. Well, they may be my family but my heart is elsewhere, with you, the Sellabie, DeBobo, and Pendle. I'm connected to all of your families and, frankly, that's where I want part of my estate to go. When I die, Swee, my house is to be sold, and the money given to you. That's my restitution for my boys' destruction of your home and your life in Pachacuti. What you do with that money is up to you. And you won't have to wait long to collect. I've had inoperable breast cancer for some time now. It has metastasized and I don't expect to be around much longer. All of this tragedy, in the past and now Dunn's death, has eaten me up. I'm ready to move on with a clearer conscience.

Your cancer can't be treated? There are lots of options these days.

You know, I waited too long because I didn't think that my life was that important. But my death can do some good and that's what I want. So, that's the story, Swee. My lawyer will take care of everything when I return home.

Olive, I'm so sorry you didn't act soon enough for your cancer. I never felt that you were responsible for your sons.

If not me, then who?

The truth, Olive, is that your sons are a product of the history of this country, of their times, and of their community, not just their parents and family. Look at the rest of us. We are also products of history, our time, and community. Black folks have as much hatred in their breasts as white folks but, as individuals, we have to master that, as you've done. That's the way. The world in which we live will always make some folks feel they're better than other folks. Listen to that shit talk from Habboey about homosexuals. She didn't learn that in her family, and her family has no responsibility for the way she is. That's how it is with your sons. You didn't teach them that stuff. It was all around them and still is around them, around all of us. We have to understand it and make up our own minds about what we believe is right and good and true. Your sons are in charge of themselves. You're not in charge of them. And you owe me nothing.

Nevertheless, that is what I want to do because, as you say, that is what is right, good, and true.

Okay, Olive. If that is your wish, I will respect it. I can't say, though, that I will look forward to that day when I get a call from your lawyer.

Just remember me, Swee. I'm that old white woman who tried to buck the system.

Swee and Olive circled the block and returned to Trique's house. Everyone was beginning to say their goodbyes and heading to their cars parked on the street. Swee went to Trique.

Trique, after everyone leaves, can I stay and talk with you?

Sure, Swee. I was hoping that we could have some time together.

Okay, I'll tell Amity and the rest to leave without me. Can you give me a ride later to my hotel downtown?

Of course.

After Swee informed the others that she was staying longer, she joined Trique in his study while William went through the house collecting glasses, plates, and trash. Then he arranged the furniture to the original locations.

This has been someday for you, Trique.

It's not exactly how I thought things would go.

Don't you feel a little bit better now that you know about Alfred?

Swee, Alfred is a blessing that I can't begin to understand. He's come into my life at the right time; there's no doubt about that. But, losing Dunn is something that even Alfred doesn't change. I loved Dunn as, I understand now, only a parent could love. One child doesn't replace another child. The mistakes I made with Dunn are not forgotten because another child, who seems a whole lot better adjusted to the world than his brother, is now in my life. You know, Swee, it's really ironic that the black child has a surer footing than the white child did. You would think that the white child had all of the advantages, but, no. Alfred has a family that kept him safe and gave him good direction. What did Lee and I give Dunn? Confusion. Nothing but confusion, about his race, my sex, and our love. I failed him, Swee, and because I failed him, he is dead. That's my fault. I'll never get over that.

Trique, you're feeling sorry for yourself for things that you couldn't have changed. You loved and married a white woman. Why is that a bad thing? You may have been stupid to fuck a white girl and get her pregnant in the segregated South but you married her and raised your child in this place where all of you could be safe. Yes, Dunn was mixed race, and I'm sure he had trouble trying to decide on which side of the color line he could be comfortable. But, his struggle out of confusion was no different from any child's struggle about who he is and where he belongs. That's what growing up is about, Trique, nothing more than that.

I didn't help him find his way, Swee. He didn't feel the love I had for him. He only saw a faggot father.

Trique, Dunn had to find his own way and that is what he had started to do. In any case, you probably did no better or worse than any other parent. My girlfriend, Gulley, has done everything a mother could do for her son, and Bone is still a disaster. Is that her fault? I don't think so. Children are their own selves; parents can't make them be something other than what they are destined to be. That's my belief based on my experience. Trique, you, me, and Mosey, are all queers. Did we want to be queers? Of course, not. You and Amity like men and women. Did you decide that is what you wanted to do or was that simply who you are? But, if you ask me or Mosey or Amity if we want to be something or someone else, the answer would be, no thank you. We're okay with who we are. That's what makes you different from us, Trique, and that is the only thing that makes you different. You question why you are Trique, why you are the way you are. In fact, there's no question. You are. That's it. That's all. End of story. Does being Trique, being yourself, cause you trouble? Yes, because our world doesn't understand, yet, queer people and especially queer people who love men and women. That's what happened with Dunn. He didn't understand. It's too much for some people to understand. And, that, Trique, is their problem, not yours. Don't make someone else's problem your problem. You don't have to explain yourself to anyone, including your ex-wife, your family, and your friends. Look, you have a sweet boyfriend who seems to love you. You've got a wonderful home, a good job, a living son who does accept you, and a family that loves you. Look at that, Trique, and not what seems to be missing because you'll never find what is not there.

Swee, I hear what you're saying and, really, it makes a lot of sense. You can understand, though, that right now I can't feel what I can hear. However, having you, the family and, now, Alfred, here and giving me your support is giving me some hope.

You couldn't have said anything that gives me more comfort than that, Trique.

I think that, eventually, I'll be all right, Swee. I'll think about everything that you've said and say some prayers.

Well, if praying works for you.

It might. I haven't tried it before but now may be the time. Let me take you to your hotel now. You must be tired; I am.

When he returned home from driving Swee downtown, Trique sat on the leather sofa and stared out of the window onto the patio. Bill, he said, Alfred is coming for breakfast at 10 tomorrow. Would you mind if just the two of us were here?

I have things I can do tomorrow. You go ahead and meet with your son.

Thank you. Bill?

Yes?

Thank you.

You said that.

I know. I wanted to hear myself say it. I appreciate everything, Bill. You really helped me. What do you think about today?

Which part?

The family thing, Lee having twins and giving one away. And now Alfred's here, coming tomorrow for breakfast and, before today, I didn't even know he existed.

I think that you are lucky, Trique. You've lost a son and gained one. You have people who love you. They were here for you today. They stood beside you.

Yeah. Their faggot relative.

Trique, I'm a faggot too but I don't have people like you do who stand by me. I've had to stand by myself. I've found men like you—I found you—who made me feel good and satisfied my needs. I hope that it will always be like that with us too. I hope. But I don't regret who I am and I will keep on being who I am with or without you. You asked me what I thought about today. I think that good things or bad, Trique, you've been making yourself unhappy, and no one can change that but you. From everything that I've heard, Dunn did exactly what you are doing; he made himself unhappy. Maybe Alfred will help you but, in my opinion, even he can't make you happy. That is completely up to you. I'm going to finish straightening up and go to Hollywood tomorrow to visit friends. I'll see you, later, in bed.

Trique sat at the kitchen table. There was so much to think about. Dunn. Alfred. Lee. William. And himself. In the midst of all that had happened during the day, he had forgotten that the casket with Dunn's body would arrive in Los Angeles the next week. He and Lee had already decided on the burial plot and would have a private ceremony with the just the two of them, Lee's friend, Brenda, and William. They would say goodbye to Dunn and, then, try to move on with their lives.

FOUR DAYS
Sunday

Swee met Mosey for breakfast and they walked from their hotel, a small, inexpensive place downtown, to a diner nearby. A middle-aged white man in black pants and pink shirt escorted them to a booth at the rear of the room, near the kitchen.

See, That's how they still treat black people, Mosey. Put us back here out of sight. But I don't care. I'm so happy to have this time with you. Do you know what you're going to have?

This menu is huge, so many choices. I think I want bacon and scrambled eggs and toast. I wish they had grits.

How about some potatoes? They have home fries. I bet that they're good.

Yeah. Home fries. What about you?

Sausage patties and pancakes, and fried eggs. That's the ticket. Are you having coffee?

Yes.

Black or cream?

Black.

Here comes the waitress.

They ordered and the waitress brought glasses of water, cups of coffee, and small glasses of orange juice that came with their meal.

Mosey, you look pretty good for an old man. You're what, thirty-nine now?

Right.

And what is going on in your life? I know that you're living with Lucille after your apartment burned in the riots or should I say rebellion?

You think that all of that killing and destruction was a rebellion?

Yes. Folks are tired of being treated like shit, as if they don't matter at all. Aren't you tired of it?

To tell you the truth, Swee, I never thought about it. For me, life just is what it is.

But, Honey, your life, our lives could be so much better if we didn't have all of these racial and sexual obstructions in our way.

I guess that you're right. Anyway, Lucille is a flaming fairy but he's been good to me, letting me stay in his place.

You two have a thing going?

We did, well, sometimes, we still do. See, before, there was this white guy named Red that we met in a joint. He liked the three of us together, you know, everybody going at everybody. So, me and Lucille got it on with Red. Then, I was with Red without Lucille. But that got to me and I didn't see much of Lucille until the riot and fire. He took me in right away. It's temporary, of course.

The waitress arrived with their meals.

Let's see: Sausage and pancakes for the lady, and scrambled eggs with bacon for the gent. Anything else, folks? More coffee?

Yes, for me. How about you, Mosey? Oh, and the toast.

Okay.

Just take this check to the front when you're finished. Have a nice day.

I'm starved. This looks good. So, tell me, what are you doing at Lucille's and what are you planning to do to be back on your own?

Swee, I'm not doing much. I take care of Lucille's place. Keep it clean. And cook. I make his lunch to take to work—he's a bus driver—and his dinner. I go for walks. Watch the television. We go out to joints sometimes on weekends. We get some action, you know. That's about it.

But what about a job for you, Mosey? If you're not staying with Lucille, what are you going to do?

Swee, I don't know. There ain't work in Detroit for a one-armed, uneducated black man. I can't even get a factory job which is about the only thing that pays good money. Can't work in a kitchen no more with one arm. And since the riots, there ain't as many apartment buildings in the city that need janitors. I can't work in the suburbs. No way to get there or stay there; they're all white.

Mosey, I hear what you're saying but I find it hard to believe that with all of those black folks in Detroit, somebody can't give you work.

Swee, I've honestly tried. White folks are scared to death; they're leaving the city in droves. Black folks don't seem to have the wherewithal to step up and take over. Something is going wrong there. I see it all around—poorer, blacker people, Swee. Not a lot of opportunity and I'm at the bottom of the barrel, it seems. I'm even too old to sell my ass. Don't think I didn't think about that.

It's honorable work. Some women wouldn't survive otherwise.

I have to tell you, Swee: That Red wanted me to live with him. He wanted to take care of me.

So, what happened?

I couldn't. I couldn't see myself, as a black man, taken care of by a white guy.

Tell me, Mosey, why that's different from living with Lucille?

Lucille is black, Swee. That's it. That's the whole thing.

Really?

Of course. You wouldn't let some white woman take care of you, would you?

Well, interesting that you should say that. Yesterday, at Trique's, Olive asked me to go for a walk with her. We walked around the block, and she told me that, in her will, she was selling her house and giving me the money because her boys burned down my house. She has terminal cancer and doesn't have long. I may be in for some serious money soon.

She did that?

That's right.

The Boston boys must have stroked.

They did but she said that's what she wanted. So, Mr. Mosey DeBobo, this Sellabie has a white woman taking care of her, and I'm loving it.

But, Swee, that's not the same thing. Olive isn't expecting you to live and sleep with her.

No, but old Olive could probably burn up the sheets given a chance. Here's the thing, Mosey. You're making this out to be about race. Red is white; Lucille is black. That's the choice for you. But why? You know and I know and Olive knows that we've got black and white in us already. Your own momma had a white mother, Soonie Fleet, Olive's sister. You may have been too young—I think that you were five—when your momma, Loissey, died in 1934. But she could have passed for a white woman. Do you remember her?

I remember her.

She loved you, Mosey. Crazy as she was. She died after your brother, Phessin, was born. That's why you came to live with me. The Sellabie took you in when your own family couldn't raise you and all those other babies. You are part white. So what's this about not wanting to be taken care of by a white guy?

Being part white and being white aren't the same, Swee, and you know that. That poor Dunn was white but he didn't think that he was. Everybody thought he was white but inside he knew he was black. He lived between black and white and you can't do that in this country.

How do you know about Dunn, Mosey?

He told Aunt Xantha.

So, what's your point?

It doesn't matter what's on the outside. We know inside what and who we are, and what and who we are in this white man's world determines everything else.

So, you're saying, that because you are a black man in your head, that fact, and that fact alone, determines how you treat the world?

Because that's how the world treats me.

But one white man in this world wanted to treat you with love.

His idea of love.

A white idea of love?

Yes.

Mosey, I have another theory.

What's that?

Trique and Lee fucked up your head. You have never gotten over Trique having a girlfriend—a white girlfriend and wife, or former wife—you haven't moved on.

That's not true. When Trique and me broke up, I met Waite. I loved him. If it wasn't for that damn fool that cut off my arm, I might have been able to stay with Waite. We could have been together but my arm changed everything. Waite couldn't afford to keep me. I didn't want to hold him back. But I loved him, Swee. Trique had nothing to do with that.

You fell in love with Waite who, because of your arm, you couldn't stay with him? Mosey, I understand the effects that losing your arm had on you, and, because of your arm—actually because you believed that Waite couldn't afford to support both of you—you decided that you had to take care of yourself somehow. You are a DeBobo and DeBobo are proud. But they know how to depend on other folks when necessary. So when someone comes along and wants to take care of you, like I took care of you and raised you, you take that help because you need it. It's not about pride, Mosey. It's about what we need in this world and pride has its place but nobody expects you to suffer in order to be proud.

I can accept help. Habboey and Critton helped me. Lucille is helping me.

But Red? Why can't he help you? Because he's white? Mosey, you've tried to take care of yourself; you did the best you could with no education, no skills and a major handicap. You're living with a man who is giving you a temporary home. You have sex or have had sex but he's not your love, is he?

We still have sex but he's not my lover. I like Lucille but, no, I don't love him. Maybe he loves me.

So, Red did love you also but you can't love him because he's white. See, that's where I think Trique and Lee messed up your mind. A white took your lover away from you.

A woman.

A white woman. I don't think her being a woman matters. Listen, Mosey, as I see it, you are letting your anger over Trique and the fact that you lost him to a white affect your feelings about someone who had nothing to do with any of that.

Swee, I'm not going back to Red. That's that. And it's not because of Trique or Lee. I'm a black man. It doesn't matter to me about my momma or any of that stuff. I'm black and I'm going to live a black life, in a black world. I'll find a way. I'll get work. I'll take care of myself. I'll be okay. I'll always remember Trique and Waite but I have moved on. I'm still moving on. Thank you, Swee, for everything you've done for me and for your thoughts now. I'll make it on my own. Don't worry.

Mosey, you know that you are like my own child, the only child I'll ever have. You may not agree with me but think about what I've said. I say it with love. Give me a hug and let's get back to the hotel. We've got to leave this afternoon.

Having finished their meal, they paid the check, left a tip for the waitress, walked back to their hotel, got their bags, and headed to the airport where they said goodbye. Swee and Amity boarded a flight to New York; Mosey caught his plane to Detroit.

III

INWARD PASSAGE

DETROIT II

Lucille's apartment was small; there was a living room, dining room, one bedroom, kitchen, and bath. It was on the top floor of a four story walk-up in a shabbier part of one of Detroit's black ghettos on the east side. Lucille did have a few nice things, however, inherited from his mother who got them as cast-offs from a white woman whose house she cleaned. When the woman decided to buy more modern furniture—heavy dark mahogany pieces, she let Lucille's mother take what she wanted—cut glass lamps, Victorian settee, hand-carved cherry end tables—before putting the discards out with the trash. Since Lucille tried to take as much of his mother's things, as possible, his apartment, small as it was, was a bit crowded, like a second hand store. Nevertheless, the place had class and style. Mosey was careful cleaning everything. His experience as a janitor and as a cook served him well, even with only one arm. Actually, caring for Lucille's place was easy because Lucille was neat, almost obsessively so. Mosey was less neat and found himself cleaning up mostly after himself while annoying Lucille with his cups, glasses, papers, and clothes left helter-skelter. Mosey wasn't a slob; he just wasn't as compulsively neat as Lucille. But, since he made sure the place was presentable and dinner was ready when Lucille finished his bus-driving shift, Lucille mostly overlooked Mosey's things being out of place. A not too subtle sigh and a little eye-rolling usually told Mosey when things were amiss.

Usually, on Friday or Saturday night Mosey and Lucille went out to the joints, clubs or bars catering to homosexual black men. They never went to white joints because these still excluded black men by making them feel not welcome or demanding several photo identifications. There were, now, a few mixed bars which were predominantly white but welcomed blacks. Lucille liked these bars but Mosey did not and would not go. More and more, Mosey went alone to the black joints. He knew many of the men there and had sex with some of them. But because the crowd was becoming younger and younger than he was, he was less likely to find someone with whom he had sex. Men his age seemed to have abandoned the bars. This was true for Lucille as well but an exotic, like Lucille, still intrigued some white men. Mosey had never again encountered Red even though he thought that he spotted him a couple of times.

Mosey thought that he had long overstayed his welcome at Lucille's and wanted to move out but he still hadn't found a job. There was so much turmoil still in Detroit following the rebellion that unskilled jobs weren't plentiful, certainly not for one-armed men. Mosey contacted his old friend, Parker Patterson. But neither he nor anyone else knew of anything. Some had lost their jobs because companies and stores were moving out of the city to the suburbs. Mosey called his sister, Habboey. She was distracted and unconcerned but she invited Mosey to dinner.

The Gant home was a two story brick house in a relatively affluent black neighborhood on the city's west side, not very distant from the site of some of the major rioting and destruction, and not far from where Red had his apartment in a white enclave of an increasingly black neighborhood. Critton picked up Mosey from Lucille's place because public transportation between the two homes would have taken hours. Critton drove a new model Lincoln which was luxurious. He was waiting in the car when Mosey came down to the curb, opened the passenger door and climbed in.

Hi, Critton. Thanks for coming to get me.

It's okay, Brother. When your sister says jump, I jump. You know Habby.

Critton pulled away from the curb and into traffic making a series of turns until he was on the freeway headed to his neighborhood.

How have you been, Critton?

Not too bad. How about you?

I'm making it staying with Lucille but I've got to leave there. I'm getting on his nerves, and he's getting on mine. I want to get my own place again but I need a job first. I wanted to ask Habboey to help me.

Mosey, how can she help you? She works for the post office. You can't get a job there without exams and all. And, frankly, Brother, you don't have the skills or education.

I know. But she has lots of friends in different places. There must be someone who needs a janitor or handyman.

Man, you know every nigger in this town in your shoes is looking for your job. You got to get out in the suburbs if you want a chance.

Suburbs? I can't even get across town without a car. How can I get to the suburbs? And, I can't live out there.

I hear you, Brother. You don't have what we could call prospects. But you know Habby would let you move in with us again. I could be cool with that. We could pick up where we left off, Mosey. You're still good looking to me and we had fun together. Right?

Yeah, but Habboey is down on fags. She let the shit fly in California and if she ever suspected or caught us, both of us would be out on the street if we were even still alive because she would kill us first. Besides, she's my sister and, although I was hot for you, Critton, at the time, I can't go back to that. I can't play around with you. You're married. You don't even think that you're a faggot. That's not my scene anymore.

Well, Mosey, I may not be a faggot. I don't know. I've not been with any other dudes but you. But I really liked being with you. I'd like it again. Habboey and I don't have good sex. I get off with her every now and again. But it's not like you and I had. That was something. I felt something, Mosey, something for you.

Critton, that was a long time ago. A lot has happened to me. I'm still trying to make a life for myself. Sleeping with my sister's husband is not going to work for me, even if the sex was good. I can't go there. If that is what it meant if I was to stay for a while at your house, I'd have to do something else.

Mosey, come on, man. It's no big deal. I want you to fuck me. I've been thinking about it a long time. When we were in Los Angeles, I was hoping that you and I could find some time together.

No, Critton. If you need to get fucked, go out and get somebody. There are clubs, bars with lots of men or women, whatever you want. But I'm not doing it with you.

Why not?

Critton, I don't want to fuck you. It's not what I want or need now.

Habby doesn't care what I do.

What do you mean?

She knows we've had sex. She's always known. All that talk she did in Los Angeles. It was the booze talking. Habby likes women more than she likes men. She always has.

You knew that when you married her?

No. But I figured out that I wasn't really satisfying her.

Why didn't you find yourself another woman?

I did, lots of them. But none of them did for me what you did. I never figured that out until you moved out of our house.

Why do you stay with my sister?

She's all that I got. I can't be out on my own like you, Mosey. I need her. I need to be with her. You DeBobo are something else. You make people feel like they are safe in this world. That's why I want you, Mosey. And Habby.

Critton, you'll have to find someone else. Hang on to Habboey, if you can, but I'm not part of your happiness or security.

They arrived at the Gant home with its wide front lawn and side drive. Critton pulled up to the garage behind the house. And they both walked back along the driveway to the front door of the house. Critton used his key to open the door.

Mosey noticed the plastic slip-covered furniture, the wall to wall carpeting and the bright lighting of the living room.

Habby! Mosey's here.

Habboey came into the living room from the kitchen carrying a glass with a drink.

Hey, Brother.

She came close to Mosey so that he could give her a kiss on the cheek.

Critton, fix Mosey a drink. Sit here on the sofa and let me get a good look at you. So, I see you've been eating well. How's life with Queen . . . what's her name?

Lucille.

Queen Lucille. You fruits kill me with all this sissy talk. Hell, you're not women. Why does he call himself by a woman's name? He doesn't have a pussy, does he? His ass is never going to be a pussy. Women don't have shit in their pussies, or don't you know that? I don't guess you've seen many pussies but I bet you've seen a lot of shitty asses. What do you think of Critton's ass? You ever have it? Or, did he only stick his dick up your one-armed ass? Didn't think I knew, huh?

Critton told me in the car.

Did he? He wants your dick again. You know why?

He said it satisfies him.

I'll say it does. But, Brother Mosey, that's okay with me because he won't be getting my pussy anymore.

Why are you telling me this, Habby?

I'll tell you why! I'll tell you why! You went off to live with Swee after momma died. I had to stay home and take care of our baby brothers, Cullios and Phessin. I had to stay with those boys and daddy. I had to raise them until I met Critton. And then I got out of there. I didn't love Critton. Hell, I didn't even like sex with him. I just wanted to be with you and Swee. You had what I wanted. You had Trique. You were living the life I wanted to live.

Why didn't you find a woman like Swee found Amity?

A woman couldn't get me out of the house like Critton did. And I didn't know I wanted a woman; I wanted to be in a home with a woman like you were with Swee. You had a new mother and all I had was dicks. Well, a dick got me out of the house and got me here. So, now, no more dicks.

Just pussy.

You got that right, Brother Mosey.

Critton returned to the living room with drinks.

Here, Mosey. Habby.

Oh, don't worry, Mosey. Critton has heard all of this before. He knows that I'm not going anywhere soon. Besides, I can have what I want and none of the problems. So, you see, Brother dear, you can move back here with us and it won't bother anyone. You get what you want. Critton gets what he wants. And I get what I want.

Habby, Mosey doesn't want me.

You're kidding? Mosey, you would turn down a fine man like Mr. Gant here? For what? That queen you live with?

Habby, nothing's wrong with Lucille. He's sweet, and he's been a good friend. The best, I would say. But he needs his place to himself. He didn't intend, and I didn't intend, for me to stay with him forever. But I would like to stay here, temporarily, until I can get a new job, my own place, and back out on my own again.

Mosey, you can come back here. And who knows, you might even get it on with Critton. He'll certainly try to convince you, won't you, dear?

I won't bother Mosey.

Well, we'll see. You hungry, Brother? Dinner's ready. Let's eat.

Habboey prepared a big meal of roast pork with mashed potatoes, collard greens and biscuits. The men seated themselves while she brought the serving dishes from the kitchen and seated herself. She insisted that everyone say a blessing and then began passing the food. Habboey sliced the pork for Mosey. Otherwise, he helped himself.

Dinner conversation turned to other topics—changes in the city and neighborhood, the trip to Los Angeles, the memorial service, and the latest news about the family. Following dinner, Critton drove Mosey home without much conversation, and Mosey said goodnight and entered Lucille's apartment.

Mosey told Lucille the next day that he would move to his sister's house again. Lucille asked him why, and Mosey replied that he was imposing on Lucille's hospitality and that he didn't want to jeopardize their friendship by overstaying his welcome. Lucille was surprised.

Mosey, I don't know why you would think that.

This is your place, Lucille. You didn't invite me to stay indefinitely.

But I like having you here, Baby. You take good care of the place. You cook. We have fun, don't we?

Yes, but I need to get my own life together. We won't stop being friends. We were buddies before; we'll still be buddies. Only, I won't be in your way and I can find my own place again.

Mosey, I hate to see you go. I like having you here.

But, I need to work.

You can stay here and still look for a job. You don't need to move to do that.

But I think it would be better for me to be with my sister and not impose on you.

You keep saying things like impose. It's not an imposition. Mosey, you're beginning to sound like you did when you were talking about Red. Why can't you let people, who want to, help you? You run away from folks, always running back to your family, to that sister of yours who is bat-shit crazy. Excuse me for reminding you that she is one raging bitch. And that double-dealing husband of hers. Mosey, this can be your home. We have fun together. I like you; you like me. What's the problem except that you don't seem to want anyone in your life? You left Trique. You left Waite. You left Red. Now, you want to leave me. And don't tell me it's because of your arm. This lady is no fool. With or without an arm, you just don't want anyone close to you. Well?

Lucille, I don't know what it is. Maybe, it's too many disappointments. Maybe, it's being a fairy. How can fairies live like other people? We can't make families and live like other folks live. We have our sex and good times and then what?

Excuse me? Didn't you live with two lesbians when you were growing up? Didn't they have a home? Weren't you part of a family?

But women can do that. I don't think that men can.

Why not? What are we doing here? What is this if not a home with and for fairies?

But we don't love each other. We're just friends. Not a family.

Mosey, we've never tried to love each other. At least you've never tried. I've always been very fond of you but your eye has been elsewhere. Look at me, Mosey. I'm a man that you've fucked.

I've slept with you. We've partied. We've lived in the same home. The only thing missing is we haven't let ourselves love each other, you know, like Swee loved Amity.

I don't see how that could happen?

Why not? Because I'm not your type? I'm not Trique or Waite or Red? Well, I am Lucille and, Baby, give me a chance and I'll show you.

Lucille, you're sweet and good to me but I can't see it happening. I'm going to my sister's place. Maybe, in time, I'll see what you are saying. Maybe, everything you say is right. But it's not right for me. Not right now. You know, I think I do love you, Lucille, but I can't love you the way you say. Not now.

Mosey moved back to the Gant's basement, actually, a finished room with wood paneling, carpeting, and acoustic tile ceiling. The furnace and laundry room were separate from Mosey's new quarters. There was a fold-out sofa bed and dresser, a few tables and lamps. Mosey had virtually no possessions except for his clothes—some shirts, trousers, jackets, overcoat, and shoes, all of which fit into one big suitcase. He was not completely self-contained in his basement room because he had no toilet, shower, or cooking appliances. He was free to use the upstairs bathroom and kitchen which he visited only when, he felt, Habboey and Critton were otherwise busy or absent from the house. This was his routine for several months.

Mosey sat at the kitchen table. Both Habboey and Critton had left for work. The morning newspaper lay on the table. Mosey flipped through the pages to the want ads. There were no jobs for janitors or handymen. But one notice caught his attention: Civil Service applications were requested for museum guard positions. This was something that Mosey had never previously considered as a possibility for himself. A high school diploma was required as a minimum qualification. Mosey had only completed tenth grade in Pachacuti before he and Trique fled to Atlanta and he never had the opportunity or interest to finish high school. At thirty-nine, he couldn't see himself going back to school. He went to the telephone and dialed the number in the want ad. A woman answered in the municipal Civil Service office.

Civil Service, personnel office. Miss Townsend speaking. How may I help you?

I saw this ad in today's paper for a museum guard.

Yes, sir?

It says a high school diploma. I've only got grade ten.

Well, sir, you would need your G.E.D.

What's that?

General Educational Diploma. You would have to take classes for adults in the evening at one of the local high schools.

How long would that take?

Depends. But call the Board of Education. Ask about the G.E.D, and when you get that, you can apply for a job with the city, like the museum guard. Okay?

Thank you.

Mosey sat for some time, thinking. After an hour, he got the telephone book, searched the number of the Board of Education and called.

When Habboey and Critton arrived home that evening, they found a note from Mosey saying that he was at Central High School where he was enrolling in an adult education class to get his G.E.D.

It wasn't easy. Mosey had never been a good student and his Pachacuti education had been inferior. His math, English, and reading skills were rudimentary, at best. On the other hand, the other students didn't seem to be in any better shape. The teachers, male and female, were patient and considerate. Above all, they encouraged and they criticized. Mosey considered quitting after a week. He listened to the complaints of the other students and realized that learning was difficult but not impossible if he worked at it. He asked for extra help. He teamed up with another man, older than he, but who seemed to be better prepared. They studied together, became friends.

Prince Henry Walker, Mosey's new friend, was forty-seven years old, married with three children. His wife worked. Prince was a laborer in the Packard automobile plant until it closed and the company went out of business. He had made good money but now, after a series of low-paying jobs, he was laid off. Although he grew up in Detroit, he never had a decent education for anything other than factory work. He had started working in his teens because he wanted the money. Now that his own children were finishing high school and planning for college, he felt ignorant. He was determined to change himself so that he could be an educated man like his children. And, maybe, with an education, he could get a better job in another factory. That was his plan.

He liked Mosey. Mosey presented himself well—dignified, handsome, despite having only one arm. And he had a good mind even if he didn't have a lot of education. He was working hard trying. Sure, it was difficult after all of those years, but hard work would get Mosey and Prince to their goals. He wondered about Mosey being a single man. No wife. No girlfriend. No interest in women, really.

Mosey, don't you plan to get married and use all this education to make yourself a family?

No, Prince, I'm not getting married. Who wants a one-armed husband?

But there's no woman in your life?

I've got women in my family.

But not a woman of your own. How come?

I'm not interested in women at my age.

What do you mean, at your age? Since when do healthy men stop being interested in women? Nothing like riding those hips.

I'm just not interested, Prince. Some men are; some men aren't.

Yeah, but those who aren't, are usually pansies.

That's not the worst thing in the world.

I wouldn't have anything to do with a pansy.

Why not?

Ain't right. Ain't natural. Something's wrong with those pansies. Ain't part of god's plan.

How do you know that?

How do I know? Everybody knows. Don't you?

I've known pansies, and they are like anybody else.

No, Man. You're wrong. They are against nature. Nature made women and men to go together. That's all there is. That other stuff is against nature. There was a pansy on the assembly line where I worked. I didn't want him anywhere near me. He was like some freak. A sissy.

Do you think that all sissies are like that?

Sure, you can always tell.

Can you?

I can.

Really. I can't.

Well, as part of your education, I'll point them out to you.

You do that, Prince. It should be some education.

You got that right.

Mosey and Prince completed their G.E.D.s, Prince before Mosey. But Mosey stuck with school and, despite the struggle, began to learn that he could learn. He called the city Civil Service again and was told that there were no longer any openings for museum guards but he could fill out an application and take the next Civil Service exam.

He went to the City-County Building where the city offices were located, got the application, and filled it out. When the exam was given, he took it and felt that he did reasonably well. Although there were no guard positions, there were openings for janitors, and Mosey got a job at a city recreation center. Mosey started work immediately. There was one other janitor for the center so he shared responsibilities for maintaining the boiler, taking out the trash, and cleaning the floors and restrooms. Despite his handicap, Mosey was adept with a broom and mop. He could manipulate the stump of his severed arm with agility so that gripping the cleaning utensils was not difficult. The strength in his intact arm allowed him to heft trash cans and other heavy objects. He never deferred work to his co-worker, a white man named Julius Schmidt. Julius was older than Mosey by about ten to fifteen years. He had worked most of his life in automobile plants but when DeSoto shut down, like Packard, he had few options. He felt lucky to get a janitorial job with the city and, although he was white, he had long worked with blacks and welcomed Mosey. Julius was a widower with four adult children. He cared for his widowed mother who lived with him in an all-white neighborhood on the city's far west side. Julius opened the recreation center in the morning and worked until afternoon. Mosey's shift began at midday and lasted until evening when he closed the building. The recreation staff conducted the programs for clientele and maintained all equipment. There was little interaction between staff and clients with Mosey or Julius. They were invisible in their coveralls despite the fact that they worked throughout the building during its hours of operation. Mosey liked his job. He made good money and soon found a little apartment in midtown near several bus lines. His was a one bedroom apartment, the nicest he had ever had. It was small—a living room, bedroom, kitchen, and bath but it had lots of windows and it was on the second floor overlooking a tree-shaded residential street. He got some second-hand furniture. None of it matched or was of any quality but Mosey didn't care. He was on his own again, paying his own way, taking care of himself, and not dependent on anyone.

He began to remember his dreams which he recorded in his journal. He would wake up in the morning, open his eyes, and look around his bedroom. The shades were drawn over the two windows facing the street. He stared at the ceiling, at the moldings at the top of the walls. He remembered dreaming about his mother, Loissey, and his father, Adelpho. He couldn't remember what they were doing, just that they had been present. His mother had smiled but she seemed unhappy. His father was quiet. Mosey got up to pee. He slept in his boxer shorts and undershirt, both of which needed laundering. He fiddled with the fly of his shorts with his right hand and grasped his cock to aim. When finished, he gave it a couple of shakes and slipped it back into his shorts. He flushed, turned on the bathroom light—the light from the window was inadequate—and looked in the mirror. He looked his age now that he was over forty. His sharp features had begun to soften and sag. Oh, he knew that he was no longer youthful and that meant that he might not have as much luck in the bars and joints as he had had in the past. While his missing arm had been unattractive to some men, to others it didn't seem to matter. They found him handsome and when they reached for his crotch, they were more than delighted. And Mosey knew how to use his short arm; it was versatile and strong. Mosey smiled at himself at the thought.

He went into his little kitchen, put the coffee pot on the gas stove, and started brewing a couple of cups. He looked in the refrigerator for some eggs, made toast in his toaster, sat down to eat at the table in his living room, and finished his meal with black coffee.

After returning the dishes to the kitchen sink, he stripped off his underwear, took a shit, ran water in the bath tub, bathed, and shaved. He dressed in work-clothes—his overalls were in a locker at the recreation center. He still had a couple of hours before reporting to work so he walked to the New Center area past the Fisher Building, to the General Motors headquarters to look at the new cars on display in the ground floor corridors. The autos were big, glossy, highly polished, and gleaming. They were seductive. Mosey wanted a blue Oldsmobile but his salary wouldn't permit that, and he never had a driver's license. A car was not in his future, just public transportation. But he had the desire, as did the crowds in the corridors and lobby who crowded around the cars to peek inside at the interiors. Only the ropes held by stanchions kept Mosey and everyone else from pressing close and spoiling the polished finish with fingerprints and hot breath. There were blacks and whites, old and young, men in business suits, women in dresses, kids in jeans, the well to do, and the presentably shabby; they mingled together in General Motors' stately halls. Albert Kahn, the architect, had created the perfect expression of automotive power, wealth, and influence. G.M.'s headquarters was the Versailles of Detroit, the seat of the city's real royalty. Everyone knew it. Since coming to Detroit over twenty years ago, Mosey had become immersed in the auto culture. Ford, General Motors, Chrysler, Packard, American Motors, they were the pillars of the city. Packard was gone now but the others were strong.

Mosey moved through the crowds to leave the building and catch his bus. He joined the end of the queue. Mostly black folks stood in line. A bus arrived. Mosey was amused that the driver was Lucille.

Hey, Lucius, he said as he dropped his fare into the fare box.

Hi, Mosey. Step back, folks. I can't operate the bus until you're past the white line. Talk to you later, Mosey.

Mosey gripped an overhead handhold and braced his legs as the bus lurched into traffic. The aisle was crowded. Mosey focused on the street as the bus moved to the next stop. There were still gaps in the storefronts where buildings burned during the rebellion. It didn't seem that they would ever be rebuilt. Maybe, it was best if all of those old buildings were torn down and something new replaced them. That was what people said. Mosey heard it all the time. People also said that what had happened in Detroit was not a riot but a rebellion against oppression. That's what some thought. In any case, white people were leaving the city which meant that blacks could move to neighborhoods that were formerly closed to them. But it also meant that whites were taking their businesses and money with them and, so, there were fewer jobs in the city. But, Mosey had a job and a nice place to live. He was doing well. When he came to his stop, he left by the rear door and didn't have a chance to speak again to Lucille. He would call him sometime to go out to a joint, maybe get together for sex. He liked Lucille, liked his company, and now that he was on his own again, he didn't feel obligated or dependent.

He walked several blocks from the bus stop to the recreation center. It was an older brick building, two stories with a swimming pool and gym on the ground floor and meeting and activity rooms, as well as offices, on the second floor. The boiler and storage rooms were in the basement. That's also where the janitors and staff had their lockers. That's where Mosey headed to get his overalls and equipment. He found Julius cleaning the men's restroom. Julius asked him to take care of the women's restroom before mopping the main entry. This, Mosey did and then took a break with Julius in the employee lounge in the basement.

Not too busy today, Julius?

Nah. People don't come in like they used to. Before, this place would be packed with retirees, women, and little children but, now, it's mostly retirees and not a whole lot of them. I think the city is going to close this place someday, too much money to operate for too few people.

I don't know, Julius. This was a white neighborhood and now, what? It's mostly black. Black people never felt welcome here so it will take time for it to catch on with them.

Well, that could be as you say but I don't think that blacks weren't welcome. They just did other things. You know, like hang out with their own kind. Didn't you do that?

Yeah, because us black folks couldn't get into places like this.

Who kept you out? This is public property.

Julius, we weren't welcome. Nobody said, maybe, you can't come in here but if you came here and people, white people, stared at you like you came from the zoo, or made comments for you to overhear like "What are they doing here?," you might not feel welcome. Listen, I grew up in the segregated South, lived in Atlanta and Cincinnati, and I can tell you that Detroit, when I came here, wasn't a whole lot different from those places. Don't kid yourself. White people in this country have wanted black people out of their sight and out of their lives except to cook, clean for them, and take care of their babies. Oh, and they like to fuck our women. Strange, huh?

Well, I don't know about all of that. I've been around colored all my life in Detroit.

In your neighborhood?

No. They have their own neighborhoods, you know, like the Jews live together, us Germans, and the Italians. That's how people are. But we've all worked together in the factories. Some of my best friends in the factory were colored.

I'll bet. Do you still see them?

No. We got different lives now.

I see.

Hey, don't give me that shit like I'm some racist or something. I never done no harm to colored. With me, it's live and let live. I've got to finish my work now and leave.

Mosey also went back to work changing light bulbs, emptying trash, and mopping floors. In the evening after everyone left, he shut off all but the emergency lights and locked the doors. He took a bus home but stopped at a neighborhood restaurant and had meatloaf with mashed potatoes, some overcooked carrots, and coffee.

When he arrived home, his phone was ringing. It was Lucille who wanted to meet him at a bar not far from Mosey's place. At nine, Mosey headed out. He walked the fifteen blocks to the bar and went inside. Music was playing. Cigarette smoke filled the place. Lucille was at the bar.

You got here in a hurry, Lucille.

Honey, I was just around the corner when I called you. I've been here getting mellow.

Mosey ordered a beer.

So, Miss Thing, tell Lucille everything and don't leave out the most interesting details.

I haven't been fucking around.

That's not what I heard, you sly bitch.

Well, that's the truth. I got this job as janitor at the Kendall Recreation Center. Afternoon shift. There's another janitor—white, but a pretty decent guy—who has the morning shift. I hope it's just temporary until there's a museum guard opening.

Well, good for you, Miss Thing. Employed and all. So, how's your new place since you haven't invited me over for tea, yet?

It's pretty nice. Small. Not much stuff. But it's my place and I like it.

Miss Lucille is still pissed that you left her. Now, she has to clean her own place and make her own meals, you selfish bitch.

Hey. You've got your place to yourself again. And you can entertain your gentlemen callers in peace without a one-armed butler in your way.

I wish that you would get off that story about your being in my way or whatever. I'm going to hit you with my high-heeled pump if you don't stop that.

Okay, Lucille. I feel a whole lot different since I got my G.E.D. and this new job. I feel like I'm finally on my own and going somewhere.

When you get there, send me your new address.

Lucille, you're something else.

Honey, don't look now but someone you know just walked in, and he has red hair. And he's coming over here.

Hi, Mosey.

Hey, Steven.

Hello, Lucille.

Hello, Mr. Red. Long time no see. Excuse me. I must go change my sanitary napkin. You two talk until I come back, if I come back.

How have you been, Steven?

Pretty good. Busy with work. The accounting office is real busy. We are hiring and need more space. The rumor around the office is that we're moving to the suburbs from downtown. There are lots of new office buildings out in Southfield. We might move there. I'm already living out there. My old neighborhood went downhill pretty quickly after the riots.

Too many niggers, huh?

Mosey, that's not it and you know it. White people got scared.

Like you?

Like me. They left the city for the suburbs where they feel safer.

And where there are no niggers.

There are some black people, Mosey, people with money who want nice neighborhoods and safety. My old neighborhood filled up with poor people.

Poor black people.

Mosey, they are the only people who will to pay the rents.

Tell it to someone else, Steven. White people created ghettoes and now that niggers are breaking out of them, you white people are heading for the hills.

Okay, Mosey. It's just like you say. I'm not here to defend racism. I only want to have some drinks, a good time. Bartender, give me a draft, please. So, how are you?

Thanks for asking. I've got another janitor job with the city until I can get a museum guard job.

That's great.

Yeah, it's great for a nigger.

Mosey, what did I ever do to you that you dislike me so much? I told you that your leaving was breaking my heart. I loved you, Mosey.

How could you love me? Steven, you like black dick. That's all. There's no love. Not for me as a person.

Can I sit here beside you?

Go ahead.

Listen. I may not have had as clear a picture of things as you did at that time and I may not have been as tuned into the race thing as I'm sure you were and are, but I cared for you deeply. Sure, I like black men. So what? But you were more than just a black man to me. You were a smart, sexy, very aware guy who I wanted to be with. You were good to me and good for me and I wanted you and I didn't understand—and still don't understand—why you didn't want me, why you were so hostile.

Hostile? Steven, I didn't trust you. I couldn't trust you. You are white. I grew up in a world where white people hated me and my kind, treated us like we were nothing.

But, Mosey, I didn't treat you like that.

But you were, are, part of that world.

Mosey, I can't help that I'm white just as you can't help that you're black. But that shouldn't mean that we can't be simply two people. Wasn't that Reverend King's dream?

It sounds good, Steven, but it doesn't work that way. King is dead now, killed by a white man.

Yes, but you can't blame all white people for what one man did. You're blaming me as if I was someone that I'm not. My attraction to you is as real as anything in my life. You just won't accept that, will you?

I guess you're right.

I'm sorry, Mosey, that our skin color is such a barrier for you. It isn't for me. But, I hear that you won't change your mind about me or us. I'm sorry that I've wasted your time. I'll see you around. Bye.

Miss Mosey, did you send that man away again?

Not really. I only told him how the world is.

Not how the world is, how you are. Mosey; you're one fucked up, mean queen. Men are falling all over you and you're offended. If it's not race, it's something else. You don't want to be happy with anyone, Honey. It's a good thing Miss Lucille likes the smell of your shit because, Baby, you're dragging a sack of it around with you.

It's getting late. I have to cover my partner's shift tomorrow. He's got a doctor's appointment.

But, Baby, we haven't scored this evening! I thought that we could spend some time together.

You score. I've got to go. Night.

Goodnight, Miss Thing. Miss All-Responsible-And-Up-At-The Crack-Of-Dawn Thing.

Bye.

Mosey headed home, undressed, and pulled the covers over himself. When he awoke, he realized that he had been dreaming again about Pachacuti. This time, he saw a dream version of Swee's house but no one was in it. He walked through the central hallway of the house out the backdoor into the yard. There was a chicken coop with chickens. Beyond was the forest with dense vegetation. Then his mother appeared on the rear steps of the house. She was speaking to him but he couldn't hear what she was saying and that dream ended. Variations on this dream re-occurred during the next year. Sometimes, his mother was in Swee's house or outside. Sometimes, a man whom Mosey didn't recognize was with her. Sometimes, Swee and Amity were present. One time Trique appeared. When he did, Mosey felt sexually stimulated and ejaculated in his boxer shorts.

He telephoned Swee to talk with her. He discussed his janitor's job, his apartment, his evenings with Lucille, and his dreams.

Swee, Why do you think I'm having these dreams about my momma? I was five years old when she died. You've been more of a momma to me than she was?

Gee, Mosey, I don't know. Loissey was a strange and beautiful woman. She was seven years older than me and there were the other two kids between us in age—Prellis and Daphet. I was the baby and they all took turns taking care of me. Loissey was always kind to me, as I remember, but she was also very quiet and, somehow, distant. When I later found out that she had a different mother than me, I understood why she didn't seem to fit into our family. My mother, Darissa

McKree, did treat Loissey different, less loving, I guess, less close than she behaved towards her own children. I didn't know Loissey's mother, Soonie, Olive's sister. When I was told that Soonie was a white woman, I remember looking at Loissey and seeing her as a kind of white woman—she was a whole lot lighter than the rest of us. Maybe, it was her difference that made her seem apart, strange. I don't know, Mosey.

Who do you think the man was?

You got me there, Mosey. You say you didn't recognize him?

No.

Was he black?

Yes.

How old?

I don't know, maybe, my age now.

So, forty-ish. Hmm. It wasn't your daddy, Adelpho?

No. I would have recognized him. I was ten when he died. That's when they sent me to live with you.

The only other men in your family and my family, other than your brother, Phessin, are your uncle, Teatus, and my brothers, Littell and Prellis. But you didn't know my brothers. They were never around.

Maybe, it was Prellis because you talked about him even though I never saw him until they lynched him.

Maybe. But why would you be dreaming about Prellis?

I don't know. Maybe, it's all part of that stuff when we ran from the Boston boys and they burned down your house.

Could be, Mosey. Let me ask you this: Do you ever dream about losing your arm?

Not that I remember.

Isn't that odd?

I don't know. I don't think much about how I lost my arm.

Well, that's probably for the best.

How's Gulley and the kids?

They're fine. That knuckle-headed Bone is finally getting himself together and not causing trouble. Thing is he's really smart, and now he seems to be using his smarts to better himself and stop creating so much turmoil in our lives. Have you heard anything from Trique?

No. He hasn't called, and I haven't called him.

Why don't you? He could probably use some encouragement.

I suppose you're right.

Well, I've got to go. Love you.

Love you, too. Bye.

After his conversation with Swee, Mosey's dreams of his mother ceased, and he had no further dreams of Pachacuti. But he thought more and more about Trique and Waite. Since he saw Lucille frequently, he didn't think about Red. And he didn't see Red in any of the usual places.

Late at night, Mosey dialed Trique's telephone number.

Hello.

Trique?

No, this is William.

Oh, William. This is Mosey DeBobo in Detroit.

Hi, Mosey. How are you? You want Trique? He's not home yet. A late meeting, I think. Shall I tell him to call you when he comes in?

Yes, please. How are things out there?

Not bad. We're doing okay. Things are fine between me and Trique. He can tell you about Alfred.

Good. I'll expect his call. Thanks, goodbye.

Mosey went to bed at midnight. The telephone rang at 2 am.

Hello.

Mosey?

Yeah.

It's Trique. What time is it there?

What? Wait. It's after two.

Hey, Man. I'm sorry. I got in late but I didn't think about the time difference. When Bill told me you called, I was so excited I called without thinking. Are you awake?

Yeah. I think so. I was dreaming about Pachacuti. That's funny. I haven't dreamt about it in a long time and then, after I called you and went to sleep, that's what, I guess, was on my mind.

Is this a good time to talk though? I just woke you up.

It's good, Trique. Let me get out of bed though and turn on some lights. Okay.

So, what's up, man?

I was thinking about you. About us way back when. We didn't have a chance to talk when I was out your way at Dunn's memorial.

Yeah. That was a bad time for me, Mosey, with Dunn's death and finding out about Alfred. Bill and I were having a hard time then, too. Swee spent a lot of time with me, though, talking about all of these things.

So, how is it now?

I still have a terrible hurt about Dunn but I'm getting some distance on it now. It's been, what, almost three years? Lee and I don't talk much anymore. We've really gone our own ways. But Alfred and me are getting real tight. You know, he is cool with me, and with me and Bill. Maybe, because he didn't grow up with me, like Dunn; he's got more distance between us. And Teatus and Iolithe raised him right. Well, Xantha kept an eye on everything too.

Man, you sound better. Not so depressed like before.

You know, Mosey, I'm getting cool with myself. I could never, you know, understand this thing for guys and women. I couldn't get why I was after Lee while I was with you. It confused me.

So, what do you understand now?

I like dicks and cunts, to be honest. But what I really like is being with someone who is good to me. Bill is really good, Mosey.

And he's black.

Yes, he's black. I thought I could handle the white thing with Lee but I couldn't. Still can't. It's like we're two different species.

How did you ever let that happen in the first place?

Mosey, it was Pachacuti. She came on to me, a white chick, forbidden fruit, Man. Shit. Niggers got lynched for looking at white chicks. I was full of myself, and I was a horny kid, Mosey, always was. You and I had good sex but pussy was something new for me. White pussy, man, the holy grail. I was crazy. I was a kid. We were all kids, and crazy, all of us.

So, you think it was just crazy?

Yeah, don't you?

I don't think it was crazy. I was in love with you. I thought you loved me. I thought we would be together like Swee and Amity. I wanted you, Trique, even after Lee. In Atlanta, I was still in love with you. But you went after those other women and men. I wasn't enough for you. I wasn't what you wanted. I didn't know what you wanted, and then I knew that you didn't want me. I left you but I still loved you. And I still love you.

Mosey, I was an idiot. What can I say? I've learned a lot since then. I've changed, I think. I can't apologize anymore for being a crazy kid. I'm not a kid anymore and neither are you. I still have love for you, Mosey, but that doesn't mean I can go back to what was over twenty years ago. I don't think that you mean that you want to go back?

No, Trique, not back. You're right. A lot has happened, we've both moved on.

But, what?

But you broke my heart, Trique.

Mosey, I'm sorry but how can I change that? I know how you feel. I've had my heart broken, too. Dunn's death felt like I had died. I think that I was close to suicide. I think I could have killed myself because I thought I caused his death by being his faggot father. I thought I caused your injury by cheating on you. I thought I caused Lee to lose her family because she married a nigger. Mosey, I've lived with all of this pain and guilt and remorse and, yes, I could have ended it all. But would Dunn be alive? Would you have your arm? Would Lee, well, that's a whole other story. Mosey, I've got Bill. I've got my son, Alfred. It's good for me. How can I make it good for you? I can't change the past. I can only change today or, maybe, tomorrow. So, what can I change for you now?

Trique, I guess I'm happy for you. You're right. You can't change what's done. You're not going to leave Bill for me, and I don't know now that that is even what I had in mind. But, maybe, I did or at least I wanted you to say that you still wanted me. But I feel you still love me and that's something. I guess I have to fix my own broken heart. But how, Trique? How did you fix your broken heart?

Simple, Mosey. I loved someone other than myself because I couldn't love myself. Don't you love somebody, Mosey?

I loved Waite but he's got someone he loves. And, there was this white guy here, Steven. I might have loved him.

What happened?

Well, it's like you and Lee. I couldn't get over the white thing.

I understand that, Mosey. Poor Dunn was at war with himself trying to be white or black or both. Alfred, thank god, never had that conflict. Both of us, Mosey, come from black and white. Your grandmother, Soonie Fleet, was white, as was her father, Murray Fleet, who was my grandfather. But we didn't have to struggle with that because we grew up black around black folks. But, when you think about it, Mosey, this race thing is just in our heads. Yes, we sort out from one another by skin color but skin color isn't everything or even anything. It's in the head, in your head, in my head. In the heads of our families and this whole fucked up country. It affects everything. It rules everything. But, it's in our head and, if we can get a grip on our heads; we can see that shit for what it is. Shit. Listen, Man, it must be really late for you. Let's talk again at a different time.

Thanks, Trique. Say hello to Bill and to Alfred next time that you talk to him.

Okay, goodnight.

Mosey had trouble falling asleep after his conversation with Trique. He went to the kitchen for a drink of water. Then, he had to pee. When he got back in bed, he started to cry. He stared at the ceiling and thought about everything from Pachacuti to Atlanta to Cincinnati to Detroit, from Trique to Waite to Steven. He needed to talk to Waite.

Mosey got the morning shift at the recreation center. His co-worker, Julius Schmidt, had a heart attack and received a medical leave. The replacement on the afternoon shift was a younger man, in his twenties, and also black. Calvin Erskine didn't seem like a serious worker to Mosey. He seemed more interested in smoking weed and watching women than in completing his work. Mosey found that he often had to do or re-do things that were Calvin's responsibility. As a result, there were more complaints from the staff and clients about the center's state of cleanliness and maintenance. Mosey did the best he could but he was unable to motivate Calvin or get a sympathetic ear from his supervisors at the center or from the parks and recreation department overseeing the center.

He went downtown to the City-County Building to inquire about a transfer to a museum guard position. As he got off of the bus, he noticed that there seemed to be far fewer people on the streets than in the past. Also, more stores were closed or had changed to lower quality merchandise appealing, apparently, to lower income customers. At the personnel office, he scanned the listings for job openings. He was surprised to see one for museum guards. He asked a clerk and was told that it had been recently posted. He mentioned that he had made an application years ago and had made subsequent inquiries at least a couple of times a year. Why hadn't he been informed since he was a city employee? The clerk shrugged. It wasn't her responsibility. He could make a new transfer request. That was it. So, Mosey filled out the form and left.

At their usual spot, Mosey sat with Lucille and complained about the personnel division of the city. Lucille seemed disinterested. Mosey finally noticed.

What's up, Lucille?

First of all, call me Lucius, my given Christian name.

Why's that?

Times have changed, Mosey. This queen has become a king. The Reverend M.L. King liberated my black ass. Now, those crazy queens in New York have liberated my gay black ass.

Gay?

Yes, Honey. Gay is the new faggot. I'm gay, proud, black, and a king. Now, the second thing is Mr. Lucius has been your friend and, sometimes, fuck buddy and he has listened to your shit patiently and sympathetically for years. I mean years! Decades! And I don't remember one time in all these years when you asked about me. Oh, you told me how I must be feeling about this or that but you never seem to want to know what I think or what I'm doing. Why is that, Mosey?

I've always listened to you.

Have you? Have you ever asked me anything about me?

I'm sure I have, haven't I?

I don't think so, Mister I'm-suffering-Because-I-Can't-Love-Anybody-Who-Loves-Me.

That's not fair, Lu . . . Lucius. You don't talk about yourself.

No, you're right. You suck all of the oxygen out of the air.

Come on. You talk all the time just not about anything serious.

Well, let's get serious, Mosey. Do you know where I'm from?

Detroit? Right?

No. I was born in Atlanta. I came here in 1942 when my momma, Mary Lou, died. My daddy, Ephraim Collins, re-married a woman with her own children. So, my brother and sisters had to make do.

I didn't know you had family.

Of course not. You never asked.

You never mentioned them.

Well, my brother, Hollister, is the oldest. He's still in Atlanta. So is my younger sister, Clea. They both have families. My older sister, Callista, died in '64. She never married but she had kids that my sister adopted after Callista's death.

Sounds like what happened in my family.

Dammit, Mosey, this is about me. I know everything there is to know about your family. This is my family, my life I'm talking about.

Wait a minute, Lucius. Let me put this together and I'll listen to you all night long. You had a sister, Callista Collins?

Yes, that's what I said, my older sister in Atlanta.

When I was at Dunn's memorial service, my Aunt Xantha told us about Lee's twins.

I know that.

What I didn't mention was that Alfred's wet-nurse was Callista Collins. Was that your sister?

What? Wet-nurse? Mosey, she did wet-nurse to get money. She wet-nursed Alfred?

I guess she did. So, you and I have a family connection. You're part of the whole DeBobo—Sellabie—Pendle clan!

Jesus-fucking-Christ. That makes us kind of cousins in a way, Mosey. I can't sleep with you anymore. You're family.

Kissing cousins, you could say.

Well, more than kissing. It's a good thing I didn't have your baby.

Well, it wasn't because we didn't keep trying

This is amazing.

So, how did you come to Detroit?

My father sent me to live with my mother's people, the Seyburn. I went to school here. Graduated, unlike some, and got a job driving buses.

And the Lucille thing?

My mother's sister was Lucille, bless her soul. She called me "Little Lucille" because I was always such a queen, but a king now.

Lucius, I've always liked you as a queen. You were fierce.

And I always loved you, Mr. Mosey, because you were so sweet to a lady. And you know how to handle that thing swinging between your legs.

Lucius, you're quite a friend.

And you, my dear, could be quite a lover.

When Mosey awoke, he remembered that he had been dreaming again about Pachacuti. However, this time he was in the town's only business district. Stores lined both sides of the main street. There were black people and white people. He saw his mother, and she smiled at him and then moved away. Then, he was above the town looking down at its streets, buildings, railroad tracks. A train was moving through town heading north. He was in a bigger city, something like Atlanta or Cincinnati. It seemed more like Atlanta. He was on a busy street. There were only black people. He saw his mother again. She went into a shop. He felt a pain in his arm. The dream ended.

While he was dressing to leave for work, the phone rang. It was Waite calling from Cleveland.

Mosey, my mother died last night. She had a heart attack.

I'm really sorry, Waite.

The funeral is next Saturday, in Cincinnati. Could you come? I would really like for you to be here and meet Woodward, my boyfriend.

Uh. I'd have to take off from work. I don't know if I could get someone to cover for me. This kid I work with is, well, let's say he's not very reliable.

If you can, will you come?

I'll see, Waite. I can't promise. It won't be easy.

Well, if you can come, the funeral is at the Mt. Olivet Baptist Church at noon. If you come, you can stay with us at my mother's place so you won't need a hotel or anything. We can pick you up if you come into town. Here is the telephone number; I hope you can make it.

Mosey hung up the phone, finished dressing, and left for work. When his co-worker, Calvin, arrived for the afternoon shift, Mosey told him about the funeral. Calvin immediately told him that he would cover for him. Not to worry. Mosey wasn't so sure but he decided that he wanted to go. He called Waite that night, got all of the information that he needed and made his plans.

He took a Greyhound bus. The trip was surprisingly quick on the new interstate between Detroit and Cincinnati. When Mosey had come to Detroit from Cincinnati, there wasn't such a highway. Now, he glided through the landscape to Toledo, Dayton, and Cincinnati. Waite arrived with his car to pick Mosey up at the bus station. They put Mosey's suitcase in the trunk and got into the car.

Where's Woodward?

He's waiting for us at my mother's place.

It looks like Cincinnati has changed.

Yeah, I noticed that, too.

Not like Detroit which seems to be going downhill.

It's the same thing in Cleveland. People are moving out to the suburbs. There are lots of empty buildings. You look good, Mosey, real sharp. You always were good-looking. Now, you look positively dignified.

You look pretty good yourself, Waite. I always thought that you were the handsome one.

Well, I guess that's what got us together; we were looking for hot stuff. You know, Mosey, you were the first guy I had sex with. I was always interested, curious, you know, but I was always a little scared. I didn't even know how guys had sex but I decided to take a chance. You were good, Mosey, real good. You not only showed me what to do but you also made me feel like it was more than, you know, sticking it in and coming.

I learned a lot with Trique. He was the one who tried different things. I mostly went along because, man . . .

What, Mosey? Mosey!

Trique made me feel so good. I thought that I would be with him forever. I wanted to be with him all the time. Even after Lee, and the other women and men. Then, I couldn't stand it anymore. He was out of my reach, no longer mine to have. I felt cut off from everything, everyone.

Then you met me?

Hah! Yeah, I met you, you sweet guy.

Mosey, why did you leave me after your accident?

You know, Waite, I couldn't work; you couldn't support me.

You wouldn't let me support you.

That's true. I didn't want to be your burden or anyone's burden.

But you decided you were a burden which you weren't, not when I wanted to be with you and take care of you. I knew that someday you would work again, and we could make it.

Well, you're right again, Waite. I can see now that I've been pulling away from people for a long time ever since Trique. Maybe, even before. When my momma died and my family sent me to live with Swee, I've felt unwanted. Swee was like a mother but she wasn't my mother. When Trique came along, I found what I wanted. When I couldn't have him to myself, I sort of just closed off.

But, you opened up to me.

Yes, I did. But that crazy nigger cook who took my arm changed everything.

Mosey, people get over stuff.

Everyone has been telling me the same thing. But some things don't change so easily.

Mosey, twenty years . . .

Yes, twenty years and, maybe, in a few years or twenty more years, I'll get over everything. You've moved on, Waite.

Yes. I'm happy with Woodward. He's a nice, guy. You'll like him.

Waite, with Mosey, arrived at May Easter Carvey's house in Walnut Hills. The modest two story white wood frame house on a quiet street shaded with tall trees seemed somber without its lively matron. Waite's sister, Arleeta, opened the door for them. The living room was full of people.

Hey, everyone. This is Mosey DeBobo from Detroit. Mosey, this is my sister, Arleeta, you remember her. This is her husband, Wilson Patton. And this is Woodward Templeton. This is my brother, Cassius, and his wife, Savannah. And my baby sister, Willa, and her husband, Frederick Oldeen.

There were lots of hello's around. Woodward took Mosey's bag upstairs to the guest room. The rest of the family settled back into their conversations. Waite took Mosey into the kitchen where several older family members were setting out platters of food.

Mosey, this is my aunt, Julia Carvey Smith, my father's sister, and his brother, Hampton, Jr. These are my mother's kin—my aunt, Ornella Easter DeVoe, and my uncle, Jetty. Mosey stared at the food—fried chicken, ham, and roast beef. There were dishes of greens, beans, pans of macaroni and cheese, mashed potatoes, sweet potatoes, dressing and rice. There were rolls and cornbread, pies, and a lemon layer cake. Waite pulled Mosey away from the food and back into the living room. Woodward joined them. Woodward asked Mosey about himself, about his job, his apartment, and his family. Mosey reciprocated. Meanwhile, the food was brought to the dining room table, and the family members began taking plates and filling them up. Nearly everyone also had a drink. Cassius served as bartender. Towards evening, the family started to depart. Some had taken rooms at a downtown hotel. They all agreed that there was a time when black folks couldn't stay in downtown hotels unless it was one of those little places for Negroes only. There was some amusement and bitterness about this. Cassius and Willa lived in Cincinnati and returned home to their families; Arleeta and her husband stayed at Cassius's house. Waite and Woodward stayed in one guest room of May Easter's house and Mosey stayed in the other. These had formerly been the children's rooms. Waite, in fact, slept in the same room as he did growing up with his brother, Cassius.

The next morning after breakfast, they headed to Mt. Olivet Baptist Church. The pastor, Reverend Eustis M. Lassiter, conducted the service. It was open casket, something that startled Mosey and irritated Waite. The church was crowded with family and many friends of May Easter. She received a moving, emotional send off, and the casket was finally closed. Everyone left the church for their cars and formed a cortege that moved through Cincinnati streets to the black cemetery outside of the city. Reverend Lassiter conducted the graveside service. Symbolic shovels full of dirt were thrown over the lowered casket, and everyone returned to the church for a meal.

At May Easter's house after the meal, the family re-assembled. Woodward started a conversation with Mosey in a little sitting room at the back of the house.

That was a good ceremony.

Yes, it was, more like I'm used to.

What do you mean?

When I went to Dunn's memorial service, it was in an Episcopal church. Everything was so quiet. No shouting, no people crying and calling out.

Well, you know Baptist preachers feel that people have to get the spirit and let themselves go, some crying, some yelling, maybe even a sister who has to be restrained until she gets that feeling out of her. It's a kind of an exorcism.

A what?

You know, driving out the demons.

Oh, That's what they call it?

Speaking of demons . . . I was surprised that Waite called you to come here, and I'm more surprised that you came.

Why?

Well, I didn't think that the two of you were that close any more.

Hey, Woodward, we're not that close if you think something is going on. We just have a little life together, memories. That's it, nothing else.

That's not what I'm getting. He's been talking about you and not just since his mother died.

Talking about me?

Yes. And he doesn't hide the fact that he misses you.

But he told me that he is very happy with you.

He's happy, all right, because I'm with him but, sometimes, I think that he would be happier if he had you.

Don't worry, Woodward. I'm not going to be part of his life or your life. I've got my own life in Detroit. That's all I want.

Let's make sure it stays that way. You'll be on your way tomorrow, right?

Yes.

Good. And let's say that you don't call Waite.

Waite called me?

You just don't call him. That's between us.

Don't worry.

Waite drove Mosey to the bus station Sunday morning. On the way, he noticed that Mosey didn't have much to say and seemed distant.

Mosey, you're quiet. Was all of this too emotional or too hectic for you, all these family members?

Yeah, I guess so.

It seems like it might be something more. Did I do something or say something?

No.

Did somebody say something to you?

In fact, Woodward did.

Woodward?

He's jealous.

Of what?

Of us.

What about us?

He says you still have feelings for me.

I do, Mosey, but I don't want to leave Woodward.

I know that but he doesn't. Waite, why did you call me? We haven't seen each other in twenty years. We've kept in touch but we haven't seen each other. We both have different lives now.

I know that, Mosey. But some people are just important. My mother, I think, loved me more after you left, not because she wanted you to leave but because she knew that your absence left such a hole in my life. She tried to fill that by getting me to find my own life through school. She got me out of my sorrow and inertia, and I discovered I could create a new life. She even got Woodward to go out with me and that was how we got together. You know, I'm sorry if Woodward is feeling insecure. That's his problem. Don't make it yours, Mosey. I love you pure and simple. But I'm not giving up my life with him for you or anyone else. He shouldn't have said what he did but don't let anything he said come between us. We're friends, Mosey. We have a past together. That is important to me and I won't let Woodward take that from me, from us. Okay? Do you hear me?

On the bus home, Mosey watched the fields, the forests, the towns, the cities, the seeming unending flatness of western Ohio and southern Michigan. He got out at the rest stops, listened to people. His seat mate for the last leg of the trip was an elderly white man who reminded Mosey of his co-worker, Julius Schmidt. They talked about their visits. The older man had been to Dayton but worked in Detroit. They talked about work; the older man, Frank Carella, worked at the Dodge Main automobile plant on the assembly line. He complained about the working conditions but he liked the money which, with his wife working, allowed them to own a house, two cars, and send three kids to college in Detroit. He asked Mosey about himself.

You married?

No.

How come a good looking fella like you ain't married?

Never was much interested in the ladies.

Not interested or never found the right gal?

Not interested and never looked for the right gal.

Is something wrong with you? I see you're missing your arm. Hell, some women don't care about that. Well, I guess I'm talking about white women. I don't know about black women. Is it your arm?

No.

What then?

I'm not interested in women because I like to have sex with men.

Men? Oh, Jesus. A faggot? Jesus. I don't get it. A nice looking, upright guy like you does what? Suck cock? Take it up the ass?

Sure and more.

You do that stuff? You're not shitting me?

Yes, I do. That's the truth.

Holy-motherfucking-mother-of-Jesus-Christ-god-almighty? Man, you are the first faggot I've ever met.

I doubt it.

Huh?

Gay men are everywhere. You just don't see them.

Oh, I've seen the swishy types but not one like you.

That's the point; there's a lot like me, black and white.

No, not white! Blacks, maybe, but not white.

Oh, yes. White too. I've had sex with them.

With white guys?

Of course.

You know, I think you must be putting me on. You're fucking with me. You're no faggot. You don't do that stuff.

What do you want me to do, prove it?

Oh, no, no, no! I ain't never done nothing like that and don't intend to.

So, what's so hard to believe?

You don't look the type.

But I am. There is no type. Men who like men come in all types; they even look like guys like you.

Come on, that's impossible.

Don't say something's impossible unless you know for sure.

That's so?

That's so.

Okay, if you do that stuff, what do you get out of it?

What do you get out of fucking your wife?

It makes me feel good. But we also made four kids, three in college and one still in high school.

Well, it makes me feel good too but, so far, I haven't made any kids.

But when men and women do it, they sometimes get together, like I did, to make a family. Can two guys or two gals get together and make a family?

I know gay people—that's what we call faggots now—who've done that.

But not you.

Not yet. Not yet. But I might some day.

Two faggots, I mean two gays, making a family?

Yes.

Jesus, Mary, and Joseph. The pope is probably crying himself to sleep.

I don't know about the pope and I don't care about the pope but gay people are living their lives, sometimes together just like you. Sometimes, they have kids even.

How?

The old-fashioned way and then raise them with their gay partners.

You mean fucking up kids minds like that?

Sometimes kids get fucked up just like in your families. Sometimes, kids grow up like any other kids.

I can't believe that.

You don't have to believe it but it's true. You say a thing is not true simply because you don't believe it.

You lost me there.

What's true is true even if we don't believe it's so.

And you believe that?

I didn't until I said it.

Holy fucking mackerel. A gay philosopher. You know what, Mosey. I'm glad we had this conversation. I never talked about this stuff; I've made jokes about fags, uh, gays, but I never really knew any of this stuff. I can't say that I believe it but you seem like a real straight guy. So that means something. Thanks.

That's the first time that I've been called straight.

Huh?

When Mosey returned to work on Monday morning, everything seemed to be in order. The floors were clean, as were the toilets. The trash had been emptied. Calvin did a good job. Calvin arrived in the afternoon, and Mosey gave him fifty dollars for covering for him. Calvin took the money and told Mosey that he now knew that could run the place all by himself.

At home that evening, Mosey had a letter from the city personnel department. He was being transferred the following Monday to the Institute of Arts as a guard. He called Lucius and when they finished cheering, he called Swee.

How did you know I wanted to talk to you?

What do you mean, Swee, I'm calling you with news?

But, I've got news. Olive Fleet Boston died, and I've got an official notice from her lawyer that she left me the money from the sale of her house.

That's great, Swee. What are you going to do with the money?

Gullley and I have a lot of bills. We've never had a vacation anywhere. There's lots that I can do with this money. Anyway, they held the funeral for Olive. All of the DeBobo were there; Trique and Lee attended the funeral too. That's the first time Lee has been to Pachacuti since she left.

Did William go with Trique?

Yes, he did. And, Lee brought her girlfriend, Brenda.

Girlfriend?

No, not like that; they're only best friends. People in Pachacuti were impressed that all of those folks from Los Angeles showed up for Olive's send off. They must have thought that Trique and Lee were some kind of movie stars. By the way, Alfred is going to move to Los Angeles. He's going to college, like his daddy, and maybe become a banker or something.

That's great.

What's your news?

I got the museum guard job. I start next Monday.

Oh, Baby, I'm so proud of you. Mosey, this is making something of your life. Now, all we have to do is get you a boyfriend. How about Lucille?

Lucius.

Lucius?

He's a liberated gay now. He's Lucius.

Well, okay. How about Lucius?

He's sweet but, really, we're only friends. Dear friends but not my heart's desire.

Well, we'll find the right one, Mosey. Don't grow old without someone, you hear me?

Swee?

Yes, Dear.

I never understood about Olive leaving you the money from her house. Why did she do that?

She did it because she felt real bad about my house.

But, it wasn't your house.

She didn't know that. Nobody but the Sellabie, Amity, and you knew that, and I told you to never tell anyone.

And I never did.

That house actually belonged to Olive's daddy, Murray Fleet. He bought it secretly from that black undertaker, James Morton, so everyone thought that it still belonged to Morton. He gave it to Olive's sister, Soonie, after she became pregnant with your mother, Loissey, but nobody knew because Soonie never lived there. Before she died, Soonie told the Sellabie to give it to Loissey, and Loissey gave it to me. I told everyone I rented it from Morton, and that's what Olive believed. So, Olive, in effect, gave me her own house as penance for her sister's house that her own dumb-fuck sons burned down. Now, if that isn't some kind of justice I don't know what is.

Listen, Baby, I got to go. Gulley and I are celebrating tonight with a Broadway show and dinner in a restaurant. Be good. I love you.

I love you too. Goodnight, Swee.

When Mosey awoke in the morning, his dream came to him. He was on the main street in Pachacuti. There was no one else. He turned and saw in the distance his mother waving to him. He waved back. He couldn't explain to himself that a sudden thought long buried in his memory that came to him—he wanted a new arm. Although it would be artificial, it would give him a sense of being whole again.

Whole again.

SWEET TEA SELLABIE

The lives in this story don't end with this history. All of the living characters are pursuing their lives quite energetically. However, the history that I want to record does end here in 1972. As I ponder what I have included in this story, I have become aware of some things that were not apparent until now. Men in my extended family feature prominently in this story: Mosey de Bobo, first and foremost, Trique Pendle, Waite Carvey, Hanton Sellabie, Dunn Pendle, and Phessin DeBobo. Male ancestors as well as male friends of these family members often dominate my narrative. I have wondered about this. Is it because the men are the main actors of history, the ones who move the story forward, or is it because I have perpetuated a male-gendered perspective? Certainly, women also play an important part in this story: I would, of course, include myself—Sweet Tea Sellabie, Martalee Boston Pendle, Xantha DeBobo Pendle, and Olive Fleet Boston. There are other women, as well, who play an important role in this story: Amity Lowe, Gulley Atkinson, May Easter Carvey, Soonie Fleet, Habboey DeBobo Gant, and, certainly, Loissey Sellabie DeBobo. However, have I treated the women as fairly as the men? Have I inadvertently given women a secondary role to men? I must admit that I think that I may be culpable in creating a history in which men's lives and decisions sideline those of women.

If I had decided to write an autobiography instead of a family history, I would have taken a female-gendered perspective. I would have focused more on women and our lives because our concerns, desires, and foibles are just as important to me. Mosey's, Trique's, and Dunn's stories would have been less important. But, then, such a story would not have been an accurate family history because I, Martalee, Xantha, and Olive did not set in motion the critical events. Even as I write this, I am nagged by realization that this is not true. The truth is that a white woman, Martalee Boston Pendle, by having sex with Trique Pendle, was the dynamite that blew up our families and homes. When the pieces fell back to earth, we were a different family set on paths to new homes—East, West, North, and South. Did her race and gender blind me to the agency of her actions? I must resign myself to the story that I've written in the way that it is written. I can't go back and start over again. The facts don't change although the perspective could. Maybe this is why history is written and rewritten as we learn more about our world and ourselves and we come closer to the truth.

As I finish this history, the war that killed Dunn continues. It seems that this country always has some kind of war—with other people and with its own people. The war at home has killed Malcolm, Martin, and Bobby. It has taken too many lives overseas and at home so needlessly and thoughtlessly. I cannot see a brighter future for the world. I often ask myself who is to blame for this? Is it the people in power—our president, our congress, our politicians? Is it corporate America that seems to buy the politicians? Is it the media that tells us half-truths or perpetuates outright lies about our country and the world? Is it us, blacks and whites, who often don't seem to be able to rise above our tribal instincts and work for the greater good? I ask these questions but I certainly don't have the answers. I do know that my family, which is such a tiny representative of the larger world, is probably as good as good can be. It is the hope that I see in my family that gives me encouragement about my world. All of us, Sellabie and DeBobo and Pendle and Boston, are doing the best we can and that has made some of us better folks and our small part of the world a better place.

215

BOOK TWO

PORTAL

OF

RETURN

I
SWEE

When I finished my story about family and history, I thought that I had recorded everything that I could in order to preserve for future generations what I knew. That was in 1972. It is now 2009 and there is more, much more, that I need to say. I was 61 in 1972; I am now 98 and I see the world and our families' histories a lot differently from the vantage point of my final years. I need to finish what I started before my time is up so that these histories are not only more complete but also clearer regarding what it means to be who we are in this country. So, I return to where I ended my story in Book One and continue from there. I have not changed anything in Book One because that book continues to stand as a document from the perspective of 1972. Although Book Two continues the story, it often reflects on and is informed by events from the first book and sometimes re-considers those events from this new perspective. The facts, as such, remain the same but the facts can be interpreted differently. This is what I've come to learn is how history becomes history.

While Book Two is about families already noted in this history, it is also about other families not related by blood or marriage but are chosen. Friends, colleagues, and acquaintances often assume a greater "familial" bond than actual blood and marriage folks. These chosen families have eased me through my final years.

II
FIRST DAYS

When Mosey awoke from sleep, he remembered his dream. It had been so vivid to him that his wakefulness was dull by comparison. His bedroom was silent and mostly dark although early light pressed through the edges of the shades on his window and gave a hint of impending morning. He guessed that it was about six; he would rise at seven—wash, shave, toilet—have a light breakfast and catch a bus at seven-thirty to his new job at the art museum. He wanted to think about what all of that would be like but another hour's sleep cancelled those thoughts until the alarm rang and he got out of bed.

At forty-three, Mosey was still fit and trim. Hardship kept him lean. Good and frequent sex made his body taut and his reflexes quick. As he sat on the side of his bed gently kneading his scrotal sac, he sketched a plan to celebrate his first day of work at his new job with a visit that night to his favorite joint where he was sure to find someone interested in his short arm. Most men, in Mosey's experience, ignored his missing left arm because they became so enamored with the one between his legs. To his constant puzzlement, many men found him attractive, white men too. When he looked at himself in the mirror, he couldn't see what they saw. He looked okay but he didn't find himself to be his idea of handsome. Trique was handsome. Waite was handsome. Even Red was handsome. Lucius was not handsome but Lucius had personality to spare. Mosey didn't think of himself as particularly handsome or personable but, then, why should he worry as long as other men desired him for whatever reason?

Mosey dressed in dark blue slacks and white shirt and a clip-on black tie. He had been told that he would be issued a guard's jacket at the museum. As he zipped his pants, he wondered what was ahead. He had been briefed on his duties by the municipal personnel office but his specific routine would be outlined for him by the head guard when he signed into the security office at the museum. His new job was a short bus ride on Woodward Avenue, the city's main and, intermittently, grand artery. Mosey's neighborhood was not grand at all although he lived near Grand Boulevard. The museum's district was the most elegant section of the city with its collection of classical buildings and the adjacent campus of Wayne State University. However, a poor black neighborhood pressed against this enclave of culture and education like a very shabby and mostly unwelcome guest. Over time, the museum and its dignified neighbors would systematically demolish the offending neighborhood to give the cultural district a cordon from the surrounding black city.

Mosey knew the area well because his first job as a janitor had been in an apartment building exactly three blocks from the art museum. The riots, that some now called a rebellion, took Mosey's place of employment and other buildings in an uncontrolled conflagration that effectively advanced the cultural center's plan to blot out the black neighborhood. Mosey also knew that the museum was really a white institution run by whites for whites in an increasingly black city. White as the museum was, it was, ironically, a department of the municipal government not a privately run operation. So, the hiring of the staff had to conform to the new color-blind regulations of the city's Civil Service. For this reason, and only this reason, Mosey had been hired as a new guard. He knew that he would never have had the chance otherwise—his good record as a city janitor at a neighborhood recreation center provided his only credential for this new job. With his meagre qualifications—a G.E.D. and work experience as a janitor and cook—he knew his good fortune. His bus ride on Woodward Avenue gave him time to think about what was ahead. He would be working in, possibly, the most revered building in the city. A sanctuary, really, a place that few black people ever visited not because they weren't welcome but because the place seemed so alien to black Detroit. White Detroit created and sustained the art museum. They knew what was inside and seemed to revere its contents, its symbolism, its sanctity. Mosey had never been inside the building despite the fact that, when he was a janitor, he worked and lived so close to it. But no one he knew ever mentioned the place, certainly never said they ever were inside of it. He realized that he had no idea of what the place was like and that began to make him a little nervous. He looked around the bus. There were only black people. He suddenly wondered what had happened to the white people who used to ride the bus? He glanced out of the window at vacant stores and boarded up buildings. Why hadn't he noticed this before? And the few people on the sidewalks were black. White people seemed to have disappeared from this part of town. That is, until Mosey reached his bus stop in front of the public library that stood in magnificent serenity across the wide avenue from the equally august art museum. These two buildings with all of the other structures that constituted the cultural district created a magical, gleaming white marble world so unlike the surrounding city with its shabby houses and apartments and decaying commercial strips. Mosey, who had never paid any attention to any of this before, felt that he was becoming conscious of his surroundings for the first time in his life. He was born in the little town of Pachacuti, Georgia. He had lived in Atlanta with Trique and in Cincinnati with Waite before moving to Detroit. And, although he had been in the city for over twenty years, he had never really noticed this place or any place. He had always paid attention to people, not places. His family, his boyfriends, his buddies were all that concerned him. Now, he saw, as if for the first time, the city in which he lived and where, in a few moments he would start a new adventure.

He had been told to use the employee entrance at the rear of the building. So, after leaving the bus and crossing Woodward Avenue, he walked along the side street bordering the grounds on the north side of the marble building. When he reached the nondescript rear entrance, he became very nervous. He was about to cross the threshold into an unknown world. Funny, in his nearly forty-plus years, he hadn't worried about what might be ahead of him. When he fled with Trique from Pachacuti—Trique had good reason to fear for his life but Mosey didn't; he only wanted to be with Trique—he never considered where they would end up or how they would survive as teenagers. At the time, they didn't even know where they were headed. Lucky for them, the freight train they hopped brought them to Atlanta. Trique, the outgoing one and the one who seemed to assess their situation accurately, asked a black rail-yard worker where the colored section of town was located. That was in 1945 and two colored boys, on the run, with no money and no family or friends in Atlanta were prime candidates for hardship or disaster. But Trique made some quick calculations. They would make their way east across town to Auburn Street, the colored heart of Atlanta, and survey their prospects. They were hungry, had no place to stay —no knowledge of Atlanta, its pitfalls or rewards—but certain knowledge that two black boys in an unfamiliar white world would have precious little time to organize and situate themselves. Trique took the lead, walking with determination and purpose but not so as to attract the attention of any white people, especially the police. They made their way through white Atlanta to Auburn where they began seeing people who looked like them. Satisfying their hunger was their first concern. They hadn't eaten in a day. Trique thought of asking for work in a little restaurant as a way of getting food and prospects for work. After trying a couple of places without success, they found Osgood's, a ramshackle hole-in-the-wall eatery run by Vereatha Osgood herself, an aging but agile mammy who was cook, waitress and janitor. And the place looked it. Vereatha recognized two desperate and hungry boys who seemed to be from a much better background than their circumstances suggested. In any case, she would never refuse anyone food. She made enough money to get by and didn't begrudge two boys a free meal. She had no family and no help. When she learned they were looking for work, she decided that she could use a couple of good-looking and healthy boys. She also took them, after the day's work, to her neighbor's house nearby because her neighbor had a spare room to rent. It would take almost all of the money they earned at Osgood's to pay the rent but they had a place to stay. And food and jobs. All that without a moment's forethought when they raced out of Pachacuti and caught that freight.

Mosey's reverie, as he passed through the security doors of the employee entrance, calmed him and took his mind off of whatever was ahead of him. A white museum guard behind a thick glass window asked him his business and Mosey handed him, through a slot in the glass, his employment papers.

Well, you're going to be a new guard, huh?

Yes, sir.

You want to go through those doors and turn right. Look for the office marked Paul Bosch, Head of Security. Give your papers to him.

Thank you.

And Mosey was buzzed into the inner sanctum of the museum. It wasn't what he expected. There was a concrete block wall hallway with fluorescent lighting and linoleum-covered floors. Doors lined the hallway with name tags on each of them. He knocked. A woman answered and told him to enter. Seated at a desk covered with file folders, a potted green leafy plant, little plastic figures, and a plate with two donuts was a smiling white woman who had already eaten a few too many of the donuts—she had a nameplate on her desk with name Patricia Szabo. Mosey didn't know how to pronounce her last name. Under the name was her title—Secretary.

Hello, I'm Mosey DeBobo, a new guard. The man at the door said to come here.

Well, hello, Mr. DeBobo. You're in the right place. We were expecting you. You transferred from Parks and Recreation. Right?

Yes.

How long were you there?

About two years.

Well, good. Now you'll talk with Mr. Bosch. But, first, you'll need to see the administrator and fill out employment forms. After that, you'll come back here and Mr. Bosch will explain your duties, give you a manual of rules and regulations, get your photo I.D. taken, and give you your assignment. Okay?

Yes. Thank you.

So, go out to the hallway and turn left and look for a door with Thurmore Pierce, Administrator, on it.

Mosey did as he was told, found the office, knocked, and was told to enter by another female voice. To his surprise, the woman inside was black. Alice Compton, as her desk nameplate identified her, was a young, trim, dark-skinned woman with a soft voice and sincere manner. Her desk was tidy with a small stack of papers and nothing else except framed photographs that Mosey could not see since they faced away from him.

Good morning, Ma'am. Missus, uh, Patricia down the hall . . .

Do you mean Mrs. Szabo?

Oh, yes. Szabo. Is that how you say it? I didn't know.

It's okay. You'll find a lot of names like that around here.

Mrs. Szabo said to come here and fill out employment forms. And that I should meet Mr. Pierce, the administrator.

Oh, yes. I'll get the forms for you. You can sit at that table and fill them out. Mr. Pierce is out of the office for a meeting with the director. He should be back by 10. Would you like a cup of coffee?

Yes, please.

With milk and sugar?

Yes. If you don't mind.

No problem.

Alice stepped into an adjacent room with filing cabinets. Mosey could hear her pouring coffee. She returned momentarily and placed a mug of coffee on the table where Mosey sat.

I put two sugars in your coffee. Is that okay?

Yes, thank you. I like lots of milk and sugar. That's how my people drank it in the South.

Is that where you're from?

Yes. Pachacuti, Georgia.

That must be a small town

It is. Is your family from the South?

Well, yes and no. Originally, yes, from Virginia on my mother's side. But my great-grandparents on my father's side, they were free Negroes in Massachusetts. My great-great grandmother escaped slavery to the North. One of her daughters met my grandfather here in Detroit. So, my family hasn't had much contact since then with the South. Do you still have family down south?

Yes. In Pachacuti still. My brother is the mayor.

Really? I didn't know that there were blacks in authority down there.

Well, yes. Things have changed.

I guess so. I see you lost your arm. Did that happen in the South?

No. Not really. It happened in Cincinnati when I lived there. I was working as a cook in a restaurant and another cook—he was the head cook—swung a meat cleaver at the owner. I tried to stop him but had my arm chopped off for the effort.

Oh, I'm sorry. That must have been awful.

Well, it certainly changed my life.

Why don't you finish filling out those forms? I have phone calls to make and Mr. Pierce should be here shortly.

Thank you, Mrs. Compton.

Miss Compton.

Oh, Miss Compton.

But call me Alice.

Mosey finished the forms and sat at the table while Alice Compton busied herself with phone calls and typing. Presently, the door to her office opened and a tall, black middle-aged man dashed in, saying nothing, then entered an inner office and shut the door. Alice looked at Mosey who had followed the man's sudden appearance and immediate disappearance.

That's Mr. Pierce, she said in a lowered voice. I'll tell him you're waiting for him and I'll give him your forms.

Alice knocked on Mr. Pierce's door and entered un-beckoned. She returned seconds later and gestured to Mosey to enter.

Mr. DeBobo, is it? Have a seat.

Yes. Mosey DeBobo.

Unusual name.

It's southern. Probably from Louisiana although my people are from Georgia.

Well, yes. All of that is very interesting. You're starting work here today, right?

Yes, sir.

Don't sir me. This isn't a plantation. You're a man like any other man here and you don't have to be second class to anyone here. Do you hear me?

Yes.

Mosey stared hard at Mr. Pierce. He was surprised that Pierce was a Negro. He had a mustache, graying temples, and a coldness and precision about him right down to his tweed jacket, crisp white shirt and knitted tie. He wore horn-rimmed glasses and didn't smile. But he looked at Mosey with a barely concealed curiosity. Something in that fleeting look reminded Mosey of men in the homosexual bars and joints. Mr. Pierce wore a gold wedding band. Mosey knew that didn't mean anything one way or the other. The husband of his sister, Habboey, had had sex with Mosey often and enthusiastically. So, being married, in Mosey's view, didn't preclude a man going down on another man. And, Mr. Pierce was attractive. But this was new and strange territory so he assumed that Pierce was simply giving him a routine once over.

So, Mosey, tell me something about you. Where have you worked and why do you want to work here?

I had been a cook until I lost my arm.

And, if you don't mind me asking, how did that happen?

I was working with a cook who drank and he got crazy one day and went after the owner with a meat cleaver. I tried to stop him and he accidentally hit me with the cleaver. I was pretty young then.

So, with one arm, I'm assuming, your job possibilities were limited.

Yes. And I hadn't finished high school then but I got a job as a janitor for an apartment building. Then I got a job as a janitor with the city. I finished my G.E.D. and applied for this job. That's how I got here. I want to improve my life and make myself more useful and better off.

You'll find that there are a lot of men like you working here. Not much education. Limited skills. But you'll need another quality and we'll see if you have that. Do you know what I'm talking about?

Not exactly.

I didn't think so. Listen. This museum contains great treasures. It's more important than a bank because a bank only has money and money can be replaced. The treasures here can never be replaced. They are all one of a kind. Your job here—and you have to understand this the first day —is to protect these treasures. That's it. Nothing else. You're not to be friends with the public. You're not here to party with the other employees. You are not here as decoration. You're a museum guard. And you will guard the museum's treasures or you won't be here long. Is that clear?

Yes.

Don't come to work late, drunk, high, or with any excuses why you can't do your job. Otherwise, you won't have a job. There are no second chances. You either perform your work as I've described it or you are out the door. And, by the way, don't get involved in any way with another employee here. We don't think that you can concentrate on your work if you are mixed up with someone else in this building. Now. I'm going to send you back to Paul Bosch's office. He's the head of security and he'll get you situated and assigned. That's all here.

And Pierce turned in his chair to attend to some papers. Mosey, realizing that Pierce was not going to say anything more, got up and left Pierce's office, closing the door quietly behind him.

Pierce had made things very clear to Mosey and Mosey liked that. It was all above board. Guard the treasures. Nothing else should or would get in the way of his job. Mosey knew that he could do that. He would find out from Bosch how to guard the treasures and he could focus on that exclusively. Nothing would distract him. He wanted this job and he would do it well. Nothing would interfere with that. Except. He found Pierce very attractive. In his adult life, he had never had such a strong feeling for another man without a seduction. And, he knew that Pierce was not trying to seduce him despite the look that he had given him. Pierce might be interested in men, and, maybe, even Mosey. But he didn't seem the kind of man who would go against the rules that he had so explicitly stated. No. Pierce wouldn't cross that line so Mosey could put Pierce out of his mind, focus on his work. Do his job and enjoy his good fortune.

When Mosey returned to Bosch's office, his secretary showed him in immediately.

Come in, Mr. DeBobo. Mosey, is it?

Yes. Mosey.

Call me Paul.

Okay.

Well, this is your first day with us and I hope that there will be many, many more. We have a good crew here. Thirty-five guards. You are number thirty-six. You've met the administrator, right?

Yes.

I'm sure he told you what the museum expects from its guards.

He did.

Well, Mr. Pierce can be a little harsh in his viewpoint but what he says is important. We love the things in this museum and we protect them. But those things are here for all people to enjoy and so we don't want to interfere with their experience. However, we do want to let people know when they are endangering the objects and you will learn when to be gentle and when to be forceful. You won't learn all of that today or even this week. You'll learn from the other guards, the curators, and from your experience with the public You'll get it. You seem like an intelligent fellow to me. You'll get it.

Bosch explained the details of the guard uniform, the need for professional appearance both as a symbol of the museum and as a figure of authority. The guards were the museum's police force; their presence had to be obvious, their jurisdiction unquestioned. To protect the treasures, no one, not the public nor the staff could interfere with the guards' duty.

Ah, there was one important exception and every guard had to know exactly how this applied: the curators who supervised the collections could and did intervene in the care of the treasures. They could touch, move, or otherwise make decisions about objects as long as they caused those objects no harm. If a curator came to remove an object, relocate it, or administer some treatment, the guard should know that the curator had ultimate authority. However, the guards had to know each curator and the objects under his supervision. So that, if a curator exercised authority over objects not under that curator's jurisdiction, a guard had the imperative to question or even stop any action. This was a delicate matter because two lines of authority crossed in a gray area. Ultimately, a higher authority might have to be involved—the chief of curators, the museum administrator, or even the director of the museum. In such a situation there was a bottom line— protect the treasures even if a guard crossed the limits of his authority. Mosey hoped that he could never be in such a situation but if he was, he knew that he would protect the treasures.

Mosey listened. He compared how Pierce, a black man, had treated him with Bosch, a white man, who spoke to him so kindly. It wasn't that he was surprised—plenty of white people had treated him with respect and plenty of black people had treated him badly. And vice versa. It was that, somehow, he expected Pierce to be more warm to him because Pierce had looked him over —however briefly and impersonally—with a knowing glance. Well. Enough of that.

Bosch continued. I want to introduce you to some of the other guards and take you on a tour of the museum to familiarize you with the layout and the things we really have to watch closely. But first, we'll take you to the guards' locker room and get you a jacket. Are you ready?

Yes, sir.

Paul. Call me Paul.

Yes, Paul.

Bosch escorted Mosey out of the office and into the corridor. After a series of turns they arrived at the locker room and Bosch retrieved a jacket from storage for Mosey.

We'll get a name tag for you later so that when you're on duty, people will know who you are.

When Mosey had put on the jacket, Bosch assigned him a locker and, then, they headed out again. Bosch explained that the floor that they were on was the street level ground floor. Below that was the basement with the storage rooms, work rooms for carpenters, and so forth including the building's boilers and utilities. The public was not allowed under any circumstances in the basement. At the street level ground floor, there were administrative offices and the guards' room, also closed to the public, and there were some galleries that were open to the public, and there was the lecture hall. The non-public areas were clearly marked and, with permission, authorized persons could enter these non-public areas. Bosch showed Mosey the other areas on the ground floor and pointed out the main means of entrance and exit as well as stairs to the other levels of the museum. Mosey had been interested in seeing the administrative areas of the museum, but when they entered the ground floor galleries, he was quite unprepared for what he saw. He couldn't even put a name to the kinds of things before his eyes.

Have you ever been here before, Mosey?

No. this is my first time.

This stuff is really something, isn't it?

I've never seen things like this.

Wait until we go upstairs to the main floor.

What are these things?

You know, I've been here fifteen years and I still don't know much about this stuff. You can ask the curators if they will take the time to tell you. Let me tell you something about that bunch. Now, some of them are nice—and you'll find out soon enough who they are—and some of them won't even see you unless they're pissed about something. All of them, though, think that their shit doesn't stink—if you'll pardon the expression. They are the kings and queens around here. Only the trustees rank higher than them but you won't see any trustees, normally. But if you do, treat them like royalty. Oh, and the director. He's a regular guy. You'll see him in the galleries. Do whatever he says. No questions.

What about the curators?

That's more complicated. We'll deal with that later. So, as I was saying, if you want to know about any of this stuff, ask a curator. They may or may not help you. Don't take it personally, Mosey, but we haven't had Negro guards here too long and, since all of the curators are white, they don't really expect much from you guys. Listen, I'm just giving it to you straight. Black, white, it doesn't make any difference to me. But these curators, I don't know what world they live in. It doesn't seem to be this one. So, they can be pretty high-handed with everybody. Hell, they even treat me like dirt, not that I'm anybody special. But I am the head of security and I make sure that everything and everyone in this building is safe.

Paul, can I ask you a question?

Sure, Mosey. Ask me.

Why is this stuff here? Where did it come from?

That's two questions but, okay. The second one first. These things come from all over the world. That's what the curators told me. And some of these things are thousands of years old. Thousands! I don't even know what that means but that makes them very important. So, now your first question: Why is this stuff here? Because these things are old, or valuable, or, I think, because the curators like them—who knows why? They are here for safe-keeping and to let people see them, to see things right before their eyes that they probably would never ever see otherwise. Look, Mosey. You've never been here before; you've probably never even seen these things before, and you are amazed already and you haven't seen hardly anything yet. That's what it's about: people come here; they see this stuff that they've never seen before and they are amazed. Really. I see it all the time—little kids, teenagers who don't seem to care about anything, and adults—they all find something here that amazes them.

How did these things get here?

I think a lot of it was donated, that means someone gave it to the museum. Some of it was purchased. That's what the curators do. They get this stuff, one way or another and put it in the galleries. They are always going somewhere and talking to people to buy things or to convince them to give things. Sometimes, the curators bring guests into the museum—sometimes when we are not open to the public—to show them things to convince them that whatever they might give or buy will fit in somehow. I've seen it a lot. Most of the curators are good at it. You'll see. Am I making any sense to you?

Yes, Paul. I'm getting an idea of it. You're being very helpful. Thank you.

Okay. Let's go up to the main floor. Oh, let me introduce you to some of the guards first.

After the introductions, Bosch and Mosey went to the main floor of the museum. As Mosey climbed the stairs to the lobby, he felt he was entering another world, this one was unlike the ground floor and unlike anything he had ever seen in his life. He couldn't quite focus on what made this ascent to the main floor so overwhelming but he saw that the space was vast with high ceilings, higher than anything he had ever seen. It was like a gymnasium at the recreation center where he had worked, or a train station. But more beautiful and quiet, filled with light flooding through the immense windows. There was a stone floor, not wood. Colors, huge doorways, gigantic chandeliers. It was grand. It somehow meant wealth and some kind of power. This was how he imagined rich people lived. This was a rich person's building. And then it struck him that the treasures in the museum came from rich people. This was where they kept their things. And he was here to protect their wealth.

Mosey, this is the main entrance on Woodward Avenue. There is always a guard here to watch people coming and going and to shut the entrance in any kind of emergency. The fellow there is Earl Gladney. Hey, Earl, this is the new guy, Mosey DeBobo.

Pleased to meet you.

Same here.

Earl, I'm showing Mosey around to give him a feel for the place.

See you around, Mosey.

Yeah, okay.

All right now. Up these stairs we enter the Great Hall. This is where they keep the armor. Pretty impressive, right?

I don't know what to say. I've never seen anything like this. This room is so big. It's just a big room.

I know. I guess they just wanted to impress people and it works. It really works but you ain't seen nothing yet. Come on, straight ahead to the next room. I'll bet you've never seen anything like this either. This is what we call the Rivera Court. A Mexican artist named Diego Rivera came here during the Depression at Mr. Edsel Ford's expense—he was the son of Henry Ford; you'll be hearing a lot about the Fords around here. Anyway, Edsel Ford was chairman of our board of trustees at the time and he hired Rivera to paint all of the walls in this room from floor to ceiling. The paintings are all about the automobile industry in Detroit. Hey, that's our bread and butter here—why shouldn't it be right here in the museum? The factories, the workers, all of it in glorious color. What do you think?

Mosey didn't know what to think. He couldn't begin to make sense of what he saw. Sure, there were scenes in factories, with big machines and conveyor belts and lots of workers. But there were also big naked women lounging at the top of the walls and airplanes, and fire and smoke and—it was overwhelming.

You said a Mexican painted this?

Yes. Rivera.

Why a Mexican?

He was real famous at the time. Worked fast. People love this room They see themselves here. This is what this city is about. If there wasn't any automobile industry, there wouldn't be any Detroit. This is why we have over a million people here. People making good money. All kinds of people. White, black, yellow, brown. All kinds, all working together for Ford and all the rest of them—General Motors, Chrysler. There used to be more, like Packard, but they're gone now.

Hell, the auto companies employ more American people and make more money than any other industry in this country. That's why there is so much money in this city, why people have such good jobs, and why this museum has all these treasures. It's automobile money that made this place and keeps it going. That's why you and I have jobs. See. Rivera put all of that here, right here in this museum for everybody to see. And people come from all over the world to see the Rivera Court. You'll see. Let's go in the next gallery here. I'll introduce you to a guy who's been around here a few years. You'll stay with him today to get a feel for things. I have to go to a meeting but if you have any questions, come see me. This here is Swayne Pitken. Swayne, keep an eye on him. Show him how we do things and, Mosey, I'll come back for you at the end of the day.

Sure, Paul. See you later.

Bye, Mosey.

Bye, Paul.

Mosey is it?

Yeah.

What kind of name is that?

What do you mean?

I've never heard that name before. Were you named after somebody?

Nobody that I know

Mosey. Is that like Moses?

I don't know. I never thought about it. Nobody in my family ever talked about it. It's just a name.

No. Really. Names have meaning.

Oh? What does your name mean?

Swayne? It's a funny spelling like Wayne with an "s" in front of it. But it's pronounced Swain. In olden times, a swain was a young man or servant. So, I'm a young man and I'm a servant of this museum.

And your folks knew when you were born that you would work for the museum?

Of course not. But my family always has worked for other people. We're natural servants. So, tell me about you.

I was born in Georgia. I came to Detroit a little over twenty years ago and I worked as a janitor at a city recreation center before I came here. That's about it.

I'll bet there's more than that but that'll do for now. Believe it or not, I went to college here just a few blocks away and got a degree in Romance Languages.

What's that?

Ah, you know—French, Italian, Spanish.

You can speak those languages?

Yes. Pretty well but I want to continue with courses in graduate school. Languages come easy to me perhaps because my parents came from Europe and speak several languages at home. I'm a first generation American. I'm working here to save money. I figure that . . . wait a minute. Madam. Excuse me, but don't touch the sculptures. You can harm them. See, Mosey, you've got to keep an eye on people all the time. I mean after a while you almost sense when someone is going to do something they shouldn't. Most of the time they aren't thinking—it's not like they intend to damage something but they just want to touch things like they do everywhere else. But here, they can't. So, you explain the rules to them and usually they cooperate.

And if they don't?

You go tough. Escort them to the exit. Threaten to call the police. As long as I've been here—and that's been three years—that hasn't happened. But it could and you have to be ready for that. Uh oh. Look up. Here comes a curator. He's one of the good ones, Vincent Kinneally. Good morning, Dr. Kinneally.

Good morning, Swayne. Is that a new man with you? I've never seen him before.

This is Mosey DeBobo; this is his first day.

Hello, Mr. DeBobo. I hope that you'll like our little family here. You look like one of the sculptures in this room with your missing arm. Anyway, carry on, gentlemen.

Kinneally is the curator of these galleries, the Ancient art collection—you know Egyptian, Greek, and Roman and the earlier civilizations.

Can I tell you that I don't know anything about what you're talking about? Egyptian, Greek, Roman. I don't know what that is.

Hey, in a little while, you'll know that and a whole lot more. Wait and see. Anyway, Kinneally is really a good guy. He's friendly with the guards. He explains things to you. He tells you what to look out for. Now, the ones you want to avoid are Gale King and Isador Waas. King is curator of Contemporary art and Waas is his assistant.

"His" assistant? Isn't Gail a woman's name?

Ah, what was I saying about the meaning of names. It's G-A-L-E not G-A-I-L. And he's a pretty stormy character. Waas is his assistant and he is best avoided, if possible. He behaves very friendly but look out. It's hard to know what his game is but he has caused a lot of people around here a lot of problems.

Why do they keep him then?

That's a mystery and I don't know the answer. Take my advice, when you see him coming, find something to do so you don't have to talk to him. And if you are assigned to the Contemporary art collection, make yourself invisible when he's around. Hey, it's break time. My relief will be here in a minute. Here he comes. Henry Bibb, this is Mosey DeBobo, the new guy.

Nice to meet you, Mosey.

Same here, Henry.

Henry, we'll be back in fifteen minutes but if I take a little longer to show Mosey a few things, is that okay?

Sure, but no more than twenty minutes. I've got to relieve the guy in the American Wing.

We'll be back for sure. Come with me, Mosey. So, are you married?

No.

Neither am I.

Where do you live?

Near Woodward and Grand Boulevard.

I live on the far east side. Yeah. Me and my dog, Wolf.

What kind of dog?

She's a cocker spaniel. I don't know much about dogs. She's a little dog, black with long hair. Really sweet. When they're pups, they cut their tails off, you know.

Why do they do that?

I don't know. I think it has something to do with the way they look. It doesn't really make any sense but that's the way she was when I got her.

You say that names are important. Why did you call her Wolf?

That's funny. You know what? I never really thought about it. When I got her, she was so tiny and kind of helpless. I called her Wolf maybe to make her strong, and she is now. So, Mosey, we're on the ground floor now. This is the lecture hall. They use this for concerts sometimes.

Let's go over here to the other side. This is the Kresge Court. At one time all of this was open to the sky before they put the skylight over it. They say that this courtyard is a copy of one in Italy. It's beautiful, isn't it?

It's big.

I think that this museum is unlike any place else in this city. I love to come here to work everyday. I feel like I'm in a magical place. Do you see what I mean?

A little bit. I don't really understand this place.

Mosey and Swayne continued walking through the museum to the guards' room where they had a coffee. Then Swayne took Mosey upstairs again to the main floor.

We don't have much time so I'll just take you through the European Wing back to my station in the Ancient galleries. All of these rooms have art from Italy, France, and Spain mainly. There are lots of paintings. And this room, they say, came from a French chateau.

What's a "chateau"?

That's some kind of French house in the country, I think. I've never been to Europe. I only know what I learned from my parents, college, and what the curators tell me. Let's turn here, and now here we are back in the Ancient art galleries.

Thanks, Henry. We made it back in time.

Sure. See you guys later.

Swayne, with Mosey, made the rounds of the Ancient galleries. He pointed out some of the important objects and reminded Mosey that people are not to touch anything although they constantly did.

Swayne continued his instruction. More important than touching, however, is vandalism. Although rare, it did happen and, when it did the curators were furious. The guards are always blamed, not the vandals, who seldom are caught. Vandalism is a quick way for a guard to lose his job. So, guards have to be detectives and anticipate who might be a vandal before they act. Sometimes a trouble-maker is obvious by his appearance or behavior. You keep an eye on them; let them know that they're being watched. It's the ones who aren't obvious—sometimes, kids who act on impulse; sometimes adults who a guard had to spot the moment they made an unusual move—who can harm the art. Fortunately, vandalism is rare. Nevertheless, no guard can relax in his vigilance. That is the essence of the job.

For the remainder of his first day at the museum, Mosey stayed with Swayne. From him he learned a lot more about the museum and guard duties. Towards the end of his shift, when the museum's galleries closed to the public, Bosch returned and escorted Mosey to his office. He asked if Mosey had any questions about his job or the museum; he made sure that he understood the basics of his work; then he gave Mosey a handbook with a list of all museum employees and their titles as well as all rules and regulations for guards. He showed Mosey a bulletin board with photographs of all the employees and, in particular, pointed out the director, assistant director, curators, and department heads. He strongly urged Mosey to familiarize himself with the upper administrative staff in case any of these people came through the gallery where he was stationed. When Bosch finished his briefing, he informed Mosey that he would be stationed in the Dutch and Flemish art galleries of the new wing on the following day and he should arrive promptly at work at 8 am. for any news or changes in assignment prior to the opening of the museum to the public. When Mosey left the museum, via the employee entrance, and headed to Woodward Avenue to catch a bus home, he felt myriad emotions. He was happy that the day had gone smoothly, nearly everyone was friendly and helpful. They seemed to accept him, in fact, welcome him. On the other hand, although being a guard was not demanding or strenuous — nothing like the kind of work he had done all of his life — the fact that something could go terribly wrong, virtually without warning, left him uneasy. And, then, too, those comments about curators — how could he avoid getting into trouble with one of them?

At his apartment, Mosey opened his mail — a few bills — changed clothes, and sat. He stared out of his small living room window — not at anything in particular — but just to provide himself a focus. Everything that had happened that day replayed in his mind. When his phone rang, he refocused on his room and picked up the receiver.

Hello.

Hey, Baby, it's Lucius. Well, Mr. Museum Guard, Mr. Lucius wants to hear everything. How about we go to Maude's for some barbecued ribs and then to Ace for drinks and good time?

Sounds good to me. What time?

Let's get to Maude's early, at 6:30, so we can get a good table. Is that all right with you, Honey?

I'll be there.

Maude's was a short distance from Mosey's apartment, and he decided to walk there. The sun was lowering in the sky casting long shadows across the street. Mosey fastened his jacket against the chill he felt as the temperature dropped. There was a lot of car traffic but few people walking. Papers littered the path. Mosey noticed that several storefronts were empty. They had never re-opened after the rebellion of 1967. In fact, in Mosey's neighborhood, there were fewer and fewer shops and services. He had to travel longer distances on the bus downtown and further uptown to find a clothing store or a cleaners or even a grocery store. Well, it was part of life in the city. When he reached Maude's, he found a table near the back by the entrance to the kitchen. Since he was a regular at Maude's, the waitress, Murleen, didn't rush over to him immediately. Instead, she told him that she would take his order shortly. He let her know that he was waiting for Lucius, another regular. Mosey glanced around the place. It wasn't yet busy, only a few customers. The metal tables with their metal chairs were bare. After they ordered, Murleen would bring a sheet of white butcher paper to cover the table top, and then silverware, a bottle of hot sauce, and a bottle of barbecue sauce, and glasses of ice water. For now, Mosey sat.

Mr. Mosey, Baby, Lucius has arrived. How's my favorite nigger?

Hey, Lucius. Am I your favorite nigger?

You know you are, you sweet thing. Let me come over there and give you a big kiss. Oops. I guess I can't do that here. Later, at the Ace of Spades.

Mosey noticed, for the first time, that Lucius had gained weight. He also seemed tired despite his gay mood.

Honey, I want to hear the whole story; don't leave out a detail. But, first, let's get . . . who's working tonight? . . . oh, Murleen. Murleen, darling, could you take our order?

I'll be there in a minute.

What could she be doing that's more important than us? Murleen, Honey, were starving and we want to get out here before the riff-raff arrive.

Okay, Lucius. I'm coming now. Now, Here's your water, silverware, napkins, menus. Let me put the paper down first. I'll be back with the sauces.

What are you having, Baby?

A slab of ribs, a side of greens and macaroni and cheese. And cornbread.

Boy, those folks at the museum must have worked your narrow ass off today.

No. I just feel like celebrating.

Well, okay, Mr. Mosey. I feel like fried chicken tonight—and, no, not that kind of chicken—with smothered cabbage and fried corn. I'll go tell her. What do you want to drink?

A beer.

Okay, Honey, Mr. Lucius will be back in a minute and I want you to start your story.

When Lucius returned, Mosey told him about meeting Pierce and Mosey's feeling that Pierce was giving him the once over. He also described his talks with Bosch and Swayne.

It's a big place, Lucius. There's a lot there and it's full of things, all kinds of things. I don't even know what I'm looking at but I know that they think these things are valuable and important and I have to make sure that nobody touches them or damages them. If something gets broken, I'm out of a job and I'll tell you, I don't want to go back to janitor work. I like this job. I only have to watch things and people and keep to myself. I can do that. Hell, I want to keep this job until I can retire. This is my chance, Lucius, to make it on my own. It's a good job, a city job like you have with the buses. For me, this is as good as it gets. I'm gonna do a good job, be a good guard, and retire.

Does that mean that you can settle down with some good man, like me, and raise a family?

Lucius, you know you're my man. You're my friend.

And your piece of ass.

That too, but I'm not going to live with anybody again. I've done that.

Yes, when you were a kid. Now, you're getting on, Mosey. You're going to need somebody in your life.

You're in my life.

But I might find Mr. Right and Mr. Lucius won't be available for you whenever you think you might have time for him. This might be our last opportunity, Mr. Mosey.

Come on, Lucius. Don't go getting all serious on me. This is my night to celebrate.

I've told you before and I'm telling you now this prize will not be available much longer. In fact, I have some news for you. You're not the only person starting a new life. I've met someone quite wonderful. Not as wonderful as you, Mr. Ten Inches, but wonderful nonetheless. He's young and little silly, but he's sweet and he satisfies Mr. Lucius.

Their meals arrived. They ate in silence. When they both had finished, Lucius said: Let's pay the bill and go to the Ace so I can tell you more about Mr. Wonderful.

The Ace of Spades was a bar for gay black men that was patronized by a few gay white men who liked sex with black men. There were only black men present when Mosey and Lucius arrived. The bar was dim, as usual, and smokey. After taking a table and ordering beers, Lucius returned to his description of his new boyfriend.

His name is Leon.

Leon?

Yes. Leon Ross. He's twenty-two.

He's a child, Lucius.

Age of consent, my Dear. He's legal and he's mine. He's finishing college. Imagine, me with a college boy. And he's smart. He's not a man like Mr. Mosey, but he's good in bed and he's talking about living with me.

I guess that's what you want.

Mosey, that's what you said you wanted at one time.

I know and maybe, someday, I'll want that again. But not right now.

Mosey, that's why I decided to move on. It was silly for me to hope that you might want me someday.

Lucius, I was always honest with you.

I know. I was a dumb queen then but I'm rising up now. Some men, like you, once they've been disappointed or had their hearts broken, can never get over it. They can't see that their life is ahead of them not behind them. Everyone from your past—Trique, Waite, Red—is in your past, not your future. You can see a future in your work but not in your love life. What is that, Mosey? Why can you move forward and take a chance on a new job, take a risk, learn new things, open yourself up to new possibilities, adventures, experiences, and in your love life just sit down because you can't have what you once had? And you were, what?, sixteen? Red loved you, wanted you and you wouldn't even give him a chance with all of that bullshit about white and black, and you're as high yellow as anybody, from folks who, for generations, have been white and black. I realize right now, Mosey, that you're not going to change. You can't change. You're out in the world but closed up inside yourself. I really feel sorry for you and I feel sorry that on the night of your first day at your new job I am finally cutting you loose in my mind. But I've got to move on. I'm stuck in a dead-end job driving a bus but my real life is inside me and I want someone, maybe Leon, to share it with me. You'll be my friend, Mosey, but you won't spend another minute in my fantasies.

Lucius, you know my story so I don't have anything more to say about that, and I don't think I'm responsible for your feelings. I never tried to be anything to you but a friend. You're right about me living in the past but I know, and I've told you, that I can't go back to what once was. I'm not even trying. I just haven't found anyone who can be part of a future. It's not about Trique, Waite, you, or Red or anyone. It's just that I am who I am. I sometimes get interested in someone—Pierce, today, really got me going—but that's just a crazy fantasy. I think that if the right guy came along, I would change. I would want a life with him.

"If" and "would," Mosey. You're just going to wait? What are you doing about it like when you finished your G.E.D. and got this new job?

What should I do, Lucius?

Come on, Man. Get out there. Look for something more than sex. Look for that man who could be in your life. Don't just wait for him to find you. Get busy. Open up, Mosey. You're not always going to attract men like you always have. Those days may be coming to an end. Let somebody know that you want them.

Can I buy you a last beer? I need to go home and get some sleep so I can be on top of things tomorrow at work.

Mosey, You always want to end this discussion. Fine. I've had enough beer. I've got an early start tomorrow too. This is the last time I'm bringing up this subject so we can say good night. I know that you are going to be the most famous guard the museum has ever had. Who knows. Someday, you may be director.

Yeah. A black, one-armed director with no education and no training.

But who is drop-dead gorgeous, Honey.

Mosey looked around the galleries. He was assigned a section with four rooms for him to patrol. Bosch told him to move from room to room periodically so that he could keep track of everyone in the section. Actually, there was no one in the area, only another guard who patrolled the remaining rooms on the floor. There were mostly paintings in these rooms, dark, strange paintings, Mosey thought. One that caught his attention showed some kind of cemetery under dark trees and a stormy sky. He looked at the tag beside the painting but he couldn't pronounce the name of the artist. Mosey was startled to realize that a group of people had come into the room while he was looking at the painting. He stepped aside and repositioned himself at the entrance. A woman advanced ahead of the group and walked over to a painting. The group formed a semi-circle facing her and the painting.

Now, Ladies and Gentlemen, we've come to the Flemish and Dutch galleries. In this room, we can see three masterpieces from the fifteenth to seventeenth centuries. The earliest, behind you, is the *St. Jerome in his Study* by the fifteenth-century Flemish master, Jan van Eyck. His greatest painting, in the town of Ghent, in present day Belgium, is the *Ghent Altarpiece*. Some of you may have seen it. Here, on your left, is *The Jewish Cemetery* by the seventeenth-century Dutch master, Jacob van Ruisdael. In front of you is the painting I want to discuss; this is one of the rarest paintings in this museum. It is *The Wedding Dance* by the sixteenth-century Flemish artist, Pieter Brueghel. Most of Brueghel's paintings are in a museum in Vienna. Only a couple of his paintings are in this country and our museum has this one.

Mosey listened carefully even while he kept an eye on the group as well as other people who began to come and go in the galleries. He circulated through the other rooms just to check that nothing was amiss. When he returned to the entrance of the room with the group, he heard the woman continue her discussion.

So, Brueghel often painted scenes showing the life of the common people in sixteenth-century Flanders. Several of his paintings concern weddings and others show dancing. This one is called *The Wedding Dance* because many of the guests at the wedding have joined in a vigorous and, frankly, sensual dance. We can tell that this is a wedding celebration because the banquet table is here in the right background. The bride was seated in front of the draped cloth with a paper crown attached; this marks her special place at the table. You'll notice that she is not seated there now. In fact, she is dancing but I'll bet you can't guess which one of the women she is.

Mosey quickly scanned the painting to see if he could find the bride. He surprised himself that he was even interested in the game. Nothing in his whole experience up to this point had put him in such a frame of mind—he was curious.

One of the reasons that we, today, have difficulty identifying the bride is because, in our culture, brides wear white. Well, in sixteenth-century Flanders, the bride wore black. So, this woman near the center of the group of dancers in the front is the bride. Now, we can't be sure that she is dancing with her husband; maybe her companion is a family member. You have undoubtedly noticed that most of the men seem to be sexually excited by the dancing. Part of the explanation of the prominent protrusions in their groins is simply a matter of costume. Many men during that time wore trousers that laced in the front—there were no zippers in the sixteenth century—so they wore a piece of cloth over the front of the laced area for modesty. In time, however, this piece of cloth was used as a kind of purse. It grew in size to a pouch. This bulging cloth was called a codpiece and that is what you see in the painting, of course. Brueghel has exaggerated the codpiece so that it looks like an erection and that, we think, hints at his deeper meaning of this painting. You'll notice in the far background of the painting several couples making love in the open fields. Their love-making, the sensual dance, the wedding celebration all create the idea that this painting is about procreation, about the perpetuation of the family and the preservation of the community of mankind.

Mosey listened to this explanation and when the group had left the gallery, he went over to *The Wedding Dance* and looked closely at the things that the woman with the group had mentioned. He had been staring at the painting for a few moments when he heard more people entering the room. So, he turned away from it and resumed his surveillance and patrol of his section.

Swayne, a group came into my gallery today with a woman who talked about the paintings.

Yeah, she must have been a docent.

A what?

A docent. Was she dressed real nice and looked like a rich lady?

I guess so.

She was a docent. They're volunteers who learn about all of these things in the museum and they give tours to groups.

She wasn't a curator?

Naw. The curators don't usually give tours unless they're showing some rich or important person around. You won't see the curators doing that touring stuff. Just showing off. That's all.

So, how did this woman know all of those things?

The docents take classes, and the curators in the education department train them to give tours. Someday, you'll see one of the training classes in the galleries. Those docents can be a real pain in the ass, by the way, because they act like they own this place. Most of them live in the suburbs, like Grosse Pointe and Bloomfield Hills. They're all well-to-do. Some are real snotty. But you're a guard; you can tell them what to do or not do if they are violating the rules. Be tough with them or they'll run right over you.

This woman seemed to know a lot.

She probably did. Some of them are real smart. Some work really hard and give good tours. You can learn a lot from them. Listen to their talks; it's a good thing. But don't forget to keep your eyes on what's going on around you; don't ever forget your job.

Mosey had never thought about a painting; he had never really looked at a painting before. And, now during his hours in the Flemish and Dutch galleries, he returned to *The Wedding Dance* again and again when no one was around. He looked at the dancing couples, the enormous codpieces on the men and found that he was aroused by the phallic shapes. He stared at the bride —she was so homely. He noticed musicians to one side, one playing what looked like a leather sack with a horn attached which the musician was blowing. There was a man at the edge of the crowd who was watching with an expression of amusement. Mosey thought about the things the docent said. He had difficulty understanding how this painting could mean so many things if what she said was true. But, there he was, looking at a painting and thinking about it. He looked at some of the other paintings and could see nothing but people, buildings, trees, and other objects. He couldn't see anything but what he saw. How did that docent see those things that weren't there? How did she do that?

On his way out of the building after the museum had closed to the public, Mosey encountered Thurmore Pierce.

Well, DeBobo, how is it going with you?

Just fine, thank you.

I'm getting good reports so far that you're punctual, attentive to your duties, and learning fast. That's good. But remember, you fall down on your job and you're out of here. Good day.

Mosey watched Pierce as he exited the building and headed to his car which was parked in a reserved spot.

Excuse me. (The remark was addressed to Mosey.) You're blocking the doorway. God, these people are so inconsiderate. Why are they hired here? Do you see, he only has one arm. We're hiring the lame and the halt. What's next, the blind? Two men brushed past Mosey and exited. Mosey turned to the guard at the exit. Who was that?

Curator of Contemporary art, Gale King, with his assistant, Isador Waas. It was Waas who was talking. If I were you, I wouldn't get in his way again. Really nasty guy and his assistant can be even nastier. Watch it.

Oh, Good evening, Dr. Vilbliss.

Good evening, Eustis. Do we have a new guard here?

Yes, sir. This is Mosey DeBobo. He's new. Been here a couple of days.

Mosey, I'm Harry Vilbliss, the director. I'm glad to have you on our team. I'll bet there is a story about your arm. Come by my office any time so that I can get to know you. See my secretary for an appointment. Good evening.

When Vilbliss had left, Mosey followed him out of the building. Vilbliss headed to his car which also had a reserved spot, and left the parking lot. Mosey headed to his bus. Now, he had met the director who seemed to be nice and the curator of Contemporary art and his assistant who were mean. He had been warned and now his first contact with King and Waas was negative. But, perhaps, King wouldn't remember him. Forget that. How many one-armed Negro guards were there in the museum? One, exactly. No, King would remember him. Shit. That night Mosey went to the Ace for drinks. He was on the lookout for someone who might want to have sex. To his complete surprise, Red entered the bar. He spotted Mosey and came over to him. Mosey invited him to sit at his table.

When did you start coming here?

This is my first time. Do you come here often?

Yes, I don't live far from here now. I have my own place and a new job.

Good for you. What's the job?

I'm a guard at the art museum.

Really? How did you pull that off?

I applied for it after I got my G.E.D. and they called me in. I started this week.

Good for you, Mosey. Good luck.

How are you, Steven?

I'm doing okay. I've moved to the suburbs. Southfield.

Southfield. That's a long way from here.

It's a quick trip by freeway.

But why come all the way back here?

You know why; I like black men.

Why, exactly, is that?

What do you mean?

I mean what's with you and black guys? Dick is dick, black or white.

That's a funny thing coming from you since you've always made such a big deal out of how different blacks and whites are. Now you say it doesn't matter?

It matters for people but not for dicks.

Mosey, dicks are attached to people, in case you haven't noticed. Your dick belongs to a black man and it's the black man I like, not just his dick.

Or stump.

Oh, I remember your stump. I'll never forget that.

Tell me, what's it about black men that you like?

I like their personalities. There's something different about them from white guys. I like their bodies which are also different—different shapes, skin textures, and color. I love the color, the hair, the attitude. Black men are special to me. I've never been with a white guy who turned me on like a black guy. Does that answer your question?

I guess. So you liked me just because I was black?

I knew you would say that. You know, Mosey, you can't accept that I like you, really like you because you're Mosey. Of course, your being black is what attracted me to you but I got to know you as a person, not just my fantasy or fetish. You can't get that, can you?

No, I can't. When you met me, I was a one-armed, uneducated janitor living in a basement room with no prospects, no nothing.

Sure that was you but that wasn't all there was about you. Mosey, you're a sexy man—you know guys are attracted to you—and handsome, really handsome. I would say that you're beautiful. Really. You don't look like other men, especially other black men. You stand out. But all that is just appearances. Nice, sure, but it's the hook. What I really like about you is your personality. Mosey, you're strong, really strong but not in an obvious way. A person has to know you to see how strong you are. You're tough too. No one pushes you around or tells you what to do. But I think that the thing that is most attractive about you is that you're tender. You try to hide that but I've felt it and that is something I've seldom experienced with another man. Don't get me wrong when I say this but you're tender like a woman and I think that all of those women in your family that you told me about, taught you to be tender and gentle. You may not want to seem that way— and you act like you aren't most of the time— but it's there, inside of you, Mosey.

Mosey was quiet for a long time. He took a swallow of beer.

Steven, I told you I live near here. Do you want to see my place?

Do you mean do I want to go to bed with you tonight?

Yeah.

Mosey, I wished this had happened before but not now. I had made up my mind to forget you. I'm not ready to change now. Maybe if we see each other again soon and you still feel the same way, then we could try it.

You're mad at me?

Not mad, exactly. Just cautious. You pushed me out of your life and I had to accept that. I'm not ready tonight to forget all of that for sex. Although the idea of it really gets to me. Right now just thinking about you naked in bed with your stiff cock standing straight up, I could give in and, then, regret that I did. Oh, shit. Fuck. Damn. I can't resist you. Let's go. I can't turn you down no matter how I might feel later.

Mosey turned on the light in his living room. The sparsely furnished room had the barest necessities.

It's not much. Not your place where you used to live.

It's a start. You don't need a lot of stuff.

Yeah. That's right. It's just me here. Nobody else has seen this place, not even Lucius.

I'm the first?

Yup. You want something to drink?

No, I had enough at the Ace.

So, the bedroom is this way. At least I have a real bed.

I see. Hey, where's the bathroom? I've gotta go first.

Next door down.

While Steven used the toilet, Mosey undressed, pulled back the covers and sat on the side of the bed. He heard the toilet flush and Steven came into the bedroom and started to undress.

Mosey watched him. It was as if he was seeing Steven for the first time. His skin was very pale, almost colorless. His red hair seemed out of place against such pale flesh.

Hey, how come your dick hair isn't red too?

I don't know. It's always been brown.

Is that just you or all redheads?

I've never been undressed with another redhead. I could ask you why your cock hair is a lighter brown than your head hair.

I never thought about it. Nobody ever asked before.

Mosey, you still have a good body. I remember how you didn't seem to have any fat on you. Lean and trim, with those hard muscles under your skin. I know I've put on a little weight. I don't have any muscles. Just freckled white skin.

You look okay. Kind of soft looking but nice.

Steven went over to the bed, sat beside Mosey, and put his arm around him. He leaned over and kissed Mosey on the neck, then on the cheek, then on the mouth as he felt for Mosey's stiffening cock with his other hand. Mosey lay back on the bed and Steven shifted position to kiss Mosey's chest, then belly, then erect cock. As the cock slipped into Steven's mouth, Mosey thrust up causing Steven to gag.

Hey, Man, I'm sorry. You got me going there.

Steven resumed to work on Mosey's cock. He then stood, pulled Mosey to his feet, turned his back to Mosey, bent over feeling behind him for Mosey's cock and guided it to his anus. Mosey braced his legs, held onto Steven's hip and slowly thrust his cock into Steven's ass. He rhythmically slid in and out, thrusting deeper and pulling out completely. Steven stood up, pulled away from Mosey, turned and led him to the bed where Steven lay on his back, legs spread and bent at the knees, inviting Mosey to straddle him and begin thrusting again. Mosey quickly came with a suppressed groan, pulled out and lay on his back. Steven sat up, leaned over Mosey, took his cock in his mouth again and began masturbating himself. When he felt himself coming, he sat back on his haunches and shot his cum onto the sheet, then he lay on his back beside Mosey.

Mosey?

Yeah?

I have to go; I've got a long drive and I have work tomorrow. I know that this is just something that happened. We didn't plan it or know that we would see each other tonight. But, now that it's happened, I want to see you again. If you don't want to, say so. I'll go and this will be another memory.

You know what, Steven?What?

You came here to my place. We fucked in my bed. You're in my world. If you want to be in my world, I'll see you again.

Can we say that we will be in each other's world?

Okay. Each other's world. But remember, I still don't have a car so you'll have to spend more time in my world.

Okay. I'll get dressed and go. Give me your phone number. I'll call you.

Steven?

Yes.

Was I tender?

No. You were hard and that part of you I also like.

II First Days 249

Book Two   Portal of Return   250

III

SHOW TIME

Show biz is tough. Amity Lowe found that out in no time even after she caught a couple of breaks as a dancer in small clubs and Off-Off-Broadway theater in downtown Manhattan. With her now blonde hair, fair complexion, and trim figure, she was an exotic. While she didn't seem white, she didn't seem black either. She was exotic. The name "Lowe" also threw people off. Was she Jewish? Who knew? She got jobs dancing and that was what mattered to her. Her boyfriend, Hiram Brown, loved her, shared his home with her in Harlem, and willingly provided her financial support when gigs were few and far between.

They lived in the Hamilton Heights section of Harlem in a brownstone that Hiram bought when prices were still a bargain. He fixed it up and made it a kind of showcase for the neighborhood. He and Amity had lots of friends nearby and loved to entertain other black theater and art types who made their homes in Harlem. Hiram knew about Amity's previous relationship with Swee, that they had lived together as lovers in Pachacuti, and had moved together to New York. Hiram first met Amity when she was dancing in a Harlem club. He recognized her natural talent as a dancer and choreographer after she took over as dance captain in the club. He got her the first dance jobs downtown and then she began making her own opportunities. It was slow at first until she met some dancers, like Zipper Schiele, who had been involved in a downtown experimental theater.

That theater, Sault Sainte Marie, called as its home an old school building in the East Village. Several theater groups used the building but Sault Sainte Marie was, by far, the most active and innovative company. It was also one of the few companies that not only attracted, but also gave prominence to black, as well as white, performers and theater professionals. The creative team was also mixed racially. Amity was both performer and company choreographer. She had developed into an expressive, disciplined dancer and impressed her colleagues with her original and distinctive choreography that was inspired mainly by the avant-garde ideas and abstract work of choreographer, Merce Cunningham. In between her projects for Sault Sainte Marie, she danced in clubs, Off-Off-Broadway shows, and occasionally in Off-Broadway productions. These were rare opportunities because blacks—even those as light-skinned as Amity—were not hired in shows that did not have a black theme, black story or black characters. Amity knew that she often got a break because of her fair skin and straight bleached blond hair. Unlike her darker-skinned sisters, she didn't immediately turn-off white casting directors. But the color line was closely policed and enforced. Sault Sainte Marie was different because, other than Amity, the other resident creative staff were white, leftist Jews.

Hattie Harmon and her husband, Ammon Harmon, founded Sault Sainte Marie and served as the creative directors. Hattie directed their productions and managed the company's business. Ammon was technical director who translated the production designer's ideas into the staging. Martin Fromm was the resident playwright and dramaturg who wrote most of the company's many original scripts. He collaborated with A.J. Freeman, a composer of original music, Shona Weisberg, the company's chief designer of sets, costumes, and lighting, as well as Amity, Hattie, and Ammon. Their work was truly collaborative in that the lines of responsibility were not rigidly drawn and anyone could and did suggest ideas outside of their own area.

The company enjoyed modest success in the downtown experimental theater scene. It had a loyal audience of young New Yorkers who were eager to be challenged by unconventional theater and performance. The audience was also mixed racially because black performers were frequently incorporated, even showcased, in productions. That's how Amity found her place in the company, first as a featured performer and, then, and a member of the creative team.

As 1976—the bicentennial year of the independence of the USA—approached, the company considered staging an ambitious new work that would address two hundred years of American history. The creative team, including Amity, began a series of informal meetings to thrash out ideas. As an experimental theater, the company was not going to stage a historical pageant. But certain historical events, or even historical periods, could be the core of a production. Over a series of months in 1974, the group considered and discarded such obvious themes as the arrival of the first Europeans and the appropriation of land belonging to, and occupied by, indigenous people. The struggle of the colonists for independence from England was deemed "too Broadway." The conquest of the West and suppression and annihilation of the native inhabitants seemed "too Hollywood." The Civil War, industrialization, immigration, World Wars, rise of the cities, the Civil Rights Movement—these themes seemed already imbedded in theater history.

Amity listened to these discussions. She realized that these well-meaning, talented people were missing a story that was at the heart of America's history: The enslavement of Africans in America and their struggle for freedom and equality were bound to ideas of race. Racism—a construct in the USA to distinguish people of African descent from those of European descent—was and is a force that permeated all other aspects of American life. This was a topic that determined and continued to define the destiny of the USA. While receptive to her argument, the other members of the creative team were unconvinced. They felt that race and racism as embodied in slavery, Emancipation, Jim Crow, and the Civil Rights struggle were important, as Amity said, but these themes were too broad and not adaptable to the company's approach to theater without some specific and compelling focus. Amity made up her mind to persist and find a way into the topic that would convince the creative team.

One evening, when she and Hiram were home, she told him about her ideas and the creative team's resistance to them. He was not surprised by their reaction and told Amity so. It seemed to him that there wasn't a story in her idea that could become a good, provocative, and moving production. Besides, if Amity was to create choreography for the piece, what would be her inspiration? Amity listened. She was surprised by Hiram's sensitivity to the situation. Though they had known each other and lived together for over thirty years, they seldom had this kind of conversation. Mostly, he talked about his work in real estate; he had long ago left his job in a furniture store and gave up his interests in show business to become a very successful real estate agent. He was one of only a few blacks who entered and navigated the housing market in Harlem. Amity would listen to him attentively. Occasionally she discussed her own successes and failures. It seemed to her that Hiram listened but clearly he wasn't really interested. He had grown accustomed to Amity and greatly admired her beauty but he had long ago lost interest in any intimate contact with her other than the comfort of having her as his partner. Amity had never been wholeheartedly sexual with him, and he never had the sexual drive to desire her fully. She was a faithful companion, as was he, but she was not monogamous. Both were content to be almost siblings to one another. But this theater project not only hooked Amity but also intrigued Hiram. Years of witnessing slow racial progress made him want to see creative folks, especially those at Sault Sainte Marie, take a stand. The company that Amity was involved with was a perfect opportunity to focus attention on race and racism.

Hiram was as dark-skinned as Amity with light-skinned. All his life, his blackness was used against him by whites as well as other lighter-skinned blacks. He harbored deep resentments that he had only recently begun to acknowledge. His initial attraction to Amity was, he now realized, due to his desire to be attractive to a light-skinned black woman. If he had had the nerve, he would have tried to attract a white woman. However, that impulse had long passed. He was more interested now in racial progress, and Amity's ideas touched him.

He looked around their living room. It was comfortably furnished with upholstered chairs and a sofa. The old, original wood panelling contributed a certain dark grace and somberness to the room. The low level lighting softened edges and muted colors. Amity, in a chair, sat opposite Hiram on the sofa. He thought for a moment about their conversation and made what seemed, for Amity, a surprising suggestion.

Why not, he said, ask Swee what she thinks? Isn't she now finishing her PhD program in writing at City College?

Amity was so surprised at this mention of Swee that she didn't have an immediate response. She thought his suggestion over, however, briefly questioning herself why, after all of these years, he would mention Swee? Sure, Amity had given updates on Swee's life over these many decades but Hiram had never shown any interest in her reports or in Swee. Amity thought that he was either jealous of their decades-ago youthful relationship or simply uninterested in Swee's life. After a few moments, she said that Hiram's suggestion was a good one and she would contact Swee.

Swee was in the throes of finishing her dissertation which concerned black fiction literature from the late Nineteenth Century to the beginning of the Harlem Renaissance in the 1920s. She focused on the changing viewpoints of black writers to the shifts in racial progress during the period. She was intrigued by Amity's ideas but agreed with what Amity told her about Hiram's suggestions. Amity did need a compelling story that could be dramatized by the experimental theater company. Swee had an idea and it was one with which Amity was already familiar.

You know a lot about my family's history, right?, Swee started. Now that history—the different families, the various characters, the struggles and successes—it's too complex and rambling for theater. But one story brings everything together: Trique and Martalee's fraternal twins—one white and one black—Dunn and Alfred. That story: How Trique and Martalee started their affair; their abrupt flight from Pachacuti; their separation and eventual reunion after Martalee gave birth; her giving up the black child to a wet-nurse and moving with Trique and Dunn, the white child, to Los Angeles; the black child, Alfred, fostered into his grandmother's family; Dunn's death in Viet Nam; and the surprise reunion of Alfred with his parents at Dunn's funeral—Honey, that's a story.

Amity let this suggestion settle into her thinking. She had long known much of this story but it had been packed away in the back of her mind. Now, brought forward, and in the context of a framework for her theater, she agreed. It was a story with many possibilities for the company although she would have to find a way to present it to the creative team. Amity thanked Swee, wished her good luck with her dissertation, and asked her what her future plans were. Swee replied that she would continue to write and there was a possibility that she could also teach a writing class, as an adjunct, at a local college. Her advisor, who had first encouraged her to continue with her education and helped her get a scholarship so that she could quit work and concentrate full-time on school, had found a part-time teaching job for Swee if she could take it. She had talked it over with Gulley who agreed it would be a good opportunity.

At the next meeting of the creative team, the director, Hattie Harmon, asked everyone for their best idea. Martin Fromm, the playwright and dramaturg in residence, thought that a story about an immigrant family coming from central Europe and struggling to settle in New York would present a lot of possibilities for dramatic theater. Yes, he acknowledged, it was not a particularly new idea. In fact, there was a rather long and well-developed theater history of such plays. But he argued that the very familiarity of the theme would allow the company to take the idea in some new directions. In effect, they could experiment. There was nodding agreement among the group. A.J. Freeman, the composer, proposed using various European and American musical forms and traditions as the basis for a production. The musical forms could be woven into a story. Hattie, Martin, and Amity were enthusiastic to this concept. Amity thought that this was the opportunity to state her proposal and spoke up. She presented the idea suggested to her by Swee and argued that their theater should present a story that was not familiar. The Bicentennial was an opportunity to open up their theater to the story of people whose lives had not been well-represented on stage. European tales were well known as Martin acknowledged; the stories of black people, especially interracial families, was little known. Furthermore, her story would not only allow for an interracial cast—something in keeping with the times—but would also lend itself to a choreographic staging that might transcend their usual stage productions.

Martin finally responded: Who's going to be interested in an interracial family's tribulations? That's something for a black theater, not us. We have to consider our audience which is majority white. Relatively few black people attend our theater.

Amity answered: That's true. And, maybe the fact is that we never offer blacks anything that would interest them because our work is never by them or about them. This is a story that concerns both both races—black and white—because the story is about this country's past, present, and future.

Martin: Most whites have nothing to do with blacks. They don't know them. Why would they be interested in this story?

Amity: What you say is true. Very true, and that is why this story is important and should be presented to our audience. For too many whites, blacks are invisible and, when they are visible, they are often considered undesirable. Why is that? How did we, as a country, get to be that way? Blacks did not come here voluntarily. We were enslaved in Africa and brought to this country by force and then made to work to build this country without compensation until we died. When slavery was abolished, we suddenly became unwanted in this country—an embarrassing reminder of slavery's history—and forced to be invisible and without the full rights of citizens. That's what the Civil Rights Movement is about. The Black Power movement and the Black Panthers have made the invisible visible and many whites are not happy. But, through this tragic, brutal, and inhumane history, some whites not only desired blacks but mated with us and produced people like me. Where do I fit in? How does my story get told? How much longer will people, white people that is, ignore and deny what this country is really about? These are the reasons that an interracial family matters as a theatrical event in the bicentennial year. This country's two hundred year history is about race. Race is at the foundation of everything else. It was at the heart of our country before there was a country called the United State of America.

Again, there was silence.

Shona Weisberg spoke: You know, I get her point. I must say that I never thought through these matters and it's all still a bit sketchy to me but I hear something essential and something neither we nor anyone else has done or is doing. Even if there have been productions about interracial families, I doubt that any have been produced from the perspective of blacks.

Martin interjected. Well, that's a problem. We don't have a black playwright our team.

Amity replied: I have a candidate, a soon-to-be PhD, black female writer.

Martin: Who is that?

Amity: An old friend, Swee Sellabie. We've known each other from our days in Pachacuti, Georgia.

Hattie: Would she be interested in talking with us?

Amity: I think so. I'll ask her if everyone is agreed.

Hattie: Well, what say all?

Heads nodded affirmatively around he room. As the meeting broke up, Martin approached Amity.

I think that you've got a good idea even though I'm still concerned about our audience. But, if we don't do this now, when will we do it?

Thank you, Martin, and I hope that you will bring your theater genius to the project.

I'll try.

Swee was delighted when Amity announced that the theater group had accepted her idea and wanted to begin development despite the fact that she was finishing her dissertation. She promised Amity an outline of the story within a week. And she met her deadline. Amity distributed copies to the creative team, and Hattie scheduled a development meeting to include Swee.

They met at the theater in the conference room. Hattie introduced everyone to Swee and opened the discussion:

Hattie: I want to begin by thanking Swee for her prompt preparation of a story outline. Indeed, on paper this is a compelling concept and I think that it is one that suits our needs as an experimental theater. Of course, your outline, Swee, must be a starting point for our team's collaborative vision; the end point may be very different. But, I expect that you and Amity will keep us true to the core meaning and importance of this story as we each bring our own dramatic and expressive ideas to your text. Martin, as resident playwright, will you tell us your initial thoughts of how we stage Swee's story?

Martin: Sure. Swee, as you probably know, I was initially resistant to this story because I didn't think that it suited our audience. But, now, I see that we have an opportunity to take our audience in an unfamiliar direction while challenging them to think about issues that few of us white folks have taken seriously. For this reason, I think the production should feel totally unfamiliar to the audience, disorienting in fact, and should bring them into a new world, a new experience, a new reality.

Swee responded: That's a lot to put on a story don't you think?

Martin: Not really, Swee. We've had a lot of experience with different theater forms. What we don't want to do, which is what your outline suggests, is a naturalistic drama. As we see it, naturalism is best for literature which, I understand, you have mastered, Our theater requires something different. We need a theatrical vision of your text which means a visual and aural experience that moves the mind and drives the emotions.

Swee: How do you see doing that?

Hattie: I think that we are going to rely a great deal on Amity's talents as a choreographer to re-imagine some of the text as movement and dance. There might be some spoken dialogue but much of it may also be sung to music as in musical theater or opera. I'll ask our resident composer, A.J. Freeman, to tackle a score, and Shona Weisberg, our resident designer, to visualize the production. A.J., have you had a chance to think about music?

A.J.: Actually, yes. My initial instinct was to take an atonal modernist approach but I think that drawing upon American musical traditions, of both African and European origin, would be in keeping with my original suggestion for a bicentennial piece. I am thinking now of using some black musical forms within a modernist framework and use those to contrast with some recognizable white musical forms, where appropriate. I could write music for text used as song in arias, duets or choruses.

Hattie: Thanks, A.J. Shona, anything yet for the visual production?

Shona: I would like to hear first what Amity sees for movement and dance.

Hattie: Amity, what are you thinking?

Amity: What I visualize are the principal characters appearing onstage as called for in the text. They will move as dancers but they may also sing or speak. There will also be a group of dancers —representing blacks or whites—who may also sing and speak as in a Greek chorus. They may also interact with the principals. The entire production should flow and move with the music, with speech and movement coordinated seamlessly. Does that help you, Shona?

Shona: Very much so. Do you see having separate black and white groups of dancers?

Amity: No. We can select the best and most versatile dancer/singers regardless of race. They could be "racialized" by masking and costuming.

Shona: What do you mean?

Amity: A black dancer might wear a white mask and costume to designate a white person and a white dancer might wear a black mask and costume to designate a black person. Or, vice versa.

Shona: That's helpful. Given that approach, I think that sets, as such, are unnecessary. Lighting, some props maybe with costumes and masks will do the job. The stage and staging should support not overwhelm the performers.

Thanks, everyone. It seems that we are all onboard with a way to bring Swee's story to the stage. What do you think, Swee?

Swee: Let's get started.

Hattie: I like this story and now this concept of staging it. If we can keep all of the elements moving forward and in sync with one another, we may accomplish our goal. It could be very exciting, innovative, and provocative theater. Hey, it's us! It's what we do.

Hattie concluded the meeting by asking the team to consider the budget implications of their ideas. It would be necessary once the plans begin to take shape to approach donors for financial support. The production costs could be quite huge.

The casting call for actors/singers/dancers went out four months after the initial meeting of the creative team that Swee attended. In the interim, members of the team worked long hours with many consultations to develop and refine their project. All of the elements began to take shape. A.J. Freeman's score, which he played as sections were finished, really excited the team. The music was lyrical and melodic but also often ominous and nervous. There were tuneful melodies and occasional dramatic dissonance. Hints of gospel and jazz inflected the score as well as some references to white country and popular music. As the score evolved, the team began to hear how seamlessly Swee's story had been reborn in music, lyrics, and dialogue. It was going to be musical theater that moved on stage like ballet. Amity and Swee were pleased. Both felt that the essential elements of the story had been retained. Amity saw clearly how her choreography would bring the performers to life on stage. Due to the content of the story, the white characters gained an unexpected prominence. While that might please the Sault Sainte Marie audience, the black characters would, nevertheless remain critical to the story. Amity was anxious about the casting call because she wanted certain kinds of dancers who could move with agility and precision. A huge number of dancers—black and white—appeared for the audition. Many were immediately eliminated because they lacked the range of abilities required. About thirty made the cut. Casting the principles was easier. There was an abundance of talent, black and white, that not only suited the team's vision of the principal characters but also sang and acted beautifully. While not necessarily accomplished dancers, they could move with sufficient confidence to suit the choreographer and director.

The first rehearsals, however, satisfied no one. What had seemed so clear and integrated as a theatrical vision was muddled and disjointed on stage. The anticipated seamless flow wasn't seamless and didn't flow. The team huddled in the conference room to analyze the problems.

Hattie: Can anyone put their finger on what is not working and what we can do to fix it?

Amity: My movement is not working as I imagined it. I think that Martin's music is perfect and the performers are mastering the vocals and dialogue. It's the movement that's not pulling things together. I'm sorry.

Hattie: I hate to say so, but I agree. The movement is the right approach for this piece but your choreography seems too busy and complex. It needs to be simplified and, at the same time, heightened, made stronger and more distinctive. This is a difficult piece to pull together. We've got a little time for you to work things out. Maybe discuss the movement with some of the dancers. Oftentimes, they can pinpoint problems and offer simple solutions.

Martin: I don't think that all of the problems are with the choreography. I believe that we should economize on dialogue and exposition in favor of bolder imagery. For instance, Swee's story unfolds with a lynching in the rural South of a black man who is a relative of one of the main characters. This is the essential backdrop to both the romance between the two young black males and the sexual encounter between one of these youths and the seductive young white girl. I think that we could accomplish that opening with Shona's visuals and Amity's choreography supported by A.J.'s score. The music and lyrics can move us quickly through this opening of the story and into all that follows.

Hattie: I see what you mean.

Amity: So do I but I need to re-think the movement to make the visuals stronger.

Hattie: Okay. Give it a try.

After the meeting, Amity and Swee sat for a few minutes on the stage. Some of the dancers were practicing.

Swee, what do yo think I should do?

Honey, this is a big job for you. You've done something wonderful here but you need another perspective on it. Ask one of the dancers as Hattie said. That gal over there is a standout. She really gets your moves. Maybe she can help. She's also gorgeous. Get my drift?

Oh, Swee. I'm not interested in young women.

That's your business. I've got to run. My dissertation defense is next week. I've got to run and prepare.

Bye, Honey.

Amity sat alone watching the dancers. She watched the young woman Swee had mentioned in particular. Indeed, she understood Amity's choreography as if it were ingrained in her own body. Amity called to her.

Dianna, can I speak with you for a few minutes?

Sure, Miss Lowe.

Dianna Primus was twenty-five. Dark-skinned. A deep rich, silky chocolate. Slender, with her natural hair pulled up on top of her head into a puff. She sat in a chair beside Amity.

Call me, Amity. You're Dianna . . .

Primus. Dianna Primus.

You are a very good dancer, Dianna. You seem to understand my choreography instinctively.

Well, yes, I do. It fits me as if the moves come from my own body.

Yes. You've got the movement perfectly and if my choreography was as good as your performance, I wouldn't feel so troubled.

What do you mean?

The choreography doesn't seem to be working for the whole piece. The creative team agrees. Something's not working and it isn't you dancers. It's my vision that's not working.

I think that your vision is great. That's why I like dancing your moves.

Thank you, but the choreography isn't working for the piece as a whole.

I think that you could fix that.

What? What do you mean?

I mean fixing it could be easy. I've watched the rehearsals. The dancers are all terrific and they work well with the main actors. But there are too many of us on stage at a time. It gets pretty busy and crowded out there. You could try this: Have a few dancers move while the rest remain still or in the background. When you want to emphasize something, put all of the dancers to work. Otherwise, keep the movement to a few bodies.

Amity sat back in her chair, lost in thought as if she were reviewing the entire production speeded up in her mind, revising it as it unfolded. After some minutes, she turned to Dianna and said: You're right. It might work. I'll go through it tonight and try out some changes tomorrow at rehearsal. Do you have any other suggestions?

Yes. Two. Give me more to do because I love your choreography. And, join me for a drink.

Amity was so surprised that she didn't know how to answer Dianna.

If you can't make it, that's okay.

Oh, I can make it. I just haven't been invited out by a beautiful young woman, well, lately.

Are you married.

No. But I've lived with a man for some time now.

A boyfriend?

A companion. To be perfectly honest, my collaborator who was with me a little while ago was once my lover.

So, you go both ways?

Sort of. I guess that I just became attached to certain people at different times in my life. Right now, it's a man. A very nice man but not sexual.

So, how about that drink?

I'd love to.

They walked to a little cafe near the theater, sat at table and ordered glasses of wine. The cafe was quiet and dim.

I'm curious. How did you become part of this theater? I haven't met many black women choreographers, especially here downtown. Uptown, there are a few in Harlem but down here, rare.

I was lucky. I was always looking for an opportunity and I happened to work as a dancer for Hattie Harmon, the director. She's one of the few whites I've met in this town who sees beyond color.

But, excuse me, it doesn't hurt you to be almost white. Are you white?

I'm mixed race. My father was white; my mother was black and native American. But you're right. Being near white is an advantage. But what about you? Beautiful, talented, intelligent. That's quite a package.

Maybe so. But you'll notice that I'm a lot darker than your shoulder bag. Dark-skinned women are at the bottom of the pecking order regardless of attributes.

I can't argue about that. But, that's why I'm using my luck to bring more of us along. If we don't work for our own, who will?

Amen, Sister.

Funny, you say "sister." I never had a sister. Swee was a kind of sister to me as well as my lover. We lived and worked in Pachacuti, Georgia.

Pachacuti? Lord, that sounds so country.

It was and is country. But I grew up in Tallahassee. I'm a southern girl.

Not much southern left.

Well, no. New York changed all of us, I guess.

So, Amity, what about my suggestions?

I'm working on it even as we speak.

More dancing for me?

I think that I can work that out.

Great. Well, I've got to run. It's a long train ride out to Saint Aubins in Queens.

You commute from there?

Yes, Ma'am.

You could stay sometimes at my place in Harlem if we're working late.

How about tonight?

But it's not that late.

That's not why I want to stay.

Amity smiled. Asked for the check, and they left the cafe to catch a train to Harlem.

Boy, is Hiram going to be surprised.

Is he your companion?

Well, yes, as of this morning. I'll guess we'll see how this works out.

Hiram was not happy. The woman that Amity brought to their home was a threat to him. Nothing like this had ever happened in their relationship. Although they both felt free to pursue their own lives, neither of them had brought another love interest to their apartment. Hiram knew that Amity had lived with Swee and still had an attraction to women. Nevertheless, this young, attractive woman that Amity had brought home unsettled him and he could not conceal his upset.

Amity invited Dianna to sit on the sofa. Amity sat beside her but not too close. Hiram sat in an upholstered chair across from them.

Hiram, Dianna is one of he best dancers in our company's new production.

Is that so?

Yes, she's really good, really understands my choreography and has made some important suggestions about how I can make it better.

Good for her.

I'm thinking of giving her a bigger featured part as the wet-nurse who takes the black twin from his mother and saves his life until he is adopted into his grandmother's family.

Yeah. That's great.

Hiram, you seem to be in a strange mood tonight. What's up?

Why did you bring Dianna here?

She's got a long commute home to Saint Aubins and it's late. I offered her our place to stay the night.

Yeah? Where is she going to sleep?

I thought you wouldn't mind sleeping on the couch. You often do that anyway.

Well, tonight I'm not interested.

Why?

I don't want the two of you sleeping together.

Why not?

Dianna interjected: Uh, Amity, I think this was a mistake. I don't want to cause Hiram or you any trouble. I can make it home on the train.

No, really, Dianna. Stay. Hiram, I don't understand why you said that about not sleeping together. Why do you care? You've never said anything like that before.

You never brought another woman home before.

That's right. But you know my history.

Yes, but I also know that you've never brought another person into our life since you've come to New York.

Hiram, you haven't been my only lover but you are my dear companion. Since, I didn't feel that you were still romantically interested in me, I don't understand why Dianna being here is so upsetting to you. Why is that? We haven't had a physical relationship in a long time.

So what? Have you wanted one?

I guess not. But it seems that neither have you. However, I have wanted affection and attention from you.

Amity, I've always been affectionate to you.

I guess you have but not always attentive.

May I say something here? This is a little awkward but I feel I'm the cause of this discussion. Hiram, I am greatly attracted to Amity for a bunch of reasons and I told her so. I'm guessing here, but it may have been a long time since someone told her she was a hot momma. I wanted her to know that and, honestly, I thought that telling her that would help me. I'm not ashamed to say it. I want to stand out in this show. It is going to be a big hit and I want people to notice me in it. Frankly, when the chance came to speak to Amity, I let her know how I felt about her and I couldn't help but feel that, if she responded as I thought she would, that would help me. I'm ambitious.

Dianna, you're something else. You certainly are the right dancer for the job. Hiram, I made a mistake. Bringing Dianna here like this was disrespectful to you and to the love and affection you've shown me all of these years. I apologize. And, to you too, Dianna. I was carried away by your beauty, talent, and directness. Stay the night. On the couch. Tomorrow, we'll work on the show. Is that okay with you, Hiram?

Yeah. It's okay.

Hiram, how about some drinks?

I'm on it. And, Amity, I've always loved you.

When Amity presented to the creative team the changes she wanted to make, a shock went through the group. Each one seemed to realize a new potential in their individual areas. Martin streamlined the text; much of what had been dialogue became lyrics. A.J. devised new musical sections for his lyrics as well as new musical bridges between scenes. Shona invented several startling visual effects with slide projections, film, scrims, and lighting. Everyone agreed that these contributions sharpened and tightened the production. However, given the direction that the production was taking, Hattie suggested bringing in a few new collaborators for the project. She wanted a new technical advisor for Shona's visual effects. Howard Mickelson, who had worked periodically on several Sault Sainte Marie productions, had studied theater in Japan, dance ceremonies in Africa, and filmmaking in Hollywood. He could review the current plans and perhaps suggest some additional ideas. Also, Zazie Moore, who was a gifted black poet, had an intimate knowledge of black literature and history. Hattie felt that she could collaborate with Martin on the lyrics to achieve greater power and expressiveness of language. All were agreed that these additional collaborators could help refine the project and they did.

During the ensuing rehearsals, dialogue and lyrics, music, movement, and stage effects all began to merge into the desired seamless story. The opening of the production, which had undergone many revisions as each team member critiqued what worked and what didn't work, finally took shape to nearly everyone's satisfaction. The team decided to bring up the lights gradually on an empty raked stage as singing voices were heard off-stage. Women and men wearing black masks entered from both wings in single file but in step to the rhythm of their singing. The movement was a kind of march with the figures leaning forward. As the files reached the center of the stage, they formed a circle, then continued a step in place. The figures leaned into the circle and out, then to one side and the other, all in unison. The singing became joyous with individual voices rising above the group. The movement became more animated and individualistic but still in the circle formation.

In the background, the silhouette of a large tree with spreading branches began to rise from the level of the stage until it was in full view stretching almost to the wings and into the fly above the stage. The singing and dancing crowd lowered their voices and became still. A second group of men and women wearing white masks entered from the wings and gathered at the center of the stage but behind the first group that kneeled down in their circle. The second group also sang, raucously, and turned to face the tree. Hanging by a rope from one of the thick lower branches was the silhouette of a dead lynched man, his body aflame. The second group turned from the tree to face the first group and continued singing a kind of chant. The first group slowly stood and moved in file with lowered heads to the wings, leaving two men in place. The men sang and danced together in intimate movements suggesting a sexual encounter that reached an ecstatic climax with an embrace and kiss. Then, they separated and one of the men left the stage; his partner remained in place.

At this point, the group in the background, moved to the wings leaving one woman and three men in place. The woman, in a white mask, came forward to the man in a black mask, and began singing to him seductively. They joined in a duet which culminated in a passionate embrace, kiss, and an ecstatic sexual coupling. As the couple sank to the stage in climax, the three men in the background sang a threatening trio, then disappeared into darkness along with the hanging tree.

A projection of a house appeared in the background. Threatening male voices sang from off-stage. Onstage, the man and woman frightened by the voices, stood and began running back and forth as the offstage voices grew louder and more angry. A woman and a man in black masks entered from the left. The running couple moved toward them. The four sang a quartet in which the frantic couple explained to the anxious and confused man and woman that they were being chased. The three men in white masks arrived from the right. There were a series of solos, trios, and duets and ensemble songs with the three men in white masks leaving the stage on the right and the other two men in black masks leaving the stage on the left. The two women remained alone on the stage. There ensued a duet between them at the conclusion of which the woman in the white mask ran off the stage to the left as the projected house begins to burn. The lights dimmed to black.

This opening scene condensed Swee's story of the lynching in Pachacuti of her brother, Prellis, by whites; the romance of Mosey and Trique; the meeting and tryst of Martalee and Trique; the discovery of their transgression by Martalee's three brothers; Trique and Martalee's flight to Swee's house; the explanation of their tryst to Swee and Mosey; the arrival of Martalee's brothers and their threatening departure; Trique and Mosey's departure; Martalee's departure; and the burning of Swee' house. This scene compressed and simplified Swee's introductory text for theatrical effect and set the template for the remainder of the production.

One critical passage in the story also changed many times before all of the elements achieved their desired effect. This passage was the pregnancy of Martalee—who was known in the production as Annabeth—and the birth of her twin sons, Dunn and Alfred—renamed in the production as Hughes and Baldwin. Swee had provided a script with dialogue which Martin and Zazie changed mostly to lyrics for song by Annabeth and a chorus. The character of Annabeth, a seventeen year old pregnant white girl from a small town in Georgia, received an extended scene that presented her life just before, during, and after the birth of her sons. This scene was chosen to end the first of two acts.

Hattie sat midway back in the darkened theater as the cast rehearsed act one. She was joined by one of the wealthy board members of the company who was invited to the rehearsal because the production was running short of cash. Barbara Steel, who had been a longtime backer of Sault Sainte Marie, whispered to Hattie asking what she thought of the production thus far. Hattie was pleased with the opening and middle passages of the act. Now, came the transition to the act's closing.

Annabeth was alone on stage in a room suggested by a rear slide projection on a backdrop. She sat on a wooden chair downstage center and began to softly sing a lullaby:

> "It's my time. It's my time. It's now my time to see this through. To see this happen. To see this life. To live my life. To be so free. So free of them. So free to be. To be. To be. To be. To live in my time. My own time. My time to be free and free to be me. And to live my life. This is my time. For the first time. And my time it will be. For me. To

be me. To be free. So free to be me as I have never been before. Before, I was not free. I could not be me. I could not live free. Could not live free as me. As me. As now I am me. And free. In my own life. In my own time, I'm free."

While she was singing this lullaby, the chorus emerged silently from both side of the stage dressed in black and wearing masks with white faces. They lined up against the backdrop of the projected room and sang in a kind of low murmur:

"Free? Free? You're not free. Never free. Never free to be free. You can't be free. It isn't your life. Never. Never free. We won't let you be free. You can't be free from us. Never Free."

Annabeth continued singing more insistently:

"It is my time. It is my time and I am free. I say that I'm free. I will be free. Always free. Always free to be me. You can't hold me. You can't change me. You can't make me who you want me to be. No. No. No. I'm free. I'm here, not there. Never again there. Never. Never again. Never again one of you."

"I miss Mama. I miss my Mama. Mama, how I miss you. How I miss you, Mama. Mama. Mama, I miss you. Do you miss me? Do you? Do you miss me your only daughter? The daughter that you loved? How I miss you. Miss you. You loved me. I know that you loved me. You told me that you loved me. You did. You did tell me. You did tell me. I know that you loved me and still love me. I hope you still love me. Can you still love me as I still love you?"

One of the members of the chorus stepped forward from the group and approached the chair.

"Yes, my love. I love you still. Love you still. How could I not love you still? You are my only daughter. My only daughter and I love you still. I will always love you. Love you as my only daughter. They can't change my love. They. They don't love. Not us. Not us do they love. What they love is themselves. Only themselves. Selfishly unloving. Unloving, selfish they are. Not us. Not us. We love because we need to love, not hate. Not hate. They love hate. They hate and do not love. Their lives are not ours. Our lives are love and loving. Being loved. Being loved. Yes, I love you and always loved you. And always will love you. My love."

The chorus member rejoined the group. The chorus' murmur changed to a staccato chant.

"Wrong. Wrong. You're both wrong. Wrong. It's wrong. It's wrong. We won't have this wrong. No. No. No. No, wrong."

Annabeth stood and paced the stage:

"I'm not wrong. I didn't do wrong. Nothing I did is wrong. It was love. I was in love. I loved. And I was loved. Really loved. I only loved. And he loved me. That's not wrong. I know it's not wrong. It's not wrong. It wasn't wrong. Was it wrong, Mama? No. You know it wasn't wrong. They are wrong. All of them are wrong. Always wrong. I was loved. I only loved. And was loved. Yes. Yes. Loved. Really loved. Mama, I loved as you loved me. As you taught me to love. To love. To be loved. You taught me to love and I loved the boy who loved me. He loved me. I loved him. I still love him. I hope that he still loves me. I'm not wrong. They are wrong. Always wrong. Wrong."

"Mama, they did something wrong to me. To me. They did something wrong. Really wrong. So wrong. So awful. So full of hate. So, so wrong. I know that it was wrong. I couldn't tell you but you knew something was wrong. Really wrong. I couldn't tell you. I couldn't tell you. They couldn't tell you. Wouldn't tell you. Didn't tell you. You didn't know. And, yet, you knew something was wrong. You knew something, something terrible, was wrong. Very wrong."

The rear projection changed to a dense woods.

"What they did. They did something wrong. I knew it was wrong. They knew it was wrong. But they did it. They did it. They did it one night. One night. One spring night. At night. In the dark. In the woods. The woods. In the dark. They took me there. In the woods. At night in the dark. They took me there. I didn't know why. I didn't. I didn't know why. They were laughing. They were joking. Laughing and joking and having fun. Having fun laughing and joking. I didn't know. I didn't know. It was because of him. Because of him. They knew that I looked at him. They didn't like me looking at him. They made up their minds. She can't look at him. Can't. We won't let her. We won't. Won't. I didn't know. I didn't. They were laughing, having fun. In the woods. At night. In the dark. They pushed me to the ground and held me there. Held me. Covered my mouth. My mouth. Held me there in the woods. In the dark. At night. On the ground. One pulled up my skirt. Pulled it up and pulled down my panties. My panties. I tried to yell. I tried. I did. I tried. Another stuck his finger in me. In me. Between my legs. In me. And pushed. Pushed his finger in me. I couldn't yell. They covered my mouth. I cried. I cried, Mama. It hurt. Hurt. He hurt me. They were laughing. Laughing. It hurt. They stopped. Stopped and said, "Don't look at that boy again." My brothers said that. They said that. My brothers. "Don't look at that boy again." My brothers. My brothers. Your sons. Your unloving sons."

Three chorus members stepped forward and chanted:

"Don't. Don't look. Don't look at that boy. Don't look at that boy again."

Annabeth continued singing:

> "It was wrong. They were wrong. I was not wrong. But I couldn't tell you, Mama. I couldn't. I didn't. It wasn't my time. I couldn't tell you. I couldn't. But I still wanted that boy. That colored boy. That beautiful colored boy. And he wanted me. I know. He didn't say it. Couldn't say. Wouldn't say. But I knew. I knew. So, I asked him. I asked him. I told him I wanted him. Just him. Him. To love me. To hold me. To kiss me. To be inside of me. In love. In love with me. To love me. Just love me. And make a baby. A baby. I wanted the colored boy's baby. A beautiful baby. Our baby. I wanted a baby. His baby. A beautiful baby. Our baby."

> "My brothers knew. I don't know how they knew. But they knew. They came for us. For us. While we were in the woods. We ran. We ran to where he lived. Where we might be safe. But we weren't safe. They came. All three of them. They came. Yelling and screaming. Hateful. Full of hate. My beautiful colored boy ran and ran. Without me. He ran with his cousin. His cousin. Out of town. Why? Why his cousin? His cousin. Gone. Gone. My brothers took me home. Hateful. Hating. They told you. Told you. You cried. I cried. They were hateful. I left. Secretly. Secretly. Silently. I left home. Our home. My home. I left town. I came here. With his child. Our child. And now it is my time. My time. Our time. Me and my child."

The rear projection changed back to the room. The entire chorus came forward moving back and forth, side to side, chanting:

> "Your child. Your child. What will that child be? Your child. His child. What will that child be? Will he be like you? Will he be like him? What will that child be? If he is not like you. But like him. What will that child be? He will be a dead child. A dead child. He can't be with us. Never. Never with us. Not our child. Not our child. Your child. What will he be? Like you? Like him? Dead. Like him. Dead. We won't have him. Never."

Annabeth raised her arms to silence the chorus. She continued singing forcefully, deliberately:

> "My child. His child. Can he be our child? Like me. Yes. Like him. No. No. My child can't be like him. How could I keep him? Where would I keep him? Not with them. Hateful. Hating. They would kill him. How could I keep him? How? Where? There must be a way. I would love him but I could not keep him. How? Where?"

One member of the chorus stepped forward now wearing a black mask:

> "I will help you, child. I will help your child. I know what you've done. I know who you loved. How you loved. You've loved like you shouldn't have loved. But you loved. And, now, the child. His child. I will take his child and keep him safe. Loved.

> Safe and loved. Forever. Safe from them. Safe. From them. I will keep him when your time comes."

Annabeth replied singing:

> "It's my time. It's my time now. Now. Right now. My time is now. My child is here. Now. Now. Ahhh. My child."

A baby cried, then a second baby cried. Annabeth sang:

> "There are two. Two. Not one but two. Two. How could there be two? My children. Two. Boys. Two boys. Are they my children or his children? My children? Yes. One. One is my child. The other? No. Not my child. His child. One is mine. One is his. One and one. Two. I can keep the one. The one. My child. I cannot keep the other. The other. His child. I can't. I can't. How can I keep him? He is not mine. Not mine but he is mine. My child. My child. They are both my children. Both. Not just one but both. Both. Both."

The woman with the black mask sang:

> "They are your children. Your children. Your beautiful children. Keep one. Just one. That one you can keep. I will keep the other. The other one. The one you can't keep. You can't. Can't. You can't keep the other one. He will never be safe with you. Never. How could he be safe? Where could you keep him? Safe. They will never let you keep him. Not safe. Not safe. No. Never. He must stay with me. I will keep him safe. Let me have him. I must have him. I must take him from you. You must let him go. Save the one. Keep the one. Let me have the other. He will be safe. He will be loved. He will live. He cannot live with you. He can never live with you. He will not have a life with you. Never. It is what is best for him and for you. For him and for you. For him. For you. He will be safe."

Annabeth sang:

> "No. No. No. I can't. I can't give my child to you. I can't. I can't give my child away."

The woman sang:

> "Do you want him to die? To die? He will die with you? With you he will die. You may die with him. With him you may die. Then. The other child may also die. The other child. All may die. And why? Why? It's your time to be a mother. Be a mother to the child you can mother. You can't mother this other child. You can't. You know you can't. For him. For his time. Let him go. He will be loved. He will live. He will have his time. His time will come."

"I will take him and keep him to be his kind. His loving kind will keep him safe and see him grow and become a man. He will be strong among his kind and know that his kind, his kind alone, will keep and protect him. We will love him. He will be one of us. Always one of us because he can never be one of them. He will not want to be one of them and they will never want him."

"You are his mother. You will always be his mother but he will not know you as his mother because you cannot keep him, love him, and help him grow into a man. You cannot keep what you cannot protect and love. We can protect and love and we will, without you. Ever. Forever. Take the other one and love him. He is truly yours. Not this one. Not this one. He is ours to keep."

Annabeth dropped to her knees and sang:

"I know that I can't keep him. I know that I can't keep him alive. They won't let me. I know they won't let me. He must live. He must. He must. Take him with you. Keep him safe. Love him. Give him his time that his mother cannot give him. Tell him I loved him. I did this for him. For him. Not for me. For him. For his time."

Annabeth took one baby and the woman took the other. The chorus, now in black masks, surrounded the woman and she and the baby disappeared into the chorus and faded into the shadows. They chanted:

He is ours. He is ours. We will keep him. We will keep him safe. We will keep him alive. For his time. His time. It is his time.

Annabeth was left alone with the other baby. Stage lights out.

Barbara Steel was puzzled as she watched this performance. It was a challenging production because of the story but it was also difficult to grasp because, visually and aurally, it was so unlike anything she had previously seen. And she had seen nearly everything the company did during its five-year life. She knew the company needed more money to pay the production costs, including the large cast and staging, until ticket sales could sustain the show but she was unsure about investing further in something that left her so adrift in her feelings.

Hattie sat next to her in the otherwise empty theater seats.

What do you think, Barbara?

Hattie, it's a stunning show but I don't know what to make of it. It's about black people! And white people. But it's really about black people. Do I understand correctly that the story is about a black and white relationship and one black child and one white child who result from that relationship?

Yes, that's the core of the story.

But if one parent is black, how can there be a white child?

Barbara, look around you. Have you ever looked at black people? They're not all black in color. That's because ever since black Africans were enslaved and brought to this country, white folks have been having sex with them. That's why many blacks in this country don't look anything at all like many Africans today. This is the reality of this country. Black people have had to live in a white world with white ancestors in their own families but having to make choices about who they are based on how they appear to white people and how they want to live their lives.

I never knew.

Of course, you never knew. You or I have never had to know. In fact, we would prefer not to know. This show changes that and, sure, people—white people—are not going to understand immediately, but we've got to put this in front of them if they are going to begin to learn.

Barbara pondered long and hard. She talked with friends, with her family, with her husband. Everyone was skeptical, even antagonistic. She made up her mind and wrote a check for $10,000 and promised to get the other board members to help underwrite the remaining expenses of the production.

Initial reaction to the show was similar to Barbara Steel's puzzlement. However, the puzzlement triggered a lot of discussion among the downtown theater crowd. Quickly, Sault Sainte Marie's show became sold-out for its scheduled run. As more people saw the show, the more its story and production were discussed. Critics for major newspapers took notice and began to write often ill-founded analyses of the show. But that, in turn, increased the volume of discussion and debate. The company was compelled to extend the run. When that sold-out, a larger Off-Broadway theater offered its venue and, after a half-year run at its home theater, Sault Sainte Marie moved *Domus Niger* to the new venue for a run that lasted almost two years.

Amity, would you have slept with Dianna that night when you brought her here?

Hiram, I don't know. I was flattered that such a beautiful young woman was interested in me. And, she is sexy. I hadn't been so flattered in a long time. I was curious and excited and suddenly horny.

Maybe, I shouldn't have made such a fuss. I don't think it matters to me if you have sex with another woman or a man. I just didn't want to lose you. I know that we haven't had a great sex life—I'm no stud—but I didn't feel or think that you wanted someone else. If you did, I hoped that it would only be sex for you, not love.

Hiram, I know I want to be with you. You've been a joy to me. Kind, thoughtful, loving, supportive. Sex. I can live, and have lived, without sex but I want affection and attention. I want to feel your love not just know it. Is that okay?

You've got it, Baby.

By the end of the show's run, Amity and Dianna had, in fact, become lovers as well as collaborators. Dianna moved into Harlem so that she and Amity could be closer. Amity began to spend more time at Dianna's place than at Hiram's apartment but she maintained her non-sexual relationship with him. Amity discovered that Dianna, who had studied theater at City College, had many innovative ideas about theater that complimented Amity's experiments with movement and choreography. Together they began to imagine a kind of theater different from that of Sault Sainte Marie.

You know, Dianna, I thought that I was happy with what we created out of Swee's story. I mean, it was good and dramatic theater but it was missing something but I don't know what.

Honey, I can tell you what it was missing. Do you want to hear this?

Of course.

It wasn't black theater. Although it was based on a story by a black woman about black people, it was filtered through the perspectives and perceptions of the white folks at Sault Sainte Marie. It became a white interpretation of a black experience.

How do you mean?

Think about it. Although the creative team were all sympathetic and even sensitive to the story Swee brought them, they could only see it in terms of their experiences which, I think that you would agree, are not our experiences. None of them has lived as black people although they may think that they know a lot about us. But, they don't live in our skins.

Are you saying that a creative person cannot create something authentic outside of their own experience?

Yes. I think that to be really authentic you must have lived in that frame. In other words, to create something authentically black, you have to be black. Otherwise, it is a filtered creation.

But if what you are saying is true, then a woman could not create an authentic experience about a man and vice versa. Or, Jew could not create an authentic experience about a Muslim.

That's what I'm saying.

I don't think that I agree.

Okay. Let's say that a group of black folks took Swee's idea and made it a theater production. Do you think that the results would have been what was created by Sault Sainte Marie? More importantly, if those black folks had made their production for a black audience, would it have been like the one your collaborators made?

Probably not but can you suggest how Swee's story could become black theater?

Yes. I would have conceived it as a kind of trial of Martalee with her son, Alfred, as the prosecution. Her story would be told as a response to Alfred's indictment that she had abandoned him because of his color. The trial, in effect, would be a trial against whiteness and that is the foundational issue of this country.

That would be quite a different approach.

And that is my point. We blacks would have made something different because we are different from whites, not because of our color, but because our culture and history. We see things differently and we have different impulses and stimulants and satisfactions. We really live in a different world much of it of our own creation. Sometimes, we can't see our world because it is immersed in the white world. But when we step back, we know what we know and we know what we feel and we know who we are and how we are different.

You know, I grew up in the South and, despite the fact that I'm not the blackest woman, I have always known that I was black. I never really examined what that meant. I guess that you have.

Bingo.

So tell me, what would you do with this knowledge?

I would create a black theater here in New York City for black audiences with productions by and about black people. I think that the time is right and that would be where I would want to devote my talent and time.

That takes money and we ain't got none.

But there are black folks who do and maybe we could interest them in such a project.

Let's keep talking about this and see if there are any opportunities.

Okay.

Although Amity and Dianna pressed their vision of a black theater with like minded folks, without the financial backing and, more importantly, without a cultural and social environment that understood the importance of such a theater, their dream languished.

III Show Time 275

Book Two   Portal of Return   276

IV

BITCH

You fucking son of a bitch. You lying, cheating, low-life asshole. You punk-fucking pile of shit. You fucked my girlfriend? You fucked her? My girlfriend! You couldn't be satisfied with those punks you've been fucking and who fucked you? You had to fuck my girlfriend too? I should cut off your dick and shove it up you ass except that you would probably enjoy it. Fucking faggot nigger!

Habby, what are you so excited about? Yes, I fucked Jackie. A couple of times. She seemed to enjoy it. But what was it? Just a fuck. Nothing more.

Why her?

Why not? She's always around here. She knows me since you've told her everything about me. Maybe, she wanted to see what punks bend over for. She's just a freak like you and like me. I don't know why you're getting so worked up about her. She wouldn't be your first girlfriend that I've fucked and probably not the last. Habby, we've been married, what, almost forty years? This is how it's been from the beginning. What's changed? You sleep with your girlfriends. I sleep with your girlfriends. We've done threesomes. Yes, I've done punks. What the fuck is different now? Why does Jackie, of all people, matter that much to you? Tell me, why her? Why now?

Habboey was silent. Her anger was so intense. Her feelings were so conflicted that she couldn't answer her husband, Critton Gant.

Habby, you've known me a long time. We were teenagers when we met in Pachacuti. You wanted to get out of your family home, away from your sisters and brothers, away from the responsibility of taking care of the younger children after your parents died. I was fifteen, the same age as your brother, Mosey, when we met in 1944. We left Pachacuti for Detroit so that we could live with my brother. I lied about my age and got a job in a factory at Ford, made some good money. We got married when I turned eighteen in 1947, rented a house, then brought it. I've taken good care of you. I never hurt you. I've tried to give you everything you've wanted.

You got a job at the post office. You make your own money, have your own friends. I've never been troubled about your fondness for pussy. You like pussy. So do I. And dick too. Yes, I had your brother, Mosey, when he stayed with us but you knew that and said nothing because, Habby, you didn't care. You only care about yourself. That's the truth, Baby. I don't really matter to you and that doesn't bother me anymore. We both get what we want when we want it. So what's this about Jackie? I don't give a shit about her and she couldn't care less about me. We fucked. Over and done with. She's still yours if you want her so I don't get your anger. What makes you so angry?

Habboey was still silent. Brooding, trying to think back over her life and how she was, at sixty years old, upset because a woman who seemed to care for her was, in fact, sleeping with a husband who didn't care for her, or for who or what he put his dick into. Yes, Critton had taken good care of her, let her have her own life and love interests, and kept his business to himself. What had upset her? Betrayal? Abandonment? Deceit? What? Who had betrayed who? Had Critton betrayed her, Habboey? Had Jackie betrayed her? Critton hadn't abandoned her nor had Jackie. Was she deceived? She had no illusions about Critton or Jackie. Habboey knew that she had behaved like both of them most of her adult married life. Habboey was unhappy, with her marriage, with her girlfriend, with her life. Why? She had long thought that she was jealous of her brother, Mosey, because he had followed his instincts and impulses and found satisfaction in male lovers. As a youth he had been sent to live with his mother, Loissey's half-sister, Swee, and her lover, Amity. Habboey had wanted that kind of life for herself. She wanted to live with Swee and be free to love another woman. Instead, when Critton came along, she took him as her partner and means of escaping her family and Pachacuti. Critton didn't seem to mind that she didn't love him or even want to have sex with him. He could have sex with anyone—male or female. He stayed with Habboey at first, because she was older than he and she was smarter. Clever, in fact, and no one would mess with her because she had a sharp tongue and used it viciously. She was a free woman, he thought, in a marriage with no marital demands or expectations. She could have women and enjoy their sex without answering to her husband or anyone else. Certainly not her family. In Detroit, she had much greater freedom and opportunities than in Pachacuti. But she wasn't happy. This vexed her, made her more angry and resentful and made even her female friends and lovers wary of her. Coming out of reverie, she looked at Critton and said, Why don't you get the fuck out of my face, Nigger? Critton got up from his chair, put on his coat and hat, and left the house. His parting words were, I'll be back late tonight. That was Thursday. Friday, Habboey was expecting her bridge club. They were meeting at her house because it was her turn to host. There were nine women in the club, counting Habboey. Eight played bridge at two tables of four each and the ninth was host providing refreshments and dinner after the bridge games. Habboey had planned her menu and shopped during the week. The women loved her baked chicken with roasted potatoes and collard greens. Dessert was ice cream and cake, an angel food cake that Habboey had baked. A bridge party was a lot of work. Not only planning and preparing food and drink for eight very demanding black women but also cleaning house, cleaning dishes, glasses and silverware, and setting up two card tables with folding chairs. Everything had to be perfect. This was the bridge club's expectation.

These women were particular. They all had professional working lives. They were teachers or school administrators, secretaries, clerks, and one was a nurse. Although most were married with husbands that worked, they prided themselves on their financial independence. Several had completed college. All were proud that, as black professional women, they had risen in status in their families and communities. And, they were excellent bridge players.

The club had formed over time with, first, four women, then expanded, as friends were invited to substitute when a regular was unavailable. Eventually, enough women were compatible as players and friends to create two tables of four with a ninth as host. The initial group had formed around two sisters, Helen and Kathryn. In planning an evening of bridge, each had invited one friend to make a foursome. Helen asked her best friend, Loletta, and Kathryn brought Urcelle. Later, Helen included two old friends—Cora and Margaret—while Kathryn wanted a relatively new friend, Betty. The guests all served as substitutes. Eventually, Betty asked if her friend, Jackie, could join and that made eight permanent players at two tables of four each. When food was added to the club meeting, a ninth, non-playing member was needed. So, Betty also asked if her friend, Habboey, could join; she became the ninth and final permanent member of the club. Habboey never quite fit into the group. She was a professional of sorts, after years of working as a cleaner in the post office and after passing an exam, she was promoted to the position of mail sorter. But, it was not her background that was a problem; it was her manner. She had a sharp tongue and, although she never used it against any of her sister club members, when she discussed other people or situations, she could be both crude and vicious. Everyone tried to avoid provoking her by sticking to light chit-chat in her presence. But Habboey would seize upon the most harmless topic to vent her anger or disgust. She could be very unpleasant for no particular reason. There were those in the club that would have liked to ask Habboey to drop out. But, no one wanted to take the initiative. It seemed best to ignore her and move on to another topic or just concentrate on bridge. Ironically, the members looked forward to Habboey's hosting because, one, she would be pre-occupied with her hosting duties and, two, she was an excellent cook. The food would be plentiful and delicious.

Habboey had cleaned house, set up the card tables and folding chairs—one in the living room and the other in the adjoining dining room with the dining room table pushed out of the center of the room up against a wall. The dishes, glassware and tableware were set out on the dining room table as would be the food that was to be served buffet style. The women would play bridge first and have drinks and snacks, then eat and converse. The bridge game would start at 7:30 pm. and the group would eventually break up about 11 pm.

Habboey had taken a leave day from work that Friday to prepare the house and the meal. She didn't expect Critton to stay home with her to help nor did she ask him or care when he would be home after work. She took extra care with preparing the food because she knew the women expected an exceptional dinner. When all was ready, she took her bath, dressed, and did her hair and make-up. As she checked herself in the mirror, she suddenly thought about Jackie who would be arriving soon. Habboey was angry with Jackie for sleeping with Critton. Had she seduced him or had he seduced her? It was just like Jackie to sleep with her husband simply because she knew he would sleep with almost anyone. Habboey convinced herself that Jackie wanted to make her angry because she lived with a man while desiring women. Habboey convinced herself that Jackie was the seducer; Critton was simply an opportunist because he wouldn't have had a special attraction to Jackie. Jackie wanted to piss-off Habboey. That was Habboey's conclusion. But did that mean that Jackie wanted Habboey to herself? Did she want more than casual sex? Did she want Habboey as nobody in Habboey's life wanted her? Why was she not loved like her brother who everybody seemed to want? But was Mosey ever really happy after Trique betrayed him with Martalee? What was it about the two of them—Habboey and Mosey? Why the persistent dissatisfaction and the inability to change their situations? Why, after all these years, couldn't Habboey find someone—a woman—with whom she could live her life? Could Jackie be the one? Well, the bitch had fucked her husband. That made Habboey mad and vindictive.

She had met Jackie through Betty. Betty was a schoolteacher and single. Never married. They had met at a party, and Betty, who was quite the talker—had told her all the gossip about her colleagues at school, including Kathryn and Jackie, also both single and never married. They were all about the same age in their late fifties and early sixties. Betty suggested that they get together some time for a bridge game and Habboey could meet Betty's colleagues. They might have something in common. Betty eventually arranged a little bridge party for the three of them and a fourth woman, Earlean, whom Betty knew somehow. At the bridge party, Habboey was immediately attracted to Jackie who was tall, slim, the color of cafe-au-lait with smooth, long black hair that she pulled tightly into a bun at the back of her head. She was smartly dressed and spoke in an amused tone punctuated with frequent sarcastic laughter. Habboey noticed that Jackie frequently addressed her directly although she was talking to the group. Habboey got the hint—Jackie was flirting. Habboey flirted back by giving Jackie a look that unmistakably said: If you want me, you can have me. That was when they started their affair. Habboey spent as many nights and weekends at Jackie's apartment in Lafayette Park as her schedule permitted. Jackie wanted Habboey to leave Critton, divorce him, and be her companion. Habboey couldn't do it. Not because she wanted to stay with Critton but she wasn't convinced that Jackie would be as constant a partner with her as Critton had been. There was love in her and Jackie's relationship and certainly great sex—neither was a feature in her marriage with Critton—but Habboey lacked confidence in Jackie. Jackie was all about Jackie. She was self-centered and oblivious to anyone else's needs. She did what she did with Habboey because it was what Jackie wanted. She never asked nor did she seem to care what Habboey wanted. Habboey, in fact, had trouble expressing what she wanted because she felt she never had the opportunity or encouragement to say what that was. She knew that she wouldn't give up Critton for someone who offered her even less constancy. So, Jackie's response was to sleep with Critton. Habboey thought: What a shit-pot her life had become. And, now, Jackie and the other members of the bridge club would be arriving and Habboey would have to keep her temper in check. She wanted to smack the bitch upside her head. Cool it, she cautioned herself. Any display of anger at Jackie—and Habboey was sure that some of the women, perhaps all of them, knew about her and Jackie—and the other women would turn on her. They were all so cool and polite to Habboey. She knew they didn't really like her. They didn't like her opinions or the way she had of expressing them. They were too polite to say anything to her. They just smiled and ignored her. The bitches.

Habboey made a last minute check of everything. Put some music albums on the record player— Sarah Vaughan and Dinah Washington—and awaited the first arrivals. The doorbell rang. Habboey opened the front door. Betty and Kathryn were the first to arrive; they drove together. Kathryn, a school administrator, and Betty, a primary school teacher, were complete opposites. Kathryn was soft-spoken while Betty was brusque and given to loud, dramatic exclamations. They were close-friends, possibly once lovers. As they entered, three more women arrived at the door—Helen, Kathryn's sister, who was a secretary, her best friend, Loletta, also a secretary, and Urcelle, another school administrator. All three women were talkative and entered the house in a conversation that began when they drove together to Habboey's house. They left their husbands at home. As the first five guests settled in, shared stories, and complimented one another on their stylish and tasteful attire, the doorbell rang, and Habboey let Jackie in. Jackie was effusive, hugging Habboey and giving her a kiss on the cheek. Jackie was a teacher who taught at the same school as Betty. Before Habboey could say anything, the last guests—Cora and Margaret arrived at the door. They were driven separately by their husbands but met on the street after being dropped off. Cora was a nurse, petite, easy-going, and quick to laugh. Margaret was a secretary and seemed perpetually distracted as if in a drugged fog. As all of the women exchanged greetings and news, they drew lots to find out at which table they would sit and who would be their bridge partner. Jackie and Loletta became partners at the living room card table as were Margaret and Betty. Helen partnered with Cora, and Kathryn with Urcelle at the dining room card table. The first set commenced. All were good players but Helen and Cora and Kathryn and Urcelle had the best cards and emerged winners of the first set at their respective tables. To begin the second and final set, Helen and Cora changed places with Jackie and Loletta so that at the dining room card table were Jackie and Loletta, Kathryn and Urcelle. Margaret and Betty, Helen and Cora. were at the living room card table.

Helen: Well, partner, shall we show these gals how to really play bridge?

Cora: Just keep dealing me some good cards and we'll see what happens.

Betty: I've heard all of that big talk before. You two don't know what you're up against here. Margaret and I are going to show you how this game is really played.

Margaret: Betty, let's not get too far ahead of ourselves here. I've got to focus on my cards.

The women continued their conversation after Helen named the suit for the winning bid.

Betty: I'm thinking of buying me a new Mercedes. You know, one of those small convertibles. They're beautiful.

Cora: Really? They must be paying you school teachers too much money. I could never afford a Mercedes on a nurses' salary and my husband, who is a lawyer, couldn't afford one either. Together, we couldn't afford one.

Betty: I'm just one person. No husband. No kids. I can afford it.

Margaret: I guess that's what also comes from having a union. We secretaries don't have a union and our paychecks show it, and my husband works at Ford on the assembly line and we still couldn't buy a Mercedes on our income. Not to mention that even if we could afford one and did have one, he couldn't drive it to Mr. Ford's factory and park in the company lot.

Helen: I wouldn't mind having a Mercedes. But, you know, we're a Chrysler family; my husband works for Chrysler and he couldn't drive anything but a Chrysler car to work. But I don't think that he would own any other car anyway. He's always been an auto man. His whole life. It's Chrysler this and Chrysler that. But, hey, I'm not complaining. He gets good pay and now that the auto people are letting black folks do something other than the dirtiest, most dangerous jobs in the factories he's moving up to management. He thinks that he's going to get a plant manager job soon.

Betty: Manager? He's going to be some big nigger if that happens.

Cora: Isn't the same thing happening in the public school system for black women? Aren't they moving up?

Betty: Yes, Ma'am. We're being promoted to principals in the schools and administrators in the district offices. But I wouldn't want an administrative job. Our kids need us in the classroom. Lord knows they don't get much at home in terms of support or encouragement. You know these parents today don't value education like we did growing up. Maybe because they don't see education as a way to rise up and get ahead. Where are they going to work in Detroit now? How are they going to make enough money? Blacks, like us, with a little money send their kids now to private schools in the suburbs. The poor blacks send them to Detroit public schools where, if it wasn't for teachers like me, they wouldn't get any education at all. That's why I want to stay in the classroom and, believe me, It's not easy. These kids have no discipline. They'll call you nasty names, cuss at you. Say all kinds of things you wouldn't believe kids would say. In my day, if I said anything like that to an adult, I would have been knocked into next week.

Margaret: I sent my two girls to private school in the city. Catholic school. I didn't want them associating with the lowlife in public school.

Betty: Lowlife? Honey, we all came from lowlife. We all came from poor working-class families. Nobody here was born with a silver spoon in her mouth. But our parents wanted to lift us up. They told us that we were going to have opportunities that they never had. And we had better take advantage of it and do well, or else. That's one of the reasons they all left the South. They didn't want us to have to work in the factories like they did. They didn't want us to be forever at the bottom of the pile. We wouldn't be here now playing bridge and being ladylike if it wasn't for the hard work and sacrifices that they made for us.

Helen: And that I was determined to make for my child. I sent my son to Catholic school, too, here in the city. I didn't mind if he attended public school with other neighborhood children but I didn't think that he would get as good an education in the public school as he got in the Catholic school.

Cora: Well, I never had children so I didn't have to make that decision. However, if I did have children, I would send them to public school. If we don't support the public schools, then they will be bad for everyone. They won't have parents who will insist on the things that make the schools better.

Betty: Amen, sister.

Helen: I wasn't going to sacrifice my child's education for a cause. In my opinion, the public schools are terrible and always have been for black kids. You public school teachers don't do your jobs. You are nothing but babysitters, keeping the kids off the streets and not providing them a good education.

Betty: I'd like to see you handle a class of 35 kids. Most of them can barely read and write. They have no interest in learning. They have no respect for anyone including themselves. Many only have one parent, if they have any parents at all. Too many of them live with a relative who doesn't have the time for them or doesn't really care about them. They are not being raised in whole, complete families any more. There are too many drugs out there. Too many distractions. Too many temptations. They can't focus on school. They are disruptive and menacing to the few students who want to learn. They contribute to a school environment that is everything a school shouldn't be. You say we are overpaid. I say we aren't paid enough to be teachers and social workers and policemen and therapists and wardens. I dare you to spend a day in my classroom and see what I have to deal with everyday, five days a week.

Cora: Listen. It's the same at my job. At General Hospital, we nurses see the worst of who lives in this city. Not only are people shot up, stabbed, on drugs and alcohol, but also out of their minds. Screaming and acting crazy. Hysterical and angry. Violent. Abusive. Unwashed. Unhealthy. We see the worst of the worst, and there are more and more of them these days. We try to treat them. Try to show them some loving care. They don't care. They don't seem to have any motivation. No purpose or drive or ambition except to drink, drug and act up.

Betty: This is the way it has been ever since Detroit began to lose its auto companies. All of those jobs gone. To Kentucky and Tennessee, Canada and Mexico. All of the money went with those jobs. And, without money and jobs, what are folks supposed to do? They never had much education. They didn't need it to work in the factories. Now, what can they do? What jobs can they get? They're stuck here in the city because they can't move to the suburbs where there are jobs. The white folks don't want us out there. They fled the city after the 1967 Rebellion leaving it to us black folks. And, now, they fight like hell to keep us from moving out of the city to the suburbs. Who wants to deal with that? So, poor black folks drink and drug and act up. But, we have to do what we can to help those who still want something and are willing to work hard to get it. That's why I stay in the classroom for the one or two students who want what we have.

Cora: We're blaming the victims for being victims of forces and decisions way beyond their control. This city was a different city when there were jobs and money. People worked and worked hard. They saved their money. They sent their kids to school. They took care of homes and each other. They believed that it was possible to get ahead, to make a better life than any of their parents and grandparents knew in the South. That city has changed. We've got to see that it has changed. The opportunities for poorly educated, poorly motivated black people are simply few. When it seems that there is nothing worth fighting for, what are folks supposed to do?

Helen: Let's change the subject. This is too depressing.

Betty: Well, one more thing: This is 1984. Did anybody read the book?

Margaret: I did.

Betty: Case closed.

During the second set Helen and Cora again got the best cards and became overall winners. It was the club's custom to give prizes to the winners and Helen and Cora received gift certificates to a local department store. During this pause in the evening, Habboey refreshed everyone's drinks and then brought out the food for the buffet placed on the dining room table. The women took turns getting their silverware and napkins and a plate for helpings of the roasted chicken, potatoes, and collard greens. Once they had their food, they settled back into their most recent seats and began to eat. Conversation dropped off as they concentrated on their food. They did compliment Hobboey for her cooking as everyone was pleased with the tastiness of the meal. Music filled the background—Count Basie, Sarah Vaughan, Duke Ellington and Nat King Cole.

The women in the living room—Helen, Cora, Betty and Margaret were the first to hear someone at the front door. They alerted Habboey who came from the dining room and headed to the door as Critton stumbled into the living room. He was clearly off-balance and clutching his chest and stomach. Before Habboey could say a word, Critton lurched forward, vomited on the carpet, and slumped to the floor. Blood trickled from his mouth. Margaret was nearest to him and was the first to react.

Margaret: Oh my god, he's bleeding!

Helen: What happened to him? Habboey, call emergency; Cora, take a look at him. Is he dead?

Cora bent down to him and took his pulse.

Cora: There's a pulse. Very weak. Help me turn him on his back so I can clear his mouth. Habboey, call emergency then get something to clean up this mess.

Betty: I'll get a pan and water from the kitchen. Habby, call emergency now!

Habboey went to the phone in the den. The women in the dining room crowded into the living room. Betty returned with a pan of warm water and dish towels.

Kathryn: What happened to him?

Cora: We don't know. I don't see any injury. He is certainly sick but, why, I can't tell. We're seeing similar cases at the hospital. All men. Sudden onset of nausea. Bleeding. Sores. It's something we haven't seen before.

Habboey returned to the living room.

Betty: What did they say?

Habboey: An ambulance is on the way.

Loletta: Urcelle, help me clear the dishes.

Kathryn: I'll take care of the dining room.

Margaret: I'll give you a hand.

The four women swiftly removed the dishes and silverware and cleared the buffet. They scraped plates, loaded the dishwasher, and put away the left-over food. While they worked in the kitchen, Jackie quietly made Habboey sit on the couch and sat next to her with her arm around Habboey's shoulder. Cora, Betty and Helen attended to Critton. Helen got a blanket from the bedroom to cover him. When they heard the ambulance siren, Cora went to the front door and directed the

EMS to Critton. EMS brought a stretcher, lifted Critton onto it, and carried him to the ambulance.

Jackie: Habboey, aren't you going with Critton to the hospital?

Habboey: Yes.

Jackie: Do you want me to come with you?

Habboey: If you want.

Habboey and Jackie got up from the couch and followed EMS to the ambulance.

Jackie: Do you have a set of house keys to leave so that the gals can lock up after they've finished?

Habboey: Look in the covered box on the bedroom nightstand.

Jackie retrieved the keys, left them with Cora, and followed Habboey to the ambulance. Cora closed the front door.

Helen: What is going on?

Betty: I'll bet he has that new disease.

Helen: New disease?

Cora: It's called AIDS—Acquired Immune Deficiency Syndrome. We're seeing it in drug addicts and homosexuals.

Helen: Is Critton a drug addict?

Cora: I don't think so.

Helen: Then how could he get this disease? He's a married man.

Betty: Not all married men are strictly or even mostly heterosexual.

Helen: Are you saying that Critton is homosexual?

Betty: He's been known to swing both ways.

Helen: You're kidding!

Betty: No, I'm not. Cora, what do you know?

Cora: I've heard the same stories but what concerns me is not his sexuality but the fact that he's been having sex with Jackie. I know that he and Habboey haven't had sex in years.

Helen: What?

Cora: Yes. Isn't that true, Betty? You're close friends with Jackie and Habboey.

Betty: I think that you're right. You know Jackie's big mouth.

Cora: Well, this AIDS seems to be a highly contagious disease and we don't know how it is spread but we do know that sex and blood have something to do with infections.

Helen: Damn! He was bleeding all over the floor.

Cora: Yeah. We need to get something to disinfect that and make sure that everyone washes their hands. Let's go in the kitchen and help the others finish cleaning up.

Cora, Betty, and Helen joined the others in the kitchen and shared their recent conversation.

Kathryn: I didn't know that Jackie was fooling around with Habboey's husband.

Urcelle: That's not the half of it. Jackie and Habboey were getting it on and have been doing so a long time.

Kathryn: I don't believe you.

Urcelle: You don't have to believe. Ask Betty. She knows all of the dirt.

Kathryn: Is that true?

Betty: I don't have photographs of them going at it, but I know from Jackie that they have been.

Kathryn: I can't believe it!

Betty: Why not?

Kathryn: Because all she talks about is her boyfriends.

Betty: Yeah. That's a pretty good cover.

Kathryn: Cover?

Margaret: She's not the only one here with a cover.

Loletta: What are you saying?

Margaret: There are more swinging doors here than Jackie and Habboey.

Loletta: Who?

Margaret: Ask Betty.

Loletta: Betty? What about Betty?

Margaret: Ask her if she bites the pussy.

Loletta: Margaret, really!

Margaret: Ask her.

Betty: She doesn't have to ask. I like women. I've had women. Who here hasn't tried another woman?

Margaret: Well, I haven't.

Kathryn: Neither have I.

Urcelle: Kathryn, why are you telling a lie?

Kathryn: It's true!

Urcelle: Let me remind you that when we were young, many, many years ago, we had a fling.

Kathryn: We didn't do anything!

Urcelle: Maybe you don't consider it anything but I remember some pretty heavy groping and tongues poking.

Kathryn: That was kid stuff.

Urcelle: Okay. Kid stuff. But it was still sex.

Kathryn: I can't believe that you're bringing that up.

Urcelle: Why not? I'm not ashamed. Hell, I think a woman's body is much more attractive than a man's, and I know what a woman is feeling. Who knows what a man feels except that he's getting his rocks off?

Cora: I agree with Urcelle. I'm happy with my husband and, no, I actually have never had sex with another woman but I can see that it might be a different and satisfying experience. I mean look at us. Those of us who are married are probably no longer having sex with our husbands. That thrill has long worn off. Wouldn't a woman know how to please another woman in our post-post-menopausal years better than a man? You have to admit that most men are really only interested in their own orgasm. What happens to us, for them, is incidental and inconsequential.

Helen: Amen. Loletta, why are you laughing?

Loletta: Because I'm hearing the truth. But, you know, for women who desire and have sex with men, it doesn't matter. The male body is what we want and gotta have.

Margaret: Amen to that, Sister.

Kathryn: To tell the truth, I've never wanted a man's body but I never thought that a woman's body was the answer either.

Helen: So, you're happy with your toys?

Kathryn: Did my sister just say that about me?

Helen: Isn't it true?

Kathryn: No truer than you and your toys.

Helen: Well. I guess we all have to entertain ourselves now and then.

Cora: Guilty!

Urcelle: Guilty!

Betty: Girls, let's go before this turns into an orgy.

The women laughed, finished putting away the washed pots and pans, dishes, glassware and silverware. They folded up the card tables and folding chairs and put them in the basement. Put away the record albums, turned out the lights, left through the front door and locked it.

Critton was admitted to emergency at Detroit General while Jackie stayed with Habboey in the waiting room. The attending doctor told them that Critton was resting and that they could visit him. The doctor was unsure what was wrong with him. It would be several days before the blood tests results would be available. At that time, he could tell them what might come next. Jackie told Habboey that she would come and stay with her until Critton was released from the hospital. Habboey agreed. The next week involved more tests for Critton, many hours for Habboey beside him in the hospital room, and nights together for Habboey with Jackie.

Jackie was very comforting to Habboey and took care of the house and meals. Habboey took vacation time from work to spend her days beside Critton. She noticed his condition did not seem to improve. He had no appetite. He seemed to be losing weight. He looked pale and drawn. After several days, the doctors had news; the lab test results were in. Critton was infected with the HIV virus. He had symptoms of AIDS. The doctor advised Habboey to be tested immediately and anyone else whom her husband may had had sex. Habboey didn't know about HIV or AIDS and asked for more information. The doctor provided her a copy of a recent medical article that discussed the disease. That night she showed the article to Jackie and explained that both should be tested. Jackie was furious.

Are you saying that your goddamned husband gave me some kind of disease?

I don't know. The doctor just said that anyone who had sex with Critton should be tested.

That son of a bitch. Why did I ever get mixed up with him?

Why did you?

I wanted to piss you off.

Why?

Because I wanted to be with you and you didn't seem to care about Critton.

Maybe I didn't then but you didn't seem to really want me. You liked the sex and the fun but you could have had that with anyone, not just me.

I like having a good time. You liked having a good time. What more did you want?

What we have now.

What is that? Me taking care of you?

You taking care of me and me taking care of you.

That's for lesbians. I told you I'm a good time girl.

But you could be a partner to me, a lover, a wife. Lesbians can have that too.

This? This is temporary. All I want is the good time. We can do that.

I don't know. I don't think so. Critton getting sick has changed my life. I guess I never really thought what my life would be without him.

You don't even love him.

Maybe I didn't know that I loved him. What I feel now is love for him, and I feel love for you. But Critton was always there for me. He fucked around, yes, but he was there for me, always.

And I'm here now.

Only for now.

I'm not a wife. I don't want to be a wife.

I know.

A few days later, Habboey decided to make a phone call to her brother.

Hello.

Hi, is this Steven?

Yes. Who is this?

This is Mosey's sister, Habboey.

I've heard a lot about you.

I'll bet you have. Well, I've heard a lot about you too. So, you and Mosey are living together?

Yes. For some time now.

In Lafayette Park, right?

That's right. I moved from Southfield back into the city because Mosey could never and would never move out of the city to a suburb.

I don't blame him. White folks don't want niggers living beside them.

Habboey, you know I'm white and I live with Mosey in an integrated neighborhood.

Yeah, I know all that and that doesn't mean anything to me just because a few white folks like you are nigger-lovers.

Habboey, is there a reason you called because this conversation is upsetting to me. I've been through all this stuff with Mosey for years and we understand and love each other. So, can you tell me what you want?

Steven, I never thought that I would say this but I'm happy for Mosey and I'm happy for you. White people may be the scum of the earth but you've been good to, and for, Mosey. I understand that, if it means anything to you. I think that you're one of the good ones.

I'll take that as a compliment. Now, you called about something?

I want to talk to Mosey.

He's not here, now. He'll be back shortly.

Steven, I need to talk to him. My husband, Critton, is dying from this AIDS thing.

Oh, no! How?

Getting fucked by guys.

He's bisexual?

He's everything. He would fuck a cow.

Jesus!

Steven, you've probably fucked a lot of guys. How come you didn't get this AIDS?

Habboey, it was pure luck. I've done a lot of things I shouldn't have done. I was stupid in thinking that there could be no consequences. But there were. Venereal diseases. Crabs. Bloody shits. I was lucky and so was Mosey.

Critton wasn't lucky. He's in the hospital dying.

I'm sorry, Habboey.

You know what, Steven, I'm sorry too. We've had a messed up life together but we've had a life together. I don't know if it was love but we stayed together. And, I realize now that he may have saved my life.

How's that?

Even though we both ran around with other people, we always came back to each other. I was a bitch to him and he was a bitch to me but we were each other's bitches. I don't think that anyone else would have had me. And you know what?

What's that?

No one could have had Mosey but you. Mosey and I were alike. We had a strange mother. She may have loved us but we didn't feel it. Mosey kept to himself. When he found love, he got hurt bad, and it became hard for him to love or be loved again. I never thought that I would find love because I took the easy way with a man when what I wanted was a woman. When I finally found women, I couldn't love them or let them love me. I see that now, and now the man that I never really wanted is dying and I know that he loved me as best he could and I loved him as best as I could. This is all messed-up.

Habboey, I've had a messed-up life too but, lucky me, I've got the man I've always wanted and he wants me. It's not too late to tell your husband what you feel. It won't keep him from dying but it may do him some good. Listen, Mosey just came in. I'll put him on the phone.

Habby?

Yeah, it's me, Brother.

You've been talking to Steven?

Yes. Mosey, that man loves you. You better love him back. You've got this chance. Don't let it go.

I won't, Habby. What's with you? I've never heard you sound like this.

I don't think that I've ever felt like this. Mosey, Critton is dying in the hospital with AIDS.

Oh, Shit! Habby, can't they help him?

They say it's just a matter of time. There's no treatment or cure. He's got sores, pneumonia, kidney problems. Everything is going wrong. He's on painkillers and sedatives. Tubes everywhere. There's no hope.

What can I do, Habby?

I want to talk to you, Mosey, not on the phone but face to face. I've got to understand some things and I think you can help me.

Anything, Habby. Just tell me when and where.

Can you come to my house tomorrow evening? I'll even make dinner for you.

Sure. What time?

Six.

I'll be there.

The next evening Steven dropped Mosey off at Habboey's home. Mosey was shocked to see how much the neighborhood had deteriorated. There were many vacant lots where substantial houses once stood. Other houses were boarded up and a few were partially burned. Habboey's house stood out in its almost pristine condition.

Mosey rang the doorbell and waved goodbye to Steven. Habboey opened the door after undoing several locks.

Hey, Brother.

Hi, Habby.

Come on in. Let's sit at the kitchen table. Dinner is ready. Pork chops and rice with peas. I also made some cornbread.

I'll have to ask you to cut up the pork chops for me because I still can't use my artificial arm to hold a knife.

Oh, stupid me. I forgot about that. I'm sorry, Mosey.

That's okay. I do pretty well with this thing.

Sit down here. I'll serve your plate.

Habboey, I have a lot of memories from staying here with you and Critton

You make me laugh, Mosey. You and Critton were getting it on right here in this house and I think you thought that I didn't know.

Habby, I'm really ashamed of that. I mean, after Trique and losing my arm, and leaving Waite, I had no focus. Critton was not a lover but an opportunity for sex.

I know that and it doesn't upset me. He had his sex life and I had mine. In a way, I was happy for you and Critton because you were "keeping it in the family."

Now, you're making me laugh.

I'm serious. Family is what I wanted and felt that I never had.

We had a family—a father, a mother. Two sisters and two brothers. It felt like a family to me.

But wasn't Swee more of a family to you?

Swee and Amity?

And Trique.

We weren't a family. I don't think we were a family. We just lived together. Swee and Amity and me and Trique.

Think hard about it. What is a family? Is a family a family because there is a mother and father and children? Or is a family people who care about and love each other? I didn't feel loved in my family. I was just another mouth to feed. No one ever took an interest in me or helped me. Swee did that for you. Swee and Amity did that for each other. They were your real family.

Habby, we had parents, aunts, uncles, cousins. That was a big family.

Mosey, that was a lot of people, yes. But what made them family beside the fact that we were related by blood or marriage? I'm telling you, a family is more than that or it is something completely different.

I don't agree. I love Swee and Amity and I'm grateful that they took me in when our sister couldn't take care of all of us. But you, Serriah and Phessin are my family. Our dead sisters and brother are family. Our parents are family. Our grandparents and their parents and grandparents are family. Aunts, uncles, cousins. All of them are our family.

And I never felt a part of it. Critton is my family. He has been there for me all these years. The rest is nostalgia.

Habby, why did you call me and invite me to dinner? We've hardly kept in touch since I left here many years ago. We've never been close or been much interested in each other and, yet, you are my sister and that means a lot to me. Doesn't being your brother mean something to you?

Mosey, yes, you are my brother and, yes, we aren't close but I'm not close to anyone in my family. They don't mean much to me. I called you because only you can answer a question for me.

What's that?

Okay. Critton is dying. When he's gone, I have no one. Well, not exactly. This is what I want to ask you. There's a woman; Jackie is her name. Jackie Braxton. She lives in Lafayette Park near you and Steven. She's my age and a school teacher. We've been seeing each other for maybe a couple of years and, yes, having sex. I like her and she likes me. Critton knows about us and never had a problem with our seeing each other. In fact, Critton had sex with her too. Jackie did it to piss me off, she said, because I stayed with Critton instead of living as a lesbian, I guess. But here's the thing: Jackie didn't like me being with Critton but she didn't want to take Critton's place in my life. She said she didn't want to play house.

Okay, what's your question?

Here it is: Should I stay with a woman who doesn't want to give me what I want? And let me be clear: I want what you have with Steven.

Yeah, but you don't know how we live together or why.

Don't you love each other?

Yes. Each in our own way.

I don't understand. If you love each other and live together, to me that's what I've wanted since we lived in Pachacuti—someone I could love and who loved and lived with me, like you and Trique, you and Waite, and you and Steven.

Habby, you're looking only at the outside. You don't know anything about what those relationships were like. I loved Trique. I was attracted to Waite and Steven. Steven did something I didn't think any white man could do: He came into my life and my world. That changed something in me or, better still, satisfied something for me that I've never had in my adult life. I could say that Swee gave me that when I was a kid but I left Swee when I was still a teenager. A lot has happened to me since then and it took a long time knowing Steven before he was ready and I was ready to be together. Do I love him? Yes, but love has changed for me since I was young. Love means a lot of different things now. It means having our own lives apart and together. It means depending upon one another but not being a burden on the other. It means being free and being committed. I still see Steven as a white man and all that that means and he sees me as a black man and all that that means. But our race no longer is a wall between us. Steven has his white friends and I have my black friends. We also have friends—black and white —together. Do we still have sex with other men? He says no. Do I have other men? No. Might we? It's possible but not likely. The point is our relationship is something between us that nothing outside can touch. I know and believe that now and that is what I want.

Mosey, would you talk to me like this if I wasn't your sister?

I don't know. Probably not.

Why not?

You are my sister and we share a past and a history of ancestors. We are connected in a way we are not with friends.

But friends are often closer than family.

True. But, for me, I need knowing those family connections.

Isn't Steven a family for you too?

Yes, he is.

Then, does it matter if family is blood or chosen?

They both are families, I guess, but the one that is important is the one that makes us who we are and proud of who we are.

Mosey, you make me proud.

Thank you. Did I answer your question?

I don't know but you gave me something to think about.

Habby, I have to say that you make me proud of you. I never thought about your life or what you had to do to survive and still be yourself. I guess that I took you for granted as my sister and that was that. Because you were part of my family, I never really saw you for who you were or why you were the way you were. You were just Habby to me. Now, I feel something that I've never felt before and that is a bond of love with you. I feel now that I want you in my life as my sister and as a friend.

Me? The bitch?

Yes. You, my bitchy sister.

Mosey, if you can love a bitch like me, I need you in my life more than I need anyone else.

I'm here, Habby. I'm always here for you.

Habboey leaned over and gave her brother a hug and a kiss on his forehead.

Habby, I have to ask you a question. You know that HIV is transmitted by sex, right?

I know it now.

And you and Jackie have had sex with Critton, right?

I haven't in years but, yes, Jackie has somewhat recently.

Could she have gotten HIV from Critton, and you, perhaps, got it from her?

Well. Jackie is nobody's fool. She made Critton wear a rubber not because she knew anything about HIV but because Jackie wouldn't fuck any man who didn't use one. And, we both got tested. No HIV.

That's a relief.

What about you?

I got tested and I'm negative. Steven is also negative.

Well, I guess we all got lucky, except Critton.

Mosey and Habboey finished dinner. Mosey called Steven to come pick him up. Steven arrived an hour later and Mosey left. Habboey cleaned up the table and kitchen. She thought about Critton and then about Jackie.

Critton died after two months in the hospital. Multiple infections overwhelmed his weakened immune system and caused systemic failures. Habboey had his body cremated. There was no funeral. Critton had no close relatives and Habboey didn't want to have a service that she thought neither her family or friends would attend.

The next bridge club meeting after Critton's death was at the home of Urcelle. Habboey had missed a couple of meetings while Critton was in the hospital. The club had invited substitutes in her absence. Now, she planned to return but only to announce that she was dropping out of the club.

Urcelle had a big house, one of the biggest of all of the club members, in the still posh section of the Boston-Edison neighborhood where Steven once lived. Her living room was so large that two card tables were easily accommodated and dinner was served at the dining room table where all nine members could be seated comfortably.

Everyone arrived on time except Habboey. Jackie, in fact, arrived first. Just when Urcelle thought that she would have to be the eighth at one of the tables, the doorbell rang and in walked Habboey.

Urcelle: Girl, I thought maybe you changed your mind and decided not to come.

Habboey: I almost didn't come but that would have been a shitty thing to do.

Urcelle: After what you've been through, I wouldn't have been surprised. Come on in. We're about to start. Everyone is looking forward to seeing you. You're at table one and Margaret is your partner. Loletta and Kathryn are at the same table.

They entered the living room from the entry vestibule.

Kathryn: Habboey! Glad you made it. We were worried you wouldn't come.

Margaret: Come on, sit down. We missed you. I'm so sorry about Critton. It must have been a terrible experience for you.

Loletta: Honey, I'm sorry there wasn't a funeral service. I wanted to come. We all wanted to come. We didn't want you to be alone through all of that but we didn't want to intrude on your life either.

Urcelle: Did you have him buried?

Habboey: No. Cremated. His body was so deteriorated that I couldn't face a casket even if it remained closed.

The women at the second table came over to Habboey, except Jackie.

Cora: When my husband was sick, I couldn't think straight. If it wasn't for Helen and Loletta, I would have lost my mind. Thank god, Stan got better.

Habboey: Thank the doctors he got better.

Cora: The doctors cured him but god watched over him.

Habboey: God didn't do anything for Critton. And neither did the doctors. He got a fatal disease and died.

Cora: I prayed to god for Stan and Critton and you.

Habboey: Well, it may have helped Stan but not Critton.

Cora: What about you? You're here, in one piece.

Habboey: I'm here but not in one piece. I feel like my life is over. The man who loved—the only person who ever loved me—is gone. What's left? A job at the post office? Dinner alone? A bed for one? A bridge club once a month, except during the summer?

Helen: You're not the first woman to lose a husband.

Habboey: You've got one so what do you know?

Helen: I know that we all lose people important to us—husbands, parents, children, friends. That's life. We grieve and move on with our lives.

Habboey: Move on to what?

Urcelle: We find people and things that keep us going.

Betty: Habboey, nobody here thinks your loss is inconsequential. You've lost a husband. But that's not the end of the world. Not your world or any other world. It's something that you have to adjust to.

Habboey: How?

Betty: Other people care about you and some even love you though you always want to play the bitch and drive people away. I've been your friend for years. I brought you into this bridge club. I gave you an opportunity to make friends here. But you didn't seem to want to be friends with anyone.

Jackie: With one exception.

Jackie got up from the second table and walked over to Habboey.

Jackie: I was your friend and everybody here knows I was your lover too. Black women don't keep secrets so don't look surprised. We know. I know how you felt about Critton. That part of your life is over. You can grieve; you will grieve. But your life isn't over yet. I was with you when he was in the hospital. I tried to fill a space in your life that I thought needed filling. I did that out of love for you. Yes, I wanted you even when Critton was alive and well and, yes, as everybody knows, I slept with him. Not because I wanted the sex but because I wanted you, and I thought that you could finally choose what you really wanted—a woman who could love you not a husband who would fuck anything with two legs.

Helen: Or four legs.

Kathryn: That was tacky.

Habboey: Helen is right but Critton loved me and stayed with me.

Jackie: I offered you love and I stayed with you.

Habboey: But you said you didn't want, as you put it, "To play house."

Jackie: I did. That was a mistake. Like you, I've had time to think about things and I've come to the conclusion that I want you as my partner and lover and I have all these women here as witnesses.

Habboey started to cry.

Urcelle: Habboey, Honey, we're all grown up here. We may not all agree about things. Some of us can't yet wrap our heads around women loving women but we know we love you and Jackie and, if you want to be partners and lovers, you are welcome in this family of women.

Helen: I couldn't have said it better myself.

Kathryn: But you would have tried.

Margaret: Okay. I'm not completely on board with this lesbian stuff; my church says that this is a sin. But, hell, who doesn't sin sometime?

Loletta: Amen, Sister Margaret.

Kathryn: Alright, can we play some bridge now so that we can eat. I'm starving.

Helen: Eat the cheese and crackers.

The women returned to their seats. Several gave Habboey a hug and kiss on the cheek. Jackie lingered and took Habboey's hand, then went to her seat. Habboey and Margaret were the final winners. The meal afterwards was superb: roast beef, baked macaroni and cheese, tomato-lettuce salad, and apple pie. It was a splendid evening that all agreed made the bridge club an essential part of their lives.

The bridge club remained a part of Habboey's life but Jackie did not. Although they tried being more than casual lovers, Jackie could not really commit herself to "keeping house," although she tried. Habboey decided that another woman was not really the answer she sought for so long. Instead, she became closer to her brother, Mosey, and his partner, Steven. And, after retiring from the post office, she began to travel, first on Caribbean cruises and then to Mexico, Central and South America. She traveled with members of her bridge club which she finally allowed to become her family of choice.

IV Bitch   301

Book Two   Portal of Return   302

V

RED WHITE AND BLACK

Steven looked across the bedroom to the window. Sunlight streamed into the room onto the bed where Mosey lay tangled in the sheets and covers. Mosey was still asleep. As he breathed, the covers rose and fell. The stub of his amputated arm rested outside of the covers. Steven liked looking at this appendage. He liked seeing it without Mosey's prosthetic which he thought looked too mechanical. He loved watching Mosey. His now gray, thinning hair was still curly but, to Steven, it made Mosey more handsome. Steven's own hair was no longer red—what little was left of it, mostly on the sides, was also gray, a kind of dingy brownish gray. He would have preferred to shave his head but Mosey objected. Mosey wanted a reminder of his long-gone red.

Steven hadn't yet bathed; he didn't want to disturb Mosey. So, he simply got out of bed and sat in the wingback chair and read from the guidebook for Rome. Steven and Mosey had arrived in Rome only the day before for a two week visit to Italy. It would include the usual stops other than Rome—Florence, Siena, and Venice. It was the first trip for both of them to Italy and Europe. They were both still out of sorts due to jet lag, and Mosey needed more rest. The trip, in 1999, was a present from Steven for Mosey's seventieth birthday (Mosey was born in 1929) and for his recent retirement from his museum guard's job. Mosey was excited about the trip because, ever since he started work at the Detroit museum, he surprised himself by his unexpected interest in art. Nothing in his background or life could have suggested such an attraction. And no one—not Steven or any of the other museum guards or curators—had said or done anything to stimulate his interest. Mosey was drawn to art because it fascinated him. He loved looking at it and wondering what it told him or made him feel. He started thinking about things far removed from his own experience. It was as if a door opened to a world whose existence was unknown to him but which beckoned him to enter and freely explore. Mosey fell in love with something, instead of someone, for the first time in his life and he felt an overwhelming desire to fill his mind with images and knowledge. Italy would be his school.

Steven watched Mosey as he slept. He was eager to get ready and go out into the city. The noise of the traffic, even early in the morning, made him want to plunge into the crowded streets. He wanted to stop at a bar and have a coffee and pastry. He wanted to see how people dressed, hear them talk, and watch the swirl of life that seemed to him so intense and beautiful and different from Detroit. He thought to wake Mosey but decided, instead, to bathe and dress and not worry about waking him. He hoped that his activity would wake Mosey, which it did, so that they could plunge into the city and head to the Vatican for their first tour. They had planned their first full day in Rome and Italy around St. Peter's Basilica and the Vatican Museums. Although both had read the guidebook and seen many images of the Vatican, they weren't sure how they would react to being in these places. Would it be overwhelming or a disappointment? Would it be similar to what they had read or somehow different? Arriving in St. Peter's Square after a taxi ride answered all of their doubts and expectations: This was unlike anything they could have imagined. The vastness of the Square, the immensity of St. Peter's Basilica, the crowds, the sounds, light, heat, sky, towering stonework, statues, everything hit them at once. Inside St. Peter's, they were beyond amazed. This was a place like no other—gigantic, stunning, complicated, intricate—beyond human endeavor and comprehension. Surely mere people could not have created all of this. They were stunned and fatigued. So, instead of continuing on to the Vatican Museums, they left the Basilica and retreated to a nearby restaurant for lunch where they tried to understand what they had just seen. Both decided to postpone the museums until the following day.

The next morning they headed again to the Vatican but this time to the museum entrance. The crowds waiting to enter were thick. Mosey and Steven waited patiently until their turn to pass through the entry doors. Once inside and having paid their entry fee, they followed the crowds up to the level of the route to the Sistine Chapel. There was so much to see along the way: Ancient Roman statues, long corridors elaborately decorated and filled with art. Then the rooms painted by Raphael that seemed so confined and crowded compared to other parts of the Vatican. Then down stairs through more rooms adorned with paintings. All this luxury and beauty struck both of them as strange for the home of the head of the Catholic Church. The expense and work involved in creating all of this was beyond them. They shuffled along with the flowing mass of humanity and then they passed through a rather non-nondescript door and without warning they were standing in the Sistine Chapel with hundreds of other people nearly shoulder to shoulder. Silencio!, boomed a voice over a loudspeaker, and the crowd momentarily quieted only to begin again to chatter first at a whisper and then in louder and louder tones until, inevitably, the voice boomed again. Silencio!

Like everyone else, Mosey and Steven stared at the ceiling. Michelangelo's astonishing creation was seemingly suspended like a canopy way above their heads. The human figures were enormous. How did Michelangelo paint such a massive work? Mosey knew about Diego

Rivera's paintings in the Detroit museum, but this was far grander and overwhelming than Rivera's amazing paintings. As much to relieve the stiffness in their necks from craning upwards as to survey the entire setting of the chapel, Mosey and Steven glanced at the walls that were also painted from floor to ceiling. Scenes telling stories, and an enormous variety of human figures, male and female, young and old, caught their gaze everywhere they looked. Mosey opened his guidebook and began reading in a low voice to Steven.

"The chapel was built by and named for Pope Sixtus IV in the fifteenth century. It is the pope's chapel where important ceremonies are held including the selection of a new pope upon the death of his predecessor. Sixtus hired a group of artists, most from the province of Tuscany, to paint the walls with the stories of Moses and Jesus. These stories represent the old and new covenants between god and his people as told in the Old and New Testaments of the Bible. As the viewer faces the altar, the story of Moses is on the left and the story of Jesus in on the right. Originally the first scenes in both stories were on the altar wall but they were destroyed to make room for the painting of the *Last Judgment* also by Michelangelo. The ceiling was originally painted blue, like a sky, with gold stars. This was removed to make way for the paintings by Michelangelo completed in four years from 1508 to 1512. Pope Julius II, a nephew of Pope Sixtus IV, hired Michelangelo to paint the ceiling. His subject was the Creation, Disobedience of Adam and Eve, and the story of Noah as told in the Old Testament, the Jewish Torah. This sequence of stories details mankind's fall from grace which is the reason for the successive covenants god made with his human creations as illustrated by the wall paintings. Furthermore, Jesus, the son of god, as told in the Bible, conferred his authority to his disciple Peter who, in turn, is considered the first pope. Sixus IV, Julius II, and later Paul III who had Michelangelo paint the *Last Judgment*, were successors of Peter and exercised their inherited authority over the Church and Christianity."

Mosey stopped reading. Steven said, What's going on?

I never really knew any of this and I'm not sure what it means.

It means that these paintings are about authority and who has the power to rule over other people.

But I'm not a Catholic. I'm not even a Christian. I've never even attended church except for funerals. So how can a pope have authority over me?

Well, I'm Jewish and I don't think that the pope has any authority over me or my people either.

So, what should this mean to us?

Not much, I guess. But to Catholics, I think that it means a lot. We Jews are ruled by the laws and teachings of the Torah and Talmud. These books give us the moral and ethical principles to live by.

Funny, I've never heard you mention any Jewish law.

That doesn't mean that I ignore the laws. I think that I generally follow the Jewish principles I learned in my family.

Such as?

Treating other people the way I want to be treated. I don't steal or cheat. I've respected my parents when they were alive. I've never killed anyone. Although I was a Bar Mitzvah boy, I never attended synagogue except for bar mitzvahs, weddings and funerals. So, I guess I don't observe the law regarding the Sabbath.

How can you pick and choose which laws to follow? Aren't laws laws?

Okay, I'm a sinner under the law but I think I'm a just and respectable person. Not all laws are just nor should they be respected. You grew up in a racially segregated town and you live in a city that still practices discrimination against black people. Much of your mistreatment was once a fact of law

But the laws that segregated and discriminated have been abolished although many white people still hate us blacks and discriminate against us despite new laws that forbid it.

And they can be punished if found guilty of breaking the law. You know, Mosey, you and your family have quite a few white ancestors and that makes you almost as much white as black. I've never asked you what you think about that and I've never heard you say anything about it.

What could I say? It wasn't and isn't that important to me. I've always felt black. I've always been treated like a black. You were interested in me because I was black. Isn't that true?

Yes, I was attracted to black men; I met you in a black joint. But, as I've told you many times, I love you for you. Black is a part of it but not the whole of it.

You've said that before. Many times. But have you thought that you were attracted to me because I was not quite black? Because I was near-white?

Come on, Mosey, you're turning this race thing upside down. How can I be attracted to you because you're black and also not black?

You just answered your own question. It is because I look like I'm between the races—neither really black or really white—that I appeal to you. Think about it. There are a lot of good-looking obviously black men but you chose me—a mulatto, a mutt, a high-yellow descendant of "massa."

Why are we even talking about this after all these years together? I've never questioned you about your choice of me as your white lover. Why did you want me?

I liked your red hair when you still had some.

Quit kidding.

I'm not kidding. If you had been black with red hair, I would have wanted you.

You're saying it's just the red hair and only the red hair and not this white skin?

What's so appealing about white skin?

I don't know. I've never been particularly interested in white guys.

And neither was I until you came along.

So, you wouldn't be attracted to another white guy?

Not really. I happen to like black people. Black guys. Always have.

Okay, for the sake of argument, think about Dunn: he had a black parent as well as a white one. Would he have been black or white to you?

You told me that Dunn felt that he wasn't sure if he was white or black.

His father's family accepted him as black.

But, you've said that his mother's family accepted him as white.

That is what they wanted to believe.

You say that but his black family wanted to believe what they wanted to believe too. Who's right?

Both, I guess.

But you always say that people are one or the other, not both just because of who's deciding.

What does the law say?

Fortunately, we no longer have laws that decide race. People decide for themselves.

And that is why in our family some folks believe that they are white even though they shared ancestors with other folks like me who believe that they are black.

What if I told you that I had black ancestors?

Did any of them have red hair?

I'm serious.

Really?

Really.

Who were they?

There was one for sure. He would have been my great grandfather on my father's side of the family. We think his name was Arkady Miller.

Miller?

Yeah. Here's the story I was told in my family: I had a distant relative in Europe named Isaac Schiff. He was probably a peddler or some other poor guy who lived in a Jewish ghetto. He and his wife, Rachel Gold, had several children, most of whom died young or left the ghetto for better prospects. One daughter, Miriam, left home and managed to get on a boat to this country. How she managed that is anybody's guess. Very likely she slept with some guy who helped her on the ship. They may have traveled as a married couple. Maybe, they were even married. In any case, they reached New York and the man disappeared from her life. She was on her own trying to find a way to survive when she met a cook, a free black man named Arkady Miller. He probably felt sorry for her or she may have been willing to fuck him for a place to stay and food to eat. This was around the end of the Civil War. They lived together for years and had a least four children. My grandfather, Nathan Schiff, was the eldest. He looked white enough to pass and did. Because his mother was a Jew, he was a Jew. He eventually married my grandmother, Rebecca Ornstein. She had red hair. They had three children, my father, Avram Schiff, was the eldest. He married my mother, Sarah Meyeroff, after he moved to Detroit to work in the automobile industry. My mother also had red hair. I'm the oldest of their children. As you know, my sister, Ariella, and my brother, Adam, don't keep in touch with me. When they went away to college, they never came back to Detroit. In the old South, I would be considered an octoroon— one-eighth black. So, I'm not as black as you but I could be considered black enough to be on the wrong side of the color line.

Why, after all of these years, are you just now telling me this?

Because, until now, Mosey, I didn't want my ancestors to be the most persuasive thing for you about me. You have always seen me one way—white. I wanted you to accept me for me regardless of who or what you thought I was. I have always wanted you, not because you are black or part black or part white or white or whatever. I want you for you.

Mosey smiled. Something finally became clear to him about Steven and about families and about life. As far as he and Steven were concerned, race did not matter because who even knew what race was? At the same time, however, he knew that in the world in which they lived, what people thought about race did matter. Their world was structured around race but their life together could continue without race as a barrier to their love.

During the remainder of their stay in Rome, Mosey and Steven visited several popular tourist attractions including the Roman Forum and Colosseum, Piazza Navona, many churches, and the Borghese Gardens. They happened upon the Pantheon quite by chance as they walked from the Piazza Navona to their hotel near the Spanish Steps. They had heard about the building but they did not consider it an essential part of their visit. However, the massive structure, with its porch of columns that dwarf mere humans, and seemingly pinched on all sides by neighboring buildings stopped them in their stroll. They sat with other tourists on steps opposite the Pantheon's front and simply gazed across the shallow square at its solid bulk. Although both of them had seen grand, impressive buildings in Rome, this was something that seemed beyond grand. It was beyond words. They decided to go inside. As they passed beneath the entry porch and through the single massive portal, they were completely unprepared for the interior. The space inside was circular, without any kind of pillars to support the round dome overhead. The only light in the interior came through a great, circular opening in the center of the dome. As they looked up, at the sky way beyond, they thought of this enormous opening as an eye of the heavens. It is, in fact, called an oculus. As they peered above, it was as if they were being watched from the sky.

After Rome, Florence and Venice were enjoyable but the spectacular appearance of Rome made the other cities seem somehow less powerful as experiences. They saw many wonderful things: Michelangelo's *David* made them both lustful and they marveled at *David*'s physique not to mention his prominent genitals. Since all the other tourists were ogling what they were ogling, they felt less self-conscious in their lust. They pondered the beautiful uncircumcised penis of *David*. Steven was circumcised but Mosey was not. Steven was puzzled by the *David*'s uncircumcised penis. He noted that the biblical David was a Hebrew and male Hebrews were circumscribed at birth. A tourist who overheard Steven and Mosey's conversation about this, offered that Michelangelo was not circumcised and didn't want to mutilate the natural beauty of his *David*. Steven listened and winked at Mosey while also glancing at Mosey's crotch.

Their return flight home to Detroit was interrupted by a stopover in New York. Mosey had never visited the city and since their international flight was roundtrip New York-Rome-New York, they agreed to spend a few days in the city before continuing on to Detroit. Mosey wanted to visit Swee whom he had not seen in person in years although they talked frequently by phone. Steven wanted to see his Aunt Judith, his father's sister and the last surviving member of the older generation of his own family. She was quite ancient as was Swee who turned 88 in 1999, the year of Mosey's visit. Judith was 89 and lived two more years after their visit. Mosey and Steven decided to visit Swee first. She still lived in her apartment with Gulley in west Harlem. Gulley's children had all left home for school, jobs, and starting their own families. Even Bone, who turned out to be not only bright but also talented in science, majored in math and physics. His success was a surprise to everyone except Gulley who had done everything possible to get him on the right track. One day when he was still young and foolish, she told him that he could become a thug or a person of worth. His choice. If he wanted to be a thug, he could leave her home now. If he wanted to be a person of worth, she would make sure he had every opportunity available to a young black boy. When he saw his best friend die as a thug, he told his mother that he would stay and try his best. And he did.

Gulley and Swee had long been retired and living, if not comfortably, at least without great financial stress. Their combined incomes from social security and Swee's modest pension and retirement account covered their needs and allowed them to stay in their rent-controlled apartment. When Mosey and Steven arrived, there were many tears. Mosey was surprised that Swee was considerably thinner than the last time he saw her. Gulley also was thinner. Apparently, they both changed their diets and began eating healthier and walked a lot for exercise. Of course, both women were gray but looking almost stylish. Swee thought that Mosey had hardly changed. He was gray too but as handsome and slim as ever. Swee had never met Steven although they talked frequently on the phone when Mosey called. She thought to herself that Steven could use a little exercise because he only vaguely resembled the man that Mosey had described to her when they first became a couple.

Mosey and Steven sat on the couch. Swee and Gulley sat in overstuffed chairs. Refreshments had been placed on the coffee table. Dinner came later. The women wanted to know about their trip —the things that they had seen, the sights that most impressed them. The men talked about Rome in great and intimate detail then Mosey mentioned Florence. He was surprised by the narrow streets and how the stone buildings were so close to the streets with barely any sidewalk. He loved the River Arno that flowed through the city. It reminded him of Detroit on the river separating the United States from Canada. The Arno, however, was so different because it was much narrower than the Detroit River and there were many bridges across it including the Ponte Vecchio which had buildings on it. Detroit only had one bridge and that was a huge steel suspension bridge. Florence felt cozy and full of surprises down every street and around every corner. And there was art everywhere—statues in the public squares; paintings in the churches; and beautifully ornamented buildings. But it was crowded with tourists, so many, in fact, that the visit was spoiled by the crowds. Sienna and Venice were the same. Too many people for such small spaces. The many things that the men had to say carried the visit to dinner time. Gulley had prepared a hearty beef stew with green salad. As they ate their meal, Steven talked about his feelings of the trip.

It was, in fact, the first time that he and Mosey had travelled together and he had wondered how the two of them would be treated as a gay, interracial, middle-aged couple. He was surprised that no one seem to take notice of them. They were just tourists, American tourists who spoke no Italian. He realized, after a while in Italy, that he was no longer conscious of race, either his or anyone else's. People were just people. The only thing that really distinguished folks was the language that they spoke. He heard French, Spanish, German, Japanese, and several languages that he didn't recognize. He thought maybe they were Russian and Arabic. Then he remembered some Africans who were speaking their native languages. Steven stopped talking. He had the sudden realization that he had seen the Africans as standing apart from everyone else. And it wasn't because of their language. It was their color. They were black. Really black, not chocolate hues of African-Americans. His sudden awareness of his color consciousness embarrassed him. He had long convinced himself that race and color didn't matter to him. He had, after all, a black man as an ancestor. But here it was in his memory, the singling out of Africans because of their color. He decided to discuss that at the dinner table.

Steven: Why did I see Africans as different? Because of their color?

Swee: Steven, you're no different from anyone else. We all see color. The point is: What do we think and do about it?

Mosey: I've always told you that you were color conscious. You denied it as if there were not color differences. But to your credit you've not seen color in a prejudicial way. In other words, you're not a bigot. We are all racists since we live in a country where some people have used color to create a racial hierarchy with white on top and black on the bottom. The white race has declared itself superior and the black race inferior. And, yet, what is race? You and I and Swee and Gulley are all mixtures to one degree or another. What race does that make us?

Swee: In truth, this is not about race or color but about power and authority with white people holding the power.

Gulley: You know, my family comes from blacks and whites just like yours. We've got a whole branch of the family that passes for white. I never had that option and, if I did, I don't know if I would have taken it. It hasn't been easy being at the bottom of the pile, being treated like shit. Excuse my language. Getting the least of everything. Knowing that you can't climb up because of your color or race. I have actually hated white people most of my life because they treated me like I was no one. Not as important as their dog or cat. They hardly ever have seen me as a person with intelligence, talents, ambitions, feelings, and goals. I've just been a nigger woman— a double curse—the lowest of the low and, yet, I have a nice home, a woman who loves me, children who are proud of themselves and of whom I'm proud, and a life that has been productive, honest, and loving. I'm somebody and I like me but if I had given in to all those whites, and some blacks, that treated me badly, I wouldn't be here now. I would be beaten down and dead like too many black folks.

Mosey: We've all been there and we've kept pushing, taking one step at a time. Seizing our opportunities. Watching ourselves and everyone around us. Staying low. Minding our own business. Squeezing out what happiness we could. Finding love. Making something of ourselves and our lives. Doing our best. Holding on to those who hold on to us. Opening our minds and hearts. Learning. Working. Planning. Helping. Being helped. Being loved. Being.

Swee: I knew that you've come a long way, Mosey. I just didn't know how far you've come.

Mosey: You've been my inspiration, Swee. You came to New York. Worked. Got your degree, and became a writer. Who knew back in Pachacuti that we would be sitting here after Gulley's delicious meal, talking about Italy, race, life?

Steven: I want to thank you, too, Swee. You were a real mother to Mosey. He's become the man he is in no small part because of you. And, Gulley, the meal was wonderful and I was very moved by your story. I know I have probably had a much easier life than anyone else in this room and it was not because I was smarter or more talented or better educated or from a better family. My color has made life easier for me because I have only had the normal obstacles that white people face. I have never felt denied or abused because of my color. Except by Mosey.

Swee: Steven, you are family. You're one of us. Even if you are only an octoroon, you're one of our people. Hey, we are a big house. All are welcome!

The next day Steven had arranged to meet his Aunt Judith at her apartment on the Upper West Side of Manhattan. Although he had never been close to his aunt—a nice Jewish boy did not like to tell his aunt that he lived with a man—he felt that at this point, late in their lives, it would be no loss to pay his respect. She welcomed Steven and Mosey warmly into her tiny apartment. The living room had too much of everything. It felt cramped and busy with objects on every surface, and pillows and throws everywhere. Aunt Judith walked slowly and very carefully using her cane to steady herself. She lowered herself into a rocking chair and gestured to Steven for him and Mosey to sit on the sofa.

Aunt Judith was a tiny woman, white haired and pale. She spoke softly but emphatically, seemingly always attentive to her point and not expecting interruption:

I always told my brother, Avram, your father, that he spoiled you by letting you do whatever you wanted. I warned him that, if you didn't have a girlfriend, you would never have a wife. And see. Here you are with this nice gentleman but he is no wife. So, does that make you the wife? Don't tell me. Some things these old ears don't need to hear. You, Mister, what is your name? Oh, yes. Mr. Mosey. Like Moses. Did you lead your people out of bondage? Of course not. That was the wonderful Reverend Doctor King. He was the new Moses. I went to that March in Washington. I was there with all those people. Black and white. And I heard him. I could hardly see, of course, I was so far away. But I heard him and I tell you, I believed him when he said that one day we would all be together as one—black and white. Well, it hasn't happened yet. But look at you two —black and white together. Not quite what the Reverend had in mind. Who knows? Not I. Maybe he did know. That Bayard Rustin, forgive me, Mr. Mosey, I think that he was the genius behind the success of the March—Rustin was like you two. A what? What do they say now! A gay? A gay. So, what is there to be gay about? Never mind. The Reverend made me feel hope for all of us. I thought the blacks would finally find their proper place in this country. Be able to live like the rest of us. The same opportunities. The same successes. Well, I guess it is happening but we still have a long way to go. Would you agree, Mr. Mosey? Of course, you would. The gays have it better too. When Avram told me Steven was gay—he didn't say gay back then. I won't say what he said but he meant gay—I told him: Dear God, someone is going to kill him. I mean I was sure that he would be beaten up and stabbed or shot. That's what happened back then but why am I telling you? You already know that. Avram. He was such a pushover about you. Judith, he says, the boy will be all right. He can take care of himself. I just want him to be happy and I said to Avram: How is he going to be happy? He'll never know family life. He'll never have children. He'll meet all kinds and probably end up a drunk or a dope addict living on the streets. This son, I told him, would never be happy and he would break Avram's heart. Well, Avram died before all of this liberation. He saw Kennedy but was spared the assassination. In 1962, when Avram died, I remember it well. Sarah, your mother, called me. Judith, she said, Avram is dead. Just like that. I nearly had a stroke. How could he be dead?, I said. He's not old enough to be dead. He wasn't even sick. Judith, he had a stroke and died. That was it. Boom. Dead. My dear brother, my only brother. I cried for days. My brother was gone. My mother, Rebecca, and my father, Nathan, were dead before you were born. My dear husband, Howard, god bless his soul, died 11 years ago leaving me all alone and childless. My only living relatives are you, Steven, and your sister, Ariella, and your brother, Adam. Thank god, they have children or that would be the end of the Schiff family. My husband's family is almost gone. Both of his brothers are deceased. One never married and has no children. The other had a son, Richard, and a daughter, Amy. She lives in New York. I told her you were coming to visit me today and she asked if she could come by and meet you. I don't know why but she should be here soon, at 3 o'clock.

Almost as soon as Judith finished speaking the building buzzer rang. Then a few minutes later the apartment buzzer rang. Judith toddled to the door and opened it.

Come on in, Amy.

Aunt Judith, it's so good to see you again. I hope that you don't mind that I brought my partner, Dianna, with me. She wanted to meet you finally.

Welcome, Dianna. Partner? Does that mean what?

We live together. That kind of partner.

Oh, well. We're having a gay party here today. Find a place to sit. Over there is my nephew, Steven, and his partner, Mosey.

I know Mosey, said Amy. I think he remembers me. Mosey, I'm Amity Lowe. I lived with your Aunt Swee in Pachacuti. You lived with us for several years, you and Trique. Do you remember me?

Mosey: Of course, I do, Amity. All these years. You look a little different. Swee has told me about your theater work. How you've made a name for yourself. She even told me that you've been living with Dianna for a long time.

Amity: Yes, Dianna, my boyfriend, Hiram, and I got an apartment together; Hiram is in real estate. We're a family. Hiram is really like a brother to me. We were once lovers but now we're just dear friends. Dianna has become my true love and we also work together as a team. I trust her creative instincts and she inspires me. And you and Steven have been together a long time too.

Steven: It took a long time before Mosey came around but we've been together almost thirty years.

Dianna: Mosey, how long has it been since you've seen Amity?

Mosey: Dianna, I left Pachacuti in 1945. In 1968, at a memorial service in Los Angeles, we met again. That was the last time I saw her. She's changed a lot since then. I remember her as being skinny.

Amity: Well, yes, I'm a little more matronly now.

Dianna: She's still beautiful even with gray hair.

Mosey: But how is it that you're here?

Amity: I think that Swee told you that I'm from Tallahassee where my parents lived and my brother, Richard, still lives. My mother was part black and part Native-American and my father was a Jew. His family came from Germany in the early 20th-Century and settled here in New York. My father, Nisan, and Aunt Judith's husband, Howard, were brothers. During the First World War my father went into the Army and ended up in Florida where he met my mother, Edouit Long-Green. Although they couldn't marry, they had me and my brother. I left Florida with a man who came to Georgia and that's how I ended up in Pachacuti where I met Swee. We moved here to New York when you, Trique, and Martalee all ran away north. My father's other brother, Uncle Aaron, helped Swee and me when we first came to New York. He's also deceased.

Steven: I know that story but I never connected you with whom I always knew as Amy, not Amity. All these years and I never suspected that I had another connection to Mosey's family.

Judith: This is too much for an old lady. Is everybody related to everybody?

Amity: Auntie, if there was an Adam and Eve, we all are related!

Judith: Black, white—all mixed up like this. Men with men. Women with women. Jews and Goyim. This isn't right. This is not what god intended.

Amity: Auntie, god must have intended this because here we are. And we're not the only ones. There are lots of gay people and interracial couples and families.

Judith: This is not the teaching of the Torah.

Amity: It may not be how the Torah is interpreted but gay people have always been here and different races have always found each other. Just because you or someone else doesn't like it or doesn't approve won't make us go away.

Judith: Okay, I'm an old woman. I learned things differently. My meshuganah brother had children with an Indian.

Steven: And your grandfather was a black man.

Judith: Steven, you should never tell that lie.

Steven: It isn't a lie, Auntie. Your aunts, Jessica and Carol, told me that story before they died. They wanted me to know the truth. Besides, what does it matter? Aren't we all one big family anyway? All people are related somehow. We've been divided up into groups so that some will have control or advantages over others. Skin color, ancestry, don't matter. Even religion. We're all humans and we are capable of loving who we love instead of who someone thinks we should love.

Judith: Old women don't change their minds just because somebody wants to change everything to suit themselves.

Amity: Aunt Judith, Dianna and I—and I think that Steven and Mosey agree—we don't want to change your mind. We just want you to see that we are here. We are happy. We live our lives without hurting other people. We love who we love and believe that all love is better than hate. We may be upsetting some ideas or rules but people make rules and people can change them. We hope that some day the rules and laws will be fair for everyone.

Steven: Auntie, we are your family. We love you even if you don't think that we conform to your rules.

Judith: Not my rules but I understand what you're saying

Steven: Okay, not your rules but the rules. Even those rules change. In any case, thank you for having us here today and having the chance to meet Amity and Dianna. I think that we will go now and say goodbye.

Judith: Forgive an old woman. I grew up in another time. Things were different. More strict and certain. I've also lived alone with no children. You and Amy are all I have. Please don't let what I believe keep you away from me. Family is everything even if it isn't kosher. Feygele. Schwarze. Who am I to judge?

Steven, Mosey, Amity, and Dianna headed to a diner near Judith's apartment. There, over dinner, they caught up on one another's lives and filled in many details of their past histories. They vowed to remain in contact after Steven and Mosey returned to Detroit. That would the first and last time they were together.

When Mosey and Steven returned to Detroit, Mosey called Lucius to tell him about their trip. Mosey was uncharacteristically enthusiastic and wanted to share every detail of what he saw, ate, and felt. Lucius listened patiently, as he often did, and finally asked Mosey about Steven's reaction to Italy:

Oh, he loved it. We talked about everything. Lucius, we had fun together. He enjoyed it as much as I did.

Did he?

Sure. You sound like you don't believe me.

I believe you.

Then, what's up?

I'm jealous, that's what's up.

Why?

Mosey, you've taken this fabulous trip with a man you've known since, since how long? Over 30 years? 30 years you two have been together. I'm still a bachelor. I've never been to Europe. I don't even have a boyfriend now. I'm jealous that you got your shit together and have made a good life for yourself with a man you wanted at one time to throw away. Now look at you, all Italian this and Italian that with Mr. No-Longer Red.

Do you want me to feel sorry for you?

Yes, Bitch. I need a little comfort right now. Mr. Lucius is getting old, too, and there aren't many opportunities left for me in this life.

Lucius, as long as you're alive and kicking, you can make your opportunities. That's what I've learned.

Easier said . . .

Than done?

That's right.

Lucius, what is really going on with you? Why, when I've just come back from my first and, maybe, only trip to Europe and I want to share with you my happiness, you want to be such a cranky old lady? You used to criticize me for being closed up in myself and not being out in the world. Now I'm out in the world and that seems to make you unhappy. Why?

Because I always wanted to have with you what you have now with Steven, and I know that he makes you happy. Being with him makes you happy. You two could do nothing together and you would still be happy. You found the only man who probably could make you happy. I'm pissed that man wasn't me.

Lucius, you know that I love you as my best friend. As a brother. More than a brother. You are my special friend who has stuck with me all these years. You could have walked away. You've threatened many times but you've always been there for me. The truth is that I could never have become who I am if I had tried to be your partner. I couldn't have become Steven's partner if I hadn't struggled on my own, by myself, to become myself. When I finally got to a place where I felt I was myself, Steven gave me what I needed for a partner—a willingness to go along with me on a journey that I didn't even know where it was headed.

Was it because he was white?

You know what? Maybe, so.

Why is that? Because white is better than black?

No. White isn't better than black. It's just different. Sometimes. You know, Lucius, it has taken me a long time to accept that I probably have as much white in me as black. I don't know why that makes a difference but it does. I've always felt different and I've always been treated differently. Because I'm black and white? I don't know. I do know that I'm not a white person and, sometimes, I think that I'm not a black person. What am I? Where do I fit in? In Italy, no one seemed to pay any attention to me as black or white. I was just a tourist.

You know what? It's funny how I've known these things about you and didn't know them or didn't take them seriously. To me, you were just Mosey, beautiful Mosey. One-armed Mosey. Big dick Mosey. I-Want-To-Melt-In-Your-Arms Mosey. But, you are right. You are different and people do see you differently and it is because you are either a white-nigger or a black-cracker.

Maybe both.

So, how is Mr. No-Longer-Red?

He's doing fine. Now that he is retired, too, we are spending a lot of time together doing things that we've often talked about but never had the opportunity to do. He's fun to be with. Smart. Sometimes too serious. Always the white boy. You know, I love him. Really.

I know. Let me be jealous of you because I love you and I'm happy for you. Always will be.

You want to know something about Steven that you've always wanted to know?

What's that?

It's brown down there.

What's brown down there?

You know, Red . . .

Oh. Brown. If you tell me it's also kinky, I'm gonna think that he has some jungle in him.

Are you sitting down?

Yes.

He does. He's a nigger Jew. I hit the jackpot!

VI

DR. PENDLE

Hello. 911.

Hello, my partner is having trouble breathing. He needs an ambulance immediately. I'm afraid to take him to the hospital in my car because he might stop breathing.

I'll send an EMS. What is your address?

One Lafayette Plaissance.

Your name? Steven Schiff.

Can you be reached by the number you're dialing from?

Yes.

An EMS is on the way.

By the time the ambulance arrived Mosey's breathing was shallow and intermittent. The EMS attendants fastened an oxygen mask to his mouth and he began breathing more deeply. But by the time the EMS vehicle arrived at the emergency dock of General Hospital, he had stopped breathing. He was wheeled into emergency surgery but his vital signs were all flat. The doctors informed Steven that Mosey had died probably of pulmonary distress. His lungs then his heart had stopped functioning.

Steven took a taxi home. He called Mosey's physician and then the funeral home with which arrangements for the body had already been made. Then he called Swee. Later, he called Lucius, then Habboey. Since Mosey's health had been declining for some time, no one was surprised by his death but all were saddened and offered their support to Steven. Habboey said that she would come over immediately, as did Lucius. Swee contacted Amity, Waite, and Lee. Later, she called Mosey's sister, Serriah, and his brother, Phessin, in Pachacuti. They promised to inform other members of the family and so it went. Word went out to all the intertwined families and friends.

Very few of Mosey's living relatives really knew him. Most of Mosey's generation and the generations before him were dead. The younger folks never knew Mosey and no one talked about him except for the tale of the man who lost his arm. Those who did know Mosey either knew him very well or at a distance. He was known by few and loved by fewer still. Steven notified the art museum from which Mosey had retired nine years previously. He doubted that anyone currently working there would even remember Mosey. Mosey had not made many friends although people who knew him liked him. But he was not anyone's best pal except for Lucius.

His first love, Trique, had died in 1990. They were born in the same year—1929. Trique was killed in a car pile-up on a Los Angeles freeway, the notorious I-405. It was a tragic death that deeply depressed Mosey. William Bass, Trique's partner who was also in the car, survived with a permanently damaged leg; Mosey and William never established a relationship. Mosey's long-time friend and sometime lover, Lucius, never quite got over his infatuation with Mosey but he was supportive of Steven because Steven also had long been a part of Lucius' life. Waite remained fond of Mosey but his life continued to be focused on his partner, Woodward Templeton. It was a small circle even counting relatives.

Mosey's body was cremated according to his wishes. Mosey had told Steven that a memorial service was okay if Steven wanted to have one. Many were still celebrating the election of the first black president of the United States and making preparations for the holidays so Steven decided to wait until March of the following year to hold the service. He arranged with a Unitarian church in Palmer Park for the memorial service and reception following. Although neither Steven nor Mosey belonged to any religious organization, Steven accepted Lucius' advice since Lucius was a member of the congregation. It would probably be a small gathering that could be held in the chapel instead of the main auditorium. With date and arrangements set, word was spread of Mosey's memorial service.

March is a chancy month in Detroit. The weather can change drastically from day to day. Sometimes there are hints of spring. Sometimes winter won't let go. As luck would have it, the Saturday in March for the service was mild and sunny. Steven and Lucius arrived early to greet guests. Several folks had indicated that they would attend. Habboey was the first guest to arrive. She was now 84 but upright and trim. Her gray hair was short in a boyish cut that made her look younger than her years. She volunteered to greet other arriving guests. In rapid order of arrival were: Phessin and his wife, Luma, with Alfred—Trique and Lee's son—and Alfred's wife, Beatrice; Swee, Gulley, Amity, Dianna and Hiram; Lee and her friend, Brenda Lessinger; and finally Waite and Woodward. Two old Detroit friends also appeared—Parker Patterson and Prince Henry Walker. But then an even larger group of folks appeared. They were Mosey's former co-workers from the museum. Swayne Pitkin, Earl Gladney, Paul Bosch, Alice Compton and Thurmore Pierce. There were so many people from the museum that some had to stand at the sides and in the rear of the chapel. The service was intentionally planned to be brief with a few remarks about Mosey from Steven, Lucius, and Swee. But after the planned remarks, folks— family and friends—wanted to come forward to tell personal stories about Mosey. For a man who seemed to keep pretty much to himself, a picture formed of an intelligent, thoughtful, honest, and loving man who, despite his reserve and inwardness, was genuinely sympathetic and kind to everyone. There was an outpouring of love for a man who, although he found it difficult to be loved, did love others. That is what they felt.

Swayne Pitkin, a fellow guard of Mosey's, wanted to speak. He moved toward the lectern and mounted the few steps to reach it. He paused before speaking and cleared his throat.

My name is Swayne Pitkin and I met Mosey on the first day of his job at the art museum. He was a handsome fellow. Very reserved but obviously curious about the place where he was now employed. He was sincere but a little anxious about his duties. In time, he became an excellent guard, one of the best, in my opinion, because he cared about the place and about the visitors. A guard has a tricky job to protect the art in the museum while helping visitors to enjoy their visit. It's a simple balance for most visitors; they know not to touch or otherwise harm the art. But for some who don't know or don't care, the guard must be firm and sometimes disciplinary. Mosey could be both gentle and fierce.

But I want to tell a little story about Mosey. One day early in Mosey's employment, we were both assigned to the African art galleries. Mosey had become very curious about art. He would ask questions and, I later found out, began to read about it. He bought books on art at the museum shop. But on this day, Mosey didn't know anything at all about African art. He asked me why it looked so different from the art in the American and European galleries. Was it made by people without skills or talent? Did Africans look like the sculptures? These questions bothered him. I told him what I knew that Africans had a different concept of art than Europeans and Americans. Their art served their own needs in religious and ceremonial practices. Their cultures were different from European cultures but that didn't mean that they were inferior. It took lots of skill and talent to create the objects in these galleries. In fact, Europeans began to admire African art, collected it, and African art helped Europeans to change the way they viewed their own art. Mosey took all of this in and some time later, he came to me and said: Swayne, I got a book about Picasso. He was one of the greatest European artists of the 20th-Century. He studied African art and used some of the African images in his paintings. He changed the way he made art because of the ideas he discovered in African art. From that day on, whenever he was stationed in the African art galleries, he became a kind of tour guide for uninformed visitors. Mosey was a man who became aware of, and proud, of his ancestry. He was an inspiration to me.

At the conclusion of the service, the crowd proceeded to the social hall on the lower level where light refreshments were provided. Swee worked her way through the crowd introducing herself to those she didn't know and chatting with Mosey's family members and intimate friends. When she came upon Alfred, he pulled her aside and asked her if they could talk later. Swee and Gulley had plans to spend time with Amity, Dianna and Hiram but Swee said that she could postpone their time together to talk with Alfred.

They arranged to meet at Habboey's house where Swee and Gulley were staying. When Alfred arrived without his wife, he spoke briefly with the other women then he and Swee went into a small sitting room where Habboey had the TV. Alfred began:

Swee, I wanted to talk with you because you know more about our families than anyone. I know that you've been writing a family history for years, collecting stories and information and tracing our ancestry.

Well, you're partially right. I have been writing a history about our families but it isn't really a genealogical history. It's more of an investigation of how our families are enmeshed in the racial, sexual, and gender issues of this country. And, I'm a kind of historian but I'm not the family genealogist.

Who is?

Serriah. Mosey's oldest sister.

Serriah?

That's right.

She still lives in Pachacuti?

She does indeed.

How old is she?

She younger than I am. She's 88. Whenever I've had a question about ancestors, I've asked Serriah. She seems to know everything about everybody.

I need to talk to her.

Why?

You know most of my history. Right?

Not really. But let me tell you what I know. I know about your birth. You and your fraternal twin, Dunn, were born to Lee Boston Pendle and Trique Pendle. Because you were a black baby born to a white single woman, your mother gave you to a wet-nurse, Callista Collins. Your grandmothers, Olive Fleet Boston and Xantha Debobo Pendle, retrieved you from the wet-nurse when they found out about your birth, arranged to place you in the home of Xantha's brother, Toetus, with his wife and children, and gave you their family name—Debobo. You were raised as one of their family but you were told that they were not your birth parents. When your brother,

Dunn, died in Viet Nam, your grandmothers decided to tell you about Lee and Trique. You met them for the first time at Dunn's memorial service. I know that when you got out of the Army, you went to Los Angeles and, I think, went to college. That's what I know.

Well, let me back up a bit first. When I was in the Army, I lucked out. I never went to Viet Nam like Dunn. I was stationed at the Presidio in San Francisco as a desk clerk. Coincidently, Dunn was also stationed there but, of course, I didn't know about him at the time. When I was discharged, I asked Trique if I could stay with him for a while because I wanted to use my G.I. benefits to attend UCLA. Trique was excited that I would stay with him and William. They gave me the guest room and told me I could stay as long as I wanted. Trique said that he wanted to formally adopt me and I agreed. With Lee, we got a new birth certificate making me Alfred Debobo Pendle. I stayed with Trique for a year then got my own apartment with a couple of other guys. I graduated in four years with a history degree and decided to continue in graduate school. While I was studying, I met a female student from Ghana named Beatrice Nhongo. We got married while I was working on my dissertation. She worked and, with my scholarship, we were able to get our own little apartment in Los Feliz. I graduated with a PhD in 1977. I taught history at the University of California, Irvine for six years then got a position at the University of Michigan where I am a full professor. Beatrice and I have two children, Maddie and Hunter. They are 28 and 23. Maddie works in Chicago and Hunter is in college in Atlanta. That just about brings things up to date.

What is your specialty in history?

My dissertation focussed on Antebellum enslavement in urban Georgia. I was interested to learn about the lives of enslaved blacks in towns and cities as opposed to plantations. Since then, I have become more concerned with plantation life but from the perspective of how the enslaved were uniquely adapted to the harsh rural conditions of the South. That interest has brought me to my current quest and that is to visit rural areas of Africa from which agricultural people were kidnapped and transported to the USA. I want to study firsthand life on farms in Africa. Beatrice wants us to go to Ghana to meet her family who live in Ghana's capital, Accra, and to tour the countryside in preparation for a longer stay later for my research.

Okay. So how can I help you?

Before I go to Ghana, I want to know as much as I can about our families' ancestors, going back to their origins in Africa.

Well, you can certainly know more about our families but I'm not sure that you can get back to any African ancestors. Our family isn't *Roots*. Here's what I can do: I'll give you a copy of my manuscript that has a lot of family history and some pretty spicy details. But if you want to go far back in time, you'll have to talk with Serriah DeBobo Fox.

Serriah still lived in the family home of her parents, Adelpho DeBobo and Loissey Sellabie DeBobo. It was a modest house like others in the black section of Pachacuti. There were three small bedrooms, all on one floor, and a sitting room. The kitchen and bathroom were at the back of the house. Over the years, Serriah made the house more comfortable and modern. However, it was still a simple working class home with modest furnishings. In expectation of her guest, Serrriah had the house cleaned to white glove standards. Her young roomer, Tracey Brown, who, in the traditions of black women in Pachacuti, was a domestic, cleaned Serriah's house to the perfection of the white homes in which she worked. Fresh flowers were placed on a table in the sitting room. Iced tea with lemon and warm ginger bread squares were ready for Serriah's guest.

When Alfred arrived, he was both pleased and dismayed. The welcome was impeccable but he was astonished by the general decrepitude of the black section of town. Although some blacks now lived outside of this ghetto in newer, modern neighborhoods surrounding Pachacuti, the historic district was nearly Third World in appearance with the exception of Serriah's house. He kept his reaction to himself. Serriah had been throughly briefed by Swee on the purpose of his visit and after an almost mandatory review of Alfred's history to date, she started in on the purpose of his visit:

Swee is my aunt, you know. She's a half-sister to my mother, Loissey. They had the same father, Hanton Sellabie, but different mothers. Loissey's mother was Soonie Fleet, a white woman. Swee's mother was Darissa McKree, a black woman. That already tells you something about how complicated ancestry is in our family and in many families in the South. Swee has already told you about some of your ancestors; I'll fill in the rest of what I know.

Let's go back generation by generation starting with your father:

Trique Pendle, was the son of Murty Pendle and Xantha DeBobo. Murty's father was a white man, Murray Fleet. His mother was a black woman, Estah Pendle. Murray and Estah, of course, could never marry because of their color—besides, Murray was already married to a white woman, Sutreen Moore, and one of their daughters was Soonie Fleet, my grandmother.

Now, your family name—Pendle—comes from Estah's father, Oscar Pendle, a black man who had been enslaved but became a free man of color after Emancipation. He married a mixed-race, formerly enslaved woman named Medan Smith. They had three children—their daughter, Estah, a son called Cutt and another son named Wheeler; the sons left Pachacuti when they were young and never returned. Estah remembered that her father, Oscar, called his mother, Creanda, but Estah could not give any more information about Creanda or her ancestors. She also didn't know anything about the family of her mother, Medan. So, those are dead ends on your father's side because the links were broken.

Serriah, how do you know this much?

We had to pass on what we knew generation to generation. It was important to us to know where we came from. It was, for a long time, all that we had. But enslavement broke up families, sent young children far away from their parents and prevented any re-connection. When white folks were the parents in our families, they often didn't acknowledge their mixed-race children, and black women often didn't want to admit to rape, even though everyone knew where these not-black, not-white, children came from.

So, there's nothing more on the Pendle side?

Well, not exactly. There's also the DeBobo. You know that your father's mother and my aunt, Xantha DeBobo, was the daughter of Adelpho Debobo and Loissey Sellabie. That not only makes you a relative of the DeBobo and Sellabie but also carries your ancestry further into the past. Adelpho's parents were Bear DeBobo and Ardeah Person. We know nothing about Ardeah's family but we know a lot about Bear's ancestors and I'll come back to that after we talk about the Boston on your mother's side.

Now that's a complicated story but important for what you need to know. Your mother, Martalee, is the daughter of Finn Boston, Sr. and Olive Fleet. There's that Fleet name again because Olive's father was the same Murray Fleet, who was your great-grandfather on your father's side. As I said, Murray Fleet was married to Sutreen Moore, Olive's mother. This was when he got your great-grandmother, Estah Pendle, pregnant with your grandfather, Murty Pendle. That means that your mother and father are distantly related to the same man, Murray Fleet, your great-grandfather on both sides of your family. That white side of both of your parents is not known beyond Murray Fleet because we weren't interested in white folks' ancestors and didn't keep track of them. Is this helpful so far?

Yes and no. Yes, it fills in some blanks but it also raises some unsettling issues about my family like was my mother attracted to my father because, somehow, she sensed his connectedness to her? And, no, it seems that we can only go back as far as enslavement, not Africa.

Well, we haven't got to the good part yet.

What do you mean?

I mean the Boston side of the family that connects with the DeBobo and takes us way back in time. As I said, your mother's father was Finn Boston, Sr. He was the son of Roy Boston, a white man, and Deerie DeBobo, a black woman. Finn was white enough to cross the color line and he did so he and his children all identified as white. Now, here's the connection: Deerie DeBobo, your maternal great-grandmother, and Bear DeBobo, your paternal great-grandfather, were sister and brother. That means that you are descended through both parents from DeBobo, and that family's history goes way back.

Bear and Deerie were born to a woman named Nattea DeBobo and fathered by an unknown white man. She was born enslaved in Louisiana and died in 1900. She remembered her own parents as an enslaved man named Midah and an enslaved woman named Jubelie. The couple were separated before Emancipation and Nattea stayed with her father. She said that Midah never knew his father but he knew his mother's name was Athena. This takes us deep into enslavement time. Nattea said that Athena didn't know her mother but her father was called Jukah and he was the son of a woman named Desirée. She, in turn, was the daughter of a man named Abediah. He was born to a woman named Onyx who was a pure African and who survived the Middle Passage. She was raped on the slave ship by a white man and was pregnant with Abediah when she was sold to a plantation owner in Louisiana. We know that Onyx was the name given her by her enslaving master. Her African name was Adwoa. She probably arrived in the USA around 1740. When she was captured in Africa, she was about 16 years old. She lived in a village a long way from the ocean. She remembered being kidnapped by Africans who were not from her village and not from her own people; they spoke a different language. She was imprisoned by white men in a building near the ocean before she was placed on a ship for the long voyage to a place she didn't know and never understood. And that, Alfred, is all what Nattea remembered and that is all I've got.

Well, that's certainly more than I expected. So, let me see if I got this straight: my father and mother both have a common ancestor in a white man, Murray Fleet, and in a black woman, Nattea DeBobo. It is through Nattea that I have a thread back to Africa but the link ends there. That is amazing but also sad because there should have been so many others threads that we could trace but no longer.

You're right. There are many ancestors out there, like stars in the night sky, that we'll never know or name. Each one that we do know or can name would lead to others and then others until we would be overwhelmed with so many stars beyond count.

Swee said that you knew more than anyone and it's true. Thank you.

Please fasten your seatbelts, secure your tray tables, and return your setbacks to the upright position. Cabin attendants prepare the cabin for landing.

Alfred looked out the window of the airliner at the carpet of lights below. The plane was on its approach to the airport and was apparently flying over the outlying districts of Accra, the capital of Ghana. He hadn't imagined that the city would be so large or that, at least at night, it would look like any other metropolis in the world. The night flight from Casablanca would put Alfred and Beatrice in Accra when everyone would be asleep. He was, therefore, surprised by the hustle and bustle in the airport. After clearing immigration and customs, he and Beatrice retrieved their two suitcases and proceeded to the exit. Alfred scanned the surprisingly large crowd waiting at the exit while looking for someone holding a sign with his name. After several checks, he spotted his name, Dr. Pendle, and his wife's, Mrs. Pendle. The man holding the sign was Tom Kpamala; he was to be their driver for the next four weeks as they traveled by car through Ghana and the neighboring countries of Togo and Benin. Tom shook hands with both of them and directed them to the parking lot where he had left the car. He loaded their suitcases into the back of a huge Toyota SUV, opened the rear passenger doors for them, slipped into the driver's seat, and headed out of the parking lot to the road exiting the airport. No sooner were they on city streets when Alfred realized that the airport was actually within the city not, as he thought, far out in the countryside. Traffic was light, virtually non-existent. Tom made several turns onto various nearly deserted streets until they were in what appeared to be a very modern downtown with large high-rise buildings and brightly lit shops. Street level neon signs abounded as did traffic lights although there was little traffic. Somehow, Alfred hadn't expected all of this—the very familiarity of a completely unknown-to-him African city. Tom drove the car into a driveway of a hotel—a modern, upscale unit of an international chain. A porter appeared who took their bags, and Alfred, Beatrice, Tom, and porter proceeded to the lobby desk. It was an atrium hotel with glass elevators to the several stories arrayed around the atrium, like the Hanging Gardens of Babylon. It was all a bit disorienting to Alfred because of the lack of sleep and the sense that he could not tell that he was in Africa. Had they somehow been transported to Las Vegas or Shanghai? After check-in, they settled on a time with Tom for what was the pick-up later that morning, and headed up to their room for what they hoped would be some much needed sleep.

Tom promptly appeared at 11 am. as planned. Alfred and Beatrice had a reasonably good but brief sleep, then breakfast, and presented themselves to their waiting driver. Their first day in Africa, in Accra, would be pure tourism. They wanted to see some of the sights of the city. They were shocked as their vehicle pulled into traffic. Where all had been deserted and quiet during the night, the streets were now jammed with bumper to bumper traffic. Street hawkers swarmed vehicles stopped at intersections for traffic lights, carrying large metal bowls on their heads filled with fruit, vegetables, packages of manufactured goods, shoes, clothing, hats, utensils, small appliances, basically everything imaginable and unimaginable.The street hawkers were mobile pedestrian stores. The sidewalks were jammed with pedestrians and more vendors. People were everywhere. Dense, moving, talking, busy. It was a teeming mass of humanity, all black folks, and dressed in western, namely American, clothing but with bare feet in sandals or flip-flops. It was an all-black version of New York City or Hong Kong.

To Beatrice, who was born in Accra, it was home, her true home. To Alfred, who certainly knew big cities, it was fascinating in its familiarity and, yet, strangeness. He couldn't quite figure out why it was strange since it seemed so familiar. But he suspected that it was this all-black world that was so strange to him. There were no white people anywhere. Everyone was black. Pedestrians. Drivers. Shopkeepers. Road Crews. Construction workers. Police. As he thought back in time to a comparable scene, he could not remember a single instance, aside from his adoptive family home, where everyone was black. Even in Pachacuti there were lots of white folks. He was almost relieved when he spotted several tourists, apparently European, examining clothing at a street vendor's stall. As he realized how out of place they seemed, he also realized that no one, other than himself, seemed to notice them. Tom steered the car to the historical section of Accra called Jamestown where the British had first established themselves as colonists on what was centuries ago called by the British the Gold Coast. The crowds had thinned out but the automobile traffic remained. They left their vehicle and acquired a pre-arranged guide who, on foot, took them to the ocean front to see several sights including the Jamestown Fort, a lighthouse, and the Mantse Palace, home to the descendants of the original African rulers of Accra. They also visited the nearby memorial to Kwame Nkrumah who led Ghana to peaceful independence from Britain. Given the heat, jet lag, extensive walking, and the adjustment to a different world, Alfred and Beatrice called it a day and asked Tom to return them to their hotel for a late lunch and nap. They wanted to prepare for an evening visit to the home of Beatrice's family for dinner and a meet and greet.

The Nhongo were not a large family. Samuel, Beatrice's father, and Elizabeth, her mother, had four children of whom Beatrice was the eldest. There were two sisters, Samantha and Barbara; both were married and their husbands were present. Their brother, Henry, was the youngest. It was odd for a 35 year old man, like Henry, not to be married but no one spoke of the matter. The Nhongo home was modest but comfortable. It was in a section of Accra some distance from the hotel where the Pendle were staying. Tom had dropped them off at 6 pm. and would return at 10 pm. to take them back to their hotel. It had to be a short evening because the Pendle were leaving Accra in the morning for the coastal towns of Cape Coast and Elmina. Alfred had never met his wife's family, all of whom spoke English, and they were eager to learn something about him, his life, work, and family. Beatrice also wanted to bring her family up to date on her life since, although they had written and telephoned, she had not seen her family in almost 20 years. She went to the USA to study on a scholarship, met Alfred, married, and had two children. Now, she was working on her degree in law school.

When dinner was announced and served, Alfred was grateful that Beatrice had already accustomed him to the spicy, hot Ghanaian dishes, like Red Red. The food was delicious and abundant. The conversations could have continued all night but shortly before the Pendle's driver was to arrive, Henry asked Alfred if he could speak to him privately. They went into the garden behind the house; Henry was clearly nervous and found it difficult to say whatever he wanted to ask or tell Alfred. Finally, Alfred said gently to Henry that whatever he wanted to say, he could say in complete confidence. Alfred already suspected what was on Henry's mind.

Alfred, Beatrice told me that you have a relative who recently died.

Yes, a distant cousin named Mosey DeBobo. Why?

Beatrice said that he was gay but his family accepted him and his partner.

Henry, Mosey was gay and so was my father.

Your father? But you . . .

He was, maybe, bisexual for a time but he decided that he was really gay and lived with another man after he and my mother divorced.

He lived with another man and your cousin did too?

Yes.

What did you think about that?

My father and his partner let me live them them when I started college. It was the most normal home that you can imagine. Not really different from your home except it was all men.

Are you gay or bisexual?

No. But if I was, I would want to live my life as a gay man.

I think that I'm gay.

I know.

How did you know?

I've learned how to tell. Gaydar, it's called.

What am I going to do? Being homosexual is against the law in this country. Sex between men is punishable by death.

Do you know any other gay men?

Yes. But most of them are married to women. They have sex with men.

Are there any single men like you?

A few. But they are scared too.

Henry, there are international gay and lesbian organizations that might be able to help you or, at least, give you some information. Also, if you could ever come to visit us in Michigan, we can help you to connect with other gay people.

My parents want me to marry. They even have a wife picked out for me.

Maybe, you'll have to get married like the other men and have sex outside your marriage.

I would rather die.

Then, as discreetly as you can, find other men. Try to live your life as best you can and, with others, work to change the law.

This is a very Christian and conservative country.

So is the USA. But the laws have changed there. In some places gay people can even marry one another.

Ghana is not the USA.

Okay. Then what is your plan?

I don't know.

Well, at least, I know about you and you can trust me. Write me. Keep in touch. I'll be your friend and try to help however I can.

Thank you, Brother.

What were you and Henry talking about in the garden?

It's confidential. I promised him I wouldn't discuss our conversation with anyone.

Did he tell you that he is gay?

What?

Did he say that he is gay? That he likes men?

How did you know?

We all know. Gaydar. Have known most of his life.

He doesn't think that you know. He thinks that everyone is trying to get him married to a woman.

Our parents are, in fact, trying to get him married.

But why if he is gay?

We want to protect him. If he is married, he won't get into trouble. People may suspect that he is gay but they will accept the fiction that he is a straight married man.

But what about his wife?

The woman my parents have chosen is also gay. She's a lesbian and she will be protected as well. They can live together as husband and wife and still have gay relationships with whoever. People here prefer the appearance of heterosexuality than the actuality of it. As long as everything seems normal, everyone is happy.

And you prefer that too for your brother?

I prefer a brother who can live in relative peace and still be who he is even if he must maintain an act in order to live his life in this country. What would you have him do?

I must admit that I don't have a practical solution although I did suggest some ideas to him.

Like what?

Like working with others to change the laws. Like coming to stay with us for visits where he could be openly gay. Like contacting international gay and lesbian organizations for support.

Those are okay but he has to live his life now in this country and he must be safe. A wife gives him that security and can give a gay woman security as well. Two people are protected and the family can reinforce that protection by supporting the fiction.

I'm glad that my father and Mosey and Swee could live freer as gay people without this deception.

Yes. Deception isn't the best solution but the alternatives in this case are worse. I wish that my brother could live like Mosey or Swee or your father did. But there is a different reality here in Ghana.

Traffic in Accra was heavy on the freeway ring-road heading to the highway for Cape Coast, a town west of Accra. One of the largest fortresses built by the Portuguese and British dominates the Atlantic coast of the town. The fortress, Cape Coast Castle, was, among other things, a prison for captive Africans. Tom drove Alfred and Beatrice to Cape Coast Castle as their first stop on an overland tour of Ghana to visit and learn first hand of rural life and the vast enslaving operation that for several centuries forcefully kidnapped Africans, removed them from their homes, marched them in shackles and chains often hundreds of miles from the African interior to the Atlantic coast to prisons such as Cape Coast Castle, to await being packed into European and American ships for transport to the Americas. Cape Coast Castle was, just one of hundreds of such prisons on the coast that served as the terminus of the Africa leg of the journey and the gateway to the months-long sea crossing in ships—the Middle Passage—to enslavement in the Americas.

The castle was impressive, built on the ocean's edge and rising on a promontory of land with sweeping views of the sea and the land. As a fortress, it guarded the colonials' strategic position and protected the colonial administration within its well-defended walls.

Alfred and Beatrice entered the main gate of the castle and joined a group of tourists, mostly Europeans, but also a handful of Africans, about to begin a tour with a Ghanaian male guide named Jeremiah. He discussed the history of the fortress explaining how it grew from a defensive stronghold to an administrative center for the British colonial government, to a prison for enslaved Africans. The sheer immensity and solidity of the place impressed Alfred. Curiously, Beatrice seemed less moved by the fortress than her husband. After touring the above-ground structures and pointing out the spacious governor's quarters with their airy, sunlit rooms affording panoramic views of the town, ocean, and distant countryside, Jeremiah guided the group back to the ground floor where he noted the entrances to the underground prison chambers segregated by gender—men's entrance on one side of the courtyard, women's entrance on the other side. The group then descended into darkness down stairs minimally illuminated with electric lights. Down they went into fetid darkness arriving finally deep underground in a high vaulted chamber. The only illumination and air came through a few small windows high above the chamber's floor. No one could possibly reach the windows even if several people managed to stand on one another's shoulders like acrobats. Jeremiah explained:

This is the main cell for the enslaved males. About 1000 men could be held here until being loaded onto ships. They arrived here often after up to several weeks trekking across the countryside shackled and chained together. Stripped of their clothing and wearing nothing but a kind of underwear brief, they remained shackled and chained here so that they could not move around. As a result, they performed all bodily functions in place. The floor that you are standing on is covered with the accumulated human waste of several centuries. It is several inches thick on top of a stone floor. The smell of human fecal waste, urine, blood, and vomit in this closed space must have been overwhelming. But here, in virtual darkness packed together in chains and shackles, not knowing where they were or why they were brought here, or what would happen to them, here they remained for weeks or months until a ship carried them away. If they hadn't already died.

When a slave ship arrived, prepared to receive its human cargo, the enslaved men who were chosen for the voyage were marched underground through tunnels to a portal called the Door of No Return which, when opened, let in the bright sunlit air and sea breeze. Down a ladder they went to the shore and to waiting row boats that ferried them out through the turbulent surf to a ship at anchor. They would never see Africa again. The women, held in a similar chamber were also marched through tunnels to the same portal and loaded onto the same row boats, also never to return.

Jeremiah told this tale dispassionately. He had recited it many times for many years. In answer to questions from the European tourists, he explained that when the captured Africans arrived at Cape Coast Castle, they entered the fortress through a special door directly into the underground prison. They never saw the grand above-ground structures where the colonials lived and worked. And, the colonials, other than the guards, never saw the enslaved Africans.

Alfred tried to imagine surviving being captured from one's home, stripped of clothing, shackled and marched for weeks many miles under a burning sun across the countryside to this prison and, then, held for many more weeks underground in an airless, dark dungeon, living in one's own and everyone else's filth, then in chains, to be packed on a ship for an ocean voyage of several months only to arrive in an unknown place and made to work day and night, year upon year, as someone's possession, like a horse or cow, without any rights, recourse, or remedy. How did people survive? How had his ancestors survived, like Adwoa, because surely they did or he would not be here looking at their prison? He wondered if he could have survived these circumstances. As he surveyed the impressive fortress and reviewed all that he had just seen, he began to cry.

Alfred and Beatrice sat silent as Tom piloted their SUV along Ghana's highways north to the city of Kumasi, the capital of the ancient Ashanti kingdom. The countryside was lush and green with dense vegetation surrounding an endless string of villages and small, tidy farms. Alfred thought of these villages and the many people that were taken from them and marched to the sea. The further north the couple travelled, the more he felt the difficulty of the trek through the countryside. The endless days of walking in chains, under the hot sun, with little food or water, to an unknown future.

In Kumasi, the British built a palace for the Ashanti kings after the British destroyed the traditional palace that the kings had built for themselves. Now that British-built palace, with the British long gone and helpfully forgotten, was a museum of Ashanti artifacts, history, and culture. While learning of the history of the Ashanti kingdom was fascinating to Alfred, he wanted to know how the kings allowed their people to be carried away, century after century, by foreigners. The answer was not surprising but it nevertheless contained a shock. The kings often cooperated, in effect, trading Africans for foreign manufactured goods from Europe. Sometimes, the kings resisted and found themselves threatened or exiled by British power and military force. They could resist but not prevail. This was not surprising. What was a shock was the fact that kingdoms, like the Ashanti, had long taken prisoners as they sought to dominate an ever-expanding swath of the countryside. Prisoners were a bounty that could be employed as servants or workers for the kingdom or traded with other rulers or merchants for goods. When the Europeans arrived in Africa, they merely muscled into this existing enterprise. However, the Europeans required huge quantities of manpower to build the burgeoning colonies of the Americas where the enslaved produced the raw materials that were shipped to Europe. Thus, the triangular Atlantic slave trade was begun: The Outward Passage—Manufactured goods from Europe were traded for African slaves; The Middle Passage—Slaves were transported to the Americas where they created raw materials; The Inward Passage—In exchange for cash, raw materials were traded to Europe where finished goods were manufactured. Everyone, except the enslaved Africans, seemed to benefit from this economic arrangement. And it thrived for centuries because African rulers were coerced to do the bidding of Europeans. Alfred heard variations of this story from a number of guides at various sites during his journey. In Abomey in the country of Benin, the guide not only told a variation of this story but also elaborated on the expansionist drive of the Dahomey kings to continuously enlarge their kingdom by coercive or violent subjugation of the surrounding countryside, conquering or destroying neighboring districts. The Dahomey expansion was particularly brutal in a region where brutality was a common affliction on village life. As Tom drove Alfred and Beatrice through the lush, verdant countryside dotted with village after village, Alfred tried to visualize the terror that would descend on these defenseless farming communities. Composed of simple farmers—peasants really, they cultivated their fields, raising crops and animals for their own sustenance. Here they were in a fertile and bucolic paradise, living in peace, oblivious to the growing labor needs of far-off continents, and without warning, snatched from their homes, shackled, and marched for days and weeks across unfamiliar territories, through dense forests, across rivers, over mountains, to prison, then boats, and then . . .

Alfred wondered how any one survived it all and still mated, had children, and created a semblance of life while enslaved.

The string of towns and cities in Togo and Benin—Kpalimé, Sokodé, Kara, and Lomé, in Togo; and Boukombé, Natitingou, Dassa Zoumé, Abomey, Porto Novo, Cotonou, and Quidah, in Benin—urban centers that Alfred and Beatrice traversed further east and north, then south, reminded them that, even as the African population was depleted of millions of people by the slave trade over the centuries, enough people remained to build what were new, vibrant societies not unlike those in other parts of the industrialized world. Modern cities dotted the landscape still dominated by rural villages. Two worlds co-existed, indeed, needed one another for the exchange of produce and labor. In a way, it was a different kind of enslavement. Rural people worked on farms for their livelihood, as city folk worked in offices, stores, restaurants, and factories for their living wages. Transportation networks knitted together city and countryside, nation with nation, and continent with continent. All of this had been built on a foundation of enslavement.

During the long drive through Ghana, Togo, and Benin, Alfred and Beatrice stopped often at many villages to observe life and to see the cultivation of various agricultural products, like palm oil, shea butter, and cassava flour as well as many different fruits and vegetables. The villages varied greatly in their development. Some were quite rudimentary with earthen walls and straw roofs for dwellings. Others were very contemporary with buildings having metal roofs and stone or brick walls. Electricity and running water were staples of more prosperous villages. Wells and cisterns were far more common in poorer villages. Very young children populated the villages and were the first to approach visitors. They were often very subdued but curious to hold hands with visitors and follow them through the village. Adults went about their chores. Many sat in doorways chatting with family or neighbors or relaxing during the heat of the day in the shade of a tree. Women carrying bundles on their heads, often with a baby or toddler strapped to their back, were ubiquitous. On one occasion, a few children who stood off at a distance from Alfred chanted a word in their native language. Alfred asked Tom, who spoke several West African languages in addition to English and French, what they were saying. Tom replied that they were saying "white man."

They are talking about you, he told Alfred.

Me?

But I'm not white.

To them you are.

But I'm dark-skinned like they are.

Not really. To them, you look white, not African.

Alfred was stunned. He could understand his brother, Dunn, being considered white but not himself. If he wasn't seen by Africans as one of them and certainly not seen by whites as white, what was he, and where did he belong?

You know, Bee, my brother, who looked white, had the same problem. He didn't think of himself as white or black. In his diary, he talked about this.

His diary?

Yes. His personal belongings, including his diary, were returned to our father, Trique. When he found out about the family story that Swee was writing, he gave the diary to her to use. When she finished copying it, she returned it to Trique and he gave it to me so I could learn about my twin brother.

What did you learn?

He felt that he didn't fit in. He couldn't figure out how he had a place in a black and white world. He was also unsure about his sexual identity. He fantasized about sex with men but I don't think he actually had a male sex partner.

Haven't you ever fantasized about same sex? I have.

I didn't have any interest in it. I knew that I liked women and wanted them sexually.

Only sexually?

No. Of course not. Haven't I proven to you that I love you for more than getting into your pants?

Point made.

I didn't have Dunn's doubts. But, then, I was clearly not only heterosexual but also clearly black. That's why my mother abandoned me but kept Dunn.

And now that you're not black, what?

Come on, you know I'm black, don't you?

I know that you have a darker skin than most white people but I grew up in Ghana thinking like other Ghanaians—black Americans are not Africans.

But we come from African people.

And white people. You don't look African to us Africans. And, remember, during the slave trade, Africans disappeared from their families and villages never to be seen again. No one knew where they went except for stories about their being taken away somewhere far away. People here had no way to know where their family members and friends went. In the confusion of assaults on villages by the Ashanti and the Dahomey, among many other African conquerors, people didn't even know if the missing were alive or dead. And, they couldn't know that the missing were on another continent where they learned to live a new life enslaved. All of this was unknown and unknowable to us Africans. And, don't forget, those of us who weren't enslaved were subjugated to colonial rule by Europeans. We had our own struggles; while not enslavement, we weren't free. Our freedom came long after yours.

But when it came, you had your own countries, run by your own people. We American blacks were free, yes, but we never have had our own country. We're still made to feel like guests— sometimes welcomed, often shunned—in our adopted country.

So you're saying you don't have a home in America or Africa?

That's how I'm beginning to feel.

But you do have a home with me and my family and your family.

Certainly with you and our kids. I would like to feel at home with your family and I wish that I felt more at home with my family.

If you want it, you can have it. But you will have to try harder to make it so.

Alfred brooded over this conversation for the next several days as Tom drove them south towards the Atlantic coast through Benin.

A visit to Abomey, the capital of the former Dahomey kingdom, stirred all of the issues about the slave trade once again. The massive and extensive palace complex built by the Dahomey kings was a shock. Elegant buildings, situated within a defensive walled compound, faced one another across broad sunlit courtyards. Originally the compound covered much of the city of Abomey. Now, only a fraction of the whole had survived the ravages of time.

It was evident to Alfred that so much splendor built by a succession of aggressive, empire-building kings, came at the expense of enslaving subject people from the surrounding countryside and from enslaving raids far north into territories hundreds of miles distant from Abomey. Again, Alfred thought about the hapless captives marched in chains across that expansive landscape to Abomey and then on further south to the Atlantic coast.

In Quidah on the coast where Alfred and Beatrice arrived several days later, they visited another fortress, the Fortaleza Saõ Joaõ Batista. Built by the Portuguese, this fort had an outdoor prison called a barracoon. High-walled with no protection from the sun or rain, the prison enclosures held hundreds of captives segregated by gender. This was a holding area until groups of captives —young, old, male and female—were marched through the town's streets to the so-called open-air slave market where European traders purchased the captives they wanted. Then, those who were bought were taken to a nearby building where they were branded, like cattle, with their owner's identifying mark or symbol. Finally, there was the last march for two miles to the coast where waiting boats ferried the captives to ships anchored off-shore. The beach was the portal of no return.

Bee, so many of the captives died before they could reach a ship They died in the raids on villages. They died on the long marches. They died in the slave castles and barracoons. They died on the final march to the sea. They died on the ships. They died of backbreaking work at the hand of brutal masters. And this went on for centuries.

And, yet, you are descended from them. You had very strong or lucky ancestors.

So many lives lost to build new countries. So much suffering and pain and grief. Why? My brother, Dunn, died in a war in a country not unlike these African countries. He was sacrificed for what? For geopolitics? For the suppression of an ideology? For the quest for territory or natural resources? For economic advantage? Why?

Alfred, when has history been different? When have any people lived peacefully without wanting something that belonged to someone else? When have humans been simply content to be and exist without intruding on other people? Humans are restless, avaricious, fearful of others not like them. Hateful of others not like them. Angry, irrational, divinely inspired, self-righteous. Nihilistic. We are, all of us, capable of good and evil. This is our history. This is our fate. And, yet, we can only live our lives.

Alfred and Beatrice were having dinner in their hotel's restaurant near the Atlantic shore. They could hear the ocean's waves pounding the beach. Both lapsed into silent eating. At the end of the meal, Alfred announced that he was going to the beach to sit and think for a while. Beatrice decided to head back to their room to pack. The next day they would begin the final leg of their journey, heading west to Ghana through Togo to Accra. Alfred said that he wouldn't be long.

As he headed out the beach, Alfred noted that the air was still and night sky clear and moonless. There were no sounds except for the waves hitting the shore and for Alfred's own footsteps on the gravel road from the hotel to the road paralleling the beach. Once he crossed the beach road, he was on sand that muffled his footsteps. The beach was deserted. Alfred sat down in the sand facing the ocean. Because of the geography of the coastline of Africa at Quidah, he was facing south. All of the thought of the past days, weeks, months, years came rushing into his brain. Here he was, alone, on the edge of a continent looking out over an ocean that he knew stretched way beyond the horizon. To the extreme south was Antartica. To the west, the Americas. And to the west the ships sailed with their human cargo. To the west many of those humans were forced into a new life. He was a descendant of some of those humans. That place was what his ancestors, and he, called home. Was it still his home? Could it ever be his home? His hands gripped the sand. This is the soil from which he came but this was not his home. He started to cry and lay back on the sand. The tears could not resolve the conflict that he felt. He could never resolve the conflict; it was too much a part of who he was. When the tears finally stopped, he opened his eyes and stared at he sky. There were stars. The longer he stared, the more stars there appeared to be. In the clear, moonless sky, there were more stars than he had ever seen in the sky. He realized that where he lived, the ambient light from human habitation obscured most of these stars. But here, where there was virtually no lights from buildings or streets, the sky had a depth that was awesome and overwhelming. So many stars, bright and dim, but seemingly infinite in number. How many billions of years had they been there? How many millions of years had people stared at them in wonder as he was now doing? His eyes began to tear again, this time with joy. These stars were his people, numberless, enduring, shining. This universe of stars was the universe of humanity. We were, he thought, all of us, like the sky. Simply there. Different but alike. Individual but part of a grander scheme than anyone could understand or explain. It just was. Serriah was right: Our ancestors are like the stars in the sky.

Out of the corner of his eye, he thought he noticed someone moving across the beach. He sat up and peered into the darkness. It was someone approaching from his left and headed, slowly towards him. As the figure came closer, he could tell that it was a man, a young man. Closer still and he realized that the man was white. Alfred was puzzled. What was a young white man doing on this deserted beach at night? There were no other hotels nearby nor anything else that would explain his presence. The man approached Alfred silently, stopped at arm's length and sat down beside him in the sand. Hi, Alfred, he said, turning and looking at Alfred. In the starlight, Alfred could see his face. It was familiar although he was unsure who this young man could be. Then, he recognized him.

Hi, Dunn, he replied. You look just like your photographs and now I remember that I saw you at the Presidio but I didn't know who you were then. But how did you know me? You never saw a picture of me.

We lived together inside our mother. I would know you anywhere without knowing how you looked. I saw you once at the Presidio and I knew that I knew you but I didn't understand how. I didn't have a chance to ask you.

Where have you been?

Everywhere but mostly in you. I exist in you, in your cells, in your mind, in your body. I know your thoughts. I see what you see. I feel what you feel.

And do I see what you see, feel what you feel, and think what you think?

There's no difference. We are two in one. I will always be with you in you, a part of you. Is that okay with you?

I think so. Do you help me to understand things?

I don't know because a lot of what I understand comes from you. I can't really separate myself from you although I know I'm not you and you are not me. There is and there is not a boundary between us. We are a duality and a singularity. It's beyond explaining. It just is.

They both moved closer together so that their bodies touched. They put their arms around each others' shoulders. Alfred leaned over to Dunn and kissed him on the cheek. They embraced.

Alfred lay back in the sand a long time. He checked his watch. He had been on the beach for nearly two hours. He thought that he should head back to the hotel and Beatrice. She was already in bed and asleep when he entered the room. He undressed and got in bed, snuggling up to his wife's warm body and wrapping his arm around her. She moved and whispered, Alfred?

Yes, Babe.

Let's make a baby.

Bee, you know we're too old to make a baby.

But, Honey, I love trying. Enter the portal of return.

VII
ALFRED DEBOBO PENDLE

Swee died in 2009 at the age of 98. Her memorial service was wonderful. All of the family and close friends who had attended Mosey's service were present including my foster siblings— Ottice, Melivia, Delanna, Ornton, and Wentell—and their spouses. The service was held in the Harlem A.M.E. church of St. Thomas. In addition to family and friends, many LGBT folks attended because Swee had belonged to that community since coming New York. It was another family for Swee and Gulley. Gulley and her children were also present with their spouses and their children. It was a grand occasion for a remarkable woman. The mood was festive and celebratory. Like Mosey, Swee was cremated, and Gulley decided to take her ashes to Pachacuti for burial in the Sellabie family plot.

Swee left me her original manuscript; it was complete except for the last chapter. That's my contribution. We had first talked about it many years ago, but at Mosey's memorial service, she told me that she wanted me to have it in the hope that I might finish and publish it someday. She also left me all of her drafts, letters, notes, and research materials, including the personal journals given her by family members whom she consulted. I have, in effect, her library and archive that I have transported to my home in Ann Arbor, Michigan.

Since Swee almost finished writing all that she intended, I am compelled, as a historian, to add this postscript. Before her death, we discussed the last chapter and she told me to complete it after my trip to Africa. I did, attempting to remain faithful to Swee's intentions. Swee's story is, as she said in her introduction to Book One, as accurate a history as she could make. "Could make" is a significant qualification because, apart from the usual problems of constructing a history—which she acknowledged—the manuscript she wrote is not, in a key instance, completely truthful to the information in her documents. I've read through her letters, journals, and notes on which she based her manuscript and now conclude that she drafted an alternative narrative concerning the events preceding and following the birth in 1946 of my brother, Dunn, and myself. Put another way, there is far more to this story than she chose to report. Therefore, it is important to present what she did, and did not, include to understand her decisions.

The events of the actual birth of my twin brother and me occurred as she described them in her manuscript. However, an alternative draft included significant details omitted in the manuscript. These details describe the actions of many of the adult participants quite differently and with greater consequence than what she decided to write. Simply put, Swee decided to create a narrative that avoided certain links between my and Dunn's birth in 1946 to what had happened in 1945 (when her narrative begins) and in 1968 (when Dunn died).

Swee reported that in 1945 her brother, Prellis, was lynched and his body burned in Pachacuti by a posse. Prellis was accused of accosting a young white woman, Myra Charles. None of the blacks in town believed that this was possible but no one had a chance to question and defend Prellis because he was overtaken by a car of men while walking home from the purported incident then lynched and burned in the woods. Everyone in town suspected who was involved in the lynching but no one identified or accused the murderers to the authorities. It is important to note here that Swee omitted mention of a Sellabie suspicion that the leading perpetrator was someone who wanted to take revenge on their family—revenge for an unforgivable transgression of the color line. Hanton Sellabie, Swee's father, had taken as his mistress a white woman, Soonie Fleet. People outside of his family were unaware of this union with the exception of Soonie's father, Murray Fleet, who had fathered a son with his black mistress; that child was Murty Pendle, my grandfather. More importantly, Swee also omitted mention that Griffin, Murray's only son by his wife, learned from his father of his sister's liaison with Hanton and of their daughter, Loissey Sellabie, Swee's half-sister. Griffin's hatred grew towards black people and particularly towards the Sellabie and Pendle. He was well-known in Pachacuti as a virulent and vocal bigot who expressed his feelings openly and often. He was also having sex with Myra Charles, Prellis' accuser. No one tried to, or would, make an accusation against him for the murder of Prellis; the violent death of another black man in the segregated South, was not a moral or even a legal concern to most whites. But black folks didn't forget such things. Swee certainly didn't forget.

Swee's unspoken suspicions about who killed her brother weren't confirmed until 23 years later when the families gathered in 1968 for Dunn's memorial service in Los Angles. As she recorded in her manuscript, Swee had a long, private conversation outside the home of my father, Trique Pendle, with my grandmother and Griffin's sister, Olive Fleet Boston. Swee wrote that Olive wanted to make amends for the destruction of Swee's house by Olive's three sons, the Boston boys, by leaving the proceeds of the sale of her own home to Swee after Olive's imminent death from cancer. What Swee omitted from her manuscript and what significantly changes her text was that Olive confessed that it was, in fact, Griffin with two of his drinking buddies who captured and killed Prellis. Griffin bragged to Olive and her family that he persuaded his girlfriend, Myra Charles, to make the false accusation against Prellis, providing a pretext for Griffin to kill him; he said all of this even before Prellis' body was cut down from the lynching tree. Olive was horrified by the murderous cruelty of her brother, by the indifference of her husband to the crime and by the amusement of her sons to the murder. But she could not go against the codes of her family and of other white people in Pachacuti and report her brother.

In order to understand the importance of Griffin to Swee's story, a quick summary is necessary of events in 1945-46: Olive's daughter, my mother—Martalee—had sexual trysts with my father, Trique, to become pregnant by him. Somehow, however, she didn't calculate that her three brothers would discover her affair and take revenge on Swee by burning down her house because Martalee and Trique had sought refuge there. Before they could be pursued by the Boston boys, Trique and his lover, Mosey, fled Pachacuti. Martalee also left soon thereafter, then Swee and her lover, Amity Lowe, departed. Swee's manuscript recounts that Olive, when she was informed by her daughter's landlady that Martalee was in Atlanta and pregnant with a child, went to her, creating a false pretext for her travel for the benefit of her husband and sons. Although she was disheartened when she learned that her daughter was moving to Los Angeles to be a family with Trique and Dunn, she encouraged Martalee because she felt that she and her family would be safe far from Pachacuti.

This is the record of events in Swee's manuscript. Now, here is the information in her alternate draft that was omitted from her manuscript: Olive also reported to Swee that, when she went to Atlanta, she warned Martalee of Griffin's rage. He had learned from his nephews that their sister not only had sex with a black boy, but that he was also a Pendle, and both he and Martalee had fled town. Griffin was ready to kill again and threatened to track down Martalee to perhaps harm her but certainly to murder her black lover, Trique. Upon hearing this, a panicked Martalee revealed to her mother the existence of the black twin, Alfred, living with the wet-nurse; she felt that the orphaned child would also be in danger if Griffin could trace her and learn the truth about the twins. Astonished and fearing for her daughter and the twins' safety, Olive immediately urged her daughter to flee to Los Angeles with Dunn and Trique. She also made a counter-intuitive decision to safeguard Alfred's life. She had him brought to Pachacuti by Trique's mother, Xantha Debobo Pendle, so that she could hide the black twin in the large family of Xantha's brother, Teatus. There, among the DeBobo, Griffin could never trace his existence and he was unlikely to track Martalee and Trique to Los Angeles. Everyone would thus be safe.

These omissions significantly alter the story Swee ultimately created for her manuscript. However, there is still a puzzling element to this narrative. In Book Two, Swee tells the story of Amity persuading Swee to create a play for the New York theater company, Sault Sainte Marie. Swee's script was based on the story in her manuscript of Martalee and Trique, who are renamed in Swee's play as Annabeth and Kamil. In the last scene of Act 1, Annabeth makes an astonishing revelation to her mother that her three brothers sexually assaulted her when they discovered her liaison with Kamil. This declaration in the play, however, was not mentioned in Book One when Swee recounted Martalee's and Olive's meeting in Atlanta. Was it simply an invention for the play or was it something known to Swee but omitted from her manuscript? Swee left no notes or documentation that Martalee's brothers sexually violated her or that Olive knew of such a crime. However, a rape is completely plausible because it offers another reason for Martalee's immediate flight from Pachacuti without even telling her mother; she probably could not continue to live in the same house with her vile brothers. Furthermore, if Olive had learned of this unforgivable act by her sons, this could explain why Olive promised Swee, not her sons, the proceeds of the sale of her own home after her death. This may have been Olive's ultimate act of revenge on her sons. Therefore, the presumptive fictional scene in Swee's play might have been a real, although undocumented, event.

The question is: Why did Swee omit all of these particular details? Certainly, these omissions change the story by concealing the homicidal violence perpetrated and threatened by Griffin. But knowing Griffin's role in the story makes the actions of Martalee, Olive, and Xantha more understandable. Hence, why leave them out? The answer derives from another, more critical, omission that is documented in Swee's draft: Olive spoke more extensively to Swee about Griffin. Olive knew that Griffin would never be tried in court for his crime even though Phessin DeBobo had become mayor by 1968. Olive confided to Swee that Griffin should be punished, in fact must be punished, and the hate he carried within him be destroyed. Swee agreed that the brutal death of her brother, Prellis, and the shadow it placed over the Sellabie and all other black folks in Pachacuti should and must be avenged. Swee told Olive that she could find a way to punish Griffin. Not to worry.

Upon returning to New York, she contacted unnamed individuals. She carefully and discreetly explained to them what she wanted: They were to visit Pachacuti and watch Griffin's movements. When he was alone and in an isolated location preferably at night, they were to overtake him. In fact, Griffin soon disappeared without a trace. He was never seen again, and no one in Pachacuti knew what had happened to him although many suspected a version of the truth. The police under Mayor Phessin DeBobo investigated his disappearance but could find no witnesses or clues. Olive did not mourn her brother's disappearance but she imagined that somewhere near the tree on which Prellis had died there might be a grave. None was ever found.

Swee omitted all of this, and the reason is plain: She didn't want to incriminate herself, Olive, and anyone else possibly involved in Griffin's disappearance. Fortunately, this important draft of a story that concerns me personally can never be verified. I've tried. All of the knowledgeable and known participants, except my mother, Lee, are deceased, and she claims, as only a lawyer could, to know nothing beyond Swee's manuscript. She maintains that the rape scene in Swee's play is a fiction created by Swee. And, perhaps, some of Swee's other notes are also fictional creations—details of a writer's invention, once considered and then dismissed, as part of her story. Griffin's disappearance and whereabouts are a mystery. Other people vanished from Pachacuti never to be heard from again. However, there was a tale circulated in Pachacuti that Griffin had, in fact, left town on his own because he thought that Mayor Phessin DeBobo would investigate the cold case of Prellis Sellabie's murder and come after him. This particular mystery is probably best left as such. Thus is history written and rewritten.

Finally, Beatrice and I decided to bring her brother, Henry, and his new wife, Clarice, to this country on a work visa; he is a computer programmer and in great demand for his expertise. Initially, they will stay with us but they may eventually move elsewhere. We hope that they might find a LGBT community in which they can be themselves, maybe find same-sex partners. Bee and I feel that Henry is our adult child; the child we pretended to make that night in Quidah.

Swee's work was a labor of love. She never stopped gathering information and stories about the people in her life. She loved them all—and those that knew her, loved her. I hope that her work will help folks understand the power of families—in this case, black families—as a black home to all.

I close with a few words about some actual black homes. There are still three ancestral family dwellings in Pachacuti belonging to members of families chronicled in Swee's text. Domus Sellabie, the ancestral home of Fairfax Sellabie, passed to Swee after the death in 1989 of her sister, Daphet. Swee transferred the property to the Sellabie of Sokodé, members of whose family now occupy it. Domus DeBobo, the ancestral home of Bear DeBobo, was ultimately bequeathed to Toetus who, in turn, willed it to his oldest daughter, Ottice, in 1992. She never occupied the house but, instead, rented it to local folks. Domus Pendle, the home built by my grandfather, Murty Pendle, was bequeathed to me after the death of my grandmother, Xantha DeBobo Pendle, in 1987. I have kept the house as a summer home and retreat for me and my family. We try to visit Pachacuti for a few weeks a couple of times each year. These homes and the families that lived in them are, of course, the origin stories of Swee's history. As physical reminders of all that has passed, they may continue to serve future generations of our families as reminders of where we came from and caution us about where we might be headed. We are the Domus Niger. In order to help the reader follow the complex lineages of the families in this history, I've composed genealogies of all of the ancestors that have been reported to Swee and me. They follow this text.

In this year, 2009, the first USA president of African descent, Barack Hussein Obama, and his wife, First Lady Michelle Robinson Obama, visited Cape Coast Castle in Ghana on 11 July.

GENEALOGIES

Genealogy A
DEBOBO I

Onyx (Adwoa)
(fl. late 17th C.)
|
Abediah
(fl. early 18th C.)
|
Desirée
(fl. mid. 18th C.)
|
Jukah
(fl. late 18th C.)
|
Athena
(fl. early19th C.)
|
Midah Debobo————Jubelie
(d.1865) | (d.1860)
|
Nattea DeBobo
(c.1860-1900)
|
––––––––––
| |
Roy Boston — — Deerie Debobo   Bear Debobo — — Ardeah Person
(1874-1926) | (1871-1902)   (1876-1924) | (d. 1912)
            | (Gen-B) |
            | |
Valiant — — | Loissey— — Adelpho —|
(1893-1921) | Sellabie   (1900-39) |
            | (1904-34) |
Will — — — | (Gen-B,C) |
(1897-1933) | |
            | Murty— — —Xantha — —|
            | Pendle   (1904-87) |
Dolly — — | (1903-45) |
(1901-25) | (Gen-B,D) Zennana —|
            | (1907-89) |
Olive— — — —Finn, Sr. |
Fleet   (1902-55)   Iolithe — — —Toetus— —|
(1903-69)   (Gen-D)   Watson   (1910-92)
(Gen-D)   (1915-98)

Genealogy B
DEBOBO II

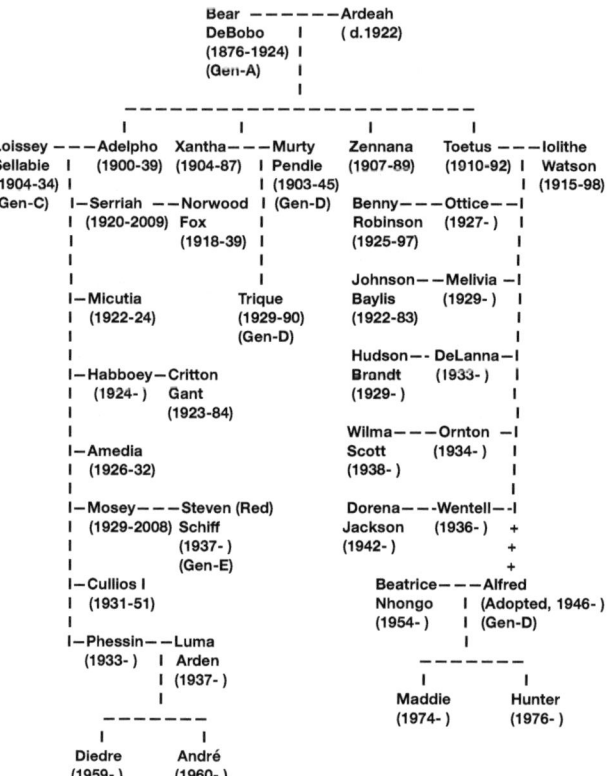

Bear ——————Ardeah
DeBobo   I   (d.1922)
(1876-1924) I
(Gen-A)   I
          I
   ————————————————————
   I   I   I   I
Loissey ———Adelpho Xantha———Murty   Zennana   Toetus ———Iolithe
Sellabie I (1900-39) (1904-87) I Pendle (1907-89) (1910-92) I Watson
(1904-34) I   I (1903-45)   I (1915-98)
(Gen-C)   I—Serriah ——Norwood   I (Gen-D) Benny———Ottice——I
          I (1920-2009) Fox   I   Robinson (1927-) I
          I   (1918-39) I   (1925-97)   I
          I   I   I
          I   I   Johnson——Melivia —I
          I—Micutia   Trique   Baylis   (1929-) I
          I (1922-24)   (1929-90)   (1922-83)   I
          I   (Gen-D)   I
          I   Hudson—- DeLanna—I
          I—Habboey—Critton   Brandt   (1933-) I
          I (1924-) Gant   (1929-)   I
          I   (1923-84)   I
          I   Wilma———Ornton —I
          I—Amedia   Scott   (1934-) I
          I (1926-32)   (1938-)   I
          I   I
          I—Mosey———Steven (Red)   Dorena——-Wentell——I
          I (1929-2008) Schiff   Jackson (1936-) +
          I   (1937-)   (1942-)   +
          I   (Gen-E)   +
          I—Cullios I   Beatrice———Alfred
          I (1931-51)   Nhongo   I (Adopted, 1946-)
          I   (1954-) I (Gen-D)
          I—Phessin——Luma   I
          (1933-) I Arden   ——————
                   I (1937-)   I   I
                   I   Maddie   Hunter
          ——————   (1974-) (1976-)
          I   I
       Diedre   André
       (1959-) (1960-)

Genealogy C
SELLABIE

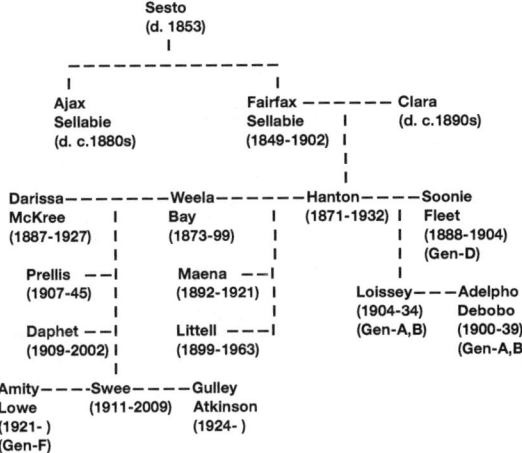

Sesto
(d. 1853)

Ajax
Sellabie
(d. c.1880s)

Fairfax — — — — — Clara
Sellabie   I   (d. c.1890s)
(1849-1902) I

Darissa — — — — — — Weela — — — — — Hanton — — — Soonie
McKree   I   Bay   I   (1871-1932) I   Fleet
(1887-1927) I   (1873-99)   I   I   (1888-1904)
                 I   I   I   (Gen-D)
Prellis — —I   Maena — —I   I
(1907-45)   I   (1892-1921) I   Loissey — — — Adelpho
            I   I   (1904-34)   Debobo
Daphet — —I   Littell — — —I   (Gen-A,B)   (1900-39)
(1909-2002) I   (1899-1963)   (Gen-A,B)
            I
Amity — — — -Swee — — — — Gulley
Lowe   (1911-2009)   Atkinson
(1921-)   (1924-)
(Gen-F)

Genealogy D
PENDLE/FLEET/BOSTON

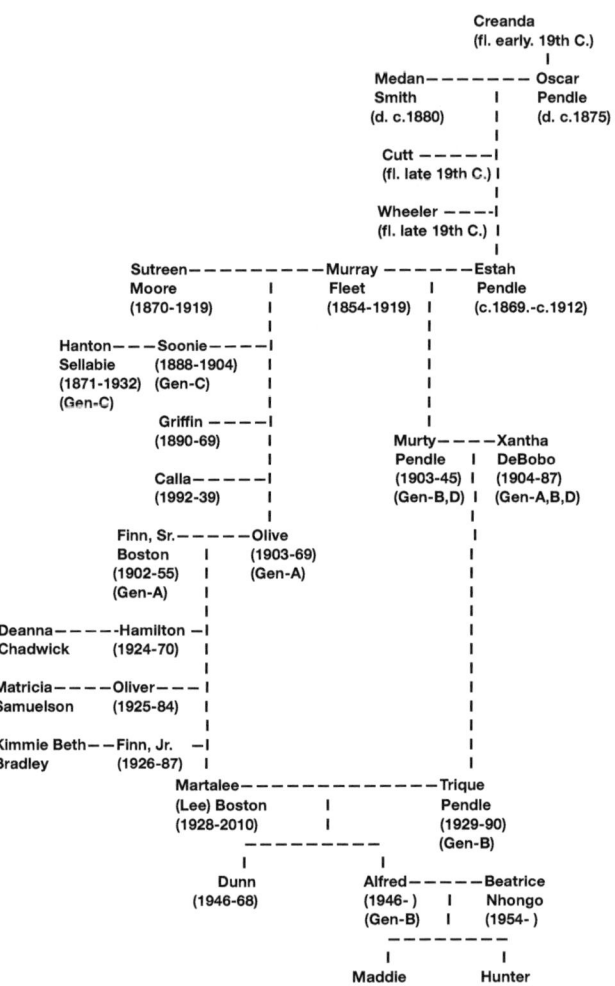

Genealogy E
SCHIFF

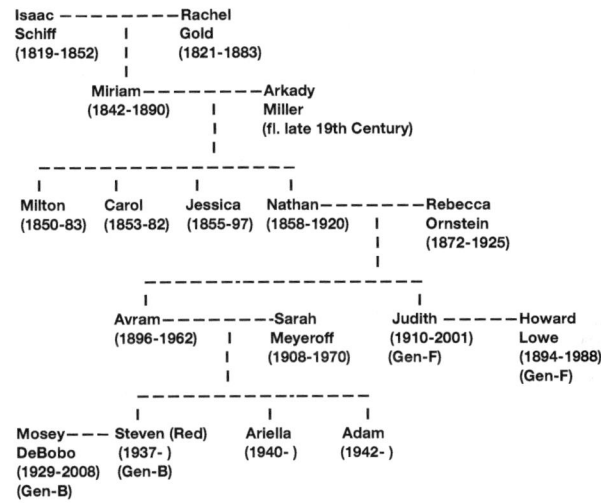

Genealogy F
LOWE

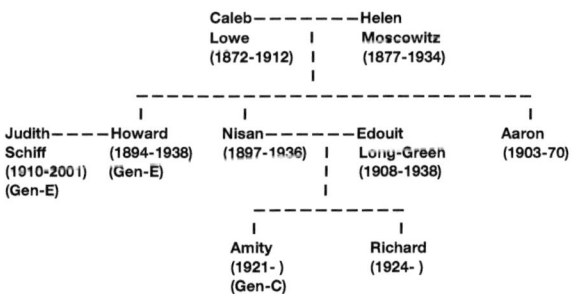

·

Made in the USA
Lexington, KY
29 October 2019